Elvi Rhodes was born and educated in Bradford. The eldest of five children, she left school at sixteen and became the main financial supporter of the family. She now lives in Rottingdean and has published five novels: *Opal, Doctor Rose, Ruth Appleby, The Golden Girls* and the bestselling *Madeleine*.

Also by Elvi Rhodes

OPAL
DOCTOR ROSE
RUTH APPLEBY
THE GOLDEN GIRLS
MADELEINE

The House of Bonneau

Elvi Rhodes

CORGI BOOKS

THE HOUSE OF BONNEAU
A CORGI BOOK 0 552 13481 3

Originally published in Great Britain by
Bantam Press, a division of Transworld Publishers Ltd.

PRINTING HISTORY
Bantam Press edition published 1990
Corgi edition published 1990

This book is set in 9½/11 pt Trump Mediaeval by
Colset Private Limited, Singapore.

Corgi Books are published by Transworld Publishers
Ltd., 61–63 Uxbridge Road, Ealing, London W5 5SA, in
Australia by Transworld Publishers (Australia) Pty. Ltd.,
15–23 Helles Avenue, Moorebank, NSW 2170, and in New
Zealand by Transworld Publishers (N.Z.) Ltd., Cnr. Moselle
and Waipareira Avenues, Henderson, Auckland.

Printed and bound in Great Britain by
Cox & Wyman Ltd., Reading, Berks.

For Mary Kennedy, with love

ONE

'Oh Madeleine,' Mrs Bates said. 'Whoever invented the crinoline didn't give a thought to having to pack it!'

She was on her knees at the side of the big trunk, helping her daughter to prepare for the journey, trying to get everything in with the least possible creasing.

'All these yards of material,' she sighed. 'Must you take so many gowns?'

'I really must, Ma,' Madeleine said. 'I want to do Léon credit in front of his family. I must look my very best.'

'Well I shall be glad when this silly fashion changes,' Mrs Bates said. 'It's been in far too long.'

'Léon says we should hope for the crinoline to be in fashion for ever,' Madeleine remarked. 'It uses so much fabric – and after all, we make our living from supplying that.'

'I suppose so,' Mrs Bates conceded. 'But in the meantime how am I to get everything in?'

'Let me help you,' Madeleine offered. 'Really, love, there's no call for you to be doing my packing!'

'I like to be useful,' Mrs Bates said.

'Useful! Oh Ma, that's an understatement if ever I heard one. I don't know what me and Léon would do without you. You spoil us.'

'It pleases me,' Mrs Bates said. 'I don't know about Léon, but you didn't come in for much spoiling when you were a bairn, so I reckon you're due for a bit now. Hand me that jacket of Léon's, will you? I think your husband's clothes are going to take up nearly as much room as yours.'

Her son-in-law was a bit of a dandy – but no, that was

7

unfair; he was just very smart, elegant as only a Frenchman could be, she thought. In Helsdon, this West Riding town where he had married her daughter and made his home, he stood out from the rest of the men. Even after – how long was it since he'd first arrived? Five years, was it? – you couldn't take him for anything but a foreigner. It was in his dark looks; in the cut of his beard and moustache which the Helsdon barber had had to learn to deal with; in his clothes, to which, though they were made in Helsdon, he somehow added the stamp of Paris.

'He likes to dress well,' Madeleine agreed. 'And you have to admit, Ma, he does look handsome in his clothes.' Her voice was warm with admiration.

'Oh yes. As they say in these parts, he pays for dressing,' Mrs Bates said. 'And so do you, love. Don't forget that I think Léon's family is going to be quite impressed by his Yorkshire wife.'

Madeleine shivered a little in spite of the August heat. Whenever she thought of what lay before her, she was nervous: and since they were leaving for France tomorrow, she thought of it most of the time.

'Are the presents well packed?' she asked anxiously. 'It would be terrible if they got broken!'

She had given a lot of thought to choosing the gifts; delicate pieces of English bone china. A cream jug and sugar basin for her mother-in-law, a trinket box for Léon's sister, Marie, for the wives of Léon's two brothers, small bon-bon dishes, and for the men, cravats. The older children would receive tins of Yorkshire toffee and the smallest ones wooden toys. She hoped they would all be acceptable. She hoped *she* would be.

'Oh Ma, do you really think they'll like me?' she asked.

She had been married to Léon for more than two years now, and in all that time she had never visited his family. At first it was the mill which had prevented it; they were expanding so fast and there was so much which needed attention. Then last August, when the mill closed down for Helsdon Feast week, their plans to visit her in-laws had broken down because her mother was ill with the pleurisy, and couldn't be left.

'Of course they will, love! You must have asked me that a hundred times!'

'I know! I'm sorry, Ma!'

'And I always tell you the same thing, don't I? Just be yourself, no need to try anything fancy, and they'll take to you right away.'

How could anyone not take to Madeleine, Mrs Bates thought. She was guiltily aware that if she had to choose a favourite amongst her three daughters – which she wouldn't like to do – then it would have to be Madeleine. She was good to look at, with her dark curling hair and soft brown eyes, her slender, yet shapely figure, her height; and above and beyond all that, the liveliness, the sympathy, the intelligence, which shone out of her for all the world to see. Oh, who wouldn't take to her?

'That's what Léon says,' Madeleine admitted. 'Be yourself and you'll be all right.' But still she remained doubtful.

'I'd feel better if only I knew a bit more French,' she said. 'I hardly know any.'

'I thought Léon was teaching you?'

'Oh, he is, but there's never enough time. The business takes it all. That's the trouble with prosperity, it gives you responsibilities and leaves you with no time.'

'Now Madeleine! Don't let me ever hear you grumble about your position!' Mrs Bates's tone was suddenly as sharp as the north wind which blew over Helsdon moor. 'Have you forgotten what it was like, living in Priestley Street? Have you already forgotten what it was like to go hungry? If you have, then I haven't. No, nor never shall! You should go down on your knees and thank God for what life has brought you since then!'

It was all so recent to Mrs Bates that sometimes, still, she dreamt about it, waking in the night in a cold sweat of terror. That loveless marriage to her husband, Joseph Bates; then his death, which in one way had been a merciful release, but had left her destitute, not knowing which way to turn, how to keep food on the table and a roof over her head, until Léon Bonneau had come to the rescue and employed her as his housekeeper before he took Madeleine as his wife. No, she would never forget any of that!

'Oh, I do,' Madeleine said. 'Most of all I thank God for Léon. And no, I *don't* forget those other times.'

But in a way it was the lowliness of her upbringing which sometimes, and almost always on social occasions, caused her insecurity. Léon's family were comfortably off. His upbringing had been quite different from hers.

She moved around the beautiful bedroom which she shared with him. Come to think of it, she had been afraid of coming to live here, as mistress of Mount Royd, where once she had been a servant. But that had worked out well enough, hadn't it?

'Ma,' she said suddenly. 'Do you remember when I went to Paris before?'

It had been to the trade exhibition of 1855 with her employer, Albert Parkinson, and his daughter, Sophia. Though both girls had been the same age, her role had been to chaperone Sophia when her father was busy. Miss Sophia had been a pig – when wasn't she? They had quarrelled fiercely. But it was in Paris that Madeleine got to know Léon better, and that had made up for everything.

Mrs Bates rose to her feet, slowly because her joints were stiff. It was the cold, damp winters of Helsdon which caused the rheumatics which stayed with her right through the summer. Madeleine put out a hand to help her.

'I remember all right! You wore one dress and packed

10

one other, and that was it! Not like now! It was the green one. Your father gave you the material.'

'It was the only thing he ever gave me in my life,' Madeleine said.

'Yes, well . . . he didn't have much to give, did he?'

'He could have given me love. It costs nothing to give love!'

And there, Mrs Bates thought, Madeleine was wrong. There were times when it cost a lot to give love. Many was the time she would gladly have left her husband had it not been for the love she had for her children. But she knew what Madeleine meant, and she had a point.

'You can't give love if you don't have it in you,' she said. 'Now is there anything else at all to go in this trunk, love? I do hope not.'

'I don't think so,' Madeleine said. 'But we won't fasten it just yet in case Léon has something when he comes in.'

'Well, I'm going to pack you a nice hamper of food for the journey. You can eat it on the train.'

'Thank you very much, Ma. I'm sure we'll be glad of it.'

Madeleine was still in the bedroom when Léon arrived home. He ran up the stairs, calling her name, and when he came into the bedroom he took her in his arms.

'There, my love!' he said when he released her. 'Everything is in order at the mill, and since, after tomorrow, it will be closed down for a week, we can leave with a clear conscience. The maintenance man will be in to check the machinery, but Rob Wainwright will see to him.'

'It was a good day when you found Rob Wainwright as mill manager,' Madeleine said.

It had been totally necessary to have someone in such a position, since with the expansion of their business Léon had to travel from home more and more. Trade throughout the West Riding had grown, and was still growing, by leaps and bounds. The easing of the tariff which had existed between England and France, which had made it difficult to sell there, had created a world of difference.

And when it came to selling to France, Léon Bonneau had a head start. Not only was Bonneau's cloth top quality, it was different from the rest, in the designs and in the blend of colours. Mostly, they were Madeleine's designs, and they grew better and better, her inspiration seeming never to flag. And since Léon knew his own countrymen, knew how they thought and felt, and could converse with them in their own language, a great deal of the cloth woven in Bonneau's found its final home on the back of some smart French lady or gentleman.

'You look excited,' Madeleine observed. 'I'm sure you're glad to be going home?'

'I must admit,' Léon said, 'I am pleased at the thought of seeing my family, and even more at taking you with me. It's high time you met them.'

Madeleine smiled and said nothing. She had already said more than enough about her qualms. She was determined from now on to keep quiet about them.

'And I'm sure you are looking forward to seeing Paris?' Léon said. 'Didn't I always say that one day I would show you Paris again – though I would have preferred it to be in the spring?'

'You did, my love – and yes, I do look forward to it, very much indeed.'

'Good!'

'You know that if I had my way, I would accompany you on some of your travels,' Madeleine continued. 'Or I'd even go alone. You know that selling is something I've always wanted to do. Oh, not in France, of course, because of the language – but there are places in England where I daresay I could do quite well.'

Léon sighed. It was a subject on which they could never agree.

'My love, we've discussed all this before, and I don't doubt will again. Selling is *not* a woman's job. . .'

'Nor is textile designing, but I do it,' Madeleine interrupted.

'That does not take you all over the country. How could you travel around the country alone?'

'Well, let's say around Yorkshire then? I could do that.'

'You would be laughed at – and so would I for allowing it. If I were to let you do that I would be thought to be – how do you say it? – petticoat ruled. No, it is impossible!'

'I did it once,' Madeleine pointed out. 'I went to Henry Garston's in Leeds and got the first big order we ever had.'

'I know. You did well,' Léon conceded. 'But it wouldn't have happened had I not been ill, unable to keep my appointment.'

'All the same I did it,' Madeleine persisted. 'Why shouldn't other merchants take to me if he did?'

'Well, as we now know, Henry Garston likes a pretty face – and whose face is prettier than my darling Madeleine's?'

'It was *not* my pretty face!' Madeleine said. 'I did the job well!'

'Well, since we both hate to quarrel, my dear, and it's a subject on which we can't agree, let us not discuss it any further at the moment. Besides, think how valuable you are to me in your designing. How could I spare you?'

What he never says, Madeleine thought, and what I'm sure is in his heart, because it is in mine, is that by now my time should be occupied in bringing up our children. Her seeming inability to conceive a child was a deep and constant ache. After more than two years of marriage, they had almost ceased to speak of it. I am barren, she thought. I am not a real woman.

Yet in the marriage bed she was a real enough woman. They made love frequently, and with pleasure and complete satisfaction to both of them – which made it all the more heart-breaking that, though month after anxious month she hoped and prayed, there was never a sign of pregnancy.

13

Will he grow tired of me because I don't give him a child, she sometimes asked herself? Will he meet someone, on his travels, who will mean more to him? Oh yes, she knew they were stupid questions. He was as kind and loving as ever. But nothing could quite dismiss such thoughts from her mind. And now they were about to visit Roubaix, where both Léon's brothers had four children each, and no doubt more to come.

'Have you anything more to pack?' she asked.

'Last-minute things only – and not in the trunk.'

The following morning it was all rush. They were up before dawn to travel to Leeds for the train.

'Have you got the food hamper?' Mrs Bates asked.

'I have it here,' Madeleine said. 'Now mind you take care of yourself, Ma. Don't work too hard.'

Mrs Bates stood on the wide porch of Mount Royd and waved them off. She would miss her daughter, though it was only for a week.

'I just wish I knew more French,' Madeleine said to Léon when they were on their way. 'Everyone says "be yourself" – but how can I be myself if I must remain silent? And will your family despise me for not speaking French?'

'Of course they won't,' Léon assured her. 'And don't forget that my sister speaks fair English, and my mother a little. My brothers' wives, however, don't know a word, so it will be harder going with them. But don't worry!'

It was not the thought of her sisters-in-law which worried Madeleine; it was Léon's mother. How *could* Madame Bonneau feel well disposed towards her? She had taken her son and tied him by marriage to another country. As foreign to her as France is to me, she thought.

'But before we go to Roubaix there is Paris,' Léon reminded her. 'We will both enjoy Paris.'

And so they did. The heat of August was tempered by a breeze from the Seine, and in the Champs Elysées trees in full leaf threw a welcome shade.

14

'Everything looks better than I remember it,' Madeleine said as they walked along arm-in-arm. 'It's all so . . . rich. So alive!'

'That is partly because Monsieur Hausmann has completed more of his beautiful boulevards, but it is even more because we are married, and in love,' Léon said. 'Our short stay in Paris will be like another honeymoon.'

'If it is possible,' Madeleine said next morning as they lay in bed, 'it is even better than our first honeymoon! Oh Léon, I do love you so much!'

But why, when their lovemaking was such perfection, did she not conceive a child? The question tore at her. When they had breakfasted – the fresh bread and strong coffee brought to their room – they dressed, and went out into the sunshine.

'We will go by boat to Notre Dame,' Léon said. 'It will bring back so many memories.'

Inside the cathedral they stood and gazed at its magnificence. They had last been there with Mr Parkinson and Sophia at the service to celebrate victory in the Crimea, and on Madeleine's part to thank God for bringing her brother Irvine safely through that war.

'Léon,' Madeleine whispered. 'I would like to offer a prayer for Mr Parkinson. But for him I would never have come to Paris.'

'He was a good man,' Léon said. 'The world is a poorer place without him. But don't forget that you and I met first in Helsdon, not in Paris.'

'I couldn't forget.'

She would never forget that as a servant at Mount Royd, and he a visitor, she had fetched and carried for him.

Paris, though, had given her more than her husband. It had been the starting place of her Catholic faith, here in this cathedral. But perhaps both had been waiting for her since the beginning of time?

She knelt and said a short prayer for Mr Parkinson. And then, because the thought was never far away, she prayed for herself. 'Please God, I want a child! Please! Nevertheless,' she added as she had been taught, 'not my will but Thine.'

Do I mean that? she asked herself. Don't I, this time, want *my* way?

Emerging from the cathedral, they blinked against the strong sunlight. All too soon for Madeleine it was time to catch the train to Roubaix. She sat in apprehensive silence for most of the journey, in sharp contrast to Léon who, with every mile of track, grew more and more excited. She could see it in his eyes, hear it in his voice as he pointed out the landmarks.

Arriving in Roubaix, Léon called for a cab. When they reached the house it seemed to Madeleine that every member of the family was there, lined up in the entrance hall to greet them: Madame Bonneau, her two sons and their wives, Léon's sister and, playing on the tiled floor until they were called to attention, a group of children of varying ages, presumably Léon's nephews and nieces.

There was a second's silence, then everyone spoke at once – and all of them in French, including Léon.

There was no doubt of the affection with which Léon's family greeted him. Madeleine had never seen so much kissing in her life. His sisters-in-law, Simone and Charlotte, were a little less exuberant than the rest. His mother held him close for a moment, then released him, but Marie flung herself at her favourite brother and he took her in his arms and kissed her fondly.

'Oh Léon, it's so good to see you!' she cried. 'It's been so long!'

'You are prettier than ever,' Léon said. 'Don't tell me you haven't got a string of beaux because I won't believe you.'

'She has a dozen. Our sister is a little minx!' Marcel said.

Madeleine strained to make out the foreign words, and to tell from their expressions what they were all saying. It was no good. In her nervousness she understood nothing.

16

All that came over to her, and that most strongly, was that they were a family, close and united. Shall I ever be one of them? she asked herself. Shall I ever be one of this circle? She so wanted to be, for Léon's sake as well as for her own. Then Léon turned to her, took her hand and drew her forward.

'*Maman*, allow me to present my wife, and your new daughter-in-law!'

Hearing the pride in her husband's voice, seeing the loving smile on his face as he introduced her, Madeleine felt better. In careful French she stammered the greeting she had prepared – and was mortified to hear how awful it sounded, how altogether different from the accents of her in-laws. Madame Bonneau kissed her formally, and replied in rapid, impossible French.

'My brother, Marcel, and his wife, Simone. Pierre, and his wife, Charlotte,' Léon said. 'And this is my sister, Marie.'

Madeleine was suddenly too shy to attempt to voice the few words she had intended for Léon's brothers. She would only make a mess of it. But Marie stepped forward, kissed her warmly, and spoke in English.

'Welcome, Madeleine!' she said. 'Now I shall be able to practise my English with you!'

Oh bless you, bless you! Madeleine thought. Was it possible that she had found a friend?

'That will please me very much,' she said. 'Perhaps you will teach me some words of French. I'm ashamed that I know so little.'

She resolved once again to try her very hardest to get on with the Bonneaus. They were Léon's family, and he loved them, and so would she. It would be easy enough to be fond of Marie, but of the rest she wasn't sure. She felt considerably in awe of Madame Bonneau: so upright, though by no means tall; so much the lady. Can I possibly live up to her expectations? Madeleine asked herself.

Madame Bonneau spoke now to Léon, and he quickly translated.

'We are to have my old room,' he said, smiling. '*Maman* will show us. Not that I don't know the way, but she insists!'

Side by side with Madame Bonneau, Léon a step behind, Madeleine climbed the broad staircase.

'Well, my love,' Léon said when his mother had left them. 'Here we are at last! That wasn't so bad, was it? What did I tell you?'

He sounded so pleased that she was glad she'd managed to hide her feeling of isolation. Clearly, among all the chatter, he hadn't noticed her near-silence.

'Your sister is particularly charming,' she acknowledged.

'Marie is a friendly little thing,' Léon agreed. 'We must have her to stay with us in Helsdon, don't you think? But never mind Marie! Give me a long and loving kiss before we change for dinner!'

I would like not to go down to dinner at all, Madeleine thought. I would like to stay here in your arms; safe.

'And now take a look at my room,' Léon said. 'I've slept in this room all my life.'

'Until you came to Helsdon.'

'Of course!'

It was a plainly furnished room, with mementoes of his boyhood around. Madeleine could imagine her husband growing up in this room.

'Was it always like this?' she asked.

'More or less. I see *Maman* has put pretty new curtains at the window; in your honour, I'm sure. And, of course, moved in a double bed in place of my narrow one.'

Surely, Madeleine thought, adapting Léon's room to the both of them was a way of welcoming me into the family? Deeds speak louder than words, as her mother was fond of saying.

She began to unpack the trunk, which had already been brought up. Yes, here were the presents! She took them out carefully. They emerged from their wrappings safe and sound.

18

'We'll take them down before dinner,' Léon said. 'And perhaps we should get ready. *Maman* doesn't like meals to be kept waiting.'

Well, thank heaven her clothes would be a credit to Léon. She chose a dress of palest cream interwoven with shades of deeper cream and gold, a design of her own of which she was particularly fond, and woven in the very finest worsted, as light as a feather.

'Will this do?' she asked Léon, holding the dress against her.

'It is perfect,' he said. He thought how well it enhanced the contrast of her dark hair and fair skin.

All the presents were well received. Marie and Madame Bonneau seemed particularly pleased, and both of them thanked Madeleine in English.

Dinner, though totally delicious as far as the food and the wine went, was for Madeleine not so easy. Everyone chatted to everyone else, everyone talked at once, and all spoke in French, which sounded more and more confusing as the meal went on. Though she tried her best, she understood little. Didn't they realize this? Even Léon seemed to have forgotten that he could speak English, and gabbled away in his native tongue. Only Marie, sometimes seeing the lack of comprehension on Madeleine's face, translated a few phrases or tried to explain a joke which had caused so much laughter among the others.

'We are a noisy family when we are together,' she said. 'And everyone's favourite pastime seems to be teasing me!'

Madame Bonneau, sitting upright at the head of the table, was quieter than the rest. From time to time Madeleine caught her mother-in-law looking in her direction. If she can speak some English, as Léon says, then why doesn't she say something to me? Madeleine thought unhappily. Anything! Anything at all! It would make such a difference.

It was the longest meal she had ever sat through, but at

last it was over and they left the table and moved into another room. Madeleine began to wish she had an excuse for leaving the company and going to bed. She was sure they wouldn't miss her, in any case. But good manners alone, as well as the desire not to disappoint Léon, meant that she must stick it out. She quickly took a chair next to Marie so that they could at least have a little conversation.

In fact, it was Madame Bonneau herself who came to the rescue.

'Léon, I think Madeleine is looking a little tired. It is late, and it has been a long day for both of you. If you wish to retire we shall all understand.'

She spoke in French, but this time Madeleine got the gist of it, and was filled with gratitude.

'You are quite right, *Maman*,' Léon said. 'I am tired, and Madeleine must be quite worn out. If you will excuse us, we will go to bed.'

He came across to Madeleine and took her by the hand.

Pierre made what she took to be, from the look on his face and the giggles from her sisters-in-law, a ribald remark. Madame Bonneau frowned at them.

'Perhaps it is getting late for all of us,' she said. She moved towards Madeleine and kissed her good night in her formal manner.

In their own room, Madeleine was quickly in bed. She buried her face in the pillow – that horrible, hard French sausage of a pillow instead of the lovely, soft feather one she would have had at home. Oh, how she longed to be back in Helsdon! Tears sprang to her eyes.

Léon touched her on the shoulder and she turned her head.

'Oh, my little love!' he said. 'You're crying! Why? Whatever is wrong?'

'It's nothing,' Madeleine said. 'I'm being foolish – and I daresay childish. I'm sorry!'

'Are you not happy here?'

'Of course I am. Just for a moment, I was the teeniest bit homesick.'

20

'I didn't mean to neglect you,' Léon said. 'It's just that it's a long time since I saw my family. And as Marie said, when we're all together we're noisy.'

'I do understand,' Madeleine said. 'And you didn't neglect me. It's mainly that I couldn't understand what was being said. Everyone spoke in French all the time. And oh, Léon, I think perhaps your mother doesn't like me! I did so want her to like me!'

'I'm sure you are wrong,' Léon said gently. He sat beside her on their bed, stroking her hair. 'My mother is not an easy person to get to know. Believe it or not, she is shy, and for this reason often appears aloof. Also, her English is no better than your French. But you are mistaken when you say she doesn't like you. I can tell that she *does*. But she needs time.'

'We don't have time,' Madeleine reminded him. 'We have only three days here.' And oh, she would be so glad when those three days were over and they could go home. But this *was* home to Léon, she thought miserably. Perhaps in his heart he wished to stay here? The thought sent a shiver through her.

'Oh Léon, is it possible that one day you might want to live in France?' she asked. She had to know.

'And what would you say if I did?' There was a serious look in his eyes as he countered her question with his own.

What *would* she do? Could she possibly live in this alien place? But since Léon was her husband and she loved him dearly, there was only one answer.

'If it was what you wanted, then I would do it. No matter where you chose to live, I would go with you.'

'To the ends of the earth?' he asked. 'Tell me you would go with me to the ends of the earth, Madeleine.'

'To the ends of the earth!'

'Well, have no fear, my darling. I shall not ask you to do so.'

He undressed quickly, and came to bed.

'I'm sorry I was upset,' she said. 'It was stupid of me.'

21

What's the matter with me? she asked herself. Why am I thinking about myself all the time? Léon spends so little time with his family, and I see mine every day, yet here I am, resenting the fact that they speak in their own language! How can I be so selfish?

'Oh Léon, I am a fool!' she said. 'Please forgive me!'

When Madeleine went down to breakfast next morning there were only the four of them, herself and Léon, Madame Bonneau and Marie.

'You slept well?' her mother-in-law asked formally, but in English.

'*Oui*! *Merci*,' Madeleine replied.

Madame Bonneau turned and spoke to Léon, in French.

'*Maman* is reminding me that last night I promised Marcel and Pierre I would go down to see the factory this morning,' he said to Madeleine.

'Then I will go with you,' Madeleine offered quickly. She would be interested to see what they were doing.

'I'm not sure that that would be a good idea,' Léon said doubtfully.

Madame Bonneau broke in with a stream of French, all the while looking at Madeleine. Marie quickly translated.

'*Maman* says the factory is no place for a woman. You wouldn't enjoy it. In France, she says, the women stay at home while the men go out to work.'

'You mustn't mind my mother,' Léon put in quickly. 'She's just a little old-fashioned.'

But surely Léon has told her the part I play in Bonneau's mill, she thought. That I work alongside him?

'Please tell your mother that it is the same in England,' Madeleine said. 'But not every woman. And while there are no children. . .'

Léon looked uncomfortable. He would have translated his mother's remarks more tactfully, but tact had never been Marie's strong point. So when his mother spoke again he rushed to explain to Madeleine.

'My mother says of course you are free to go to the factory if you wish. But she wanted you to stay behind because she would like to get to know you better. It would please me very much if you would do that, my love.'

'Of course I will,' Madeleine agreed.

'And I will stay as interpreter,' Marie offered. 'Don't be late back for lunch, Léon. Hortense Murer is coming.'

'Hortense?' Léon sounded pleased and surprised.

'She is back in Roubaix. *Maman* thought you would be pleased to see her again.'

'Of course,' Léon said.

'Who is Hortense?' Madeleine asked.

'A friend of the family,' Marie replied. '*Especially* a friend of Léon's, in the old days. But do not worry, Madeleine! It is you my brother married, and anyone can see he is in love with you!'

'You will feel at ease with Hortense,' Léon said. 'She speaks excellent English. And now if I am to be back early I must go.' He rose from the table, then bent to kiss Madeleine. 'I shan't be long, my love. Try to enjoy yourself.'

'I'll do my best,' Madeleine promised. She really would try.

As the three women left the breakfast table, Madame Bonneau spoke to her daughter.

'*Maman* says she does not need me,' Marie said to Madeleine. 'I am to give Brigitte a hand in the kitchen while *Maman* shows you the garden.'

Madeleine's heart sank a little as Marie left them. How would she and Madame Bonneau carry on a conversation?

'Come!' Madame Bonneau said.

Madeleine followed a step behind her mother-in-law around the pretty garden. At first, as she had feared, little was said, then Madame Bonneau began to tell Madeleine the names of the flowers in French. Immediately, Madeleine offered the English equivalent. In no time at all it became a kind of game in which they could both take part, and it quickly eased the tension.

'*Rose!*' Madame Bonneau said.

'Rose,' Madeleine replied.

'*Le Lis!*'

'Lily,' Madeleine said. 'And this little one is a pansy.'

'*En Français, pensée,*' Madame Bonneau said. 'It is for thought.'

'Pansies for thoughts,' Madeleine cried. 'Of course! Country people sometimes call it "heartsease".'

'Heartsease,' Madame Bonneau said carefully. 'I like that.'

'You have a beautiful garden, Madame,' Madeleine said. '*Très beau jardin.*'

'*Jardin*, garden,' the older woman said. 'But to say Madame is not *nécessaire*. You must say "*Belle-mère*". It is French for how you say mother-in-law. And you are my *belle-fille!*'

'Daughter-in-law?'

At the bottom of the garden they sat on an old bench, in the shade of a pear tree. Could I get to like it here, Madeleine wondered? It isn't nearly as bad as I thought.

'French is a beautiful language,' Madame Bonneau said haltingly. '*Très belle*. But if you do not understand it, perhaps not. It is the same with English, *n'est-ce pas?* – of which I know so little. But here comes Marie!'

When Marie joined them, Madame Bonneau spoke to her at length.

'My mother says you are very welcome in our house and she welcomes you as her daughter-in-law. She wishes you could stay longer. So do I, Madeleine! I really do!'

'Then you must visit us in Helsdon,' Madeleine said impulsively. 'And now will you please tell your mother that I am pleased to be her *belle-fille*, and to be part of your family. Tell her also that when I return to Helsdon I will make sure that Léon teaches me a little French every day – so that next time I come to Roubaix you won't have to translate for me all the time.'

Léon came walking up the garden path towards them as Marie was relaying this message to her mother.

'I promise to do that,' he said quickly.

'Tell your mother that we would like her to visit us in Yorkshire,' Madeleine said quickly. 'I mean it, Léon! Please tell her.'

But when Madame Bonneau replied, Léon looked uncomfortable.

'What did she say?' Madeleine asked.

'Only that she will come eventually, to see the grand-children you will give her,' Marie put in.

Oh no, not that! A few moments ago, Madeleine thought, she had really been at ease with Madame Bonneau. Now, suddenly, she felt a failure. No matter what else she did, it wasn't enough if she couldn't conceive a child.

'Then tell your mother,' she said quietly to Léon, 'that it is my dearest wish to have a child – but it is in God's hands.'

Madame Bonneau listened to her son, then stretched out her hand and laid it, with a gentle pressure, on Madeleine's.

'I understand,' she said.

I believe you do, Madeleine thought. I really believe you do, or try to. At least you don't condemn me. And hadn't her mother-in-law's remark about visiting her grandchildren been entirely natural, exactly what an elderly lady would say?

'Thank you, *Belle-mère*,' Madeleine said.

'Marie and I must go in,' Madame Bonneau said to her son. 'We have things to do. You stay here with Madeleine and when Hortense arrives I will send her to you.'

When they had gone, Madeleine said, 'Oh Léon, I am so sorry I haven't given you any children. I know it's such a disappointment to you.'

'Not just to me,' he said. 'We share it. But for the moment we shall try not to think about it.'

'You're right, Léon. And perhaps when we get back to Helsdon, I should go to the doctor again?'

It would do no good. She had already seen the doctor. He had simply told her it was the will of God, which was exactly what Father O'Malley had said.

'Sometimes God is difficult to understand,' she'd said to Father O'Malley.

'It is not for us to understand God,' the priest replied. 'If we understood Him, we would be His equals. Our part is to accept.'

He'd spoken kindly, but she'd not been comforted. And she wouldn't accept. She just would not.

There were women who could advise about these things; she was sure of it. Women who could give you potions which would help you to get pregnant. When she'd ventured to mention this to her mother, Mrs Bates had been horrified.

'Don't you dare dabble in any such nonsense!' she'd said fiercely. 'Hocus-pocus, nothing more! All they want is your money!'

But was it hocus-pocus? Madeleine asked herself as she sat here in this French garden. And what did that matter if it worked? She was convinced, by now, that Sophia's curse that she would never have a son was taking effect – so why not the opposite? Why should she not find someone who would lift it? Once back in Helsdon, she resolved, she would seek someone out.

Mademoiselle Murer was walking along the path towards them. Oh, but she's very pretty, Madeleine thought! She was slender, dark-haired, delicately featured – and with a bright smile on her face and her hands outstretched in greeting.

'Léon! It is so long since I saw you!'

She greeted him in French. Another conversation I'm not going to understand, Madeleine thought ruefully. And how pleased they looked to see each other.

'So! This lovely lady is your wife,' Hortense said. 'I am delighted to meet you. Do you speak French?'

'I'm sorry, Mademoiselle Murer, I don't. I thought I did, a little, until I came here, but now it all sounds different!'

'Then we shall all speak English,' Hortense said. 'It is all one to me. And you must call me Hortense and I shall call you Madeleine, which is a beautiful name and suits you. But Madame Bonneau told me to tell you that lunch is ready. We must go in at once or she will kill us! As I daresay you have discovered, in France it is permitted to keep one waiting for food, but never the other way round.' She linked her arm through Madeleine's and they walked side by side along the narrow path to the house.

The meal passed off well. Now everyone spoke in English, so that Madeleine began to feel sorry for Madame Bonneau, sitting beside her, who was frequently left behind, but remained patient and well-mannered. How stupid I was, earlier, to take offence, Madeleine thought. In fact, given time, she might actually get to like her mother-in-law, her *belle-mère*.

As for Hortense, she thought, observing her at the other side of the table, chattering away between mouthfuls of food, she is nothing like I feared. She is charming. She talks to me as much as to Léon. Oh, she flirts with him a bit, but then they are old friends. So why did I worry? Why am I up in the air one minute and down in the depths the next? I don't understand myself. But now, smiling at Léon, she felt reasonably happy.

'I liked Hortense,' Madeleine said later to Léon when they were alone in their room.

'Of course,' he said. 'Who would not?'

'I didn't expect to like her,' Madeleine confessed. 'After all, she is an old flame of yours. Were you really in love with her once?'

'Come here!' he said.

He held her in his arms.

'Yes, I was. I might even have married her if I hadn't met Mr Parkinson at the wool sales in London, if he hadn't invited me to Helsdon and I hadn't met you. But these are all "ifs", my darling. I *did* come to Helsdon, I *did* meet you. You are my wife and it's you I love!'

'We shall be back in Helsdon in two days' time,' Madeleine said. 'It hasn't been nearly as bad here as I feared. Your family has been kind. Most important of all, I've seen what it's meant to you to be with them. But you won't be offended if I say I'll be glad to be back?'

Helsdon was her own place. She belonged. She felt secure there.

'I wonder what awaits us in Helsdon,' she said.

TWO

'I must say, it's grand to have you back,' Mrs Bates said to Madeleine. 'But I'm not sure you look all that better for your holiday. In fact, I'd say you look a bit peaky!'

'I'm all right, Ma,' Madeleine said. 'It's a long journey and as I told you, it was a rough crossing. I was seasick.'

'You've been back three days, love. You should be over that by now,' her mother said.

There was more to it than being travel-weary; Madeleine was young, strong, fit as a flea and seldom tired. But why am I kidding myself? Mrs Bates thought, I know full well what's wrong. It's that letter from Our Emerald. It had arrived while Léon and Madeleine were still in France, and Penelope, the little idiot, had blurted out the news almost the minute they'd set foot back in Mount Royd.

'Oh Madeleine, what do you think? Miss Sophia has had another baby!'

'Mrs Chester to you,' her mother corrected.

'Another son! That's their third son. Emerald says he's the most beautiful baby you ever saw and he weighs eight pounds and they're going to call him William.' The words rushed out of Penelope like a river in spate.

Stop it! Stop it! It took all Madeleine's self-control not to utter the words, not to shout at her sister. Of course she'd known Sophia was expecting, known that the baby was due at the beginning of August – Emerald, still Sophia's devoted slave, kept them abreast of the news – but she'd refused to think about it, pushed it to the back of her mind.

'It's not fair!' she cried. 'Why should Sophia Chester, who cares nothing for anyone except herself, have three

29

sons, and me and Léon have none? It's unbearable!'

Then she'd rushed out of the room, taken herself off until she could calm down.

Now, three days later, discussing the week's menus with her mother, she was outwardly calm again, but the sadness lay like a lump inside her.

'I thought a leg of mutton tomorrow,' Mrs Bates said tentatively. 'What do you think?'

'Whatever you like, Ma! In any case, Léon has to go to Macclesfield tomorrow. He'll be away overnight, so I'll eat with you. Oh Ma, I wish you'd always eat with me and Léon, instead of you and Penelope taking your meals in the kitchen!'

'Well, we do at weekends, love.'

'But why not all the time? We're all one family.'

'I'll think about it,' Mrs Bates promised.

It wasn't that she didn't enjoy eating with her daughter and son-in-law, but there was a bit inside her which wanted to keep her independence. Of course she'd had her own sitting-room from the beginning, to which she could retreat whenever she wished.

'What I *shall* do,' she said to Madeleine, 'is see that *you* eat. You're far too thin!'

'I'm quite all right. Don't fuss, Ma!' Madeleine spoke sharply.

Mrs Bates looked keenly at her daughter. Madeleine was just not herself these days. She was touchy. You were never quite sure how far you could go with her. But I shall take the plunge, Mrs Bates decided.

'Madeleine!'

'Yes?'

'I've got something to say to you. You might not like it, but you and me have always been straight.'

'What are you saying?' Madeleine looked genuinely puzzled.

'I'm saying that I know very well what's eating at you, you don't have to tell me, and no matter what you think, I *do* understand – but you can't go on like this!'

30

'Like what, Ma? What do you mean?'

'It's your attitude. You're taking your disappointment out on everyone else. I was ashamed of you the other day when you spoke so harshly about Mrs Chester's baby.'

'Not about the baby, Ma. About Sophia Chester.'

'Don't split hairs! It was an attitude I don't like to see. Thinking only of yourself! And it's not the only time. It's got to stop, Madeleine. I'm telling you for your own good. You've got to pull yourself together. What can't be cured must be endured.'

'That sounds so bleak,' Madeleine protested.

'Some bits of life are bleak. And there's another thing. . .'

'Yes?'

'You'll not conceive while you spend every minute worrying about it. That's a well-known fact.'

Madeleine walked across to the window and stood there for several minutes, her back to the room, looking out.

I've put my foot in it, Mrs Bates thought. Well if I have, I have. It had to be said.

In the end, Madeleine turned around and faced her mother.

'I'm sorry, Ma. You're right. I hadn't realized quite how awkward I'd been, but you *are* right – and I *will* put a stop to it. I promise!'

'Then that's all right,' Mrs Bates said. 'We'll say no more about it. You know I only want the best for you, love.'

'I know.'

Penelope came in from the garden, her hands full of freshly-picked parsley.

'Will this do, Ma?'

'Just about right,' Mrs Bates said. 'Wash it well and chop it fine. I don't like great lumps of parsley in my sauce.'

She wondered sometimes if it would be better for Penelope to take a job elsewhere. She was sixteen now, quite old enough to leave home. But when Mrs Bates first came to keep house for Léon Bonneau, even before he'd married Madeleine, Penelope had been a very young thirteen and her mother had been glad to accept a job in the house for her. There was plenty to do. She earned her keep and her small wage. But it's time she got out from under my wing, Mrs Bates thought. She'd seen to it that her youngest daughter was well-trained in everything domestic. She'd make a good servant wherever she went and, hopefully, one day a good wife.

'Madeleine, I haven't told you I went to Helsdon Fair last week,' Penelope called out above the noise of the running tap. 'It was wonderful!'

'You did? Who did you go with?'

'I took her,' Mrs Bates admitted. 'Fairs are nothing in my line, as you know, but nothing would please her but that she should go.'

When her husband had been alive, none of them had been allowed to go near the fair. All the week when the sound of the music and the beat of the drums had been loud in their ears in Priestley Street, when it seemed as if everyone else in the street walked past the Bates' window carrying favours, or prizes they had won on the stalls, they had been confined to the house lest they should stray anywhere near the fairground. Well, though she didn't herself like the noise and the dirt of the fairground, she saw no reason why her daughter should be denied the treat.

'I couldn't let her go alone, could I?' she said.

'I went on the roundabouts,' Penelope said, bringing the chopping board and the parsley to the table. 'We had hot pie and peas, and we bought some brandy snap to bring home.'

'Ma! *You* ate pie and peas in the fairground? I don't believe it! I hope no one from your chapel saw you!' Madeleine said, laughing.

'Well if they did, they did!' Mrs Bates retorted.

'There were wrestlers,' Penelope went on, 'and the fat

woman – huge she was, you'd never believe! And a pot stall, and swing-boats. And a two-headed cat which Ma wouldn't let me go in and see. She wouldn't let me go and see the fortune-teller, neither. Romany Rose, Clairvoyant to Royalty.'

'I don't hold with fortune-tellers,' Mrs Bates said firmly. 'Anti-Christian! We're not called upon to see into the future.'

But if only I could see into mine! Madeleine thought. At this moment, she could think of nothing she would rather do. And perhaps a fortune-teller was the kind of person who would tell her what more she could do to have a child. Perhaps she would give her something to take? But even if I could pluck up the courage to go, she thought, it's too late.

'I suppose the fair is over now?' she said.

Mrs Bates nodded.

'Packed up and left on Sunday morning.'

'But they've only gone to Akersfield,' Penelope put in eagerly. 'Oh, Madeleine, why don't we go, you and me? It's not that far!'

'I should think Madeleine has better things to do with her time,' her mother said. 'Besides, you've been once. Let that be enough.'

'I could go a hundred times and enjoy every one!' Penelope cried. 'Oh, Madeleine!'

'Actually,' Madeleine said in an offhand manner, 'I wouldn't mind taking Penelope again if she'd really like it.'

'Oh Madeleine! You're the best sister in the world! Can we go this evening?' Penelope demanded.

'No. There'll be nothing much doing on a Monday. We'll go tomorrow.'

Léon would be away tomorrow. It wasn't that she wished to deceive him. When he returned she'd no doubt tell him she'd been, but she didn't want an argument about it beforehand. Most of all, she didn't want him to make her postpone it to another evening, so that, if she *must* go, he could accompany her.

They took the train to Akersfield. It was no more than three or four miles away, but at the end of a full day – after seeing Léon off to Macclesfield Madeleine had spent her time partly on a new design she was working out, partly on sorting out orders – it seemed a fair distance to walk.

'Anyway, we'll get there quicker on the train,' Penelope said. 'Oh, I can hardly wait!'

Nor can I, Madeleine thought. Yet in a way she dreaded what she had made up her mind to do. Never in all her life had she even contemplated visiting a fortune-teller. She knew that some of the girls in the mill did so – and look at the way they crowded around Sadie James in break-time because she reckoned she could read the tea leaves!

You couldn't blame them. The promise of a brighter future helped them through the poverty of the present. But for her it was wrong. She knew that perfectly well, without her mother saying so. She would have to confess it, and Father O'Malley would be disappointed in her as well as giving her a penance.

Well, so be it! She had prayed hard enough; she'd waited. Now she was desperate to do something more. And everyone said the gypsies knew a cure for whatever ailed you.

It was no more than a short walk from the railway station to the fairground. It being Akersfield holiday week and the mills closed, there were scores of people heading in the same direction. To most of them the fair was the highlight of the summer; eagerly looked-forward to. Now the cacophony of music, drums, and the shouts of the stallholders, urged and lured them on to spend. Wasn't it what they'd scrimped and saved for?

'Oh, isn't it exciting, Madeleine!' Penelope tucked her arm through Madeleine's as they were swept forward in the crowd. 'I want a turn on everything!'

'Indeed! And have you brought a lot of money, then?'

Penelope's face fell.

'Not really. I did save up, but I spent it all at Helsdon

34

Fair. But Ma gave me twopence instead of a penny last Saturday.'

'That won't take you far,' Madeleine said with a straight face. 'Oh, all right! I'm only teasing, love! I'll treat you to a few things! I know well enough why you wanted me to bring you! I'm not as green as I'm cabbage-looking!'

The brandy-snap stall was the first thing you saw on entering the fairground, the snaps shining like gold on the clean white cloth which hid the trestle table. And if you were so blind as not to see it, your nostrils were assailed by the delicious aroma of butter, treacle and ginger. There was always a lip-licking crowd around the brandy-snap stall.

'We'll have some,' Madeleine decided. 'Which do you want, flat or curled?'

'Curled, please,' Penelope said.

If she could save one until she got home – *if* she could – then her mother might fill it with thick, vanilla custard.

Penelope started on hers with gusto, but Madeleine could do no more than nibble. She was choked with anxiety. Even so rare a treat as brandy-snap wouldn't go down. All she wanted was to find the fortune-teller's tent, but she would have to do it without exciting Penelope's curiosity. She hoped and prayed she'd be able to slip in there without her sister knowing, and to that end she planned to keep her sister occupied with the offer of several goes on the roundabouts or swings.

Penelope was not to be hurried. She wanted to see everything, to spend time as well as money. She gasped in admiration at the wrestlers, loudly clapped the weight-lifters, laughed with the crowd at the patter of the pot-stall man, retreated in horror from a woman with a snake coiled around her arm; all this before she spent her first penny at the hoop-la, where to her amazement she won a small dish with roses painted on it.

'Isn't it beautiful?' she cried ecstatically. 'I shall take it home for Ma. She'll be that pleased!'

At last Madeleine sighted the fortune-teller's booth, and as luck would have it, it was no more than a few yards away from the big roundabout. 'Romany Rose, Clairvoyant to Royalty. Advice given.' There was a large photograph of Queen Victoria on the board outside the tent, and sitting on a stool at the entrance was a young gypsy woman; raven-haired, attractive, with black eyes and gold earrings.

'Do you really think the Queen consults her?' Penelope asked in awe. 'Will Romany Rose go to the palace, or do you suppose the Queen will have to visit her in her tent?'

'Tell your fortune, pretty lady,' the gypsy said to Madeleine. 'Let Romany Rose tell you what's in store! You have a lucky face, lady.'

'Oh Madeleine, she means you!' Penelope gasped. 'Oh, wouldn't it be fun to go in! What do you think it costs?'

'More than we can afford,' Madeleine said firmly. 'In any case, we're not supposed to do it!'

She moved away a little, towards the roundabout. But she'll come back, the gypsy girl thought. She'd seen her sort before. They pretended they were above it, pussy-footed around, but she always knew who'd come back, sneak in when they thought no one was looking.

'I'll pay for you on the roundabout,' Madeleine said to Penelope.

'Oh lovely! Come on then!'

'Not me,' Madeleine said. 'Roundabouts make me dizzy. I'll wait here. No, I'll tell you what – I'll just walk around while you have a go. So don't worry if you lose sight of me. I'll be back here by the time you get off.'

'You won't go far, will you?' Penelope begged. There were such crowds. If she lost Madeleine she might never find her again.

'Of course I won't! But look, here's threepence. If you don't see me standing right here after the first go, you've got enough money for another two.'

She had no idea how long the fortune-teller would

36

take, but three turns on the roundabout would be quite lengthy.

'Threepence!' Penelope gasped. 'Oh Madeleine, thank you!'

Madeleine waited until Penelope was safely mounted and away on one of the large cockerels, then she turned swiftly and made for the fortune-teller's tent.

'I would like to consult you,' she said to the gypsy girl, with as much dignity as she could muster.

'You're very wise, dear. Very wise. But I'm not Romany Rose. I'll take you in to her.'

She held back the tent flap and Madeleine ducked inside. She was struck at once by the heat. It hit her in the face, sticky and steamy. And then there was the smell; a powerful combination whose ingredients she couldn't identify; oils, spices, stale scent: strange, yet not entirely unpleasant.

It was dark inside the tent. The only light came from a small lantern hanging from a hook on the wall, barely illuminating a large woman whose ample, low-slung bosom rested upon, and took up most of the space of, the small table at which she sat. What table space was not occupied by her great breasts held a pack of cards and a crystal ball, covered by a black velvet cloth. Without speaking, she motioned to Madeleine to sit down opposite to her. Madeleine trembled from head to foot as she obeyed.

'Will you have the crystal, or will you cross my palm with silver, dearie?' the woman asked. She had a low-pitched, hoarse voice but, surprisingly to Madeleine, a familiar north-country accent.

'I. . .' What should she choose?

'I'll cross your palm with silver.'

'One hand or both, dearie?'

'Oh! Oh, both I suppose!'

'Then two pieces of silver, if you please.'

She showed Madeleine the ritual of crossing her palm with the sixpenny pieces, then took both of Madeleine's

37

hands in her own and held them close to her face, scanning them intently. Well, there was a wedding ring there, a nice thick band of gold, so she wasn't looking for a suitor. Or if she was she'd no business to be!

'I see a tall, handsome man,' she said. 'He's dark, with a foreign look about him!'

Madeleine's sharp intake of breath told her she was on the right track.

'Yes,' she said. 'He's as clear as clear in your heart line. And he thinks the world of you. Am I right?'

'Yes! Oh yes!'

'But don't take everything for granted. It doesn't do to take things for granted. You're not without an enemy in the world. Which of us is, love? There's a fair woman here. You want to watch her! Do you know who I mean?'

Sophia! Madeleine nodded mutely. It must be Sophia!

'Well she's no worse for watching! That's all I'm saying about her, but you take notice of Rose, love. I see a long life and a happy one.'

That, after all, was what her customers paid to hear her say. She observed the fine cloth of Madeleine's dress, the gold brooch at her neck. She wasn't short of a bob or two, that was for sure.

'Riches aren't everything, as you and me both know,' she continued. 'Now is there something you want to ask me, dearie?'

This was it. This was what she had come for. And now Madeleine couldn't find her voice, couldn't get the words out.

'You want some advice from Romany Rose. That's why you've come, dearie, isn't it? Don't be afraid to speak!'

'I want to get pregnant!' Madeleine whispered.

The woman leaned closer, so that her bosom was almost touching Madeleine. The strange scent coming from the gypsy's skin was almost overpowering.

'Speak up, dearie! Nothing to be ashamed of!'

'I want to get pregnant. Do you . . . I mean . . . is there

38

a potion? Is there something I can take? Some medicine?'

The woman sat upright again, her black eyes searching Madeleine's face.

'You made a wise decision when you came to Romany Rose,' she said. 'Romany Rose can help. But it will cost you.'

'How much?'

Not that I care how much, Madeleine thought, if I have it on me. And if she hadn't, she would find a way of returning. She must!

'Half a sovereign,' Romany Rose said, making a swift, bold decision. The girl seemed pretty desperate. 'Children are blessings which don't come cheap.'

Madeleine took a half-sovereign from her purse and placed it on the table. The woman opened the table drawer and brought out a small bottle filled with rose-pink crystals.

'This will do the trick! An ancient formula, handed down through generations of the Romanies. And not to every one of them, but Romany Rose holds the key.'

'Thank you! Oh, thank you!'

'A pinch big enough to cover a sixpence, dissolved in hot water and taken every night at bedtime,' Romany Rose said. 'Taken regular, and in secret, until the bottle is empty. Then bury the bottle under an oak tree, and repeat your wish.'

She picked up the half-sovereign, handed over the bottle and rose to her feet. The session was over.

Madeleine hid the bottle in her pocket and went out quickly, almost bumping into the younger woman on her way in. Breathless, she hurried back to the precise spot where Penelope had left her, and was in time to see her sister, slightly pale, clinging to the cockerel as the round-about slowed down.

Inside the tent Romany Rose spoke to the young woman, who was her daughter.

'That's the last of the Epsom-salts,' she said. 'You'll

need to go to the druggist and get some more. And a bottle of cochineal to colour them up.'

'They look ever so much better, pink,' her daughter said. 'That was a bright idea of yours. But she didn't look the sort to want to get rid of a kid!'

'And if she was, they wouldn't help her. You know I wouldn't be a party to that. I don't believe in it, let alone I'd have the law on me quick as a flash. But a dose of Epsom-salts never did no one no harm. Clears the blood. No, she didn't want to get rid of a kid. She wanted to have one.'

The younger woman laughed.

'She needs a man for that! Not a dose of salts!'

'She's got a man,' Romany Rose said. 'What's more, she *is* pregnant. Oh I could tell it in her face. I always can, right from the beginning. I reckon I could tell the very next morning!'

She picked up the half-sovereign and burnished it with the tablecloth. 'All the same, I reckon she'll not begrudge me half a sovereign when she finds out for herself!'

'She might even think it's the pink crystals!' her daughter said.

At the time of Madeleine's visit to Romany Rose, Sophia Chester was lying-in after the birth of her third son, with the monthly nurse in attendance. Or rather, *not* in attendance, for Sophia had not set eyes on her since she had last required her to shake up her pillow, and that had been all of fifteen minutes ago.

In accordance with the doctor's and the nurse's strict instructions, Sophia lay flat on her back, so that her innards might slide back into their proper place. It was so boring, staring at the ceiling. It was true that if she turned her head to the left she could see out of the window, but only into the branches of a horse-chestnut tree which stood too close to the house. The tree was also boring, its leaves no longer the fresh green of spring. Also it darkened the room.

Her breasts, abundantly filled with milk, were beginning to pain her. It was surely time Nurse Merry brought the baby to be fed? She could hear him in his crib at the foot of her bed, making little mewing kitten noises. He was wanting her too, she was sure of it, but to get out of bed to attend to him was, naturally, quite impossible, simply not allowed. She knew better than to risk it. She stretched her hand sideways, picked up the bell from the bedside table, and rang; and kept on ringing until Nurse Merry appeared in the doorway, by which time the baby was crying in earnest.

'There you are!' Sophia said crossly. 'Whatever happened to you? I've been ringing for ages! I'm quite sure the baby needs feeding, just listen to him crying.'

'It could be that he doesn't like the sound of the bell,' Nurse Merry said, her voice stiff with disapproval. 'Babies don't like loud noises.'

She would stand no nonsense from this little madam, and that was a fact. She needs me more than I need her, Nurse Merry thought. Everyone, but everyone, was having babies, and naturally, she being the best midwife in the area, she was constantly in demand and could pick and choose. Why she had chosen this one was simply because she liked Mr Chester, who was a member of her church. But that didn't mean she was going to stand any nonsense from his wife.

'Well then, Nurse, may I please feed him?' Sophia demanded. 'I'm sure it's time. Apart from anything else, my bust bodice is soaking!'

Nurse Merry picked the baby out of his crib and held him against her shoulder. His cries ceased as if by magic; the magic of her sure, professional touch.

'There, my little man!' Nurse crooned. 'Did he not like the nasty, horrid bell then? Did it frighten him?'

'It wasn't the bell,' Sophia persisted. 'I'm quite sure he needs feeding!'

She felt totally powerless, lying down here with the nurse, who was tall and had shoulders like a guardsman,

41

not to mention that awesome white cap, towering over her. And I'm such a little thing, she thought pitifully. She's a great big brute!

'He seems all right to me, Mrs Chester!' Nurse Merry said. He probably did need feeding, but she wasn't going to let madam off easily. 'He seems quiet enough now!'

She held him close. Oh he was a little darling! All the babies were darlings, it was the mothers who were the trouble.

'Who's a little petsy-wetsy then?' she murmured. 'Who's Nurse Merry's little man?'

'Please, Nurse!'

'Very well, Mrs Chester. I'll change him – and then we'll see if he'd like to take a little feed. Diddums want a feed then? Diddums want a little drinkie?' she enquired of the baby.

That he didn't mind if he did was quickly shown by the way he grabbed at the nipple, taking the milk in great gulps which were too much for him so that the milk ran out down the sides of his mouth and on to his chin.

'There you see,' Sophia said. 'I knew he was hungry. A mother knows!'

A mother practically never knows, Nurse Merry thought. She didn't say so, but her sniff, the turning down of the corners of her mouth, the jerk of her head, said it all louder than words.

Sophia had not experienced Nurse Merry before. Her first two babies had been born in Thirsk, where David was an assistant teacher at a private school. A year ago he had been fortunate enough to land a new job in Ripon, as a housemaster at Whinbury, a rather bigger, preparatory boarding school. It really *was* a step up. Not only was he paid more, but this quite pleasant, though perhaps rather small, house went with the job. And in due course, though it was a long way off, when the children were old enough there would be free places for them in the school.

Oh yes, it had been a good move, Sophia reckoned, and

not least because there was so much more going on in Ripon than in Thirsk. It was, after all, a cathedral town, with all the comings and goings, all the culture that that entailed. Not that Sophia was one for too much culture, but it certainly improved the social scene.

'We would *never* have met this class of person in Helsdon,' she'd said to her husband once, as they were returning from a most satisfactory musical evening. David had had to agree.

And then there were the wives of the other teachers and, above all, the headmaster's wife herself: the Honourable Agatha Woolf. The Honourable Agatha was really most friendly and gracious to Sophia. She treats me almost like an equal, Sophia thought, her thoughts wandering as she fed the baby.

He let the nipple go, sated, and his head lolled back.

'There!' Sophia said. 'That's better! You can take him now, Nurse. I *knew* he wanted to be fed!'

You mean you wanted it, Nurse Merry thought.

'What a pity I had my dear baby in August,' Sophia said. 'Since it's school holidays, everyone, just everyone is away. Otherwise, of course, I'd have been inundated with visitors and you'd have had to be very strict and ration them, Nurse Merry!'

'I would have done that all right!' Nurse Merry's voice was grim. She didn't hold with visitors, always staying too long, always breathing on the baby; and bringing flowers, another thing she didn't hold with in a sick-room.

'My friend the Honourable Agatha Woolf would have been here every day, I'm sure of that,' Sophia said. 'Every single day. The Honourable Agatha is the headmaster's wife. Her father is a baron, you know!'

I should, Nurse Merry reckoned, getting up young William's wind, wrapping him tightly in his swaddling clothes before laying him down in the crib again. You've told me oft enough. But Honourable or not, their babies came out the same way – not to mention got in.

43

Honourables, Ladyships, Countesses, duchesses. Even the Queen, she thought – and then wondered if she hadn't almost committed treason.

'Well thank goodness she'll be back in ten days' time,' Sophia sighed.

'Who will?' Mrs Parkinson asked, coming into the bedroom.

'Mrs Woolf, Mama.'

And that was another thing, Nurse Merry thought. Patients' mothers were a thorn in the flesh – though this one wasn't as bad as some. She didn't give contrary advice all the time, as if she knew better than the nurse.

Sophia sighed again. So far her mother and the head-master's wife had not met; now she supposed they might have to, and she wasn't sure it would work. Agatha – 'Do call me Agatha, at least in private,' she'd said – was so refined, so educated.

But she needed her mother for a little while longer. Mama was undeniably good with the children; little Bertie, now four, and getting to be a handful, always wanting his own way: little Georgie, not yet two. Yes, she needed her mother – and at any rate, if she *had* to meet the Honourable Agatha, she was more presentable than her Aunt Fanny Chester, which was how she still referred to her mother-in-law. All the same. . .

'When will you be returning to Helsdon?' she enquired.

'The minute I can be spared,' Mrs Parkinson said.

She could read her daughter like a book. I'm not smart enough for the Honourable Agatha, she thought. But as long as my two little darlings need their grandmother, I shall hang on! The minute they don't, I'll go. It would suit Sophia if I stayed out of sight when her fine friend comes back. Well, though she had no particular desire to meet the Honourable Agatha, she'd reached a time of life when she was no longer going to be put down by her daughter.

'If only we had adequate staff!' Sophia said grandly.

'Then I needn't impose on you, Mama. I needn't keep you so long.'

What could you do with so little domestic help? She had only Emerald Bates, plus a young, not very competent girl to help with the children and a local woman who came in twice a week to help with the rough. It really wasn't enough; it wasn't what she'd been brought up to expect. If she'd been living at Mount Royd. . .

The thought of Mount Royd brought Madeleine Bates to mind. She refused even to think of her as Madeleine Bonneau.

'Well, little William is another one in the eye for that Madeleine Bates!' she said to her mother. 'I gather from Emerald that she's still not expecting, and married more than two years!'

'I feel sorry for her,' Mrs Parkinson said mildly. 'She'd make a good mother.'

'Mama, how *can* you be sorry for her after what she's done to me?'

'She's done nothing to you.'

'That's not true! You know very well she has. She's stolen my home. Mount Royd should be mine, not hers. It was my father's.'

Not only had Madeleine Bates stolen Mount Royd, she had somehow or other stolen Léon Bonneau, who was, Sophia admitted to herself (though never to anyone else), by far the most attractive man ever to set foot in Yorkshire. She hated him, of course – and thank goodness no one in the world knew that it was Léon who'd jilted her, not the other way round as she'd told Madeleine in that fight they'd had just before Madeleine's wedding.

She could still remember how Madeleine had gone white, looked about to faint, when she'd said she'd put a curse on her, so that she'd never have a son. I'm sure I didn't believe it myself, Sophia thought. It had been the first thought that came into her head. Uncannily, it had worked.

45

'I shall never forgive her, Mama,' she said. 'But you see how fate is punishing her? It goes to show! Perhaps her marriage isn't all it should be?' she speculated. 'Perhaps they don't . . . well. . .'

'Sophia, that's enough!' Mrs Parkinson said sharply. 'For goodness sake mind your own business!'

'Well, Madeleine Bates will never hold Léon Bonneau if she can't give him children,' Sophia said. 'They say he's away from home a lot, and no wonder. And can you imagine what he does on those trips? After all, he's a Frenchman!'

'You're talking rubbish,' Mrs Parkinson said.

'It's time Mrs Chester had a nap,' Nurse Merry said, leaving whatever she had been doing in the corner of the bedroom, while listening. It was interesting enough, but all this argy-bargy would affect the milk, and then the baby would have wind. Mothers could be so selfish!

'I'm just going,' Mrs Parkinson said.

She stopped by the crib, bent over it and touched the smooth, silky cheek of her third grandson with the tip of her finger. He pulled a face in his sleep, then opened his dark blue eyes, as yet unfocused, and was aware of her.

Each night, following her visit to Romany Rose, Madeleine took the prescribed dose of the crystals. It was an operation fraught with difficulty, mostly because she seemed hardly ever to be alone. When she went into the kitchen for hot water, like as not her mother was there, so that all she could do was take the water and carry it upstairs.

'What's all this drinking of hot water last thing at night?' Mrs Bates enquired.

'It helps me sleep,' Madeleine told her.

Almost always by the time she reached the bedroom Léon would be there. How she longed for him to sit up late; but he never did, because every morning meant an early start in the mill. He insisted on arriving there at the same time as his workpeople.

There would have been no difficulty at all had the crystals been colourless. She could have slipped them into the water and have drunk it in front of anyone. But the moment she dropped in the crystals, the clear water became a beautiful, rosy pink; totally conspicuous, not capable of explanation.

She developed various strategies. Sometimes, on plea of a headache or fatigue, she retired to bed extra early; occasionally she managed to shoo her mother off to bed so that she was left alone in the kitchen. Twice she dissolved the tablets on the stairs and swallowed the liquid before she reached the bedroom. Once she had actually had to wait until Léon was asleep before stealing downstairs again in search of hot water.

But there was no way she would miss taking the crystals, not even if it meant getting up in the middle of the night to do it! And always, after having swallowed the pink concoction, she prayed sincerely for it to be efficacious.

Disposing of the bottle was not easy, either. When she took walks in the evening with Léon she kept an eye open for a suitable oak tree. In the end she chose one in the big meadow, before the land started climbing to the moor.

At a time when Léon couldn't possibly offer to accompany her, she went down to the meadow. With some difficulty, for at the end of the summer the ground was baked hard, she dug a hole with a spoon she had smuggled from the kitchen, and buried the bottle. Then she prayed harder than ever before rising to her feet and going home. There was nothing more she could do now.

Her period was due at the beginning of September. On the first of that month she came into the kitchen, her face pale, her eyes suspiciously red-rimmed. Mrs Bates looked at her keenly.

'What's the matter, love?'

'Nothing, Ma.'

'The time of the month?'

'That's right.'

47

'And you hoped it wouldn't happen! Oh love, I'm that sorry!'

Madeleine had wakened in the night and felt the wetness, had got out of bed to take a poorly cloth from the drawer. When she got back into bed she lay with her back to Léon, the tears streaming silently down her face. She mustn't waken Léon. She couldn't bear to tell him, not yet, that once again she'd failed him. As the blood drained from her body she felt her hopes drain with it.

In the morning she went into work, set to on her designs. When tears blurred the colours she was mixing she wiped them away and got on with the job. When the mill stopped for dinner-time she carried on working. She wouldn't be sorry for herself; she wouldn't go on about it. She would immerse herself in her work. Work never let you down.

Léon came in and looked at what she was doing.

'That's beautiful,' he said. 'You improve all the time!'

'I intend one day to become the best designer in the West Riding, in Yorkshire, maybe in England,' she said fiercely. At least she would create something.

'You're too modest,' Léon said. 'You're already the best designer in the West Riding!'

Halfway through the afternoon she was suddenly aware that the flow of blood had stopped. At the same instant her inside was gripped with a spasm the like of which she'd never felt before; not a pain, not an unpleasant sensation at all, but as if everything inside her was being gripped, and at the same time resisting. The feeling was over in less than a minute, and didn't return. Nor did her period.

She didn't understand it. She said nothing about it to anyone, not even to Léon, in case she should be mistaken in what she now dared to hope.

A week later – Léon was in London at the Wool Sales – she wakened a half-hour later than usual and hurried to get up. At the moment she put her foot to the floor the room spun around, and the next minute she was leaning over the chamber pot, vomiting. She knelt there until the spasm passed, then got shakily to her feet and, without stopping to put on a dressing-gown, hurried downstairs.

Mrs Bates, stirring porridge, looked up as her daughter, white-faced yet starry-eyed, rushed in.

'Oh Ma, it's happened! I know it has! I'm certain!'

'What are you talking about? What's happened?'

Whatever it was, it was good. She hadn't seen her daughter like this for a long time. She was transported.

'I'm pregnant, Ma! I'm expecting! It's true, it's true!'

She took hold of her mother and began to twirl her around the kitchen, but before she had done three turns she dashed to the sink, and was sick.

'Yes, I think you are,' Mrs Bates agreed. 'Oh Madeleine, love, this is a happy day!'

THREE

'Oh, my darling, I am so pleased! I am delighted,' Léon said. 'And I am quite convinced our child was conceived in Paris. He will be a true Frenchman!'

'Oh no he won't!' Madeleine protested. 'Half of him will be a true Englishman, and a Yorkshireman at that!'

All the same she, too, was sure her baby had been conceived in Paris. Everything fitted. Not that it mattered, except for pleasing Léon. All that mattered was that she was pregnant, her pregnancy had this morning been confirmed by the doctor, and she had at last told Léon. It had been so difficult keeping it from him all day. She'd been determined to choose a time when they would be alone together, but every bit of the day had been taken up by something or somebody. Now they had retired to bed and no one would disturb them.

'But why did you not tell me from the start?' Léon demanded. 'I knew you were not yourself. I worried that you were not well, and wouldn't admit it.'

'I didn't want you to be disappointed. I could hardly believe it myself, and if it wasn't true, I didn't want to build up your hopes.'

'All the same you should have told me,' Léon demurred. 'If there had been a disappointment I would have wanted to share it with you.'

'Well there isn't! Dr Hughes says I must be careful, but everybody knows what an old fusspot he is!'

She hesitated. Dr Hughes had said more than that. When he'd told her she was pregnant, and she sat before him, bathed in happiness, he leaned back in his chair and looked at her with serious eyes.

'You do want to carry this child to full term?'

She'd been immediately alarmed by the tone of his voice.

'Of course I do!' she cried. 'It's the dearest wish of my life! Why do you ask, Doctor? Is there something wrong?'

'No,' he said slowly. 'There is nothing specifically wrong. I don't want to alarm you, but I have to warn you. . .'

'Warn me?' She felt sick with fear.

'Advise you, then. I must advise you to take the utmost care. You must not let yourself become overtired.'

'I won't! I really won't! I'll do nothing which could possibly cause harm to my baby,' Madeleine promised. 'My husband and I long so much for this child!'

But of this conversation she had said nothing to Léon, nor would she. Why cause him months of worry?

'No, my love, everything's fine,' she said. 'And I'm willing to allow that the baby *was* conceived in Paris, and might therefore be a little bit more French than English. Does that please you?'

'Of course it does,' Léon admitted. 'I feel that France has given us something precious.'

'It also gave me you,' Madeleine reminded him.

'And England gave me you, dear Madeleine!'

He climbed into the high bed beside her and she went at once into his arms.

He began to caress her, his hands exploring her body, his mouth on hers. She pressed close to him, felt his hardness against her, recognized his eagerness and knew her own.

Then suddenly, at the moment he was about to enter her, he drew away.

'What's wrong? What is it, Léon?'

'We mustn't,' he said. 'We mustn't go any further. It might harm the child.'

She looked at him in disbelief.

'Not make love?'

'Not until the baby is safely born, my dear one.'

51

'But that's impossible!' Madeleine cried. 'It's impossible for both of us! Oh, I daresay it's immodest of me to talk of my longings, but you've always known how I felt.'

Desire was strong in her at this moment, urgently demanding release. She wanted him. Oh, how she wanted him! She tried to draw him towards her, but he pushed her away. Then he sprang out of bed, walked to the washstand and poured himself a glass of water. The glass shook in his hand.

'And what of my longings?' he asked. 'I am a man, therefore they will be even greater than yours. But it is a sacrifice we must both make for the sake of the child.'

'I don't believe it,' Madeleine said in amazement. 'Do you mean to tell me that all married couples cease to make love when the wife is pregnant?'

'Perhaps not,' Léon said. 'But we can't judge by others. You have had great difficulty in conceiving, and you've told me that the doctor said you must take care. It would be terrible if you were to lose the child – and if I felt I had caused that to happen I would never forgive myself.'

'But seven more months, Léon! And I want you this very minute!'

'My darling, we must deny ourselves. It will be hard, but we must do it for the child. And I shan't love you one iota less. You know that.'

Madeleine slipped out of bed and went to him, stood facing him. She held herself rigid, resisting the desire to touch him, to throw herself into his arms.

'Does this child really mean so much to you, Léon?' she asked quietly.

He nodded.

'Everything in the world – after you.'

She'd not known that a man could care so much. She had thought that the caring, protective feeling for a child still such a long way from being born resided only in women. All this time Léon's longing for a child must have been as great as her own. Yet he had hidden his disappointment even when she'd shown hers. He must love me a great deal, she thought.

But was it really true that when a woman was pregnant, lovemaking must cease? Every instinct told her otherwise, but she didn't *know*. Who could she ask? It was too delicate a subject to enquire of the doctor, and she had never discussed the intimate side of marriage with her mother.

There was Mrs Barnet. Harriet Barnet had been her guide and teacher when she first went into the mill. Then when Madeleine was no longer welcome in her own home, and had no place to go, like the true friend she was Mrs Barnet had offered her lodgings and had looked after her like a daughter, right until the day of her marriage to Léon.

But they had never discussed such intimacies. Besides, Mrs Barnet had never had a child. No, there was no one.

'Then. . .' She hesitated. She could hardly say the words. 'Then we will try to do as you say – though I'm far from resigned and I'm not sure how I shall bear it.'

'But you will,' Léon said. 'I know you will. And it will be worse for me. A man's desires are stronger.'

'How do you know that, Léon? How can you measure such things?'

But she had always understood that it was so, which was why there were other outlets for men. She was not so ignorant that she didn't know of such women, even in Helsdon, though until now she had thought that they were there for men whose wives denied them; not for a wife like herself, who longed to give her love.

Would Léon . . . ? And how would she know? And would it be an everyday matter for a Frenchman to pay for such pleasure?

She couldn't believe it. She wouldn't think about it. From now on she would think of the baby, growing inside her. That was the thought she would cling to.

She held out her hands and took hold of Léon's.

'Come back to bed, darling!' she said. 'It's chilly. Come

to bed and hold me quietly in your arms.'

They lay in each other's arms like children. Madeleine was still wide awake and staring into the darkness when Léon's breathing deepened, and then his arms went slack and fell away from her. He was fast asleep.

She eased herself away from him, leaned over and re-lit the candle, and sat looking down at him. Even in sleep, without the lively intelligence which was always in his waking face, even with his penetrating, dark eyes lidded, he was so incredibly handsome. She loved him so much! How could she bear to be without him?

But you won't be without him, she admonished herself. He will be with you exactly as before – except in bed. But how could she lie beside him and not touch him? And if they touched, how could they control their desires? She wanted to do what was right, but would she be strong enough?

It was Léon himself who dealt with that problem, the very next morning.

'Dearest, I shall have a bed made up in my dressing-room,' he said. 'I shall be near if you have need of me, if you feel ill, for instance.'

I shall need you all the time, Madeleine thought – but kept silent. And when, that same night, he went to bed in his dressing-room, she felt him further away from her than on any of his absences from home, even when he had gone as far as France. From France, he came back eagerly to her bed. It would be a long time before that happened again.

'You must take the very greatest care of yourself in every way,' Léon said next morning at the breakfast table. 'You must eat well, and take plenty of rest. I think perhaps you should give up your work in the mill.'

Madeleine paused with her teacup halfway to her lips, then slowly put it down again.

'My darling,' she said. 'To be carrying a baby is not to be an invalid. It's a natural process which most women go through. Now that my morning sickness is almost over, I'm as fit and healthy as I've ever been in my life. I feel wonderful! So please don't suggest that I give up work. I can't sit around all day with my feet up. I'm not made like that.'

'I know you're not,' Léon agreed. 'But things are different now. In view of what the doctor said, your very first thought, and mine also, must be for the child.'

'Do you imagine I don't think of the child, Léon? Why, every waking moment I'm aware of him! I wouldn't do the least thing to harm him.'

'It just seems to me. . .' Léon began.

'Please, Léon!'

Léon jumped up from his chair and came and stood behind her, his hands on her shoulders, his lips on her hair. Desire shot through her at his touch. Before today she would have turned her head, tilted her face so that her lips met his. His hands would have slipped down to cover her breasts. But not now.

'I can't have *you*,' Madeleine said quietly. 'Don't deny me my work in the mill. Nothing can take your place, but work must be my substitute.'

Why was it so hard to give up her work? Was she not really cut out to be a mother? Had nature known what she was doing in not giving her a child sooner? For a brief moment she felt a sudden fear of the future, afraid of all the conflicting demands it would make on her. Would she ever be able to meet them?

Léon walked over to the window and looked out. The leaves were turning colour. A little while longer and they would fall, and then the harsh, northern winter would be here. It would be May before his son was born. The landscape would have changed yet again, and these same trees would be in bud. How would he put a curb on his desires for all that time? Yet he thought it was right. He was truly afraid of what might happen to the baby if he didn't keep apart from Madeleine.

'Do you think I shan't feel it, Madeleine?' he said

tersely. 'I'm not made of stone, as you have good reason to know!'

'Oh, I do know!'

She couldn't tell him that that was what she feared most; that with his passionate nature he would find it impossible to stay faithful to her. What if she gained a child, and lost her husband in the process?

Léon went back to her and took her hands in his.

'You must promise me you will take care of yourself. *You* are precious to me, not just the child. If you must work, then please don't work too hard.'

'I promise you that,' Madeleine said. 'I'll be sensible. I'll learn to sit instead of standing all the time. I'll eat for two. Oh, I'll do all the right things!'

'Well I shall ask your mother to see that you do,' he said. His mother-in-law was a sensible person, a woman to be trusted. 'I shall ask her especially to keep an eye on you when I have to be away from home.'

'Oh Léon, I hope you don't have to be away too often while we're waiting for the baby!' Madeleine said. 'I shall miss you more than ever, especially when you go to France.'

'I must go there,' Léon said. 'You know that. France is where your beautiful designs are most appreciated, and it is also where there is most competition. We can meet that competition because of your designs and the quality of our cloth, and the fact that our prices are good, but also because I go there myself, and I am a Frenchman. You've always understood that, dearest.'

'Of course!' she admitted. 'I'm being foolish.'

But when he went to France, he naturally visited his family, and when he visited his family he was always a whole week away from Helsdon, a week which seemed like a month to her.

'It's time I was at the mill,' he said.

'And I am going with you. I'll get my cloak; the mornings are getting cooler.'

*

56

The smell which greeted Madeleine as she stepped into the mill was the most familiar one of her life. It was the smell of the whole of the West Riding, or at least of those places where wool was being manufactured. It was the smell of the grease and the acid from the wool. It permeated the buildings, it escaped into the streets. It seeped into the clothes of those who worked in the mills. Her father had brought the smell home with him every day.

Only those people who lived sufficiently distanced from the mills, towards the edges of the town, didn't take in the odour with every breath, together with the smoke from the giant chimneys. To breathe clear, unadulterated air, you had to climb up to the moors which surrounded Helsdon on three sides. Yet Madeleine didn't mind the smell, nor had she ever heard anyone in the town complain about it. It was a smell which meant work, and therefore food and shelter, and maybe a spare copper or two on a Saturday night.

'I have a busy morning ahead,' she said to Léon as they parted inside the mill entrance, he to go to his office, she to the small room where she worked at her designs. 'I'll see you at dinner-time.'

Most of the hands, all those who lived near enough to get there and back in three-quarters of an hour, went home when the mill buzzer sounded for dinner. The rest brought food, and a mashing of tea, and ate in the small room which Léon had set aside for this purpose.

He was a thoughtful employer, to do this. Titus Salt had built a large dining-room for the workers in his mill at Saltaire – but then *he* was a law unto himself. No one could keep up with Titus Salt's beneficence. Most mills had nowhere special for their workers to eat. In fine weather you went into the mill yard and sat on the stone setts, or on the low walls: in worse weather you looked for a window-sill or a ledge, or fought for possession of a buffet. Madeleine and Léon brought sandwiches, or a piece of pie, and ate in Léon's office.

57

'I am expecting a buyer from Anderson's,' Léon said. Anderson's was a wholesale clothing firm to whom Bonneau's regularly sold fabrics for making up. 'I daresay he will want to look at your new designs.'

'Well so he can,' Madeleine said. 'But not the ones I'm still working on.' She liked no one to see those until she was satisfied with them herself. 'If I'm not in my room when you want me, I shall be in the weaving. I want to talk to Mrs Barnet about a pattern.'

Though the smell of the mill was acceptable to her, the noise of it was something she never got used to. There were more than a hundred looms in the weaving shed now, a big increase since the day Léon, on borrowed money, had taken over the weaving department of the bankrupt mill and engaged twenty weavers only. Six years ago that had been, and she had been one of the weavers he had taken on. So much had changed since then.

But the clackety-clack, thump-thump of the looms which met her as she entered the weaving was exactly the same, except that there was more of it. She had coped with it by learning to lip-read, as did all the weavers. In spite of the noise, she could carry on a conversation with the best of them.

In the weaving shed, taking care where she walked, because for one thing the wooden floors were slippery, and for another there was always the danger of being hit by a flying shuttle, she went straight to Mrs Barnet, who minded two looms, and these days was mostly engaged in running patterns to Madeleine's designs.

'Good-morning!' Madeleine said.

'Good-morning Mrs Bonneau,' Mrs Barnet replied.

Madeleine shook her head at Mrs Barnet.

'I've told you it's "Madeleine", not "Mrs Bonneau"!' She'd been telling her for two-and-a-half years. Mrs Barnet had started calling her 'Mrs Bonneau' the minute she'd married Léon.

'How can I call the mill master's wife by her first

name?' Mrs Barnet protested. 'It's not seemly!'

'If you call me anything else, I shan't answer,' Madeleine promised. 'I've been Madeleine to you since that first day my father brought me into the weaving-room, and handed me over to you to be taught all you knew.'

'Aye! And now you know a sight more than I do!' Mrs Barnet said.

'Not about weaving,' Madeleine contradicted. 'Nobody knows more about weaving than you do – which is why I want your opinion on this design. It's a fancy one and I've done it with the new box loom in mind. What do you think?'

The box loom had been perfected, in the West Riding, not all that long ago. It allowed for more than one shuttle in each loom, and was already proving a boon to the 'fancy' trade, the weaving of checks and suchlike.

Mrs Barnet studied the design carefully.

'I see nowt wrong wi' it,' she said. 'It should work out well enough.' That was the height of praise. 'Of course I shall have to see what Our John says.'

John Hartley was her nephew, and the weaving over-looker. He was good as far as tuning the looms was concerned, but Madeleine thought he would never know as much about weaving as did his aunt.

'While you're here, will you take a look at this one?' Mrs Barnet went on. 'I've done the pattern, but you weren't sure about the colour of the warp thread.'

Madeleine examined the cloth critically.

'I'm still not sure,' she said. 'I think the warp thread needs to be a deeper mauve. I was a bit dubious when those tops came back from the dye-house. But if the yarn's not right for this, it won't be wasted. I can use it in another design.'

The worst thing would be to weave it into the new piece if it wasn't exactly right. The 'piece' would be seventy yards long when finished and the warp thread went the whole of the length. The burlers and menders were very skilled, capable of repairing both warp and weft threads, or stitching new ones in if necessary; but replacing the warp thread was a long business; it could take days.

'I'll take the pattern into my room, look at the colours in a north light,' Madeleine said.

But before that she had something to tell Mrs Barnet. For weeks she had longed to tell her friend about the baby, but it would have been wrong to do so before Léon knew. Of course it would be immodest to tell all and sundry, even though it would announce itself in due course. But Mrs Barnet was different. 'Mrs Barnet, I have news for you!' Madeleine said.

'Oh yes, love? What's that then?' Mrs Barnet's attention was concentrated on one of her looms. You had to keep a close eye on them sometimes.

'Mrs Barnet, turn this way and look at me,' Madeleine commanded.

Struck by something in Madeleine's voice, Harriet Barnet at once did as she was told. Looking straight at Madeleine, she saw the glow in her eyes, the way her mouth lifted in a confident smile. She had never seen a look quite like this on Madeleine's face before. It couldn't be . . . ? But she'd bet her last ha'penny it was!

'I'm having a baby, Mrs Barnet! It's true! It's really true! I'm having a baby!'

There was a moment's silence between them. Mrs Barnet wanted to take Madeleine in her arms, to give her a big hug, but it wouldn't be right, not with others present.

'Eeh love, I'm that pleased! I can't tell you how pleased I am!' She could hardly get the words out for the lump in her throat.

'I knew you would be,' Madeleine said. 'Isn't it wonderful?'

'When's it to be, then?'

'Next May. I didn't tell you sooner. I had to be sure.'

'Then we shan't be seeing you in here much more,'

Mrs Barnet said. 'You'll have to start taking care of yourself.'

'You'll see me for quite a while yet,' Madeleine said firmly. 'I'm as fit as a fiddle and I don't intend to sit at home and twiddle my thumbs.'

'Happen not. But you'll not be able to work when. . .'

'When it shows? Oh I know that!' She was resigned to the fact that later on she would have to keep out of the public gaze, stupid though that idea was. 'But it will be a while yet,' she continued. 'That's another good thing about the crinoline; you can hide your shape under it.'

'Well just take care,' Mrs Barnet warned. 'Don't do anything daft.'

Back in her workroom, in the harsh light of the north-facing window, Madeleine scrutinized the pattern she had brought from the weaving. It was the only way to see the true colours. You had to stand with your back to the sun. The least hint of sun and the colours were tinged with gold. She put down the pattern, then picked up a skein of yarn and wound it round the back of her hand, looking at it with close intensity.

Yes, this one was better. It was a deeper mauve, almost a purple, which would bring up the other colours in the cloth. These aniline dyes are so much better than the old ones, she thought. Whatever did we do without them?

A moment later, Léon came into her room with the buyer from Anderson's. Tom Bennet was a little, fat man, with a round face and the ruddy complexion of someone whose job took him out in all weathers. 'Good-morning, Mrs Bonneau,' he said. 'I trust I find you well?'

'Very well indeed, thank you, Mr Bennet. And how are you?'

'Middling,' he said. 'Middling.'

In spite of his healthy looks he was never known to admit to being anything more than middling.

'And how is business?' Madeleine asked.

'That's middling. I was wondering if you'd got any new patterns for us? You know how Anderson's like the latest.'

'I know,' she confirmed. 'Why don't we go into the pattern room and have a look?'

It was the proper place to take buyers. She didn't like them coming into her workroom, trying to peek at what she was working on. Everything they could have at the present moment was there. In fact Léon could well have taken care of Mr Bennet, but sometimes the agents and the buyers insisted on seeing her also; just for the novelty of it, she suspected. As far as she knew, she was still the only woman textile designer in the West Riding. She supposed, too, she was the only mill master's wife who actually worked with her husband in the mill.

They moved into the next room and Mr Bennet examined the patterns, crumpling the cloth in his hand to test its resistance. All good woolmen knew by the feel of the cloth just what it consisted of. The minute two woolmen met each other, they fingered the lapels of each other's jackets, took the cloth between thumb and finger and pronounced on it.

'I see you're still managing to get cotton warps from Lancashire,' Mr Bennet said.

'Yes,' Léon answered. 'But who knows for how long? No cotton is coming from America while they're in the middle of a Civil War.'

'And that shows no sign of bating,' Mr Bennet said, shaking his head. 'If it goes on much longer Lancashire will be ruined. What good did wars ever do anybody?'

'What indeed?' Madeleine echoed.

She thought of her brother, Irvine, who had served in that terrible Crimean War, and was still in the army, though only for a month or two longer, thank goodness. And thank goodness, too, that as far as the American War went, England was neutral, so he couldn't be called upon to fight.

When Mr Bennet had examined everything of interest to him, he gave Léon a substantial order, 'Which we'd like filled as soon as possible,' he added.

'We shall do our best,' Léon promised. 'Our spinning

and weaving are both very busy but, as you know, we do our own finishing now, and that cuts the time a little.'

Mr Bennet held out his podgy hand to Madeleine.

'Good-day to you, Mrs Bonneau!'

My, she was a looker, that one! And clever with it. And, allowing his thoughts to stray, he didn't doubt, with a figure like that, and those eyes that melted the marrow in your bones, she was well up to the mark in other departments he could name. The Frenchie was a lucky fellow.

When the mill buzzer went, signalling the end of the working day, Madeleine stood in the window of her room and watched the hands rush to leave. In their dark clothes, the women with black shawls covering their heads, they looked like a murky river, streaming towards the freedom of the sea. Well, I was one of them, once, she thought. I used to rush out with the rest. Now she tidied away her work, put on her cloak and bonnet, and went into Léon's office.

'I'm not ready, my dear,' he said. 'There are things I must complete here. You go home, and I'll be with you in about an hour. Apologize to your mother and ask her to put back the meal.'

'Very well, Léon. But don't work too long.'

It was a fine evening, but already dropping dark and the first stars appearing. It was a short walk only to Mount Royd, though uphill all the way, for the house stood on a ridge of land, its back to the mill, its front sloping down again, with lawns and trees.

As always when she arrived home, she joined her mother and Penelope. This evening they were in Mrs Bates's parlour. As Madeleine walked in, her mother greeted her with eyes shining, in a face glowing like a beacon. She snatched a sheet of paper from the table and waved it in the air.

'He's coming home!' she cried. 'He's coming home!'

There was no need to ask *who* was coming home. Only

Irvine could bring that light into her mother's eyes, that trembling eagerness into her voice. My mother's been good to me, Madeleine thought. She had been a good mother to all her daughters, but she could never hide the fact that Irvine was the light of her life. It had almost broken her heart when, at sixteen years old, he'd quarrelled with his father and left home to join the army. Madeleine knew that to the end of her life her mother wouldn't forgive Joseph Bates for that.

'Irvine!' Madeleine exclaimed. 'When . . . and why? I thought he'd settle in Brighton when he came out of the army. After all, Bessie's family are there.'

They had met Bessie only once, on the day of her marriage to Irvine, which had taken place in Brighton. Sometimes, since the wedding, Mrs Bates had wondered if she would ever see Irvine again, let alone set eyes on her little grandson, who was now a year old. Brighton was so far away; the very end of England before the sea stretched to foreign parts.

'He doesn't think he can get work in Brighton,' Mrs Bates said. 'And he's persuaded Bessie to come north. Here, read the letter for yourself. Oh, isn't it wonderful!'

'It is indeed,' Madeleine agreed. 'I hope he *will* get work in Helsdon,' she added when she'd read the letter.

'He'll find something,' Mrs Bates said confidently. 'He'll not stick fast. Not our Irvine!'

'Well it'll be lovely to have him back in Helsdon,' Madeleine said. 'It looks as though he might be here for Christmas time.'

She would be pleased to get to know her sister-in-law better. There had been little time for that in Brighton. Bessie had seemed a pretty little thing, in a fair, pale sort of way; not very lively, but utterly devoted to Irvine. But you can't make a judgement on a day's acquaintance, Madeleine reckoned. She might be quite different.

'I'm so pleased I'll be able to give Irvine *my* bit of good news,' she said to her mother.

'And I'm going to have both my grandchildren right

here in Helsdon,' Mrs Bates said happily.

On Sunday night Léon packed all but his last-minute toiletries, ready for an early start next day. He was off to France, leaving on the very first train. It would be late that night before he reached Roubaix.

'Why don't you stay overnight in Dover?' Madeleine asked. 'You'd feel all the better for it next day.'

Really she didn't want him to. She wanted him to be back with her in the shortest possible time. There was something about this trip to France which left her uneasy. Perhaps it was because she couldn't send him off having physically shown her love for him. To her, their physical separation was more than just that, it was almost a separation of her spirit from his. When she tried to say this, Léon disagreed with her.

'Nonsense, my darling! I couldn't love you more, I've never felt closer than now, when you're carrying our son!'

When he turned away from her to go to his dressing-room she grabbed his arm, and pulled him back.

'Please, Léon! Just this once! Please sleep with me tonight!'

He disengaged himself.

'Madeleine, we can't.' He was gentle, but firm. 'You know we agreed!'

'We can break our agreement,' she pleaded. 'You're going so far away. I shall miss you so much.'

'And do you think I won't miss you, my dear? Of course I will. But I'm strengthened by the thought of our baby, and you must be too. Oh Madeleine, I can't tell you how much I look forward to breaking the news to my family! *Maman* will be delighted. I shall try to make her promise to visit us in Helsdon next summer, after the baby is born.'

'I wish it was next summer already,' Madeleine said.

'Good night, dearest. Sleep well,' Léon said. 'I shan't waken you in the morning before I go.'

'Oh but you must, you must!' Madeleine cried. At least she must be by his side until the moment he left.

FOUR

While Léon was away, Madeleine threw herself into her work, of which there was plenty. They were chock full of orders to be chased up and accounts to be kept up to date. It wasn't strictly her job, but Léon would never employ quite enough clerks for this. He had the strongest objection to paying out a penny more than he need to workers who were not actually producing cloth.

'It doesn't make sense,' Madeleine had frequently pointed out to him. 'We produce the cloth, we deliver it, and then because poor Arthur Parker is always behind with the accounts, we have to wait longer than we need for the money! He has too much to do.'

'Well *chérie*, I don't intend to engage another accounts clerk,' Léon said whenever the subject was brought up. 'Our resources must go into production.'

Which was why she was always welcome whenever she offered to take time off from her designing and lend a hand in the Counting House.

'If you'll trust me with them,' she said to Arthur Parker, 'I'll take a couple of ledgers home with me and work on them this evening.'

'Nay, Missus, you're t'boss!,' Arthur said in his slow, Yorkshire voice. 'It's not for me to talk about trusting you. T'other way on, more like.' But he did trust her; she was a remarkable young woman.

'I'll do my very best script,' Madeleine assured him. 'My handwriting will never be as beautiful as yours, Arthur, but I'll do the best I can.'

Climbing the hill to Mount Royd, carrying two large, awkward ledgers and at the same time trying to contend with a sneaky wind which was threatening to take her bonnet, she thought it hadn't been a sensible offer. She was unusually tired. But never mind, the work would keep her mind occupied.

Normally when Léon was away she would spend the evening with her mother and sister, perhaps helping with the household mending, or even just chatting. But not this week. For a start, her mother could now talk about no one except Irvine. His return to Helsdon occupied her entire mind. Though Madeleine looked forward enormously to seeing her brother again, she was glad this evening to have the excuse of the accounts to work on.

'You shouldn't have to do it,' Mrs Bates said. 'Now *there's* a job our Irvine could do when he comes home, if Léon was so minded as to employ him! He'd do it very well, I'm sure.'

'I daresay,' Madeleine said. 'But Léon won't employ him on accounts. He'll not take anyone extra in the Counting House. I've been trying to persuade him for more than a year.'

'We'll have to see,' Mrs Bates said comfortably. She had no doubt, no doubt at all, that any number of people would be willing to take on her son. They had only to see him.

The clock on the mantelpiece was chiming the half-hour after ten when Madeleine closed her ledger. Well, from what it showed, Bonneau's mill was doing all right!

She rose from the table, stretched and yawned. Her mother came into the room.

'It's high time you gave that up,' Mrs Bates said with a disapproving nod at the ledgers. 'I've brought you a cup of cocoa.'

'Thank you, Ma. I've just finished. I must say, I'm a bit tired. I reckon I'll not need rocking to sleep!'

She took her cocoa up to the bedroom. Getting ready for bed, she felt so weary that brushing her hair the required hundred strokes was almost beyond her. Also, it had been her intention to take advantage of Léon's absence by smoothing thick, sour milk into her face and leaving it on all night for the good of her complexion; but she had forgotten to collect the milk from the kitchen and she was far too tired to do so now. At least I'll have no difficulty in getting off to sleep, she thought.

It didn't work out that way. The moment she got into bed, stretched her arm across the empty space where Léon should be, she was wide awake again.

Where was he now? Where exactly? Was he in Paris, or in Roubaix – or some other place of which she didn't even know? Who was he talking to? Was he telling them about the baby? Oh, how she missed him!

It was a long time before she fell asleep, only to dream unhappily that she had lost something, a jewel she thought, and whichever way she turned, she couldn't find it.

Next morning, in spite of little sleep, she wakened early. It was the Feast of Saint Luke and she planned to go to church before going to the mill. She climbed out of bed and, pouring water from the flowered ewer into its matching basin, stripped off her night-shift and washed, shivering at the coldness of the water. As she left the house the first signs of daylight were streaking the sky.

Inside the church the day had not yet penetrated the high windows, but there were pools of light from the candles. She knelt in the shadow, where the candle-light didn't quite reach, the semi-darkness more in tune with her mood than the full light of day.

The words and movements of the mass hardly touched her. She was filled with her own confused thoughts: gratitude at the thought of her baby, longing for Léon – and so very much love for them both.

Father O'Malley greeted her as she was leaving after the mass but, unusually, she made no attempt to stop and have a word with him. A brief 'Good-morning, Father', and she was away down the street.

Was she all right, he wondered? He had an especial concern for Madeleine. Hadn't he given her her instruction, right from the minute she'd set foot in his study, looking like a scared rabbit? Hadn't he had the privilege of receiving her into the Church, and later of marrying her to Léon Bonneau? And, God be praised, they were well suited, those two! It was a pity they had no child, and he'd prayed for that blessing to fall on them, but it was all in God's hands. Perhaps he'd go round and see them this evening?

Supper was over and Madeleine was already immersed in more work she'd brought home with her. It was Mrs Bates who heard and answered the ring at the door.

'Oh! Father O'Malley! Good-evening! Please come in.'

Though she liked him, Mrs Bates always felt awkward with Father O'Malley. He was the only Catholic priest she'd ever met, and she felt a touch of magic about him, as if he carried those rituals of which she had heard around him like a cloak. In her own chapel the Minister was a man, like other men (though naturally to be looked up to and respected), but a Catholic priest was another matter, wasn't he? All the same, it was her daughter's affair. She'd decided long ago that there were to be no more quarrels over religion. Religion had done harm enough already in their family.

'Monsieur Bonneau is away. . .' she began.

'But Madeleine is home?' he finished. 'I thought I'd call and see her.'

'So your husband is away?' he said a few minutes later, sipping the glass of port wine which Madeleine had poured for him.

'He's in France. On business.'

'And you are missing him, no doubt?'

'I always do,' Madeleine admitted. 'Though I try to get used to it.'

'I thought you looked a little pale this morning.' There was sympathy in his soft, Irish voice.

'We're very busy at the mill,' Madeleine said.

'Is that a fact? Then perhaps you should take a glass of this very good port wine yourself, put a little colour in your cheeks!'

'Perhaps I should,' Madeleine agreed. 'Though I don't usually, except perhaps at Christmas.'

'Well just half a glass, and why not? And let me serve you with it.'

Madeleine sipped the port wine, shuddered at the strength of it, then felt its warmth sweep through her.

'Please pour yourself another glass, Father,' she invited him.

'I won't, my child. Enough is as good as a feast! But it has brought the roses back to your cheeks, I'm pleased to see. So how are you, apart from being a little tired?'

'I have something to tell you,' Madeleine said suddenly. There was no reason to keep the news of her pregnancy from Father O'Malley. There was nothing immodest in that; he was a priest, and therefore in the same category as a doctor. She took another sip from her glass, then put it down.

'I am . . . in a certain condition,' she began.

A broad smile lit up Father O'Malley's homely face. 'You mean you're expecting a baby? Is that what you're after telling me?'

'It is, Father!'

'Well the saints be praised, and thanks be to God for his goodness!'

'Thanks to God indeed,' Madeleine echoed – then for a brief moment thought of Romany Rose and her potion. It couldn't have been, because she must already have been pregnant mustn't she? But all the same. . . Then, conscious of Father O'Malley's presence, she dismissed the thought of Romany Rose. She had never confessed the episode.

'Oh, but you'll make the best of mothers!' the priest enthused. 'Haven't I always thought you were cut out for it? And the fortunate child, to be born to good, Catholic parents!'

'Thank you.'

'It's a great blessing,' he continued. 'But I'll make so

bold as to say you don't look quite as happy as I'd expect. Is everything well with the baby?'

'Oh yes!' she said at once. She was relieved at the turn his question had taken. It was easier to talk about the baby. She wanted to talk about herself and Léon, but there was no way she could do so, not even to Father O'Malley.

'Oh yes,' she repeated. 'Everything's all right. The baby's fine, and so am I. It's just that I'm a little bit tired.'

'Well then you must take the greatest care,' he said.

If there *was* something else she wasn't going to tell him. No doubt she thought he'd be shocked. He sighed. If only his parishioners would realize that he was never shocked, or at least not by what they liked to call the facts of life. He'd been a priest a long time, there was little he hadn't heard, and none of it embarrassed him. All that shocked him now was cruelty, and meanness of spirit. To those two qualities he was quite sure Madeleine Bonneau was a stranger.

'Well I'll leave you now,' he said. 'And I'll pray for you, and you'll pray for me. And the moment your husband gets back from France, give him my hearty congratulations!'

He blessed her, then as he reached the door he turned back.

'If it's a boy, you could be calling him Luke. It's Saint Luke's day, as you know. Though Patrick is a splendid name!'

'I'll think about it,' Madeleine said with a smile. 'Half the baby boys in the parish are named Patrick!'

She felt better for his visit, though she wasn't sure why. He'd said nothing of significance and nothing had altered. But from somewhere had come the beginnings of a new strength to accept what she couldn't change. And she couldn't change Léon's decision. That much was clear.

But nothing in the world, no circumstances, would lessen her love for Léon. She loved him with all her heart, and she must show that love in the coming months in abiding cheerfully by his wishes, even when she didn't agree with them. And she would make a start by not wingeing about his absence in France.

On Friday morning, towards dinner-time, Henry Garston arrived unexpectedly at the mill. Madeleine, frowning in concentration at a design which refused to please her, heard the sharp sound of the horses' hooves on the mill-yard cobbles, the screech of wheels and the shouts of the coachman as the carriage was brought to a sudden halt. Only Henry Garston's coachman drove into the mill-yard at a gallop and pulled up within inches.

She pushed away her sketches and jumped to her feet, but Henry was already in the doorway, filling it with his height and breadth.

'Oh Henry, I'm so pleased to see you!'

Madeleine held out her hands in welcome and he took them in his. She was always happy to see her old friend, but this morning she felt especially so. He would brighten up the day. Henry noted the warmth of her greeting, and was grateful, but wondered why.

'You're looking as pretty as a picture,' he said. 'But when don't you?'

'Henry, you're an old flatterer – but, as always, you make me feel better!'

'Nay lass, it's not flattery,' he assured her. 'You're a sight for sore eyes. Is that dress you're wearing one of your own patterns? If so, you've not shown it to me before. I thought I was supposed to see them all.'

It had been part of the arrangement he'd made with Léon, all of seven years ago now, when not only had he given Bonneau's its first big order, but had announced his intention of putting money into the mill so that Léon could expand: in particular, so that he could re-open the spinning, which had had to be closed down when Albert Parkinson had died, and left the mill heavily in debt.

'You know very well you always see the patterns first,'

Madeleine retorted. 'You had the nerve to turn this one down! I thought at the time you were wrong.'

'Well I wouldn't have if I'd seen it on you! You should model all your designs yourself. You'd sell everything ten times over! So where's the Lord and Master this morning?'

He should have gone to Léon's office first. He knew that; but Madeleine drew him like a magnet, always had since that very first day she'd set foot in his office. Eighteen years old and as nervous as a kitten she'd been, but doing the job as well as any man could have done it. Better. More than once he'd offered her a job working for him in Leeds, but nothing could prise her away from that bloody lucky Frenchman.

'Léon is in France,' Madeleine said. 'He's not due back until Monday.'

'I wonder he dare leave you alone so long,' Henry said. 'One of these days he'll come back to find someone's picked you up and carried you off!'

'You mean for my designing talents?' Madeleine said pertly.

'You know damn well I don't – excuse the language!'

'And you know I'd never let myself be carried off,' Madeleine said. 'So does Léon.'

'He doesn't realize his luck,' Henry said.

But I've been lucky today, he thought. How often did he get to see Madeleine on her own? Oh, there was nothing wrong in it, he'd not step an inch out of line, but he'd make the most of it.

'Then I can take you out to your dinner,' he said. 'I'll give you a decent meal. What do you say?'

'Oh Henry, I couldn't do that! I'm a married woman and my husband's away from home! How could I go out to dinner with you alone?'

'I'm not planning on kidnapping you . . . or anything else untoward,' he said dryly. 'It *is* the middle of the day!'

He was amused to see her blush.

'You don't really think Léon would object, do you?' he asked.

'Not Léon,' Madeleine said quickly. 'You're our oldest friend. But you know what Helsdon's like for tittle-tattle.'

'Then we'll go to Bradford,' Henry said. 'You'll not be well known there.'

But you will be, Madeleine thought. Henry Garston was well known throughout the West Riding. There'd be speculation as to who his companion was. But what did it matter? she thought rebelliously. There was nothing wrong in it. Anyway, she felt like doing something different.

'Really, I should be working. There's plenty to do right here.' It was a feeble protest.

'If it's work you're thinking of, well then we can discuss it over the meal. We can talk about tops and noils and twisting and spinning, and warp and weft and burling and mending, and. . .'

'All right!' Madeleine interrupted. 'All right! Thank you very much, and I accept your invitation.'

'Good!' Henry said. 'Hoskins will have us in Bradford in no time at all!'

'Well I wouldn't want to go at your coachman's usual speed,' Madeleine warned. 'You'll have to get him to slow down a bit for me. I'm not the world's best traveller.'

She wondered, too, if the coach drive over the rough roads might harm the baby. She couldn't tell Henry about that, of course. That must be left to Léon to do.

'We'll go as slow as you like,' he promised. 'Slow enough to pick flowers by the roadside, if that's what you want!'

'Do you want to look round the mill first?' Madeleine asked.

'I'll not bother. But I will take a look in the pattern room, see what you've got.'

'Nothing you haven't already seen,' Madeleine told him. 'I'm working on a new design at the moment, but it's proving a bit obstinate.'

'Well you can't keep going without new designs, and that's a fact,' Henry said. 'Not unless you just make plain cloths, which isn't Bonneau's style at all. Without new designs you'd be out of business. You must blame the ladies, always wanting something different.'

'Not only the ladies,' Madeleine contradicted. 'Fashionable men don't want last year's checks, or stripes or flecks.'

'That's true,' Henry conceded. 'Even if the stripe's only a fraction wider or the check a smidgeon bigger. Daft, really!'

'Nevertheless, I don't see you wearing last year's designs,' Madeleine said. 'And it's fashionably-dressed people, whether men or women, we set out to please in Bonneau's.'

'Put your cloak and bonnet on,' Henry urged. 'I'm hungry!'

'Before that I'll go and tell Rob Wainwright I'm going out,' she said. That would surprise the mill manager. She didn't think she'd ever before left the mill in the middle of the day.

'Do you good, Mrs Bonneau,' Rob said. 'A change is as good as a rest!' She worked too hard, that one. He wouldn't let his own wife work like that, but then his wife had three bairns.

'If this is Hoskins's idea of a moderate pace,' Madeleine said a little later as the carriage bowled along the Bradford road, 'then I wouldn't like to experience what he calls fast! I'll be glad when we reach Bradford – and thankful if it's in one piece!'

Henry Garston's only reaction was to laugh – and to be secretly thankful when the bumpy road threw Madeleine against him.

Hoskins pulled up at the King's Head, in the centre of the city. The comfortably-furnished dining-room was packed, though there were few women amongst the customers. Madeleine was conscious of the curious glances which followed them as the head waiter led the way to a secluded table in the far corner of the room. She could hardly be otherwise; they didn't disguise their interest. Several men spoke to Henry Garston as they passed. She thought they went out of their way to do so.

'Don't look so affronted,' Henry said. 'It's admiration, that's what. No woman can go through life looking like you, and not attract admiration!'

The same goes for you, Madeleine thought. Henry Garston was not a man to go unnoticed, however large the crowd. His appearance was outstanding, and he was never less than immaculately dressed. For a start he was a big man, six foot tall. And handsome, though not at all in the same way as Léon. Fair-haired, blue-eyed, where Léon was so dark; solidly built, ruddy-skinned; every aspect of him clearly inherited from Viking forbears who had invaded the northern counties hundreds of years earlier. They had left their stamp on the land, on the language, on the people.

She supposed Henry was now in his early forties. When she'd first met him, she aged eighteen, she'd thought of him as quite old. Now that she was twenty-five the gap didn't seem nearly so wide.

'What'll you have to eat?' Henry asked. 'The roast mutton is usually good.'

'Then that's what I'll have.'

'I shall have a glass of porter with mine. Shall you do the same?' he asked.

Madeleine shook her head.

'Oh, no thank you! A glass of water will be sufficient.'

It was a substantial meal from start to finish. A generous cut from the leg of mutton, roasted potatoes, carrots, and to follow, a deep apple tart with a Cheshire cheese. Too much, Madeleine thought as she struggled with the last of it – and then reminded herself that she was eating for two.

'So how are you getting on, Henry?' Madeleine's voice was gentle.

He knew what she meant. It was only a year since his

wife had died after giving birth to a stillborn child, their only child in eighteen years of marriage.

'I manage,' he said shortly. 'But I can't forgive myself. Forty years old was too late to have a first baby, and I knew it.'

'But Ellen wanted the baby as much as you did,' Madeleine reminded him.

'Well she didn't get it, did she? Not even for a minute. I should never have let her take the risk.'

He'd been punished for it. All the riches in Yorkshire – and he had his fair share of them – couldn't assuage the loneliness of this last year, from which he was just beginning to emerge. Nor would it ever be assuaged. Only a woman could do that, and the only woman who interested him now, and had interested him even when Ellen was alive, was the one sitting opposite to him. And she belonged fairly and squarely to someone else.

'Perhaps you'll marry again,' Madeleine ventured.

'That I'll not do!' He was emphatic. 'The only woman I'd ever want is already married.'

He looked directly at her, his meaning quite plain in his eyes and in the tone of his voice.

'Then you know you must look elsewhere, dear Henry,' she said. 'But any woman would be proud to have you. Any woman who was free.'

'I don't want *any* woman,' he said abruptly. 'Let's change the subject.'

Madeleine was glad to do so. She couldn't contend with it. And the reminder of Ellen Garston's death in childbirth had disturbed her. She didn't want to think about it.

'My brother is leaving the army and coming back to live in Helsdon,' she said.

'Oh! I hadn't realized you had a brother.'

'Irvine. He left Helsdon, joined the army when he was sixteen. Fought in the Crimea and after that his regiment was stationed in Brighton.'

'So what's he going to do in Helsdon?' Henry asked.

Madeleine frowned.

'I don't know. He might not find it easy to get a job?'

'Well,' Henry said in an offhand manner, 'I don't know that I'll have anything, but you could tell him to come to see me in Leeds.'

'Oh Henry, do you really mean that?'

He watched her glow come into her face, as if a lamp had been lit inside her. How little it took to please her, and how much more he was prepared to do just for the pleasure of seeing her happiness.

'What would you like to do now?' he asked.

'Really,' she said hesitantly, 'I ought to go back. I have lots to do.'

'If you must,' he said. 'In which case Hoskins can take us the long way round. We'll go over the moor road before we drop down into Helsdon, get a breath of fresh air into your lungs.'

'I have enjoyed myself,' Madeleine said. 'I do thank you, Henry.'

When Léon broke the news of Madeleine's pregnancy to his mother, Madame Bonneau was overjoyed.

'This is wonderful!' she said. 'I have waited for this day!'

'So have we, *Maman*,' Léon replied. 'There were times when Madeleine and I thought it would never come. And now we have to make sure that all goes well right up to the time of the birth.'

'What do you mean?' Madame Bonneau asked. 'Surely Madeleine is a strong-enough woman? What can possibly go wrong?'

'She is strong and healthy,' Léon agreed. 'But it has taken a long time for this child to be conceived. If by some mischance she were to lose it . . . well, I think she might never have another.'

'But why should she lose it?' his mother said sensibly. 'I should think it's unlikely.'

'I daresay you're right,' Léon agreed. 'All the same, we shall take no risks.'

'To take no *undue* risk is right, of course. But Madeleine will not thank you for mollycoddling her, that is for sure. And now we must invite your brothers and their wives so that we can pass on the good news.' My daughters-in-law will be less pleased than I am, she thought.

'This child,' Simone Bonneau said to her sister-in-law in a low voice, after they had drunk a toast to the unborn baby, 'will be considered far more important than all yours and mine put together, mark my words! Léon was always his mother's favourite, in spite of the fact that he took his money and went off to England, leaving us to look after her.'

'I'm sure you're right,' Charlotte Bonneau said jealously. 'But I don't intend to let my little ones have their noses pushed out by an English brat.'

'Only half-English,' Simone corrected her. 'That is partly the danger. The other half will be French. And because she will see the child only seldom, it will come to mean something special to *Belle-mère*. See if I'm not right!'

At the other side of the room Léon was talking to his sister.

'So you are to be married, *ma petite*? And when shall I meet this Jules Poitier who makes you so starry-eyed? And is he worthy of my little sister?'

'Oh he is, he is!' Marie said ecstatically. 'And if you were to have been here next weekend instead of now, you would have met him. As it is, he is in Paris. Just think of it, Léon, after we are married I shall live in Paris!'

'You will enjoy that?' Léon said.

'I dream of it! And you will come to my wedding?' Marie pleaded. 'It will be next June. June 1863.'

'We shall have our child by then,' Léon said. 'It will be too soon for Madeleine to travel, but I promise I'll be there.'

'It would not be complete without my favourite brother,' Marie said. 'Though I'm sorry Madeleine won't be able to come. Imagine you, a father! Are you pleased?'

'Delighted!' Léon admitted.

He was to stay in Roubaix all the next day, it being Sunday and the worst possible day to travel, and to leave for home by the first train on Monday morning. An hour before lunch-time on Sunday, Hortense Murer presented herself.

'I wasn't invited,' she said, handing a bouquet of flowers to Madame Bonneau. 'It's just that I met Marcel, who told me Léon was home, so I thought I'd call to see him. I hope you don't mind?'

'You are always welcome,' Madame Bonneau said. 'You don't need to be invited. Why, you've been coming here almost since you could walk! But you and Léon must entertain each other for a while. Marie and I have work to do in the kitchen, since Brigitte has one of her *migraines*. Please excuse me.'

'So!' Hortense said when Madame Bonneau had gone. 'And what news have you from England? All goes well, I hope?'

'Very well. And you? You are looking well, looking very *chic*.'

She always did. In all the years he had known her she had never looked less than very attractive; and though she no longer lived there, the few years she had spent in Paris had given her a polish, a sophistication, which few women of his acquaintance possessed. It was difficult to understand why she had never married.

They talked easily together: of France; of Emperor Louis Napoleon and his exploits: his love affairs, and his Empress Eugénie's jealous reaction to them, were always good for a gossip. Then there was fashion. Hortense was nothing if not fashionable, and the subject interested Léon for, hopefully, he would supply the cloth for some of France's autumn and winter outfits.

'And so you are to be a father?' Hortense said presently. 'Marie told me.'

'That is so!'

'I congratulate you. And if,' she added lightly, 'like so many husbands, you should get a little bored while your wife is pregnant, well then, you must come to Roubaix and I will cheer you up!'

Léon laughed.

'Oh Hortense! You should be married yourself, and have children. Why not? Why have you never married?'

He knew at once, by the way she lifted her chin and turned her head away, that it was a question he shouldn't have asked.

'I'm sorry,' he said. 'I take it back. Don't answer.'

She turned and looked him full in the face.

'But I *shall* answer. I have never married because the man I wanted did not ask me. I had thought he would, but he went away and chose a bride from another country. And now, I believe, he is a faithful husband. Is that not so?'

'That is so,' he said quietly. 'I didn't know, Hortense!'

'Would it have made any difference if you had?'

He shrugged. 'Earlier on, who can say?'

'But you are happily and faithfully married, isn't that true?'

'Absolutely true!'

'What a pity! But my offer stands. If you get bored, I will amuse you. And now I must go and see if your mother needs help.'

It was late on Monday night when Léon returned. Madeleine had persuaded her mother to go to bed.

Perhaps it would be more tactful of me not to wait up, Mrs Bates thought. They will want to be alone. Also, she was quite tired, glad to retire.

So now Madeleine was sitting in the drawing-room, the fire burning high, the heavy curtains drawn against the October night. For the twentieth time she glanced at

81

the clock. The last train was due into Helsdon within a few minutes. If there was a cab, he would be home very soon. If there wasn't, it would be at least half an hour before he arrived.

The moments crawled by. Clearly, she reckoned after a while, there'd been no cab awaiting the last train. She began to think of the awful things which could befall him on the lonely walk from the station. He might be set upon and robbed, or fall and break an ankle, or. . .

Her imagination was in full spate when she heard the door, and the next moment he was in the room with her. He stood with outstretched arms, and she ran into them.

'Oh Léon! Oh Léon! I've missed you so much!'

'And I have missed you too, my love,' Léon said.

He held her tightly in his arms and kissed her long and lovingly, so lovingly that for a moment she told herself that everything was going to be all right between them, that it would all be as it had been before. But when she clung to him more closely, pressed her body urgently against his, he gently disengaged himself and held her at arm's length. In spite of his gentleness, there was no mistaking his action.

He turned away and went and sat in an armchair, not on the sofa which they had always shared. He might have been a hundred miles away.

With a tremendous effort, Madeleine controlled her feelings, even smiled at him.

'Are you hungry?' she asked brightly. 'Shall I get you something to eat? There's some cold chicken.'

'I'm not hungry, my love. Just travel weary. Have you kept well?'

'Quite well, thank you. And your family? How did you find them?'

'Also well. *Maman* was naturally delighted to hear about the baby, as I knew she would be. I have almost made her promise that she will visit us next summer, after the baby is born. And would you believe, little Marie is to be married next June, and to live in Paris!'

82

'Really! How thrilling! I *am* glad all is well.'

'Everyone sent best wishes, including Hortense Murer.'

'Hortense?'

'She arrived for lunch yesterday. She'd heard I was visiting.'

'How very considerate! And how nice for you,' Madeleine said. It was an effort to keep her voice steady.

The feeling which now swept through her made her heart thump in her chest, made her feel near to choking. So this was jealousy? She had never experienced it before, never believed she was capable of it. But why should she feel like this? There was no reason. She was Léon's wife and he loved her. Hortense Murer was no more than an old friend. What was more natural than a visit from an old friend, and where was the harm in it?

'It *was* nice,' Léon agreed. 'I am always pleased to see Hortense.'

'Of course! Well, like you, I am rather tired, and it's late. I think I shall go to bed.'

Would he follow her?

She put on her very best night-shift, the one she had worn in Paris, and left the candle alight. She lay there for half an hour, waiting for him to come upstairs. Eventually, he came into the bedroom. At the sight of him her spirits rose sky high.

He came and kissed her gently, then said: 'Good-night, my dear! Sleep well!'

He turned away from her and went to his dressing-room.

FIVE

Over the next two months Madeleine's daily routine went on as usual. She worked in the mill, went to church, ventured occasionally into Helsdon. Her pregnancy was known to very few people, but that was the way of things. You didn't announce it from the housetops.

'In the first year I was married,' she'd remarked to her mother, 'everyone used to look me up and down. They thought I wouldn't notice, but I did. Now they don't bother any more. They've given me up!'

'Then they're in for a surprise,' Mrs Bates replied. 'Though I must say, you don't show. Happen a little fuller in the figure, but that suits you.'

'And I've had to let out all my waistbands!'

How lucky she was to have her mother to talk to, if only about everyday things. Some days she felt so far from Léon. Outwardly, their relationship was the same. They were polite, considerate, even loving towards each other. Léon continued to sleep in his dressing-room.

There were times when her body ached for him. She couldn't believe his didn't for her. She had seen it in his eyes. But if she tried to reach him, perhaps physically by touching him, or showing in her eyes all the longing in her heart, then he withdrew. And when he withdrew she felt as though he had flung back her offer in her face.

She'd learned to bear it, because she'd determined she would, and she loved him. She bore it by working harder than ever in the mill, and at home by concentrating on the thought of her baby. She had begun, in the evenings, to make the baby's layette. It occupied her hands, and gave herself and Léon something to talk about. She was sewing now.

'What are you making?' Léon enquired.

She looked so beautiful with the soft glow from the lamp lighting up her lovely face, making pools of light and shade on her gown. Pregnancy had added to her beauty, fining her skin, adding a new softness to her eyes. He longed to embrace her – and gripped the arms of his chair in an effort not to cross the few feet which separated them. His resolve to put his wife and the baby first still held. He wished Madeleine could understand what it cost him.

He jumped to his feet now, crossed to the cabinet, poured himself a brandy and drank it too quickly.

'I'm making a gown,' Madeleine said. 'I had no idea a baby needed so many things: petticoats, flannels, binders, day-gowns and night-gowns, caps. And sewing is not my forte, as you know. Since the material is so fine, I should use much smaller stitches, but I'm not capable of doing so.'

'I don't suppose the baby will mind,' Léon said.

Perhaps the baby might understand, Madeleine thought – who knew what went on inside a baby? – that it was done in love. Would there be any end to the things she must do, or refrain from doing, for love of the baby? Sewing, though she hated it, was perhaps the least difficult.

She snipped off the cotton, put the needle back in its case and folded the work in a cloth to keep it clean. 'I'm going to bed,' she announced. 'Good-night, Léon.'

She kissed him lightly on the cheek and he returned her kiss in a similar manner.

'You're looking rather pale,' Léon said. 'Isn't it time you took more rest? Why don't you stay away from the mill tomorrow? It's what other women would do.'

'No, Léon,' Madeleine said firmly. 'When it becomes necessary I will stay at home. But up to now I'm perfectly fit. And even when I stop going into the mill I plan to do some of my work at home.'

She couldn't rest. She felt driven. She had wanted so

much to be pregnant, she had pictured herself sailing through the nine months on a sea of tranquillity. It was all quite different. Oh, she wanted the child as much as ever, but now she longed for the weeks to speed by and for the baby to be in her arms. And for herself to be back in Léon's arms.

Next day she was in Léon's office, discussing an order, when Rob Wainwright knocked at the door and entered.

'You wanted to know about Baxandall's order?' he said to Léon. 'It'll be ready for despatch tomorrow, if that'll suit.'

'It will suit very well, Rob,' Léon said. 'It's an important order for us. I wouldn't want to keep them waiting.'

Wainwright turned to Madeleine.

'Did Mr Garston say owt about the date for his next delivery when he was here?' he asked.

Léon looked at Madeleine with raised eyebrows.

'Henry was here? I didn't know.'

There wasn't the slightest reason why she should have blushed. She was furious with herself for doing so.

'You were in France,' she said. 'His order should go out next week at the latest. He's been waiting for the new check design. It's in the finishing.'

'I see!' Léon turned to his mill manager. 'Thank you, Rob. Make sure that Baxandall's goes off tomorrow, without fail.'

When Wainwright had left, Léon turned to Madeleine.

'Why didn't you tell me that Henry had called?'

'I forgot.'

She *had* forgotten at first. There had been other things to think about when Léon came home. Afterwards, when she'd remembered, for some reason she couldn't analyse, she hadn't mentioned it.

'Forgot? But we've talked about Henry, more than once!'

'I just didn't think about it. Does it matter?'

'So what did he come for?'

'Nothing in particular, or at least he didn't say. He took me out to dinner.'

Léon looked at her in astonishment.

'He took you out to dinner? You forgot to tell me not only that Henry Garston had visited, but that he took you out to dinner? You surprise me, Madeleine, you really do!'

She flinched at his tone. It was so unlike him.

'And how do I surprise you most?' she asked. 'By going out to dinner with Henry, or by forgetting to tell you?'

'Both,' he said sharply. 'Where did you go for this meal?'

'Léon, this sounds like an inquisition,' Madeleine said. 'Am I on trial?'

'Not at all,' Léon said. 'But I think you have acted unwisely. Women in the West Riding, married women, do not go out to dinner accompanied by a man who is not their husband.'

'But men can?' she countered. 'I suppose it would be all right if you did it? It would be all right if you took out Hortense Murer?'

She could have bitten her tongue out the moment she'd said the words. What in the world was she thinking of?

'What has Hortense Murer to do with this?' Léon sounded astonished. 'I don't understand you. Hortense is an old friend. Moreover, she's in France.'

'And so is Henry Garston an old friend. And so were you in France!'

'That is quite beside the point,' Léon said. 'You surely don't want me to think you behave one way when I'm here and another when I'm away from home?'

'I don't understand this,' Madeleine said. 'Why are we quarrelling? I did nothing wrong.'

'I'm willing to believe that. . .' Léon began.

'Willing to believe me? Thank you very much, I'm sure. That's most generous of you!'

87

'But you were indiscreet,' Léon continued. 'You know what a place Helsdon is for gossip.'

'Then it's all right,' Madeleine said. 'You've nothing to worry about. We didn't stay in Helsdon. We went to Bradford.'

'Oh Madeleine! Madeleine, how could you be so foolish? It is exactly where one would go on an affair like this! Surely you realize how well-known Henry is – and by now half the wool trade will know who he was with!'

She had never seen him so angry. Well, she was angry too. She felt hot with temper. She wanted to hit him.

'It was not an affair!' she stormed. 'Don't be ridiculous! I was feeling a bit down and I accepted an impromptu invitation from an old friend, who had actually come to see you. We ate roast mutton and apple pie. I drank water. Immediately after dinner he brought me back here. That's the lot, so make what you like of it!'

'Please don't shout, Madeleine!' Léon said. 'Control yourself, or Rob Wainwright will hear from his room.'

It was too much! How dare he! 'Don't you tell me not to shout, Léon Bonneau! I'll shout from the top of the mill chimney if I want to! And Rob Wainwright knows. I've done nothing the whole world can't know about.'

She swung round, marched out of the room, slammed the door so hard that it shook on its hinges. Tears of rage and frustration raced down her cheeks. As she neared her own room Rob Wainwright came towards her. Seeing her distress he instinctively put out a hand to comfort her, but she flung him away, went into her room and closed the door.

What was all that about, he wondered? She was a lively piece, the boss's wife, but even so he'd never seen her in such a tizzy. However, there was a rumour that she was expecting, and that could play havoc with a woman. Didn't he know it! His own wife was impossible when she was in the family way.

For the rest of that day Madeleine didn't go near Léon,

nor did he come into her room. It was unfortunate that the food for their midday meal was in his office, and that by dinner-time she was starving hungry, because there was no way she would go in there and eat with him, or even collect her share. Let him come and apologize to her!

By the time the mill buzzer went for the end of the day she was ravenous. She left at once, not waiting for Léon, and hurried home. There she surprised her mother by eating almost the whole of an oven bottom cake, still warm from the oven, spreading it thickly with butter and blackcurrant jam.

'I see you've lost your appetite – and found a horse's,' Mrs Bates remarked.

'I *was* a bit hungry!' Madeleine confessed, licking the jam from her fingers. 'I *am* eating for two, you know!'

'I'd have said you were eating for a whole brass band,' Mrs Bates said dryly. 'But no matter. It's easy enough to bake more, just in case anyone else might want a bite.'

'I'm sorry, Ma! I was greedy.'

She felt better now that she'd eaten. It really had all been a quite stupid quarrel. Yet in a strange way she felt liberated by it. She'd fought for her corner, and if she hadn't won, at least she hadn't been totally vanquished. But why am I thinking in terms of fighting, she asked herself? And with my dear Léon of all people? Now she could hardly wait for him to come home so that they could make it up.

'When you were pregnant,' she asked her mother, 'were you different? I mean, did you feel different in yourself? Were you happy, contented – or were you short-tempered and touchy?' As I was today, she thought.

Mrs Bates looked quizzically at her daughter. She wasn't surprised at the question. She had seen the minute Madeleine walked in that she was upset about something, she wasn't her usual self.

'My pregnancies were the happiest times of my life,' she confessed. 'Each time I was carrying a child I felt as though I mattered in the world.' They had also been the only times when her husband had shown her any consideration.

'But it takes people differently,' she went on. 'And if you're a bit up and down, it'll all be quite different when you hold the baby in your arms.'

'I suppose so,' Madeleine said. But it was Léon she wanted to hold in her arms.

When Léon came home nothing was said of the quarrel between them. Léon read his newspaper; Madeleine sat with her sewing. It was as if the morning's scene had never taken place. Wouldn't it be better to discuss it, Madeleine asked herself? Clear the air?

Léon had decided otherwise.

It was wrong of me to upset her, he thought. I must make allowances for her condition. Let it be as if it had never happened. Presently he looked up from his newspaper.

'Are you comfortable, my dear? Do you have enough light for your sewing?'

He got up and fetched another lamp, placed it near her.

'There! That's better!'

'Thank you, Léon.'

So that was to be the end of their quarrel?

Suddenly, Madeleine could bear it no longer. His very politeness increased the distance between them.

'If you'll excuse me, I'm going to bed,' she muttered.

She hurried from the room. She couldn't bear the thought of yet another chaste good-night kiss.

She rushed into the bedroom, flung herself down on the bed and burst into tears. He didn't love her, that was plain. If he loved her he wouldn't be so aloof, so high and mighty. If he loved her he would share her bed, he would take no notice of that silly old doctor. He would just take her and make love to her!

She was still crying, her face blotchy, her eyes swollen with tears, her hair falling down her back, when Léon came into the room. She hadn't bothered even to

90

undress, but lay on the counterpane where she had flung herself.

His heart melted with pity at the sight of her. Oh, my poor, darling Madeleine, he chided himself! What have I done to you? But in the same instant that he looked at her in remorse, he was engulfed by a passion so strong that it wasn't in him to quell it. There was no thought in his mind now of the baby, only of Madeleine and his overpowering, physical need of her.

He was on the bed and his hands and lips were on her, searching and finding. She pressed against him, all softness and yielding against the demands of his body. When he fumbled with the fastenings of her clothes she came to his aid, but her own passion was mounting, there was no time to halt their lovemaking. Before she could rid herself of her voluminous skirts and petticoats he was entering her. She received him with a gasp of satisfaction, the depth of which she had not known existed, and when his climax came, and hers with it, she gave a cry of pure joy.

Afterwards, lying in each other's arms, he said: 'Oh my darling, I am so sorry!'

She put her hand over his mouth.

'Please don't say that. I'm not in the least sorry. Oh Léon, I don't think I could have borne another day without you!'

'But the baby . . . ?'

'I can't believe that God will punish us for the feelings he put into us. That was my father's religion; it's not mine. Somehow, I'm no longer afraid.'

'Then I will go to Dr Hughes myself and speak with him about this,' Léon said. 'And shall we agree together to abide by what he says – only this time in love and closeness, no distance between us?'

'Very well. I agree,' Madeleine said.

Long after Léon had fallen asleep, Madeleine lay awake. Lying close against her husband she was filled with happiness, only in the farthest corner of her mind was there still the smallest doubt about the baby. But it was groundless, she was sure. Nothing bad could come from the ecstacy which had been theirs.

Towards morning she fell into a deep sleep. When Léon wakened he raised himself on his elbow and looked at her, still sleeping, her dark hair spread on the pillow, her long, black eyelashes splayed against pale cheeks. So vulnerable she looked in sleep, and he loved her so much. He had been wrong to quarrel with her, but perhaps not wrong in that it had led to such a coming-together. How strange that the thought of Henry Garston had lit such a fire of jealousy in him – a jealousy he hadn't known he possessed.

He tiptoed out of the room. Let her sleep, he thought. It will do her good.

When Madeleine came down an hour later he had left the house.

'Léon told me not to wake you,' Mrs Bates said.

Whatever it had all been about yesterday, her daughter certainly looked a changed woman this morning.

'I shall be late for work,' Madeleine said. 'Is there anything in the post?'

Mrs Bates held up a letter.

'For me, from Emerald. It's just come.' She started to open it.

'She doesn't write often,' Madeleine said, pouring herself a cup of tea. 'It must be something good.' No bad news could come on such a wonderful morning as this.

'She writes to say there's a place for Our Penelope with the Chesters, if she wants it,' Mrs Bates announced. 'The girl who looks after the children is leaving, Emerald is going to take that on, and Mrs Chester needs someone to take Emerald's place.'

'Oh Ma, I'd like that!' Penelope cried. Life could be very boring in Helsdon. From Emerald's letters it sounded as though they had a much better time in Ripon.

'I suppose you would,' Mrs Bates said slowly. 'And I've

been thinking it might be good for you to get away. You don't want to be tied to your Ma's apron strings all your life.'

'But not to go to the Chesters!' Madeleine protested. 'Not to work for that terrible woman! Surely you'd not allow that, Ma?'

'Why do you say she's a terrible woman?' Penelope demanded. 'Emerald doesn't think so.'

'I *know* she is,' Madeleine said emphatically. 'Don't forget I've worked for her!'

'Perhaps Emerald is right,' Mrs Bates said. 'She's always liked working for Mrs Chester.'

'You don't know Mrs Chester,' Madeleine said. 'If you did. . .'

'But I know you,' Mrs Bates interrupted. 'And I think perhaps it's that you just weren't cut out to be a servant, not to anyone. You've never liked taking orders. I don't hold that against you, but Emerald is different.'

'She certainly is!' Madeleine agreed. 'Our Emerald is like a little dog, who loves the mistress who kicks it, and comes back for more! Not for me, thank you!'

'No one's offering it to you!' Penelope said cheekily. 'It's me being offered it; nothing to do with you! Oh Ma, do say I can go! It'll be much more exciting than here. Nothing ever happens in Helsdon.'

'Sooner or later everything happens in Helsdon,' Mrs Bates said. 'But you're too young to want to wait for it. I understand that, but you mustn't expect to find Ripon a whirl of excitement!'

'Please, Ma, don't let her go!' Madeleine begged. She was so happy herself, she couldn't bear to think of her sister plunging into Sophia Chester's world.

'Well she could go on a month's notice, which is what Mrs Chester suggests,' Mrs Bates said. 'That's not the end of the world. She could always come back if she didn't like it.'

'Oh I will, I will!' Penelope promised.

'If you're determined, it would be the best way,'

Madeleine said. 'But now I must get off to work.'

She ran all the way down the hill, arriving at the mill breathless and with a thumping heart. Léon watched her charge across the yard and went out to meet her.

'Whatever is wrong?' he demanded. 'You're running as if the house was on fire.'

'Penelope is going to be a servant to Sophia Chester!' she gasped.

'Well that is a surprise,' Léon said. 'I can see you wouldn't like it, but you mustn't get into a state about it, my darling.'

'You can say that because you've never been a servant. You don't know what Sophia Chester is like!'

'Oh yes I do,' Léon contradicted. 'I wouldn't want to work with her in a thousand years. But Emerald does, and Penelope might. You can't judge for everyone. But I have something of even more importance to you and me. I went to see Dr Hughes before I came to work. I think he was most surprised to see me so early.'

'Oh Léon! What did he say?'

'He said that in his opinion for us to make love would not endanger the baby, especially now that the first few months are over and there is less danger of a miscarriage. But we must use some caution, especially as the time draws near – which I, dearest, will promise to do.'

'Oh Léon, that's wonderful! Oh, I'm so happy!'

The next day a letter, not from Sophia Chester but from her mother, confirmed what Emerald had written.

'You see,' Madeleine said, 'Sophia Chester doesn't even have the courtesy to write to you yourself.'

'Mrs Parkinson has explained that,' Mrs Bates said. 'Since the nursemaid has already left, Sophia is all hands aloft with three small children. That's why Mrs Parkinson is staying there, and why she has written the letter. Let me tell you, my dear, that when you have one child, let alone three, you'll find a big difference in your life!'

Later, when Penelope had left the room, Madeleine returned to the subject.

'Ma, do you really think Penelope should go? She's a different character from Emerald; she's more sensitive.'

'Do you think I don't know my own daughter?' Mrs Bates queried. 'To a certain extent you're right, of course; but not entirely so. It's time Our Penelope began to find her own feet, and she wants to do so. Besides, she'll have Emerald for company. She might go somewhere else where she'd be lonely.'

Madeleine sighed. 'You seem determined.'

'Anyway,' Mrs Bates said, 'Mrs Parkinson invites me to take Penelope to Ripon – which I shall most certainly do because she's never travelled anywhere alone – so I shall be able to judge the set-up. If I don't like the look of it, or if Penelope doesn't settle, she shall leave at the end of the month. I'll take her on Saturday. Mrs Parkinson says they want someone as soon as possible.'

'I shall miss her,' Madeleine said. She'd always felt an especial bond with Penelope. In spite of the gap in age between them, they had been rebels together against their father. Though poor little Penelope had been less able to stand against him than I was, Madeleine remembered.

When Saturday came there was no question of Mrs Bates going to Ripon. As she bent to tie her shoelaces a fierce pain shot across the bottom of her back. She let out an agonized yell, which brought both Penelope and Madeleine running, to find their mother bent double.

'Oh Ma, whatever is it?' Madeleine cried. 'Here, let me help you!'

'I can't stand up!' Mrs Bates said in a strained voice. 'It's that dratted lumbago again, that's what it is!'

Gently, to the accompaniment of sharp cries of pain, Madeleine helped her mother to a chair.

'Oh dear me, I shan't be able to go to Ripon,' Mrs Bates moaned.

'Of course you won't,' Madeleine agreed. 'It's not to be thought of!'

Penelope burst into noisy tears.

'Oh, it's not that I'm not sorry for you, Ma,' she said between sobs, 'but I *must* go today. We promised faithfully. If I wait until you're better, Mrs Chester will get someone else and it will break my heart.'

'Hearts don't break that easy,' Mrs Bates assured her youngest. 'But yes, you're right, you should go today.'

'I'll go on my own,' Penelope said. 'I don't mind a bit.'

'I don't like the thought of it,' her mother said unhappily. 'But if there's no other way. . .'

'I'll take her,' Madeleine said. 'It's not the journey, I'm sure she'd manage that. What's more important is that someone must see that everything's sorted out – what her duties will be, her time off, her wages; see that she's not taken advantage of. Come to think of it, Ma, I daresay I shall put the fear of the Lord into Sophia Chester better than you ever could!'

'Please, Madeleine, I don't want any trouble,' Penelope said anxiously.

'Don't worry, love! If Mrs Chester gives me no trouble, I'll give her none,' Madeleine promised. 'I only want what's best for you. Now I must tell Léon I can't go into the mill this morning. He won't mind that. He's always on at me to stay at home.'

'If you were to let Mrs Partridge know, she'd come in and help out,' Mrs Bates said. 'And at the same time she can iron my back over a bit of blanket. There's nothing better for the lumbago.'

'I'm all packed,' Penelope said.

'Are you sure you've got everything?' Mrs Bates asked anxiously. 'Oh if only I could get up from this chair and see to it.'

'I haven't forgotten a thing, Ma. Underwear, night-dresses, nightcap, handkerchiefs. Face flannel, poorly cloths. . .'

'And your bible?'

'Of course.'

'And the cake I baked for Emerald?'

'Yes,' Penelope assured her. 'Oh Ma, I shall miss you. But thank you for letting me go.'

'Just be a good girl and serve your mistress well,' Mrs Bates said. 'Remember, Mrs Chester will supply your uniform and then take it out of your wages a bit at a time. Oh dear, I did so want to take you! I wonder when I shall see you again?'

'Don't worry, Ma,' Madeleine said. 'I shall see to it that Sophia Chester allows Penelope to come home from time to time – Emerald too while I'm about it.'

'It won't be before Christmas,' Mrs Bates said. 'Irvine will be home before I see you again.'

In the train Madeleine handed Penelope a half-sovereign.

'Put this in your purse and take care of it. It's yours to spend as you like, but take my advice and always keep enough back for your fare home, should you wish to come back.'

'Oh Madeleine, you are kind!' Penelope cried. 'And Ma gave me a florin. I've never been so rich in my life! I'll do as you say and keep some back, but I shan't want to run back home, Madeleine. I know I shan't!'

'We'll hope not,' Madeleine said. 'All I want is for you to be happy.'

Whinbury School was only a little way out of the town. They followed the directions Mrs Parkinson had given in her letter, and found themselves at the school gates in a quarter of an hour.

'Oh Madeleine, what lovely grounds!' Penelope said in an awed voice. 'All these lawns and trees! Do you think the Chesters are very rich then?'

'No, you silly goose! Mr Chester is a housemaster here, though I daresay the parents of some of the pupils are rich enough. Now it's School House we want and my guess is that that's the one, over to the left.'

She was right. It was a pretty house. Not big, not in

comparison with somewhere like Mount Royd, but pleasant enough.

'We'd better go round to the back door,' Penelope said.

'No!' Madeleine said. 'We go to the front!' Best start as she meant to go on. She was no snob, but she was on a level with Sophia Chester now.

Her ring at the door was eventually answered by Emerald herself, looking dishevelled, her cap awry. The poor lamb looks overworked, Madeleine thought, and for the first time was glad she had brought Penelope to help out.

'Oh Madeleine! Oh Penelope!' Emerald cried. 'But where's mother?'

'She has a sudden attack of lumbago,' Madeleine explained. 'It's nothing serious, but she couldn't make the journey so I'm here instead, love. You'd better tell Mrs Chester we've arrived.'

Sophia Chester looked more than a little put out when Emerald announced Madeleine's arrival.

'I thought your mother was to bring Penelope,' she complained.

'My mother's got an attack of lumbago,' Emerald apologized.

'Well take both your sisters into the kitchen,' Sophia said.

'No!' Mrs Parkinson interrupted. 'Ask them to wait in the hall for a minute or two.'

'Mama, what do you mean?' Sophia asked when Emerald had gone.

'You can't ask Madeleine to wait in the kitchen. You must receive her here, in the drawing-room. She is Mrs Bonneau now, and your social equal whether you like it or not!'

'Well I don't like it,' Sophia said angrily. 'I don't like it at all! The kitchen is good enough for Madeleine Bates any day of the week!'

'Perhaps it would be if she *were* Madeleine Bates. But as I've just pointed out, she is Mrs Bonneau – and whether you like it or not doesn't change your social obligations. What's more, you must give her tea.'

'Give her tea!' Sophia cried. 'How preposterous!' Nevertheless, she knew she must do it. Social convention said so, and social conventions must be followed, or where would everyone be? But to give tea, in her drawing-room, to a servant, and to Madeleine Bates at that!

'And what about the youngest one?' she demanded. 'Am I supposed to serve tea to a girl who's coming to work with me?'

'You need not do that,' Mrs Parkinson conceded. 'As soon as you've interviewed her, Emerald can take her off and give her tea in the kitchen.'

'Oh very well,' Sophia said crossly. 'But I shall get through the whole thing as quickly as possible. I can't stand Madeleine Bates!'

Mrs Parkinson cut short the arguments by ringing for Emerald.

'Please show both your sisters into the drawing-room,' she said.

Madeleine walked into Sophia Chester's drawing-room, head held high. Penelope crept in by her side.

'Good-afternoon, Mrs Chester, Mrs Parkinson. I hope you are well.'

'We are both well, thank you,' Mrs Parkinson said. 'I am sorry to hear of your mother's misfortune.'

'Yes. She was sorry not to be able to come. However, I have come instead. Penelope has never been away from home before. I'm sure you'll understand that I wanted to make sure that everything would be all right.'

The effrontery of it! *I* am the one who is supposed to be giving the interview, Sophia thought angrily. How dare she?

'As you say,' she said coldly. 'Your sister is inexperienced.'

'She has been well trained by my mother,' Madeleine put in.

'Be that as it may –' Sophia dismissed Mrs Bates's training out of hand '– she would be required to do a month's trial. And then there is the question of her references.'

'The Minister of the chapel will give Penelope a reference – though, with respect, your family has known my family for many years, and my sister Emerald is already giving you satisfactory service. As for the month's trial, well I couldn't agree more.'

Sophia looked at Madeleine suspiciously. The words were harmless, but there was something in the tone of her voice. . .

'I am sure it will work out all right,' Mrs Parkinson said pacificatorily. 'Emerald is happy enough here, and I'm sure Penelope will be.' She gave Penelope a reassuring smile. 'And I know my daughter is ready to discuss such things as wages. . .'

'And time off. . .' Madeleine said mildly.

'And time off, and duties, of course!' Mrs Parkinson agreed.

She gave her daughter a warning look. Sophia needed this girl. No way am I staying here for ever, she thought. The maid the domestic agency in Ripon had sent was only here for a few days and in any case she was hopeless. One thing you could say for the Bates' girls, they were workers. Even Madeleine, though she wasn't cut out to be a servant, had worked hard for them at Mount Royd.

'Very well,' Sophia said. 'Come here, Penelope. Stand in front of me.'

Madeleine's eyes met hers. The message in them was plain. Treat her gently or I'll take her right back with me.

Sophia asked Penelope all the questions she could think of. She was really no good at this sort of thing. It was so tedious.

'Well,' she said in the end. 'Do you think you would like to stay here?'

'Oh yes please!' Penelope said eagerly. 'I should like it very much!' She'd begun to think no one would ever ask her opinion.

Sophia shot a look of triumph at Madeleine. Mrs

Parkinson breathed a sigh of relief and rang for Emerald. But when Emerald came, she kept quiet, forcing her daughter to give the order.

'Please bring tea for three into the drawing-room – the second-best service – and take Penelope to the kitchen where she can have tea with you,' Sophia said.

It was a bitter moment, and even more bitter when she was obliged to pour tea and hand it to Madeleine. She would like to have thrown it at her.

But worse was to come. The doorbell rang and a breathless Emerald appeared again.

'The Honourable Mrs Woolf!' she announced.

The Honourable Agatha had not waited to be received; she followed only three paces behind Emerald, sure of her welcome.

Drat! Sophia thought. I'm not using the best china!

'Oh, my dear Sophia!' the Honourable Agatha cried. 'Emerald did not say that you already had a visitor!'

She stood there, waiting to be introduced. Sophia seized her chance.

'Not really a visitor,' she said. 'Mrs Bonneau is a former servant, from when we were at Mount Royd. She is here to bring her sister to take up a post.'

'Oh, I see!'

She didn't quite see. The woman didn't look the least bit like a servant. She was as fashionably dressed as ever you'd find in Yorkshire, and that was real fur trimming on her cloak.

'So where do you live, Mrs Bonneau?' she asked.

'At Mount Royd,' Madeleine said amicably.

'So . . . so you are in service at Mount Royd?' How *avant garde* of dear Sophia to be giving a servant, even a rather superior one, tea in her drawing-room. And how utterly, utterly unlike her!

'No,' Madeleine said pleasantly. 'Mount Royd is my home. I live there with my husband, Monsieur Léon Bonneau, of Bonneau's Mill.'

Stranger and stranger, thought the Honourable Agatha.

101

Surely dear Sophia had given her to understand, that Mount Royd was still in her own family, only waiting to be claimed at some suitable date in the future.

'A Frenchman, eh? And do you go to France?'

'From time to time. I was in Paris in August,' Madeleine said modestly.

'One hears that your husband is away in France a great deal,' Sophia said acidly. She simply must take the conversation away from Agatha.

'Business does take him away from time to time,' Madeleine admitted.

'My late husband thought very highly of Léon,' Mrs Parkinson said.

'So *you* know Monsieur Bonneau, Sophia?' the Honourable Agatha said to her hostess.

'I did. But one outgrows people, don't you find?' Sophia's voice was razor-sharp. She turned to Madeleine, following up her advantage.

'What a pity you have no children to live at Mount Royd. Here am I with three little darlings and I understand you show no signs at all! They do say that if you don't have children in the first two years, the outlook isn't too good.'

'What rubbish!' Mrs Parkinson said.

'But Mama, there is always a reason for these things,' Sophia continued – and now she looked Madeleine straight in the eye. 'For instance, I know someone who put a spell on someone, and she never did have children. Too dreadful isn't it?'

Madeleine met her look head on. She would never forget that awful day – they had stood facing each other in the drawing-room at Mount Royd – when Sophia had cursed her, said she would always be barren. She need no longer worry about it, but she would never forget it, nor the two anxious years in which it had seemed to be true.

'Well Mrs Chester,' she said evenly, 'I have to say that if anyone ever put such a spell on me, then it hasn't worked. In fact I'm pregnant. I expect my baby next May.'

'Well. I'm very pleased for you,' Mrs Parkinson said.

'Thank you. And now, if you will excuse me, I'll just take leave of my sisters before I go for my train.'

In the kitchen she said: 'Are you happy about staying, Penelope love?'

'Oh yes, I am!' Penelope was all enthusiasm. 'Emerald showed me the room I'm to share with her. I'm sure everything's going to be all right, Madeleine.'

'Well I hope so,' Madeleine said. 'Write home as often as you can. We shall all miss you – as we do you, Emerald.'

On the homeward-bound train Madeleine took a seat in a compartment in which there was only one other occupant, a middle-aged, amply-built lady, sitting opposite. She didn't seem talkative and Madeleine was glad to close her eyes and relax. She hoped Penelope would be as happy as Emerald seemed to be, though it seemed incredible to her.

Presently her breathing deepened and she fell asleep. When she wakened, it was with a start, with a feeling of something having happened to her. Then it came again, and she knew at once, though she had never experienced it before in her life, what it was.

She clutched her stomach and cried out. She couldn't help it!

'My baby! My baby!'

'My dear, what is the matter? Is something wrong?'

But it couldn't be, the woman opposite thought. The young woman's face was lit with a radiant smile.

'Oh, do forgive me!' Madeleine said. 'I'm sorry if I startled you. Nothing is wrong. Absolutely nothing! But you see, I felt my baby move! For the very first time I felt him move!'

'Ah!' the lady said. 'Then I know how you feel. I have children of my own.'

When the train reached Helsdon Léon was waiting on

the platform to meet her. Madeleine ran down the platform and threw herself into his arms.

'Oh I'm so glad you're here, Léon! So glad!'

'My dear Madeleine! Did you think I'd let you come home alone, in the dark?'

'Oh it's not that,' she cried. 'It's the baby. Oh Léon, I felt the baby move!'

It was all excitement at Mount Royd, at least in that part of it over which Martha Bates held sway, and not only because Christmas was so near. More important to Mrs Bates was that Irvine would be home in less than a week now. She found it difficult to think of anything beyond the fact that she would spend Christmas with her son and her grandson – and her daughter-in-law, of course.

Everything which could be done in advance, *had* been done. The plum puddings and mincemeat had been made, and put away to keep; the goose ordered, the best tablecloth laundered. Mrs Partridge had given each room its pre-Christmas clean and polish. Every surface gleamed, every pane of glass in the large windows now sparkled in the pale December sunshine.

'Though they'll not sparkle long before the smoke gets at them,' Mrs Partridge observed. 'Happen we should have left the outsides until later.'

'We're leaving nothing we don't have to,' Mrs Bates said firmly. 'When my son comes I want everything spick and span!'

'Where's he going to live, then?' Mrs Partridge asked.

Mrs Bates frowned. That was a problem not as easily dealt with as baking and cleaning.

'I don't know,' she admitted. 'We shall have to find somewhere temporary.'

'I would have thought there was plenty of space here,' Mrs Partridge observed. 'All those empty rooms!'

'We can't use the empty rooms. Monsieur Bonneau still only rents part of the house – as yet.'

It was her opinion, though, that before long Léon would take the whole of it. He was doing so well, there

105

was nothing to stop him. But that wouldn't solve the present problem, part of which was that even if she could find a little house to rent for Irvine and his family, what could they afford? Knowing Irvine, she doubted if he'd saved anything. Money had always slipped through his fingers like best butter. Oh well, they'd sort something out. The important thing was, he was coming back to Helsdon, and for good. It was the answer to her prayers.

'Shall I make a start on cleaning the silver?' Mrs Partridge asked. 'My word, it does make a difference, your Penelope not being here. She was a good little worker, I'll say that for her.'

'She was indeed,' Mrs Bates agreed. 'And I'm thankful to say she seems to have settled well in Ripon. No, we'll leave the silver until Rose Hardy comes. She can tackle it.'

Rose Hardy, due in two days' time, was to be Penelope's replacement, though as far as Mrs Bates could see, she was as different from Penelope as chalk from cheese. To start with she was a widow, recently bereaved, though still only in her early twenties. Pity was the reason Madeleine had taken her on, Mrs Bates reckoned. Well, I know what it's like to be widowed and out of a job, she thought. She'd do the best she could with her, though she hadn't been impressed at her interview and her references were no more than adequate.

'Let's hope she'll make out,' she said.

Mrs Partridge pulled a face.

'They're a feckless lot, the Hardys. Allus have been. Still, it shouldn't be beyond her to clean a bit of silver to start with, though goodness knows she'll have had no practice in *that*!'

'What shall we do about finding Irvine somewhere to live?' Mrs Bates asked Madeleine later in the day.

She had hoped against hope that Madeleine might say that room could be found for them at Mount Royd, but common sense told her it was too much to expect. Léon already had his mother-in-law – and until recently had

had his sister-in-law – living in the house. He had been kindness itself to them, though she had tried in every possible way to repay him by doing her job well, never being intrusive, leaving the married couple to themselves, though now that Penelope had left she took all her meals with them. They'd both insisted on it.

More couldn't be expected of Léon, and she wouldn't dream of suggesting it to Madeleine.

In fact, Madeleine had already sounded out Léon, but he'd been unresponsive.

'We don't really have the room,' he'd said, 'nor am I sure that your brother and his wife would be happy here. But most of all, my love, it would be an added responsibility for you, and at the present time that is not what I want you to have.'

He had never met his brother-in-law, but he was predisposed to like him. It was Irvine who had come to the rescue when Madeleine had been so brutally dealt with by George Carter. It was Irvine who had given the man the hiding of his life and sent him packing from Helsdon. For that, though it had happened before he had fallen in love with Madeleine, Léon felt indebted.

'If Irvine had given us the slightest idea of what he wants, it would be easier,' Madeleine said to her mother. 'It does seem as though he expects to arrive here and find everything laid on for him.'

Mrs Bates quickly defended her son. 'He's got a lot on his mind – a wife and a two-year-old. He does right to rely on us; we're his family!'

'Well what I suggest for the moment is that I ask Mrs Barnet if they can lodge with her until they find a place of their own,' Madeleine said. 'It will be a squash – but she has the kindest heart in Helsdon. I'll speak to her tomorrow.'

Mrs Barnet was agreeable.

'For the time being, anyway,' she said. 'Any road, I expect they'll want somewhere of their own as soon as possible.'

'Oh, Mrs Barnet, you're kindness itself!' Madeleine said. 'What would my family do without you?'

'Get away with you, soft!' Mrs Barnet's tone was brusque, but she was pleased, nonetheless. She would have done anything in the world for Madeleine, who felt to her like the daughter she'd never had.

'What's he going to work at, your Irvine?' she asked.

'Goodness knows!' Madeleine replied. 'I'm sure he'll need to find a job as quickly as possible, but you and I know how difficult that is in the West Riding. The trouble is, the army has fed and clothed him for so long now that I don't think he knows what it's like in the world outside.'

'Happen not,' Mrs Barnet said. 'Still, he did his bit in the Crimea. That was no picnic!'

Four days later Mrs Bates peered anxiously out of the kitchen window into the dusk of the short December day. It would soon be pitch dark and it was freezing cold. She was sure Irvine should have been here earlier.

'Why didn't he let us know what time he was coming?' she said for the twentieth time. 'I'm sure my son-in-law would have sent his own carriage to the station to meet them.'

'Happen he wasn't sure,' Rose Hardy said. 'It's a long way from Brighton.'

'Well that's our Irvine all over,' Mrs Bates said. 'You never know just when he'll turn up. It wouldn't surprise me if they didn't arrive until tomorrow, though he clearly said today.'

'T'kettle's boiling its head off,' Rose said.

'Then don't leave it on the fire,' Mrs Bates said testily. 'Move it on to the hob. But they'll want a cup of tea and a meal the minute they get in. As for that little bairn . . . well, it's not a night for him to be out, I'm sure!'

'He'll be all right,' Rose said. 'Children usually are.' What a fuss Mrs Bates was making! You'd think she was expecting the Prince of Wales, no less!

'Well you'd know, wouldn't you!' Mrs Bates said dryly. 'Seeing you've never had any.'

'Me and Jim weren't given time,' Rose said coldly. 'We'd not been married a year when he was killed.'

'Oh Rose, I'm sorry! I didn't mean to be sharp. I don't know what's got into me!'

'Think nowt about it,' Rose said. 'Shall I draw the blind, then? Keep the cold out?'

'Oh no! We want them to see where they are, don't we? In fact, you'd better move yonder lamp into the window.'

Rose took the lamp and put it on the wide window-sill but its soft light penetrated no more than a yard or two into the darkness.

'Now we'll just check the dining-room again,' Mrs Bates fussed. 'See everything's on the table.'

It was all there. Fresh-baked bread, butter, a dish of potted beef, boiled ham, pickles, currant teacakes, lemon curd tarts and a madeira cake. Rose's mouth watered at the sight of it.

'I'm starving,' she said. 'Supposing your son doesn't come for an hour or more and I have to wait until you've all eaten? I shall die of hunger before then.'

Mrs Bates relented.

'Go on then! If you're pent, get back into the kitchen and have your tea. But be sharp about it, mind.'

Rose needed no second bidding. A portion of everything had been set aside for her in the kitchen and she set to it greedily.

Oh, but it was good! One thing you could say about this place, the food was good and plentiful. She hadn't made up her mind whether she liked Mrs Bates or not, but there was no doubt she kept a good table. I'll stick it out for a while, Rose thought. It was a long time since she'd eaten like she had in the last two days.

She was swallowing the last, delicious crumb of cake when Mrs Bates hurried in.

'That's them! That's our Irvine! I'd know his footsteps anywhere!'

She rushed to the door and opened it wide as they came

up the last few feet of flagstones, Irvine ahead, Bessie a little behind, carrying the child.

'Oh Irvine! Oh son!'

He had his arms around her waist and was whirling her around. Not until she cried to him to put her down did she look at Bessie, standing there in the doorway.

'Oh, do come in love!' Mrs Bates cried. 'Come in and close the door, keep the cold out. Here, let me have the bairn! How are you then, Bessie?'

'I'm quite well, thank you, Mrs Bates,' Bessie said politely. 'Tommy's gone to sleep.'

'Tommy come to Grandma, then,' Mrs Bates said, taking the sleeping child, holding him close. 'My, but he's a weight! Much too heavy for you to carry.'

Her daughter-in-law was a little wisp of a girl; slender, fair-haired, pale-faced, with a quiet voice and an unfamiliar accent which was presumably the way they spoke in Brighton. Such a contrast to Irvine, him so tall and broad and healthy looking.

'I must say, Irvine, the army has done you good,' Mrs Bates said, her voice rich with approval. 'You're looking very fit.'

Well, the way she looks at him, he *is* the Prince of Wales to her, Rose Hardy thought. She dotes on him! All the same, he did look good. He was very handsome, cast in the same mould as his sister, the mistress. They must both have taken after their father. Rose was frankly appraising him when he turned and caught her at it.

'Ah, I don't know you, do I? Nobody told me about you!'

'I'm Rose Hardy,' she said. 'I've just come to work here.'

'Pleased to meet you,' he said pleasantly, shaking her by the hand. 'And this is my wife, Bessie.'

Bessie gave a wan smile. She was so tired, it had been such a long day. Most of all, she was so far from home. Why had she ever agreed to come all this way, hundreds

110

of miles from everyone she knew, from Brighton, where the air was clear and the sun shone and every day you saw the sea? Why couldn't Irvine have looked for work there when he came out of the army?

'Rose,' Mrs Bates said. 'Mash the tea and bring it into the dining-room. Mind you warm the pot first.'

She was still holding Tommy. He began to stir in her arms.

'He's waking up, the little love!' she cried.

He opened his eyes wide, and looked at her with an unblinking, grave stare, this woman who was holding him. He felt safe in her arms, also she was warm and she smelled nice. He gave her a small smile.

'Why he's smiling at me, bless his heart!' she cried. 'He's smiling at his grandma!'

'You're favoured, Ma!' Irvine said. 'He doesn't usually take to strangers.'

'That's right, Mrs Bates,' Bessie said. 'He doesn't.'

'Well he can sense I'm not a stranger,' Mrs Bates said complacently. 'I'm his grandma! Who am I then?' she asked him brightly.

'Ganna,' he said.

'There! Did you hear that? And you mustn't call me Mrs Bates, Bessie. You can call me "Ma" – or if you prefer it, "Grandma".'

I shall never have the nerve to call her 'Ma', Bessie thought. 'Grandma' would come easier.

'Here, shall I take him from you and take his coat off,' she offered.

'All of you take your coats off and we'll have our tea at once,' Mrs Bates said. 'I expect you're hungry.'

They sat round, Tommy with two cushions on his chair to bring him to the height of the table, though he was quite tall for two-and-a-half.

'Now help yourselves and make a good tea,' Mrs Bates urged. 'Everything is home-made and fresh!'

'You haven't lost your skill, Ma,' Irvine said appreciatively, biting into a currant teacake. 'You must show

111

Bessie how to make teacakes. She hasn't got the hang of it yet.'

'Well I expect Bessie can make other things I don't know how to do,' Mrs Bates said kindly.

She didn't exactly believe that. Everyone knew that Southerners didn't know how to bake. But she seemed a nice enough girl and she wanted to make her welcome for Irvine's sake.

'If you ask me do I want a piece of Madeira cake, the answer's "Yes",' Irvine said. 'And by the way, where is Madeleine?'

'She's still at the mill. She and Léon will be home any time now, but I said we wouldn't wait tea. I'm sure Léon would have sent his carriage to meet you, and Madeleine with it, if only you'd let us know what time you were coming. There was no need for you to walk from the station on such a cold evening. Anyway, I reckon he'll send you round to Mrs Barnet's in it.'

Irvine handed his empty teacup to his mother.

'Mrs Barnet's? Why would we go round to Mrs Barnet's?'

'Because that's where you'll be staying – until you find something else,' Mrs Bates said.

He took the cup from her, stirred in two spoonfuls of sugar.

'You didn't say anything about where you wanted to live. I couldn't do anything without your say-so,' his mother said.

'Oh! I suppose I thought we'd be staying here – I don't mean living here, but just till we found somewhere else.'

Mrs Bates shook her head.

'There isn't room. Anyway, you'll be very comfortable with Mrs Barnet. She's a nice woman. Our Madeleine stayed with her before she was married. In fact she was wed from Mrs Barnet's house.'

'I suppose it will be all right,' Irvine conceded. 'We'll soon get everything sorted out, I daresay.'

'But you're not to go yet,' Mrs Bates said quickly. 'No

need to go until bedtime – and Madeleine would never forgive us if you weren't here when she came home.'

'I will be,' he said. 'Don't fret! Besides, I've yet to meet my brother-in-law, not having made it to his wedding.'

'You'll like Léon,' she said. 'Most people do.'

They were just finishing the meal when Madeleine and Léon arrived. Irvine bounded from the table and took Madeleine in his arms.

'You look blooming!' he said. 'It suits you to be expecting!'

'I'm very fit,' Madeleine agreed. 'Oh Irvine, it's so good to see you! And let me introduce my husband, Léon!' She took Léon's hand with pride, drawing him close.

'Pleased to meet you, sir!' Irvine said.

Well, Madeleine had chosen a looker, all right – and from what he knew, rich into the bargain. Good old Madeleine! If she'd fallen on her feet it was no more than she deserved.

'And I am delighted to meet you,' Léon said. 'Madeleine has talked about you often. I hope you will be happy, back in Helsdon.'

He turned to Bessie, raised her fingers to his lips. Rose Hardy, coming in with a fresh pot of tea, thought: if he did that to me I'd swoon!

'I hope you also will be happy in Helsdon, Bessie,' he said. 'You and I have it in common that we came here as strangers – but you will find, as I did, that the people of Helsdon are warm-hearted and welcoming. Not a bit like their weather,' he added with a smile.

'And you must be Tommy,' he said to the child. 'Well I am your uncle, and one day you and our son will be cousins!'

What I like about Léon, Mrs Bates thought warmly, is that he's not the least bit uppity, nothing of the snob in him.

An hour or so later Bessie said: 'I think we should be making our way to Mrs Barnet's. It's way past Tommy's bedtime.' Everyone was very kind, but she was dog-tired. How many hours had they been on the way?

'Oh dear, I was hoping you'd stay longer!' Mrs Bates said. 'It's early yet.'

But Madeleine had noticed the weariness in her sister-in-law's voice.

'No, Ma,' she said. 'Bessie is right. It's been a long day. We'll save the rest of the talk until tomorrow. In the meantime, we'll go to Mrs Barnet's in the carriage and I shall go with you, see you settled in.'

When they reached her house, Mrs Barnet took one look at Bessie's weary face and ushered them up to the bedroom within minutes.

'I've fixed up a little bed I borrowed for the bairn,' she said. 'I'll bring you up some hot water in a minute and you can have a nice, refreshing wash – and then I reckon you'll sleep like logs.'

'You're very kind,' Bessie said. 'Is there anything I can do?'

'Not a thing,' Mrs Barnet said cheerfully. 'Just get yourselves to bed. I shan't waken you before I go off in the morning. Get up when you're ready, and look around for anything you want. The house is small enough, you'll soon find things.'

Lying in the big bed, sunk in the feather-filled mattress – Tommy had fallen asleep while she was undressing him and now she could hear his steady breathing from the low bed close to theirs – Bessie was suddenly and perversely wide awake. The urge to sleep against which she had struggled most of the afternoon and all evening, had deserted her. She opened her eyes and tried to make out the contours of the room, the shapes of the furniture, but the darkness was absolute, she could see nothing. No more can I see what lies ahead, she thought. It was frightening.

'Irvine!' she whispered. 'Irvine!'

'What? What is it?' He had been on the verge of sleep.

'Irvine, I'm frightened!'

He grunted, and would have gone back to sleep, but she turned and took hold of him.

'Irvine!'

'What are you on about?' Having been lively enough all evening, now he felt sodden with sleep.

'Please don't go to sleep, Irvine! Please tell me it's going to be all right! Tell me everything's going to work out.'

'Of course it is, love! Everything will be just fine. Now go to sleep. You'll feel better in the morning.'

'Hold me,' Bessie said. 'Give me a little cuddle.'

He put his arms around her and held her close, but within minutes his arms slackened and he was asleep. As Bessie lay awake her eyes became used to the darkness and she made out the objects in the bedroom: the tall chest of drawers, the washstand, a chair. True, they were no more than dim shapes, but she was comforted by the fact that the darkness was not as black as she'd thought. Presently, she too fell asleep.

At Mount Royd Madeleine and Léon were preparing for bed, Madeleine sitting in front of the looking-glass, brushing her hair. Léon came and stood behind her, looking over her shoulder at her reflection. Then he took the brush from her.

'Let me do that!' he said. 'It gives me pleasure. Your hair is so lovely, Madeleine.'

In the mirror it framed her face and fell abundantly to her shoulders, making a rich, dark frame against her creamy skin.

'If such a thing were possible,' Léon said, 'I would say that in your pregnancy you are more beautiful than ever.'

She met his eyes, hers smiling with pleasure.

'But I might not be, as time goes by! I daresay I shall be a horrible, lumpy shape. What will you say then?'

'That you are still beautiful,' he told her. 'How could you not be when you are carrying our son?'

'I hope Irvine and Bessie are as happy as we are,'

115

Madeleine said. 'I want everyone in the world to be as happy as we are!'

'Even Sophia Chester?' he teased.

'Even Sophia Chester – providing she treats Emerald and Penelope well – and keeps her distance from me.'

'I thought Bessie was timid,' Léon said. 'And undoubtedly Irvine is the boss, though that doesn't necessarily mean he's the strong one.'

'You're very observant,' Madeleine said. 'And I think you're right. I just wish I knew what he was going to do. He has to find a job quite soon.'

'Well, as I've told you before, he can have a job in the spinning – but he'll have to learn it from the bottom up and he'll not earn much until he does.'

'I'm not sure he'll want to work in the mill again,' Madeleine said doubtfully. 'He never liked being what he calls "cooped up". I daresay that helped him to make up his mind to join the army – apart from Father, I mean.'

'Let's go to bed and stop worrying about Irvine,' Léon said.

In bed she nestled against him, contented and happy.

'I'd almost forgotten,' she murmured a little later. 'Henry Garston said he'd see Irvine in Leeds. He might just be able to offer him something.'

She felt Léon's arms stiffen around her as she mentioned Henry Garston's name.

'But you are right, my love,' she said quickly. 'Let's not bother about anyone else for now. No one but you and me and our child in the whole world!'

For several days after that it seemed to Madeleine that whenever she came home from work Irvine was there with Bessie and Tommy. Sometimes they were still at the table, enjoying a meal; sometimes they had just finished a meal and Bessie would be helping Rose to clear away, while Mrs Bates, down on her knees, played with Tommy on the rug. She had started to come home a little earlier, leaving Léon to follow. At the end of the working

116

day she was unduly tired. Irrationally, because to carry on working was her own choice, she was mildly irritated at the sight of Irvine taking his ease. 'So what have you done today?' she asked him on the fourth day.

'Oh, this and that!' he replied. 'Nothing special.'

'I see. No sign of a job, then?'

'No, not really. Actually, I thought I'd wait until after Christmas. No one wants to set anyone on just before Christmas, do they?'

'Don't they?' Madeleine said. Her voice was tight. 'You know Léon offered you a job in the spinning if you wanted to learn.'

'It was kind of him,' Irvine said smoothly. 'But it's not really what I want.'

'A lot of people have to work at jobs they don't like,' Madeleine said.

'Now don't lecture me, Big Sister!' He was smiling, but there was an edge in his voice.

'I didn't mean to.'

Mrs Bates looked up anxiously at the sound. She, too, was worried that Irvine hadn't started to look for anything, nor even talked about it – but then it was early days yet. He'd find something in the end, and when he did, she knew he'd be very good at it, whatever it was. But you couldn't drive Irvine; she'd discovered that when he was quite small. All the same, she thought loyally, a better son never trod shoe leather.

'I seem to remember,' Irvine said to Madeleine, 'that there was a time when you decided you weren't cut out to be a servant. You couldn't do it a minute longer. Well I feel the same about working in the mill. I'd hate it now, and I'd be no good at it. I don't want something where I'm cooped up all day.'

The difference was, Madeleine thought, her brother had a wife and child to support. The bit of money he had from the army would soon run out.

'We have a friend in Leeds, Henry Garston, a clothing manufacturer,' she said. 'He might be able to offer you

117

something. He employs salesmen, though whether. . .'

'Now something like that would suit me down to the ground!' Irvine interrupted. 'I reckon I'd be quite good at that.'

'I'm sure you would!' Mrs Bates said. 'Why not let Madeleine fix you an appointment to see Mr Garston?'

'And so I will,' Irvine said brightly. 'But let's wait until after Christmas, eh? Only a day or two now; no point in rushing it.'

Christmas came and went, with a flurry of snow which started on Christmas Eve, and during the night grew heavier, so that next morning everything was whited over. On the moors above the town it was magnificent, transforming them into a remote and foreign-looking landscape. Even in Helsdon itself it added a certain beauty to the mills and to the streets of little houses, and because there was no horse-drawn traffic on the streets, and few people abroad, its pristine whiteness remained.

'Not that it won't be mucky grey sludge by tomorrow,' Irvine observed. 'It usually is, except up on the moors.'

They had just finished Christmas dinner. Rose Hardy had been given a few hours off to have the Christmas meal with her parents in Helsdon.

'Otherwise,' Mrs Bates said, 'she'd have had to eat on her own in the kitchen, which wouldn't have been nice on Christmas Day.'

'It's a poor do, neither Emerald nor Penelope being allowed home for Christmas,' Irvine said.

'But not the least bit unusual,' Mrs Bates pointed out. 'Mrs Chester will have a lot on over Christmas, entertaining and the like. And they *are* servants, remember.'

'A fact which Sophia Chester won't let them forget!' Madeleine said.

'I'd like to have seen them,' Irvine said. 'What's to prevent me going over to Ripon?'

'Nothing, I suppose,' his mother agreed.

'If you don't mind, I'll not go with you,' Bessie said

quickly. 'I'll stay back with Tommy. It's too cold for him to go.'

What she meant was that it was too cold for her. Oh, it was all right here, in this room right now, and Mrs Barnet's parlour was usually warm, but the bedroom was like an ice-box, with the windows frosted up and the water in the ewer frozen over an inch thick every morning. They didn't have this harsh weather in Brighton. As for snow, through which they'd trudged this morning to get here, they practically never had snow. She hated it.

'A bit of cold weather'll not harm him,' Irvine said. 'But apart from that, happen it would be better for me to go on my own.'

Madeleine said nothing, though she thought that if he turned up at the Chester's with a wife and child in tow, his reception would be colder than the weather.

'Don't forget that I've written to Mr Garston,' she reminded Irvine. 'We should hear any day now, and if he's good enough to give you an interview, you must be available.'

'I'm ready to go over to Leeds any time Mr Garston sends for me,' Irvine said.

'Shall we go out for a walk?' Léon broke in. 'While the sun is still shining? It will be dark early.'

'I'd like that,' Madeleine said. 'Who will come, then? Irvine, what about you?'

'Nothing would please me more,' Irvine said, 'except to stay in front of the fire and smoke this good cigar Léon's given me!' His refusal was tempered with a smile.

'Tommy needs a rest,' Bessie said quickly. 'Also, I'll help with the dishes since Rose isn't here.' There was no way they were going to get her out on this cold Christmas afternoon!

'What about you, Ma?' Madeleine enquired. 'Will you come?'

'Too cold for me, love!'

'Then just you and I,' Léon said, trying not to show his

119

pleasure at the thought of the two of them alone. It was not that he disliked his brother-in-law, and Bessie and the child were quite inoffensive; it was just that they were around so much of the time. At first he had not cared for the idea of Henry Garston perhaps giving Irvine a job, but now he thought it might be a good idea.

'If Henry does employ Irvine,' he said to Madeleine as they took the path towards the moor, 'I suppose he will have to live in Leeds?'

'I hadn't thought of that,' Madeleine confessed. 'I suppose he will. There'd be no point in travelling from Helsdon. Anyway, he has to find somewhere else soon. They can't take up Mrs Barnet's bedroom forever. But Ma won't like it.'

'Leeds is not the other side of the world,' Léon said. 'Though I know most people in Helsdon think it is. Do you feel fit enough to climb to the top of the moor, my love? I don't want you to tire yourself.'

'Quite fit,' Madeleine said. 'The air is so good up here.'

'Then breathe deeply! Fill your lungs, and it will be good for the baby.'

The day after Boxing Day there was a letter from Henry Garston, addressed to Madeleine and Léon.

'He suggests you should go to see him on the thirtieth,' Madeleine told Irvine. 'Unless he hears to the contrary he will expect you at eleven in the morning.'

'You must look your best!' Mrs Bates said. 'I'll launder your best shirt and press your suit for you. A commercial traveller must always look smart.'

Irvine laughed.

'I've not got the job yet, Ma!'

'Nor will you,' she retorted, 'unless you go looking decent!' But he would get it, she knew he would. She didn't have the slightest doubt.

Henry Garston surveyed the young man sitting opposite. He was very like his sister. He hadn't seen Madeleine for

120

a while, and since Léon had written and informed him that she was pregnant, he wouldn't see her now until after the birth of the baby. Common sense told him he'd have to stop thinking about her. It was no good anyway, never had been, he supposed, right from the first, from the time she'd sat in that chair where her brother was sitting now. She'd always been crazy about that lucky devil of a Frenchman. Still, there were few things he wouldn't do for her, so he'd give this brother of hers a trial. He'd not let him get away with murder, though. He hadn't worked himself up into being one of the richest men in the West Riding by being soft. A pity he was soft for Madeleine Bonneau!

'Well you've no experience, Mr Bates,' he said. 'Do you think you could do the job as I've outlined it?'

'I think so, sir!' Irvine said eagerly. 'As I understand it, when you've bought the cloth from the mills, either you have it made up into garments, here in Leeds, which you sell to the shops, or you sell them the cloth.'

'Or both,' Henry Garston said.

'I think I could do that, sir! I'd certainly like to try.' It was right up his street. Out all day, travelling around the county, meeting people. No being shut up in an office or a factory.

'The wage is small. I make no bones about that,' Henry Garston said. 'It's up to you to make it up with commission, and to do that you'll have to get out there and sell. No sitting around on your backside!'

He supposed the young man was the right type. He was reasonably well spoken; he was attractive. The ladies would like him, and although they didn't do the actual buying, Henry knew very well that the saleswomen influenced the buyers. If the traveller got on well with the First Sales, gave her a bit of flattery and the occasional present, he was home and dry.

'I realize that, sir,' Irvine said eagerly. 'You can depend on me to work hard!'

'You'll have to,' Henry Garston said bluntly. 'I carry

121

no passengers. Very well then, you can start next Monday. I expect you here not later than eight o'clock and, think on, I set great store by punctuality.'

Mrs Bates was cock-a-hoop when Irvine came home with the news.

'I knew it!' she cried. 'I never had the slightest doubt!'

She was considerably less happy when he pointed out that he'd have to live in Leeds.

'I couldn't do otherwise,' he said patiently. 'I shall have to start early and finish late. And in any case I shan't be able to afford the fares from Helsdon every day. No, it will have to be Leeds, Ma!'

'But I've only just got you back, son,' she said. 'I don't want to lose you just yet!'

'You'll not be losing me, love! It's not more than nine or ten miles on the train. You can come and see us often; every week if you like.'

'Well, I suppose that's better than Brighton!' Mrs Bates admitted.

It was not nearly as good as Brighton, Bessie thought. In a way, she was sorry Irvine had landed a job so easily. She'd almost hoped against hope he'd have had to give in and go south to look for work. But perhaps Leeds would be better than Helsdon, and at least she'd have her own home. Irvine was sure, once he was working, they'd find it easy to rent a place.

In the early hours of New Year's Day Madeleine and Léon sat side by side on the sofa in the drawing room. They had stayed up to see the New Year in. Irvine, being a dark man and the nearest they could get to a stranger in that he didn't live there, had let it in, knocking on the door for admittance as the clock struck midnight, bringing with him the customary piece of coal. Rose Hardy had been summoned from the kitchen and Léon had proposed a toast to everyone present. And now it was over. Irvine and his family had gone back to Mrs Barnet's house, Mrs Bates had gone to bed, and no doubt, Madeleine thought, Rose Hardy was already asleep in that room I used to call mine, when I was a servant here. Were there still mice, she wondered?

'Eighteen sixty-three will be a good year,' she said to Léon. 'I feel it in my bones! Irvine has a job; my mother is happy, Penelope and Emerald are settled – and as for you and me. . .'

'Yes,' Léon said. 'Only a few months and we shall have our child!'

'It will be the best year ever!' Madeleine declared.

SEVEN

Mrs Bates opened the door and took a critical look at the weather. The snow still lay on the high moor, though it had cleared from the lower ground. The sky looked unsettled, with threatening grey-black clouds, and already there was a fine drizzle borne on the wind. She closed the door quickly and came back into the warmth of the house.

'Not the best of days for our Irvine to be starting work,' she remarked to Rose Hardy. 'Let's hope the rain gets no worse.'

'Oh I'm sure your son can cope with a drop of rain,' Rose said. 'After all, he's been a soldier, out in all weathers.'

'That's true,' Mrs Bates admitted. 'But I wish I could have seen him off, made sure he'd got a proper breakfast inside him.'

'Well he's got a wife to do that,' Rose said.

Mrs Bates said nothing. Could you really rely on Bessie? She seemed to be in another world half the time.

If I had a man like Irvine, Rose thought enviously, I'd see he was well looked after. I'd see he got plenty of everything he wanted – and not only food! Her late husband hadn't been much cop – she'd married him in haste – but she missed him in more ways than one.

'I expect he'll pop round when he gets back this evening, tell me how he got on,' Mrs Bates said.

'I daresay. And I daresay Tommy and his mother'll be here waiting for him,' Rose said.

There was something in Rose's tone of voice Mrs Bates didn't quite like. Was she being cheeky? It wasn't always possible to tell with Rose, she could sound so smooth.

124

She never actually *said* the wrong thing, it was the way the words came out, and with her looking quite innocent all the while.

'My son and his wife and child are very welcome in this house,' she said firmly.

By you, Rose thought. But was that lovely man, the master, so enamoured?

'Of course, Mrs Bates,' she said primly. 'And it's always a pleasure to see your son. I reckon your daughter-in-law's a very lucky girl.'

'I reckon she is,' Mrs Bates agreed.

'He's so handsome!' Rose paused in the act of drying a dish and gazed dreamily into space.

Mrs Bates looked at her suspiciously.

'He is,' she said. 'But as you reminded me a minute ago, he's married. Don't you forget that, my girl!'

Rose lifted a shocked face to Mrs Bates, looked at her wide-eyed. 'Oh, Mrs Bates, as if I would!'

Madeleine came into the kitchen as the two women were looking at each other. What was it all about, she wondered? She wasn't quite sure about Rose Hardy; she knew she'd engaged her mainly out of pity. However, her mother had said nothing against the girl and she was the one to know.

'I'm just off to the mill,' she said.

Mrs Bates sighed.

'I wish. . .' She broke off. 'Rose, you can start on the beds now!'

She waited until Rose, scenting an argument, had reluctantly left the room.

'I wish you'd give up going to the mill,' she said. 'It's time you gave up working, and rested more.'

'Well I will in just a week or two. I've something I want to see through to the finish. But don't worry, Ma, I'm perfectly fit.'

'I want you to keep fit.'

'I'm sure when you were having your children you worked right up to the last minute,' Madeleine said.

'Why, I remember when Penelope was born you had the bed brought downstairs so you could still run everything, look after everyone!'

She remembered Penelope's birth clearly. She had been sent to fetch the midwife, a mile away; told to run as fast as she could and tell the woman to come quickly. After that she'd been banished to a neighbour's house and when she came back, hours later, there was the baby in her mother's arms, brought, she assumed, by the kindly midwife in her black bag.

'I did the same when I had Irvine and Emerald,' Mrs Bates confessed. 'Women usually did when there were other children to look after.'

'Well then . . . ?' Madeleine demanded.

'It's different,' Mrs Bates persisted. 'I didn't go out, not more than I had to. I certainly wouldn't have gone to the mill where there were all those men.'

'But I hardly show,' Madeleine protested. 'And most of the time I'm working in my own room.'

'Aside from that,' Mrs Bates persisted, 'whether you like it or not, you're different. You're the mill master's wife. You have a position to keep up! People in your walk of life don't do certain things.'

'Well I've told you, Ma. Only a few more weeks.'

Mrs Bates changed the subject.

'I wonder how our Irvine will get on today?'

'Quite well, I'd think. He's very lucky to get a job with Henry Garston.'

All the same, walking to work, Madeleine *did* wonder. Irvine had changed in the time he'd been in the army. Oh, he was still pleasant, still affectionate. He was also, she reckoned, still rebellious when it came to doing anything he didn't want to do, as he had been with their father. She recognized the same trait in herself. And it was their father, she thought, who had sown those seeds of rebellion in both of them by his impossible demands.

But the army had made Irvine dependent, expecting to have things laid on, all his needs catered for. She detected

126

a certain laziness in him, and if she was right, it wouldn't go down with Henry Garston. Henry would be a hard taskmaster. But she owed Irvine a debt she could never wholly repay. But for him she might well have been forced into marriage with George Carter. It would have been worse than loveless. It would have been a marriage of hate. She shivered at the thought.

Irvine was shivering too. Though reasonably clad, in a greatcoat with lapels high to the neck, and the hem well below his knees, his hands encased in thick, woollen gloves and on his head his new, brown bowler, none of it was a match for the raw dampness of a January day in the West Riding. The wind whistled down Briggate, blowing sudden squalls of rain into his face, as he dodged through the crowds, trying to keep up with Joe Sims. Joe had been deputed to accompany him on this first day, to introduce him to the people who mattered, and put him in the way of things.

Irvine's trouble was that his boots weren't up to scratch. The money he should have spent on keeping his feet warm and dry had literally gone to his head. The new bowler had cost far more than he could afford, but trying it on in the hatter's shop, surveying his image in the mirror – his fine moustache, the fringe of dark beard around the edge of his chin and extending up to his side-burns, which he had grown since leaving the army – the temptation to splash out had been more than he could resist. And when the salesman tilted the hat a fashion-able rakish fraction of an inch further forward over his customer's forehead, Irvine could only succumb. Now, too late because the water was already seeping into his boots, he knew that comfort must start at the feet.

'I'll do what I can for you today,' Joe Sims said. 'Show you the lie of the land. Make the introductions. But after today you're on your own because I'm moving to a new patch.'

He was a cheerful sort of fellow, Joe Sims. And well he

might be, Irvine thought. He was wearing a stout pair of boots which defied every puddle through which they were forced to wade, every shower of rain the pavements threw up at them. Also, he wasn't lugging the heavy case of samples. That had been handed over to Irvine the minute they'd met at the railway station.

'It's very good of you,' Irvine said. 'I'm grateful.'

'Not a bit of it,' Joe said. 'Of course you won't have the best places, the big stores, just yet. You'll have to work up to that. Which is what I've done, and got promotion, which is why there's a job for you.'

'So where will I be going?' Irvine asked.

'The smaller establishments, the medium-sized outlets. Mostly a bit further out from the centre of Leeds. But there's plenty of trade to be had there if you look for it. My advice to you – you don't mind a bit of advice . . . ?'

'Certainly not! I'd be glad of it.'

'Well my advice to you is to keep pleasant at all times, and not only with the buyers and the bosses – always remember the underlings – and not to push things too much. Let the buyers think they're making the decisions.'

'And aren't they?'

'Not really. If you've anything about you as a salesman you'll see to it that they buy what you want to sell, only without realizing, if you see what I mean.'

'I do. I do!'

'Persuasion, that's the thing,' Joe said. 'But gentle, not obvious. And never come away without an order!'

'Never?'

'Never! Mr Garston checks the order books himself. If you don't sell at every place you call on, then he'll soon want to know the reason why. Apart from that, of course, no order means no commission. It's either sell or starve in this game, lad.'

'I suppose you're right,' Irvine said.

'You can take it as gospel,' Joe assured him. 'Now I

have to make one call on Lester's and I'll take you with me. It's a bit high class for you at the moment, but it'll give you an idea of things. After that I know a nice little coffee house, and I reckon we're entitled to a cup of coffee on a cold morning. Only never be tempted by anything stronger. No rum, no brandy!'

'Oh I won't,' Irvine promised.

Lester's Department Store was awe-inspiring, catering, if she could pay for it, for everything a lady might wish to wear, from a pair of fine kid gloves, through skirts and blouses and gowns to outdoor capes and hats. Irvine followed Joe Sims up the wide staircase to the upper floor where they were to see a Mr Scott, a buyer.

'At least that's who we hope to see,' Joe said. 'But the buyers won't always see you. If they're that side out they'll reckon they're too busy. That's why it's best to call on the most important places early in the morning, early in the week, before they get too many customers in.'

For the next fifteen minutes Irvine stood back and watched Joe Sims at work. He was surprised at how long the two men talked of other things; the inclement weather, the fluctuations of trade, their respective states of health. Then just as Irvine was deciding that they were never going to get down to brass tacks, Joe Sims said:

'Mr Bates, open the case and show Mr Scott our best samples. Lester's buys nothing but the best. And we've got one or two nice new ones here, Mr Scott. I venture to think they're just what you'll like.'

Irvine spread out the samples on the counter.

'Very nice!' Mr Scott admitted, crushing the materials between his finger and thumb. 'A nice bit of cloth. Now show me what styles they'll be made up in.'

But when he was shown the drawings, Mr Scott pursed his lips and was less enthusiastic.

'It's a pity there's nothing really new,' he complained. 'The ladies are always looking for something new. I know my wife is, and I expect yours is the same!'

129

My wife, Joe Sims thought, is lucky if she gets one new dress a year, never mind a new fashion. But he nodded in agreement.

'You tell Mr Garston from me,' Mr Scott went on, 'that he's second to none on his best materials, but I wish he'd get a few more fashionable styles. West Riding ladies are very fashion conscious. I wouldn't put it past them to go down to London if they can't find what they want in Leeds.'

'I'll certainly tell him,' Joe said. 'He'll value your opinion.'

He took out his order book, licked his pencil.

'Now, what can I put you down for, sir?'

'I thought he wasn't going to buy anything,' Irvine said as they left the store.

'Oh, he usually does,' Joe said. 'Only you have to play it fairly cool with Mr Scott.'

'I can see there's a lot to learn,' Irvine said. But nothing he couldn't manage, he reckoned. Nothing at all.

'And now for that cup of coffee,' Joe Sims said.

'Was it right, what Mr Scott said about styles?' Irvine asked.

'Probably,' Joe said. 'Lester's caters for well-off women who can afford to follow fashion. Most of the places you go to will be more concerned with what's serviceable. All the same, I shall mention it to Mr Garston. Lester's is a valuable account.'

It rained all day. Irvine followed Joe Sims in and out of stores and shops, listened to his sales patter, and at Joe's dictation wrote down the orders, but in Joe's book. There was nothing in his own book at the end of the day to show he'd done a stroke of work.

'You're training at the moment,' Joe said. 'You wouldn't expect me to give you my commission, would you? Indeed, I couldn't afford to. I rely on it.'

So nothing but that meagre wage this week, Irvine thought.

'Halifax tomorrow!' Joe said when they parted at the end of the day.

When Irvine left the train at Helsdon he made straight for Mount Royd. It was pitch dark, he was soaked to the skin, the rain dripped off the brim of his bowler. As for his feet – it was like walking in the park lake! Meeting the warmth of his mother's parlour was like entering heaven!

'Nay, love!' his mother cried. 'You're wet through. Get that coat off at once!'

He did so, sending out a great shower of raindrops as he shook it. Tommy, sitting near, squealed with delight as the drops hit him. Mrs Bates took the coat from Irvine.

'I'll hang it to dry in the kitchen,' she said.

'It's my boots are the worst,' Irvine told her.

Mrs Bates shrieked in horror as he took them off and held them up for inspection.

'Irvine! Whatever are you doing with boots like this! You'll catch your death!'

'Well I can't get new ones until next week, Ma. I get no commission this week. You see, I'm training.'

'Commission or not,' Mrs Bates said fiercely, 'you'll have new boots!'

She reached up to the mantlepiece and brought down a jug. From its depth she poured a heap of coins, mostly small ones, farthings and ha'pennies, on to the table.

'Here!' she said. 'There's just over five shillings. Take it! Set out early in the morning and stop off in Helsdon for a new pair of boots. You can throw these away the minute you get the new ones. They're beyond repair.'

'Oh Ma, you're a brick!' Irvine said. 'You're a real brick! But I'll pay you back.'

'When you can afford it,' Mrs Bates said. 'Now sit you down and I'll get you a bite to eat.'

By the end of January Madeleine knew she must give up coming into the mill. In four months time her baby would be born. In fact, she was fit and well. Except for tiring more easily, she felt she could have carried on right up to the hour of the baby's birth, but even she had to

131

acknowledge the practical difficulties. Before long she would be too large to nip into the weaving or the spinning when she needed to discuss technical points. In the narrow spaces between the machines there would be no room for her. And she knew, though it irritated her, that the sight of her would embarrass some of the men.

'It's ridiculous!' she complained to Léon. 'There's hardly a man there whose wife hasn't borne a child. They know perfectly well what pregnant women look like. Why should they be embarrassed? It's illogical!'

'Nevertheless, they *are*,' Léon said. 'Not everything in the world is a question of logic. Also, they would wonder how I could possibly be such a brute as to allow you to go on working.'

'No they wouldn't, love,' Madeleine contradicted. 'They'd blame me, and rightly.'

'Well I'm delighted you've made the decision,' Léon said. 'And now I hope you'll take some rest. You know that Dr Hughes has told you quite definitely that you must save your strength for the birth. Please take notice of him, Madeleine – for my sake and the baby's, but most of all for your own!'

Sometimes he wakened in the night in a cold sweat of fear that something would go wrong. He would be devastated if the child was harmed, but more, far more than that, he couldn't bear to lose Madeleine. It would be the end of the world for him.

'Oh, I haven't said I'll give it up!' Madeleine pointed out. 'I've agreed I'll stop going to the mill, and I'll keep my word on that. But you must do as you promised and fix me up a room in the house where I can carry on designing. What else is there to do with my time? Mother and I between us – and your mother – have made all the baby clothes any child could possibly need. There's nothing for me to do except wait, and I can't sit with my hands folded.'

'Very well, if you must,' Léon said.

Within a couple of days all the paraphernalia of her

132

job – her yarns, drawing-board, paper, paints – had been transferred to an upstairs room in Mount Royd.

'This is a good room for your work, if work you must,' Léon said. 'A big window and plenty of light.'

'And if I can't receive any of the men here, at least I must see Mrs Barnet from time to time,' Madeleine insisted. 'There are things I shall need to discuss.'

'You shall see Mrs Barnet as often as you wish,' Léon agreed. 'She is one of the people, your mother is another, whom I trust to keep an eye on you when I'm busy.'

'Will you be away much?' Madeleine asked.

'Between now and May I shan't often be away overnight; but early in May I have to go to the London Wool Sales, and I'll go from there to France.'

'That's awfully near my time,' Madeleine said doubtfully.

'I shall be back, my dear. Don't worry. I can't alter the date of the Wool Sales, and by then I'll be more than due to see our customers in France.'

'I suppose so.'

Léon took her by the shoulders and turned her around to face him.

'Shall you go to Roubaix?' she asked.

'If I do it will be for one night only. *Maman* will be anxious to hear about you. Moreover, I intend to persuade her to visit us in the summer, when you are over the birth and she is over Marie's wedding. Marie will be sorry that you won't be able to attend that.'

'I'm sorry also. Really sorry! But the baby will be only a few weeks old.' She liked her sister-in-law, and it would be disappointing to miss out on a family wedding.

'Did I tell you what Irvine said about Henry Garston's fashions?' she asked. 'It seems more than one buyer has mentioned it.'

'You did. It was interesting, but it doesn't affect us, does it? We only make the cloth and there's never been the slightest criticism of that.'

'I know. But doesn't it seem a pity that our lovely cloth

should go into styles which aren't up to the mark?'

'I daresay they *are* up to the mark for most people,' Léon said. 'It's only the well-off few who want the styles to be changing all the time.'

Madeleine shook her head, frowning.

'I'm surprised at you, a Frenchman, not admitting the importance of fashion. I've been thinking quite a lot about what Irvine said. It's something I'd like to discuss with Henry – after you and I have talked, of course.'

It was Léon's turn to frown. He walked to the window, stood looking out over the garden, which was just beginning to come to life after the long winter.

'I can guess what you have in mind,' he said. 'You think you could design garments.'

'Yes, I'm sure I could!' Madeleine declared. 'I have lots of ideas!'

'Well it won't do, Madeleine! It won't do at all. You'll have more than enough on your plate, designing cloth and looking after the baby.'

'We shall have a nursemaid,' Madeleine reminded him. 'And more help in the kitchen – it was you who insisted on that.'

'And I still do. But a child needs a mother's time and care also. In any case, there's no way you could see Henry now, in your present condition.' And by the time the baby was here he hoped she'd have dropped the idea.

'I realize that,' Madeleine said. It was always the same when Henry Garston was mentioned. Léon immediately put up barriers. 'I wasn't expecting to see him until after the baby is born. But I really do think I might be able to design the kind of clothes which would show our materials to the best advantage. I'd have a head start there, understanding the designs and the cloth as I do.'

'There's really no point in discussing it,' Léon said.

'Oh, I can see that, for now. You're quite determined not to listen. But don't expect me never to mention it again, my love!'

In fact, she didn't bring up the subject again for several

weeks, but during that time she made sketches until she had a whole portfolio of fashion drawings. She worked on them during the day, whenever she had time to spare from her textile designing. It helped enormously to pass the time.

And then at last the days began to lengthen, and spring was in sight. Before long it would be time for Léon to go to France.

'I have a whole collection of fashion drawings I've been amusing myself with,' she confessed one evening. 'I know you're too busy to look at them at the moment, but since you're going to France, will you ask Marie to be an angel and give me any information she can about fashion? She might even be able to send me a magazine or two.'

The very next morning there was a letter from France.

'From Marie,' Léon said, opening it.

'What does she say?'

'She says that at the time of my visit to France, she and *Maman* will actually be in Paris. Marie is to see Jules about their new apartment and to make some purchases for her trousseau. She suggests I should meet them there instead of going to Roubaix.'

'Paris in the spring! Oh, you are so lucky!' Longing to be there, to shake off finally the winter gloom of Helsdon, swept over Madeleine. 'Once you told me that you and I would go to Paris in the spring,' she said. 'We haven't managed it yet.'

'I know, *chérie*, and I'm sorry. But we will.' Léon said. 'One day we will. And at least if I am not to go to Roubaix I shall be back in Helsdon a day or two earlier.'

Irvine was just getting out of bed in Leeds; they had found one room to rent. It was a wretched room in a poor area, but it was the best they could afford at present. He yawned, stretched, groaned with the effort of getting up.

'You'll be late again,' Bessie warned him. 'You've already been late once this week!'

'Now don't nag, Bessie,' Irvine begged. 'I can't stand a

135

nagging woman, and that's what you're becoming. As it happens, I'm quite tired, *and* I have a headache. For two pins I wouldn't go in at all today.'

Bessie looked alarmed.

'Please don't say that, Irvine! You've got to go! You took a day off only last Tuesday. How are we going to pay the rent, or eat, if you don't earn your commission? It was practically nothing last week. We can't live on your wages.'

Irvine pulled on his trousers, went to the sink and sluiced his hands and face in cold water.

'You don't know what it's like, my girl, tramping round Leeds and Bradford and Halifax and Huddersfield; day in, day out; folks not wanting to see you, not wanting to buy; getting to the end of the day with an almost empty order book! It's not easy, let me tell you!'

'And let me tell you, it's not easy being cooped up in one room with a screaming kid!' Bessie retaliated. 'Pretending not to be in when the rent man calls. No money to go shopping. No money for the coals.'

'We have a bit of fire every night,' Irvine said.

'That's because me and Tommy do without during the day. I light it just before you come home. And this room is freezing cold; no sun ever gets in.'

The cold didn't do her cough any good. She'd had a cough ever since she set foot in Yorkshire, and as far as she could tell, everybody else had one too. The air was raw and damp. Every day she wished she was back in Brighton, with Irvine in the army, and the money, though it wasn't much, coming in regular.

'Well, spring's on its way,' Irvine said easily. 'We shan't need a fire soon.'

'Spring! You don't know what spring means up here in this benighted place! I'm always cold. I haven't been warm since the day we set foot in it! What's more, unless you give me some money there'll be no fire *this* evening,' she warned him. 'We've used the last bit. And no fire means no cooked meal, not even a potato. Not that I know where to find the money for food!'

Irvine felt in his pockets, threw a shilling on the table.

'It's the last I've got, aside from my train fare, and I have to keep that back to work. I have to get to Bradford today. Do you expect me to walk it, then?'

Bessie picked up the money.

'This won't go far.'

'Well do your best,' Irvine said impatiently. 'You never make the money go far, that's your trouble. My mother could make a feast fit for the Queen with less than a shilling.'

'Oh your mother! We all know your mother's a magician! A miracle worker! Nobody in the world like your mother!'

Her mother-in-law came every fortnight to visit them. On each occasion Bessie sensed her criticism of their living conditions, though nothing was said. So the district was run-down? The room wasn't too clean? Well, she hadn't the energy for cleaning, and how could you make it look decent anyway: a few sticks of second-hand furniture, not even a bit of oilcloth on the floor, nor a rag rug, nor curtains at the window.

True, Mrs Bates never came empty handed. In her basket there was always a pie, or a pot of jam, a pound of butter or a new loaf. And always a small gift for Tommy; something she had made, or a cheap toy. Tommy loved his grandma's visits. He wished she would come every day. It stuck in Bessie's gullet to accept this bounty, but she had no alternative. They needed whatever they could get.

'She's been good to us, my Ma!' Irvine said.

'Nobody's denying that!' But Bessie didn't want her mother-in-law's help, however kindly meant.

'All I want,' she said, 'is for you to earn enough to keep us half-way decent, not dependent on anybody. Is it too much to ask?'

'I do my best,' Irvine said sullenly. 'Have you packed my sandwiches?'

'I have not. There's nothing to make sandwiches from.

And no, you do *not* do your best, Irvine Bates! Not any longer. The first week or two was another matter. But now you don't seem to care. You're lazy, you're idle!'

'Watch what you're saying, my lady!' Irvine warned.

'You told me you could do this selling job standing on your head! Well try standing on your head, because you don't seem to be able to do it on your feet!'

She was screaming at him now, and that made her cough until she couldn't stop, until it nearly tore her insides out. And then Tommy, upset, started to cry. Irvine put on his hat and stalked out of the house.

'And don't come back till you've got some bloody orders!' she shouted after him. It was the first time in her life she had ever used such a word.

That, Irvine thought, hearing the words as he walked away, was unfortunately what Mr Garston would say to him any day now. Why *didn't* he get the orders? He had at first. He was sure it couldn't be his fault. Perhaps the merchandise was wrong? Or perhaps he'd been given a particularly difficult round? Yes, that could be it. Anyway, he hated the job. Bessie was right when she said he no longer cared.

Crossing the bridge over the Leeds and Liverpool canal, he stopped to watch a couple of boys sitting on the bank. They were fishing; caps down over their brows, mufflers around their necks. They were free; they had no responsibilities. They'd sit there all morning and it wouldn't matter if they never caught a thing. It was with difficulty that he resisted the temptation to chuck his case of samples into the murky depths of the water.

But one day he'd do just that. He'd pitch the hated samples *and* his job right to the bottom of the Cut. Then he'd go fishing.

'T'Boss wants to see you afore you set off!' Irvine was told the minute he entered Garston's.

'What for?'

'How do I know?' the clerk asked. 'But from the look of him I'd rather you than me!'

He hadn't much time for the commercial travellers: dressed up smart, out all day seeing the world; free as air, drinking coffee or something stronger, and earning commission – while he sat nose to the grindstone, with never a chance to earn a penny more.

A minute later, in response to Mr Garston's sharp command to enter, Irvine stood before the great man's desk.

'So what are you up to, Bates,' Henry Garston said, with no preliminaries.

'I don't . . . understand, sir!'

'Of course you do! I'm talking about your order book. There's not enough in it. So either you've not been making the calls – though I see you've claimed expenses – or you've not been doing your stuff when you did call. Which is it? Have you made the calls as detailed here?'

'Oh yes, sir. I've made all the calls!'

It was almost true. There had been one or two days – torrents of February rain, biting March winds cutting his face in half – when he'd missed out on one or two and made for home – but not all that many.

'Then how do you explain no orders?'

I made a mistake, setting him on, Henry Garston thought. He's not shaping up. He hasn't a tenth of the guts of his sister.

'I . . . can't explain, sir,' Irvine said. 'Perhaps it's the time of the year? Perhaps people don't buy as much at the moment?'

'Rubbish! The other men have books full of orders, so why not you? You did reasonably well in your first month's trial, and that was the worst month of the year. So what is it?'

'Perhaps mine's not a very easy round, sir?'

'Of course it's not an easy round!' Henry Garston thundered. 'Did I ever say it would be? It's up to you to make it one, and that takes hard work and perseverance.'

'Yes, sir.'

He could think of nothing else to say. He would like to pick up the order book from the desk where it lay and throw it at Garston's head. What did he know about any of it, sitting on his backside in his nice warm office?

'Well I gave you a trial for your sister's sake,' Garston said curtly. 'And for her sake only I'll give you another month. After that, unless things improve – and I mean considerably – you're out on your ear. I carry no passengers in my company. Is that understood?'

'Yes sir!'

'Then get out and get selling!'

Bastard, Irvine thought! He'd like to tell him where to put his job, and if he gave him the sack in another month he'd do just that!

He left the building and went, reluctantly, to catch the train for Bradford. But first, he thought, he'd have a cup of coffee, and maybe on this occasion a drop of something in it.

EIGHT

Early in April, Léon went to see Mr Ormeroyd, his lawyer in Helsdon. Ormeroyd had been a good friend to him when he was trying to raise money to buy the weaving department of Parkinson's mill, after Mr Parkinson's death. Not only had he recommended him to the bank, and to various people who might help; he had actually put a fair amount of his own money into the venture. It is something I shall never forget, Léon thought. Since those days Léon had paid back all the loans, with the exception of Ormeroyd's. And, of course, there was the stake Henry Garston had in the mill, though that was an investment rather than a loan.

'I don't want to be paid back in cash,' the lawyer had said when Léon had offered it. 'I would rather keep the money in your business – if you are agreeable. I find it interesting, and it's beginning to be profitable.'

'You are welcome to keep it as long as you wish,' Léon told him. 'I am honoured by your confidence.'

This morning, though he had arrived without an appointment, he was shown at once into Mr Ormeroyd's office. Mr Ormeroyd shook him warmly by the hand.

'It's good to see you, Léon. My wife was saying only the other day that it was too long since we'd last set eyes on you and your wife.'

'Madeleine is not going out much at the moment,' Léon said.

'Of course not. She keeps well, I hope?'

'Very well. She's given up working in the mill, I'm pleased to say – though nothing I can do will make her sit back and rest.'

'Well now, is there something I can do for you?' Mr Ormeroyd enquired.

'There is indeed,' Léon said. 'But I should like my visit to be kept quite confidential. In particular, I don't want Madeleine to know.'

'Nothing wrong, I hope?' Young Bonneau looked, as always, the picture of health – but you couldn't always tell.

'Nothing whatsoever!'

'Well you know I shan't breathe a word,' Mr Ormeroyd assured him. 'I shall even forbear to tell my wife that I've seen you.'

'The fact of the matter is,' Léon said, 'I want to buy Mount Royd.'

'Buy Mount Royd?' Mr Ormeroyd could hardly believe his ears. 'But. . .'

'I want to buy it outright, and to give it to Madeleine when the baby is born. I want it to be a surprise for her.'

'And a wonderful surprise that would be! Though I must say, it will not be a straightforward purchase. You can't buy Mount Royd like buying a pound of butter!'

'I have the money,' Léon said. 'I will pay a fair price, and in cash.'

'I daresay. But other things come into it.'

'Cash on the nail, as I have learnt to call it, is powerful,' Léon said.

Mr Ormeroyd smiled. 'You are getting more like a Yorkshireman every day!'

'The French are also practical,' Léon said. 'Though the English never seem to think so. Do you think Mrs Parkinson will be unwilling to sell?'

Mr Ormeroyd shook his head.

'Mrs Parkinson alone might be more than willing, but there is the question of her son and daughter. I'm sure Roger would be also. He wants to set up in his own practice, now that he's qualified.'

On leaving school after his father's death, Roger had been articled to Mr Ormeroyd, much to Mrs Parkinson's relief, since there was no money to send him to university.

'However,' Mr Ormeroyd said, 'Sophia Chester is another matter altogether.'

'What hope does she have of ever living at Mount Royd?' Léon asked bluntly.

'None whatever! But that won't prevent her denying the chance to someone else.' He hadn't seen Sophia since the exhibition she'd made of herself on the day of her father's funeral; nor did he want to.

Yes. She would undoubtedly deny Madeleine, Léon thought. They were enemies, and had been for years. He was not sure how much Mr Ormeroyd knew of this. It was all a lot of silly nonsense anyway.

'Would you like to speak with Roger Parkinson?' Mr Ormeroyd asked. 'It will be quite in order. He acts for his mother on all matters.'

'If you think Mrs Parkinson would not be offended that I spoke to her son first,' Léon said. 'I wouldn't like to upset her. But I want Mount Royd.'

Minutes later, Roger Parkinson sat in the office with them, listening to Léon's proposal.

'I am prepared to be generous about the price,' Léon said. 'But I want the house quickly. I'm not prepared to wait around.'

'Well for my part, I'm totally in favour,' Roger said. 'And I'm sure my mother will be. We know we shall never live at Mount Royd again, and we can't pretend that we don't need the cash. Money talks, and your offer is a very good one.'

'But open for a short time only,' Léon insisted.

'And what of your sister, Roger?' Mr Ormeroyd asked. 'What will Mrs Chester say?'

'She will fight it tooth and nail,' Roger admitted. 'No doubt about that. She needs the money as badly as do my mother and I, but she won't stand the thought of. . .' He broke off. 'May I speak frankly?' he asked Léon.

'Please do!'

'She won't stand the thought of the house belonging to you and your wife. You see, she and Madeleine never got on – I'm sure I don't know why, other than that Sophia can be the very devil – and the thought of Madeleine being in Mount Royd is unbearable to her. I think at the back of her mind she believes that one day she will oust you both.'

'It's a big stumbling block,' Mr Ormeroyd said. 'Sophia doesn't have the final say, but we should need her agreement for a sale.'

'Tell me something,' Léon said to Roger. 'Would your sister object to the sale of Mount Royd, as such, or only to the fact that it was to be sold to me?'

'She wouldn't like to sell it to anyone,' Roger answered, 'though that's a feeling she would overcome, I think, for the sake of the money. But I doubt if all the money in Helsdon would persuade her to sell it to you!'

There was silence in the solicitor's office.

I want Mount Royd, Léon thought. I want it for Madeleine and I mean to have it. It will be the crown of what I feel for her. Nothing less will do.

'Tell me,' he asked Mr Ormeroyd, breaking the silence, 'have you ever sold a property without revealing the identity of the buyer?'

Mr Ormeroyd gave him a sharp look.

'I have never done so.'

'But it has been done. It can be done,' Roger Parkinson said quickly. 'There is no reason why another person could not buy Mount Royd on Monsieur Bonneau's behalf. It would be entirely legal.'

Mr Ormeroyd shook his head.

'That's quite true, but I don't like it!'

'But it is possible?' Léon urged.

'It is possible.'

'Then that's what I shall do!'

'I can't stop you,' Mr Ormeroyd said.

'And would you arrange it for me, my friend, or would you wish me to go to another lawyer?'

Mr Ormeroyd jumped up from his chair, paced up and down the office, looked out of the window.

'I am proud to be your friend,' he said at last, 'and there isn't much I wouldn't do for you. But if I were to consent to act for you in this it would only be if Mrs Parkinson knew everything, and was agreeable. Roger already knows. . .'

'I suggested it,' Roger put in.

'But you are asking Mrs Parkinson to deceive her own daughter.'

'And the alternative is that both my mother and I would have to sacrifice the money,' Roger pointed out. 'Heaven knows my mother needs the money, and I shall never have my own practice unless I can lay hands on enough cash. We're being asked to sacrifice ourselves to Sophia's vindictiveness!'

Mr Ormeroyd returned to his desk and sat down again.

'Who would you get to buy on your behalf?' he asked Léon.

'I haven't had time to think,' Léon said. 'But the man who springs to mind is Henry Garston. Also, the bid would seem natural, coming from him, since at present he has a share in Bonneau's, though I plan to buy him out.'

'Very well. Put it to him!' the lawyer said.

Léon jumped to his feet.

'I shall go to Leeds today. I want all this to be concluded quickly. I want to give Mount Royd to Madeleine on the day the baby is born; and between now and then I must go to France.'

'I'll do what I can,' Mr Ormeroyd promised. 'If Roger can arrange it, can you come here to see Mrs Parkinson tomorrow?'

'Certainly!'

How fortunate, Léon thought as he set off for Leeds that afternoon, that Madeleine is not in the mill and I don't have to find excuses for all these comings and goings. He

145

wished it was someone other than Henry Garston of whom he was to ask this favour. They had been good business friends for several years, but now he had this reserve about Henry. It dated from that foolish episode of Madeleine going to Bradford with him. She was too impulsive.

'What brings you here?' Henry Garston said when Léon was shown into his office. 'Not that you're not welcome! Were you in the area?'

'No,' Léon said. 'I have come specially. I have come to ask you a favour.'

Henry raised his eyebrows. Léon Bonneau had been getting more and more independent over the years. He'd been grateful to have money into the business to help him to open up the spinning, but the Frenchman was doing so well now that Henry guessed it was only a matter of time now before he'd ask to buy back his interest. Perhaps this was the time?

'So how is Madeleine?' he asked.

'She is very well. If you should communicate with her in any way, I'd rather you didn't tell her I'd seen you?'

'You intrigue me,' Henry said. 'What have you been up to?'

'Nothing – as yet. But I wish to be . . . up to something, which is why I ask a favour.'

'Then ask away!' Henry invited.

He listened intently while Léon put his proposition.

'I'll do it,' he said quickly. 'I don't see why not. No skin off my nose!'

He would do it for Madeleine, though no one but himself need know that.

They discussed the details, then Léon rose, shook hands, and prepared to leave.

'By the way,' he said, turning back at the door, 'how is my brother-in-law getting on?'

'Irvine Bates is not getting on at all,' Henry said gruffly. 'He's got to pull his socks up or he'll be out!'

'I'm sorry to hear that,' Léon said. 'It was good of you to give him the job in the first place.'

'I made a mistake,' Henry admitted. 'I don't often, but I did then. But no need to tell Madeleine just yet. Not a time to worry her.'

Léon nodded in agreement.

'That's thoughtful of you, Henry.'

Quite early next morning – he had been in the mill no more than an hour or two – Mr Ormeroyd's messenger came to ask him to be at the lawyer's office at eleven o'clock. When he arrived, Mrs Parkinson and Roger were already present.

'I have repeated to Mrs Parkinson our conversation of yesterday afternoon,' Mr Ormeroyd said. 'She is fully in the picture.'

Léon turned eagerly to Mrs Parkinson.

'And what do you say?'

'I would willingly sell Mount Royd. I would willingly sell it to you. Apart from the modest rent it brings in, it is a white elephant. But there are difficulties in the way. Would you not consider renting the whole of it?'

Léon shook his head.

'No,' he said firmly. 'I want to buy it. I'm quite certain about that.'

'Mama,' Roger interrupted. 'It would not help me if you were to rent it. I need capital.'

'I know you do,' Mrs Parkinson said, 'and that is one reason why I would sell it. But Sophia would never agree. I have to tell you, Léon, that you and Madeleine would be the last two people on earth my daughter would sell to. I cannot imagine what causes her to feel so strongly, but she is not, and never has been, the easiest of creatures!'

She is the most selfish, the most awkward girl in the world, Mr Ormeroyd thought to himself. She had been like that as a child and she had never changed. It was because Sophia was as she was that he had agreed to go through with this undertaking, which was not as above-board as he would have wished.

'Mrs Parkinson has also been acquainted with the idea

that you should buy through someone else,' he informed Léon.

'And what do you say to that, Mrs Parkinson?'

She sighed. She looked pale and worried, and he felt sorry for her – but not sorry enough to drop his request.

'It's difficult. You are asking me to deceive my daughter, and that I don't like to do.'

'But you yourself wish to sell, and so does Roger!'

'That is true.'

'And if I were not the buyer, would Sophia be willing, do you think?'

'It is possible.'

There was one reason which would persuade her daughter to sell. If she thought that by doing so, Madeleine would have to leave Mount Royd, then she would agree. And if she shows her hand there, if she even hints at it, then I shall have no compunction in deceiving her as to the true buyer, Mrs Parkinson thought.

'So what do you conclude?' Léon asked after a while.

'I think you may ask Mr Henry Garston to put in his offer. We will see what happens.'

'Well done, Mama!' Roger said.

'It is by no means done,' Mrs Parkinson said. 'Mr Ormeroyd, you will have to come to Ripon to see us. I go there today. And one thing is certain, Léon Bonneau's name must never be mentioned.'

She dreaded the scene which must follow, if they sold Mount Royd, when Sophia discovered who the true owner was. And there was no possible way she would not find out. It is I who will bear the brunt of it, she thought. Not these men sitting here.

Mrs Parkinson travelled to Ripon later that day. She spent an uneasy evening, trying to make conversation with her daughter.

'Mama, whatever is the matter with you?' Sophia said sharply. 'I've asked you the same question three times!'

'I'm sorry! I'm really very tired. I think I shall go to bed.'

148

But, as it turned out, not to sleep. She tossed and turned the night long. From time to time, lying wide-eyed in the darkness, she wished she had turned down the whole proposition. But that would have been unfair to Roger – and why should his future be put in jeopardy? Oh, she would be so pleased when Mr Ormeroyd had been and gone and it was all settled, one way or the other!

The lawyer, accompanied by Roger, arrived on the dot of eleven o'clock. The two women were in the morning-room, when Penelope showed them in.

'Why, whatever brings you here?' Sophia cried.

Mrs Parkinson tried to look as surprised as her daughter, though it hardly mattered, since Sophia's whole attention was on her brother and the lawyer.

'Do you have clients in Ripon?' Sophia queried. 'I'm surprised if you do.'

'None, other than your family,' Mr Ormeroyd said. 'As you know, Mrs Chester, it has been my privilege to look after the affairs of your family all my professional life. . .'

'So what do you want now?' Sophia interrupted. 'And why is Roger with you?'

She had little time for the lawyer. *He* was the man who had broken the news that her father had died penniless. What were lawyers for if not to prevent that sort of thing?

'I am here on business,' Mr Ormeroyd said. 'And Roger is with me because it concerns all three of you – you, your mother, and him. May I sit down while I explain it to you?'

He watched the different emotions come and go in her face as he put the proposition. Disbelief, then what might be genuine pain at the thought of someone else being able to buy Mount Royd; then more than a flicker of greed as he mentioned the amount of money involved. He also watched Mrs Parkinson trying to act as though she was hearing it all for the first time.

'Well!' Mrs Parkinson said. 'Well I never!'

'So what do you think, Mama?' Roger said, too eagerly.

'It's a good offer,' Mrs Parkinson said hesitantly.

'Of course it's a good offer!' Sophia snapped. 'But why should it come to this? Why should we even have to think of selling Mount Royd? I have never ceased to hope that one day it might be restored to us, that my children would grow up there!'

'Sophia, you know that's totally impossible,' Roger protested. 'There's not the faintest hope of that!'

'I believe it would have been possible had my father's affairs not been mismanaged!'

Had she but known it, the baleful look in Mr Ormeroyd's direction which accompanied her words put new strength into Mr Ormeroyd. Until this minute he had been doubtful about the transaction, even though it was legal. Now he minded considerably less.

'My client makes this offer only on the condition that the sale should go through quickly,' he said. 'I cannot press for an immediate answer, but it must be within a day or two at the most.'

'Mr Henry Garston must be a very rich man to make such an offer,' Sophia said.

'Mr Garston is believed to be one of the richest men in the West Riding,' the lawyer said truthfully.

Mrs Parkinson was watching her daughter's face intently now. She saw the flash of cunning in her eyes. She knew what was coming – and when it did, she would harden her heart, as she had promised herself she would. There would be no more sympathy in her.

'And. . .' Sophia drawled, '. . . as Mr Garston is so anxious to buy quickly, I daresay he plans to move into Mount Royd soon?'

You have done it, Mrs Parkinson thought. I had hoped that somewhere you had some decency, some kindness in you – but I should have known better. She looked in turn at Mr Ormeroyd and Roger and saw that they had realized what lay behind Sophia's question.

'Well, does he?' Sophia asked.

Roger kept silent. Mr Ormeroyd's face and voice were impassive as he replied.

'That would seem to be a reasonable assumption on your part, Mrs Chester.'

Sophia turned to her mother, then to Roger.

'Why do we need time to decide? Both of you want to sell, and for that reason I will go along with you, even though I am signing away my dear children's birthright! Let us get this unpleasant task over with as quickly as possible!'

'Then we will go back at once and prepare the papers,' Mr Ormeroyd said. He had no wish to stay in this house a moment longer.

'You must take some refreshment before you go,' Mrs Parkinson said. 'A cup of chocolate, perhaps?'

'Thank you, no,' he said. 'We must be on our way.'

They were not quite out of sight down the school drive when Sophia clapped her hands.

'You see what will happen, Mama!' Her eyes were sparkling. 'But no, I don't suppose you will see. You are not as sharp as your daughter! It came to me in a flash! Don't you realize that before Mr Henry Garston moves into Mount Royd, Léon Bonneau and his little upstart wife will have to move out!'

Mrs Parkinson felt sick.

'That would seem a reasonable assumption,' she said tonelessly, echoing Mr Ormeroyd's words.

'Who knows where they will go? Though who cares, as long as they are out of Mount Royd? But don't look so unhappy, Mama. They don't belong there, and never would. And no one can blame us for taking Mr Garston's money. You know how much Roger needs it, for one!' She was excited, exhilarated.

'That is why I agreed to sell,' Mrs Parkinson said. 'And now, really, I don't feel at all well. I've decided that I shall return home to Helsdon. I shall catch the afternoon train.'

'But Mama, why? You were going to stay a few days!'

'I know. Suddenly I don't feel well. I will be better in Helsdon. Anything which has to be signed, I can sign there.'

'You won't change your mind?' Sophia said anxiously. 'You won't go back on your word?'

'I have agreed to the sale and I shan't change my mind,' Mrs Parkinson said.

The next day Léon went again to see Mr Ormeroyd.

'The sale will go through,' the lawyer told him.

'But that's wonderful!' Léon cried. 'Tell me – I'm curious – what made Sophia agree so quickly?'

Mr Ormeroyd shrugged his shoulders.

'Who can say?' He had no intention of telling Léon Bonneau why Sophia Chester had agreed. The motive, which he had clearly seen in that instant yesterday, the light of revenge in the woman's eyes, when she realized it was in her power to have the Bonneaus thrown out of their house, was something he preferred to forget. On the other hand, perhaps Léon should be warned.

'All the same,' he said to Léon, 'there might be unpleasantness when the truth comes out. I should have a care there if I were you.'

'Don't worry, I will!' Léon promised. 'Though I'm sure there'll be nothing I can't deal with. Now can you have everything through before I go to France, or if not, then immediately I return? I expect to be back a few days before the birth.'

'Leave it with me,' Mr Ormeroyd said.

The weather was good in France. Léon had completed his visits, taken several good orders which would keep his workpeople busy for some time to come, and now he was in Paris. He took a cab from the railway station to the hotel where Marie and his mother were staying, but really, the weather was so beautiful it would have been better to walk.

He loved Paris! He always felt better for being here. The trees in their pale green of spring, the tall buildings, the boulevards, all lifted his spirits. And the women, he thought, watching them walk by as his *fiacre* was held up in traffic. Such elegance; such a way of walking, as if they delighted in their femininity. Paris was a city for women.

At the entrance to the hotel he paid the driver, tipped him generously, and ran up the steps. Possibly Marie and *Maman* would be out. They might still be shopping, though he had arranged to take them to lunch. If they were not in the foyer he would go straight to the room Marie had booked for him.

He saw his sister at once, before she spotted him. She was walking towards him across the foyer. He looked beyond her, expecting to see his mother, and to his astonishment saw Hortense Murer.

The sight of Hortense was so sudden, so unexpected, that it gave him no time to order his thoughts. Almost before he recognized her he saw this attractive woman walking towards him. On the instant, all that was masculine in him leapt with sexual desire at the sight of her.

It was over in a moment. He kissed Marie, and when he turned to greet Hortense it was no more than greeting an old friend.

'Hortense! I didn't expect to see you!'

'I hope you're not disappointed!' Her smile was brilliant. She had observed his first reaction on seeing her, and with some amusement had watched him immediately take hold of himself.

'Of course not! But where is *Maman*?'

'She has the *grippe*,' Marie said. 'A temperature and a bad headache. Oh, not serious I assure you, Léon – but it would not have been wise for her to travel yesterday, as we did. So Hortense very kindly offered to chaperone me.'

'I am sorry to hear that – I mean that *Maman* is ill, not that you are here, Hortense. Perhaps in the circumstances I should journey on to Roubaix?'

'*Maman* said you were definitely not to do so. She was sure she would be much better today. Also, she didn't want you to risk catching anything and passing it on to Madeleine, not at this particular time.'

'So you have the two of us on your hands!' Hortense said.

'And what could be more agreeable! I must go up to my room first of all, but I shall be down again in ten minutes. Can I trust you to behave yourselves for that length of time?'

Hortense pulled a face.

'Must we always behave well, *cher* Léon? It sounds so dull! Can we not sometimes, if only briefly, do exactly as we want?'

'I can't!' Marie said. 'My dear Jules expects me to be good at all times. I can't let him down!'

'But I have no such constraints,' Hortense said. 'I am as free as air!'

'Well you must keep an eye on each other until I rejoin you,' Léon said. 'Then I will take you to luncheon.'

They ate in a restaurant on the Rue de Rivoli, and afterwards, at Marie's insistence, crossed the road in the direction of the Tuileries Gardens. Marie walked quickly, and when Léon and Hortense loitered to admire a team of splendid, matched horses pulling an open carriage around the Place de la Concorde she urged them on.

'Why should we hurry?' Léon asked. 'We have all afternoon. And why are we going in this direction? I thought we might have strolled in the Champs Elysées.'

'Not at the moment,' Marie insisted. 'And we have to hurry because I promised to meet Jules at the corner of the Quai des Tuileries! He doesn't have much time. He will have left his office for a few minutes only.'

'Marie! When was this arranged?' Léon asked.

'This morning. He took us to see the apartment we're to have when we're married. Oh Léon, it's lovely! If we stand on tiptoe and look out of the window in the right direction we have a view of the river.'

'You saw Jules this morning – and you arranged to meet him for a few minutes now? And we'll see him this evening?'

'Of course! I have to make the most of every minute. Léon, you've no idea what it's like, hardly ever seeing someone you love! I can't wait to be married, so that we

154

can see each other every day of our lives! And will you do me a favour when we do meet him?'

'I expect so,' Léon laughed at his sister's earnest expression.

'Will you and Hortense walk on ahead, so that we can have just a few minutes to ourselves?'

'We could walk immediately behind,' Léon teased.

'Oh don't be so mean! Hortense, please persuade him!'

Jules was waiting at the appointed spot. He was a dark-haired, dark-eyed young man, who looked at Marie as though he could eat her. Marie hurriedly introduced him to Léon and then gave her brother a meaningful look.

'If you have a few minutes before you must go back to your office,' Léon said, 'we might stroll along the *Quai*.' He linked Hortense's hand through his arm, and walked ahead.

'He is a nice boy,' Hortense said. 'Don't you think so?'

'I don't know him, do I? He seems rather young. I think I would have preferred someone older for my sister, someone who would keep her in order.'

'Oh, they'll be all right,' Hortense said. 'They're very much in love.'

'And is that enough?' Léon asked.

'You must tell *me*. You are the one who fell in love and married your little Englishwoman. You can tell me if love lasts! Do men remain faithful?'

Almost imperceptibly she drew him closer, so that as they walked along, their bodies from time to time touched. Her shoulder was against his arm, and when she turned to speak to him he felt the softness of her breast against his side.

'So do men remain faithful?' she persisted.

'I can't speak for all men.' And it is not easy when they are tempted, as you are tempting me, he thought.

'Then speak for yourself! Do you stay faithful?'

'I do. My wife is *enceinte*, as you know. The baby is due soon.'

'I would have thought that was a difficult time – for a

man, I mean. But it seems you are a very dutiful husband. Isn't it a bit boring?'

'No one could accuse my wife of being boring,' he said. 'It is perhaps not always easy to remain true. There are times and circumstances. . .'

'Then . . . ?'

'But you are wrong in thinking it is duty which keeps one faithful. Sometimes, as in my case, it is love. I love my wife.'

'How very touching!'

She drew away from him as Marie and Jules caught up to them.

'Unfortunately I must leave you now,' Jules said. 'But we shall all meet again this evening!'

Léon was ready, about to go down to meet with Jules, when the knock came at his door. When he went to open it, Hortense faced him. For a moment he stood rooted, dazzled by her appearance. She had never looked more beautiful. Her skin, from her wide forehead, down her slender neck to her breasts, amply revealed by the low cut of her bodice, was a dazzling creamy white, except for the faint flush of pink over her cheekbones. Her hair curled on her neck and her dark eyes sparkled. He was quite unaware of the colour or style of her gown, only knowing that the whole of her appearance was perfection. He had known Hortense Murer for years and had never been so aware of her loveliness.

'Hortense! What is it?'

'May I come in?'

'Is something wrong? Is Marie all right?'

'Of course nothing's wrong – but please don't keep me standing in the doorway. I want a word with you. I won't eat you!'

She swept past him and stood in the middle of the room.

'Where is Marie?' he asked.

'Jules has arrived and she has gone down. I told her I

156

would join her in a minute or two. Léon, I have a favour to ask you. Will you grant it?'

'If I can,' he said guardedly.

'Oh Léon, don't look so alarmed!' she said, laughing. 'It's for Marie, not for me.'

'I see!' But he didn't. 'And what is this favour?'

'Will you allow Marie and Jules to give us the slip, after dinner? They are so much in love and long for a chance to be alone.'

Whatever he had expected, it was not that.

'I don't know,' he said doubtfully. 'I don't think I can deliberately leave my sister alone with her fiancé. It is my duty to protect her.'

'Oh, what nonsense, Léon!' She was laughing at him again. 'You've seen Jules. You've seen how he adores her. She needs no protection from him!'

'Even so, I'm not sure...'

'Léon, you are getting impossibly stuffy!' Hortense complained. 'You never used to be like this. My memories of you are *very* different!'

'I am not in the least stuffy,' he objected. 'So what is it you propose?'

'It is very simple. After dinner, when we leave the restaurant, we will all set off for a stroll. But the boulevards are sure to be crowded; it is spring and Paris is awash with visitors. What more likely than that we should lose sight of Marie and Jules among all those people?'

'And then?'

'Naturally, having lost us, they will walk alone until it is time for Jules to bring Marie back here to the hotel.'

'But Marie will be worried that she's lost us. They will spend their time searching for us.'

'Of course they won't! This is something I have already arranged with Marie. She thought it better that I should ask you.'

'The little minx!' Léon cried.

'No,' Hortense said indulgently. 'She is a woman, and

157

in love. But I have her promise that they will be back here before midnight.'

'I suppose it will be all right,' Léon said with some reluctance. 'Very well then. And what will you and I do?'

'I leave that to you,' Hortense said. 'I'm sure we shall find something to pass the time.'

'That was a delicious dinner,' Jules said two hours later. 'And taken in perfect company!'

'I agree!' Léon said. 'We are escorting the two most attractive ladies in the restaurant.'

'Perhaps in all Paris,' Jules said fondly.

'Léon, it's such a pity you have to go back to England tomorrow,' Hortense said. 'Must you really do so?'

'I must,' he said. 'In any case, you and Marie go back to Roubaix.'

'We needn't,' Marie said. 'We could send a telegram, stay another day! Oh do let's!'

'I would like to,' Léon admitted. 'Perhaps . . . but no, it is impossible! So let us have another bottle of champagne while we may!'

'Oh no!' Marie said quickly. 'I'm sure I've drunk quite enough. Let's go out into the fresh air!'

'Very well then,' Léon agreed. She was so transparent in her desire to be off with Jules.

They walked along the Champs Elysées, Léon and Hortense in front, Jules and Marie behind, for it was too crowded to walk four abreast.

'What a beautiful evening,' Léon said, 'unbelievably warm. And everyone out to enjoy themselves!' Helsdon seemed very far away.

Hortense looked around.

'I think we have lost Jules and Marie,' she announced. 'There's no sign of them.'

'Then you and I will sit at the next café and watch the world go by,' Léon said.

He ordered champagne.

'It suits the evening,' he said.

Hortense gave him a quick look of pleasure.

'It is the way I feel also,' she said.

They spoke very little as they sipped the champagne, and then only with lightness – about the passing scene, the fashions, the people at the adjoining tables: nothing of themselves or their circumstances. It was as if there was no past, no future; only the here and now.

Presently Hortense said: 'Shall we go back to the hotel? I am bold enough to ask you because I believe you will not allow yourself to ask me. But I know it is what you want.'

Without answering, he pulled her to her feet, flung money on the table for the wine, and hailed a passing *fiacre*.

'Hotel Carillon,' he said to the driver.

They went immediately to Léon's room. No words were spoken. In the cab he had found it almost impossible to keep his hands from her body, and now he need no longer do so. Without waiting to undress, she lay on her back on his bed, and immediately he was on top of her. He slid her gown from her shoulders so that her breasts were bare. He stared at the beauty of them, then buried his face in her softness and dug his fingers into her flesh.

It was not until his climax came that he thought of Madeleine at all. He had not been in her world, nor she in his. But when, at that moment, she rushed into his mind, filling it as if she were physically present, as if it were she to whom he had made love, he cried aloud in agony. Hortense, her own climax upon her, did not hear him, and if she had would not have cared.

The next day, after breakfast, he left for England.

'Don't blame yourself,' Hortense said in the only moment they had alone. 'It was my fault. But I don't regret it and I never shall. Nor must you, Léon.'

When he reached Mount Royd Mrs Bates came to the door to meet him, white-faced and anxious.

'She's in labour!' she cried. 'Madeleine's in labour! Thank God you're home!'

159

NINE

'I was so afraid you wouldn't come,' Madeleine said.

She had wakened from a long sleep, but her voice was still weak with exhaustion. For two days she had been in excruciating labour. At times, nothing had seemed real; the doctor, the midwife, her mother, had simply been shapes, standing by the bed, moving in the room. She heard their lowered voices, caught the anxiety in their tones, but it all meant nothing against the pain. When her mind did surface, it was of Léon she thought. Why wasn't he here? Why was he in Paris when she longed for him, desperately needed him?

'Sometimes I thought I'd die before you came,' she said. 'I thought I might never see you again.'

'Well I'm here now, my dear one,' he said tenderly. 'Everything is all right now.'

'Oh yes,' she said. 'From the minute you walked into the room I knew it would be.'

The sound of his voice, that French accent he would never lose, his strength flowing through her as he held her hands tightly in his, had been all she needed. Within an hour of his homecoming, with a shriek she had been unable to hold back, a long cry of mingled agony and triumph, she had given birth.

'I don't know why the baby came a fortnight too soon,' she said. 'I was very good while you were away. I didn't do anything I shouldn't have done.'

'I know, my love. But it's over now. We have our child.'

He looked from Madeleine to the new life in the crib at the side of the bed; leaned down to touch the soft cheek, the mop of black hair, the tiny, clenched hands. He had seen his brothers' babies, but never when they were as young as this. In any case he couldn't believe that even one of them could have been quite so perfect.

'Are you disappointed she's a girl?' Madeleine asked. 'I know you wanted a son so much.'

'Of course I'm not disappointed,' he assured her. 'Now that I've seen her, I think a girl is what I really wanted.'

It was not quite true. His first reaction on being told he had a daughter was swift and sharp disappointment. He had longed for a son, looked forward to someone who, however far in the future, would succeed him, carry on the name of Bonneau, inherit what, every day of his life, he was building for him. But he had quickly stifled his first poignant regret, had told himself that he must not hold it against his daughter that she was of the wrong sex. Nor would he ever let Madeleine know how he felt.

Madeleine reached out and took his hand.

'Never mind,' she said. 'We'll have a son next time!'

It was what he had told himself, it had been his comfort – but not for long. Now he knew that it would never happen. Dr Hughes had been unequivocal about that.

'Cherish your daughter, Monsieur Bonneau,' he said. 'Thank God for her, even though she is not a son. Your wife will never have another child. She will not be able to conceive again.'

Léon had hardly heard the details, the medical reasons why. 'Your wife will never have another child' were the only words which beat through his head.

'Does Madeleine know?' he asked.

'No. She's in no state to be told. But later on I'm sure she must be told, otherwise her life will be a series of disappointments, of hopes dashed. Her condition will in no way impair your marital relationship, it is just that she won't conceive. So when the time is ripe, you should tell her yourself.'

'Yes,' Madeleine repeated now. 'We'll have a son next time, perhaps next year.'

'Perhaps,' Léon said.

'How was Paris?' she asked. 'I thought about you a lot, wished I was there with you. Was it beautiful?'

'As only Paris can be at this time of the year. But now I think you should try to sleep again, my love!'

He wouldn't tell her that his mother hadn't been in Paris, that Hortense had been in her stead. It was not the time to do so. Perhaps later, more likely not at all. There was no need for her to know. His brief dalliance with Hortense was, in the light of what had happened at Mount Royd – the birth of his child, the brush with death which he knew had been Madeleine's – of no significance whatever. It had been the sating of a physical appetite, as a hungry man might eat when tempting food was put before him. Nothing more than that. It was Madeleine he loved, and never more than now. Any man might have done what he had done in Paris. He wished only that it had not been with Hortense.

'I will,' Madeleine promised. 'But will you stay a little while?'

'Until you fall asleep,' Léon said. 'Then I must go down to the mill. I took some good orders in France. I must see that they're dealt with quickly.'

Before he left he spoke to his mother-in-law.

'Madeleine is asleep, and so is your new granddaughter! Nurse Edmunds is there, so everything is in order.'

'She's a little beauty, my granddaughter!' Mrs Bates said proudly. 'But the more rest Madeleine gets, the better.' There had been times, during Madeleine's labour, when she had thought that neither of them would survive, but just as when you had your own children, once it was over and you were safely delivered, you forgot the bad bits in the joy of the new baby.

In fact, Léon went first not to the mill but to Mr Ormeroyd's office.

'Congratulations!' Mr Ormeroyd said.

'How did you know so quickly?' Léon asked.

'You'd be surprised how news travels in Helsdon,' the lawyer said.

'Well, I am happy to have that news shouted from the housetops!' Léon said. 'And now tell me what progress there has been on the house,' he added eagerly.

'Everything is going smoothly and quickly. In a week or so you should have the deeds in your hand.'

'Good! And I hope that bit of news doesn't travel around Helsdon,' Léon said. 'I want it to be a surprise for Madeleine.'

Mr Ormeroyd was as good as his word. A week later – a week in which Madeleine gained a little more strength each day, in which the baby started to feed greedily – and in which Léon tried to come to terms with the news Dr Hughes had given him – a messenger came to the mill to summon him to the lawyer's office.

'Everything is settled,' Mr Ormeroyd said.

'I'm truly grateful to you,' Léon told him. 'And to Henry Garston also.'

'Well let's hope it all goes just as smoothly from now on,' Mr Ormeroyd said. 'I know Mrs Chester isn't aware of the whole truth of the matter, or Roger would have told me. In any case, I rather fancy we'd have heard the explosion from Ripon to Helsdon!'

'I don't care two hoots!' Léon exulted. 'Mount Royd is mine!'

He was far too excited to go back to the mill. Twenty minutes later he walked into Madeleine's bedroom. She was sitting up in bed, drinking a basin of gruel.

'Léon! What in the world are you doing home in the middle of the afternoon?' she demanded. 'Is something wrong?'

'On the contrary! Everything is wonderfully, beautifully right. Put down that gruel at once!'

'I'll be glad to. I hate the stuff! But why?'

'I have a present for you.'

'A present?'

He flung the deeds on to the bed.

'There! Read that!'

She picked up the papers and began to read. Seconds

later she said: 'I don't understand it, Léon. I can't believe what I'm reading!'

'Then let me tell you, Madeleine. I have bought Mount Royd for you! It is my gift to you and to our daughter. It comes with all my love!'

Just for an instant he thought, it was to have been for my son – then quickly pushed the thought away from him.

'Oh Léon! Oh Léon!'

Her startled cry brought Nurse Edmunds rushing into the room.

'It's all right, Nurse! Nothing wrong! Just a very pleasant surprise,' Léon said.

Nurse Edmunds looked at her patient's smiling face, her shining eyes.

'Well, it doesn't look as though it's done any harm!' she said. She lingered in the hope of an explanation, but when none came, she went out again.

'But how?' Madeleine asked. 'How did you do it? How did you persuade Sophia Chester to agree?'

While he told her, he watched the anxiety grow in her face.

'Oh Léon, what will happen when she finds out?'

'Does it matter, my love? There's nothing she can do. She can't hurt us now.'

But for quite a time after Léon had left the room, Madeleine lay in bed and worried. Oh, it was wonderful to have Mount Royd. Now that they had their child, she could think of nothing more marvellous than owning this lovely home in which to bring her up. That it was theirs, for themselves and their children, for all time, was almost beyond belief. All the same, Léon doesn't know Sophia as well as I do, she thought; or the depth of her spite against me. She wouldn't take it lying down, especially when she realized she'd been tricked.

When her mother came into the room Madeleine told her the news and at the same time voiced her fears.

'Why, Madeleine, that's wonderful – and you mustn't

164

give a thought to Mrs Chester. What can she do to you? No, I'd say you're a very lucky young woman, and don't you forget it! Don't you go looking for things to worry about.'

Madeleine regarded her mother fondly. As usual, what she said made sense.

'I expect you're right, Ma! And please don't tell Léon I was worrying.'

'I won't, if you promise not to go on doing it. It affects the milk.' She bent over the crib and surveyed her grand-daughter. 'We don't want to give this little lamb stomach-ache, do we?'

'Isn't she beautiful?' Madeleine said. 'I'm so looking forward to getting stronger and being able to do things for her myself.'

'Well, you will, love. A little bit stronger each day. And you'll have help. By the time Nurse Edmunds leaves at the end of the month, you'll have Flora Bryant here.'

Flora Bryant was to be the new nursemaid. She was a Helsdon girl, the same age as Madeleine herself. Madeleine had chosen her rather than an older, more experienced woman because she didn't want someone who would rule the nursery with a rod of iron, not let her play with her own baby, or help whenever she had a mind to.

'Well then, have you and Léon chosen a name yet?' Mrs Bates asked.

It was almost the only privilege her own husband had ever given her, that when she had borne the child, she should choose its name. She was aware that everyone else considered the names she had chosen far too fine for their circumstances, but she'd never regretted one of them.

'It wasn't easy,' Madeleine said. 'You see, we'd only thought of boys' names.' Their son was to have been Jean Léon Bonneau. 'But yes, we have decided. She's to be named Claire Martha – after you and after Léon's mother.'

'Claire Martha!' Mrs Bates repeated the names once or twice, testing the sound. 'Claire Martha Bonneau. Yes, I like Claire. As for Martha, well I never liked the name, but I'm flattered you've chosen it, love.'

Mrs Bates thought how kindly fortune had smiled on her eldest daughter: this lovely house, now her own; enough money never to have to worry about it, and a husband who adored her. She sighed. She was pleased for Madeleine, or course she was, but it was all very different from poor Irvine's life. His home was a hovel, and Bessie, she reckoned, did nothing to improve it. She wished, not for the first time, that there was something more she could do for her only son.

The next day Madeleine received a letter from Penelope and Emerald.

'Sophia Chester is coming to Helsdon next week to visit her mother. She'll stay overnight. She's bringing Penelope and Emerald and they can stay here, and go back with Sophia next day. Here, read it for yourself.' She handed the letter to her mother.

'Well that's wonderful! Emerald says here that Mrs Chester knows how much both girls want to see the new baby.'

'My guess is that she's bringing the girls so they can take the children off her hands on the journey – and because she knows they're months overdue for some time off,' Madeleine said. 'That's why she's bringing them, Ma. It suits her own book.'

'You're hard on Mrs Chester,' her mother chided.

'Perhaps I am. I'm sorry.' She was too happy to want to be hard on anyone.

'That's because I know her. Anyway, whatever the reason, I'll be very pleased to see Penelope and Emerald. It's been a long time.'

'And if Irvine happens to call I'll have all my children under one roof at once,' Mrs Bates said happily.

But when the two sisters arrived at Mount Royd, and were at once taken to see Madeleine and the new baby,

Madeleine was disturbed to see that Penelope looked white-faced and apprehensive, and even Emerald's face was one large question mark.

'Is something wrong?' Madeleine asked. They had admired their new niece extravagantly, and now sat one on each side of Madeleine's bed. 'Penelope, you don't look at all happy. What is it?'

'Oh Madeleine!' Penelope burst out. 'Oh Madeleine, why didn't you tell us!'

'Tell you? Tell you what? I don't understand.'

'Mrs Chester told us on the train coming here,' Emerald said. 'She seemed to know all about it.'

'Told you what, for heaven's sake?' Madeleine demanded. 'I don't know what you're talking about. What did she say?'

'She said a rich manufacturer had bought Mount Royd and he would be moving in very soon, and you and Léon – and Mother – would have to leave!' The words came pouring out of Penelope. 'Oh Madeleine, where will you go? What will you do?' she wailed. The tears were running down her cheeks now. Madeleine passed her a handkerchief.

'I told Penelope I'm sure you'll find somewhere to live,' Emerald said more calmly. 'I daresay Léon is quite well-off, and I expect he'll let Mother go with you.'

'But oh, Madeleine, supposing he says you must go and live in France!' Penelope cried. 'I couldn't bear it! France is so far away. I might never see you again!'

'Come here, Penelope,' Madeleine said. 'Come closer.' She put her arms around her youngest sister, stroked her hair.

'I'm not going anywhere, love,' she assured her. 'Not to France, not anywhere. I'm staying right here at Mount Royd for as long as I live. So is Léon, so is Ma!'

Penelope lifted her head and stared at Madeleine.

'But Mrs Chester said. . .'

'Mrs Chester has got it wrong.'

'You mean Mount Royd hasn't been bought by a rich

man?' Emerald questioned. 'Mrs Chester sounded quite certain. She said she wouldn't tell us who, but before long everyone would know.'

'And so they will – but not Mrs Chester's version of the story!' Madeleine said. 'Mount Royd has been bought by Léon. It is his present to me for the birth of our daughter.'

Both girls stared at her, open-mouthed, bereft of speech.

'Yes,' she said. 'It was a surprise to me too. A great and wonderful surprise. So you can dry your eyes, Penelope – though it was sweet of you, and entirely like you, to care. But you see, I shall always be here!'

Penelope found her voice, flung her arms around Madeleine.

'Oh, Madeleine, I'm so pleased, so relieved! I must say, Mrs Chester didn't seem the least bit sorry that you were to be turned out!'

'But she was quite positive about it,' Emerald said. She sounded doubtful. 'She's not often wrong.'

'Well in this case she *is*,' Madeleine said firmly. 'Quite wrong! Emerald, look in the top drawer of my chest and you will find a large envelope. It is the deeds of Mount Royd. You may look at them before they're deposited in the bank. Perhaps that will convince you!'

During the rest of their short visit Emerald and Penelope, especially the latter, spent as much time as they were allowed in Madeleine's room. When Nurse Edmunds said there were too many people in the bedroom for her patient's, for the baby's good, Emerald left the room at once, but Penelope begged to be allowed to stay.

'I'll be as quiet as a mouse,' she promised. 'I won't say a word!'

'Very well then,' Nurse Edmunds conceded. She was a nice little thing, Mrs Bonneau's youngest sister. She'd quite taken to her. 'But mind you don't!'

Penelope watched entranced while the nurse changed

the baby, top and tailed it, and wrapped it in layer after layer of swaddling clothes.

'It's like a cocoon,' she said. 'All rolled up tight! Oh Madeleine, I do so love babies. I hope to have at least six children!'

'Well you'll have to get married first!' Madeleine teased – and was startled to see the flush on her sister's cheeks. Surely . . . ? She thought of her sister as being so young, almost a child still, but in fact she was seventeen. A young seventeen, though. Penelope had always seemed younger than her years, while Emerald had been mature even before she was out of her teens. They were not the least bit alike.

'You're not telling me you've already set eyes on Mr Right?' she queried.

'Of course not! Don't be silly!' Penelope knew she was blushing, but there was no way she was going to admit to anything, even to Madeleine. It was all so new; she had only spoken to Archie a few times. She didn't want everyone talking about it and teasing her.

'How do you get on with Mrs Chester?' Madeleine asked.

'All right. She doesn't like me, though – but then I don't much like her, though Emerald thinks she's wonderful.'

'Well if you're ever unhappy, you know you can come back here,' Madeleine said. 'You'll always have a home here.'

Emerald and Penelope had to leave Mount Royd next day soon after breakfast, to go to Mrs Parkinson's.

Mrs Parkinson herself answered the door, and took them straight into the parlour where her daughter sat buffing her nails.

'I thought you were never coming,' Sophia said crossly. 'Now help me at once to get the children ready for the journey.'

By which she doesn't mean 'help me', Penelope thought; she just means get on and do it. She didn't mind.

The children made her job bearable. And now there was Archie. She would see him tomorrow when he came for the meat order – and then again when he delivered it. Also, Madeleine was *not* leaving. Life was looking up. She began to help the children into their outdoor clothes.

'Oh Mrs Chester, ma'am!' she said conversationally. 'My sister won't be leaving Mount Royd!'

Mrs Parkinson gave her daughter a swift look. What had she been saying?

'Oh yes she will,' Sophia said, laughing. The thought cheered her.

'Begging your pardon, ma'am, she won't,' Penelope said boldly. 'Her husband has bought it for her!'

Sophia was inspecting her shining fingernails with approval. She stopped – and stared at her servant.

'Nonsense! I happen to know who *has* bought Mount Royd and it is not your brother-in-law!'

'Yes it is,' Penelope persisted. It was unlike her, but suddenly, she wasn't going to give in. 'Madeleine showed us the deeds, didn't she, Emerald? We've never seen any before.'

Sophia jumped to her feet, raised her hand and struck Penelope a stinging blow on the side of the head. The force of it knocked Penelope to the floor.

'You're a liar!' Sophia cried. 'You're a wretched little liar!'

The children began to scream. Bertie ran to his grandmother and hid his face in her skirt. Penelope lay on the floor, sobbing.

'I'm not a liar. I'm not, I'm not! You tell her, Emerald!'

Before Emerald could say a word, Mrs Parkinson spoke up.

'The girl is not lying. What she says is quite true. Henry Garston bought Mount Royd on Léon Bonneau's behalf!'

For a brief moment Sophia was stunned into silence. Then she began to shriek.

'It's not true! I refuse to believe it!' Sophia was beside herself with rage.

'It is quite true, Sophia,' Mrs Parkinson said.

'You knew! *You* did it! *You* betrayed me! How long have you known?'

Mrs Parkinson took a deep breath. She was about to tell a lie, something she hated to do and practically never did; certainly not a lie of this magnitude. She looked her daughter straight in the face.

'I learned of it only yesterday, just before you arrived.'

'And you didn't tell me? Why didn't you tell me? Why, why, why?' Sophia yelled.

'Because I didn't want to upset you,' Mrs Parkinson replied. And that was no lie! She had hoped that Sophia would hear nothing until she was safely back in Ripon, a place she herself intended to avoid for some time to come. But now this silly, innocent little Penelope had let the cat out of the bag.

Sophia felt a torrent of hate rushing through her body, welling up inside her. She wanted to strike out, to hurt, to maim.

'I'm going to Mount Royd!' she cried. 'I'll show her she can't get away with this!'

'You'll do no such thing!' Mrs Parkinson said. Suddenly, in the face of her virago of a daughter, she felt unaccountably stronger. 'You will *not* go to Mount Royd. What good would that do? What could you possibly do there? For heaven's sake, Sophia, show some dignity!'

But she knew only too well what Sophia could do in her present rage. She seemed to have taken leave of her senses. She was pacing up and down, waving her fists in the air like a madwoman. If she were to set foot in Mount Royd in this mood, then Mrs Parkinson feared for Madeleine Bonneau, and even more the baby.

'You realize what this means?' Sophia shouted. 'It means that that – slut's – children will inherit Mount Royd. It should be for my children! It should be for mine! Oh, I would like to kill her!'

'You know perfectly well that there's never been the slightest possibility of your children inheriting Mount

171

Royd.' Mrs Parkinson spoke in a firm, calm voice. 'You are living in the clouds, Sophia, and the sooner you come down to earth, the better.'

'I won't let her get away with it,' Sophia cried.

'And I'm telling you, that if you take one step in the direction of Mount Royd I shall send Emerald at once to fetch Léon from the mill. He will know how to deal with you!'

Sophia stopped her marching, grabbed the back of the chair to steady herself, tried to pull herself together. It took her several minutes, in which the only sound in the room was of the children whimpering.

'Very well,' she said eventually. She had forgotten that Emerald and Penelope were still in the room, standing there like statues. But if Penelope had been frightened by her mistress's ranting and raving, it was nothing to the cold fear which went through her as Sophia spoke now. Her ice-cold voice was more menacing than anything she had screamed in her temper.

'Very well,' Sophia said again. 'But I shall get even. Madeleine Bates will pay for this. No matter how long it takes, I will get even.'

Mrs Parkinson saw the fright on Penelope's face.

'Go into the kitchen, Emerald and Penelope,' she said. 'Take the children with you.'

In the kitchen, Penelope said: 'Oh Emerald, I'm frightened.'

'Well you have to admit, it's hard on Mrs Chester,' Emerald said. 'We all know what Mount Royd means to her.' Then she looked at her sister's face, where the marks of Sophia's fingers showed up in dark red weals.

'But she shouldn't have struck you,' she said. 'She shouldn't have struck you, Penelope.'

In the next few days, everything appeared back to normal in the little house in Ripon. Mrs Chester was her usual demanding, complaining self, the children seemed happy enough, there were no more scenes; nevertheless, Penelope remained apprehensive.

'I was really frightened,' she said to Emerald. 'I still am. Oh, not because she hit me, but because of what she said about Madeleine.'

'Don't be so silly,' Emerald said. 'She was just in a temper. And she did have reason to be.'

'Well you *would* think so,' Penelope said. 'You always stick up for her, though heaven knows why! Anyway, it wasn't her temper frightened me most, it was what she said afterwards. Do you think I ought to write and tell Madeleine, warn her?'

'Of course not, stupid!'

But Penelope continued to be far from sure. Perhaps if she were to ask Archie . . . ? She would see him tomorrow, and away from the house.

She and Emerald had two hours off in turn on a Sunday afternoon. It was about the only time off they could really call their own, and they could never take it together. Usually she went to church – not to the chapel in which she had been brought up, but to the cathedral, which she loved. Sometimes there was evensong, and she sat at the back and listened, following it in the prayer book.

But tomorrow she would not be going to the cathedral. When Archie had delivered the meat yesterday – a leg of mutton for the dining room, scrag end for the kitchen – Emerald being out of the kitchen, he had asked her if she would go for a walk with him on Sunday.

'I don't know. . .' she said. She liked Archie very much indeed, but she had never been out with a boy before. 'Just a short walk!' he'd pleaded. 'I'll meet you in the town. No one need know.'

So tomorrow she would meet Archie in the market place and, she had now decided, she would ask his advice about writing to Madeleine. She hadn't told Emerald she was meeting him. Emerald had no time for boys.

When Sunday dinner was over, cleared away and the dishes washed, she left the house and walked quickly into the town. Archie was waiting for her. They walked by the river.

'It's the river Ure,' he told her. 'It starts a long way off, up on the moors somewhere, then it comes down through Wensleydale. Usually it's a placid river, but sometimes the opposite. Have you ever seen the water-falls at Aysgarth?'

'No.'

'I'll take you one day,' he promised.

She told him about Madeleine, and Mount Royd and Mrs Chester; the whole story.

'She sounds a right horror, your mistress!' he said.

'She is. Of course I'd never tell Madeleine that she hit me. If I did that she'd make me leave.'

'I wouldn't like you to leave,' Archie said. 'I've only just got to know you.'

'I don't want to leave, not now!' Penelope said boldly. 'But should I warn Madeleine?'

'Well,' Archie said thoughtfully. 'I don't see what Mrs Chester can do, but if it would make you feel better, then I'd write, get it off your chest. I say, fancy you having a sister who lives in a great big house. Would you like to live in a big house – I don't mean as a servant?'

'No,' Penelope said. 'But I'd like to live in a little house that was my very own.'

'One day,' Archie said, 'I mean to have a butcher's shop of my own.'

'And I'm sure you will,' Penelope said.

All in all, it was a wonderful afternoon. She didn't know when she'd enjoyed anything as much. That evening she took paper and pen and wrote to Madeleine.

When Madeleine received the letter she was furious.

'Poor Penelope sounds really scared!' she said to Léon. 'She shouldn't be working for that wretched woman. It's altogether the wrong place for her.'

'And what about you, my love?' Léon asked. 'I hope you're not scared by what she says.'

'Well, I am a little,' she confessed. 'I'm not afraid for myself – I can stand up to Sophia Chester any day of the week – but I just have this feeling that she might try to get at our baby!'

'Why, Madeleine, how could she possibly do that?' Léon said firmly. 'Our dear little daughter will never be out of the sight of one of us, either a member of her family or the nursemaid.'

'All the same. . . You don't know Sophia Chester like I do, Léon.'

'I know her quite well,' he said. 'And I know that she's powerless to hurt us. You must put this out of your mind, Madeleine.'

'I'll try,' Madeleine promised. 'I daresay you're right.'

'Of course I'm right! Now please don't you worry your head about it one minute longer.'

Penelope shouldn't have written so, he thought, but he knew she would have done it for the best.

'She can still hurt Penelope,' Madeleine said. 'She can take it out on her for being the one to break the news. I'd like to go to Ripon and bring Penelope right back here!'

'Well you can't!' Léon said. 'You're still lying-in. And I'm thankful you can't. It's best left alone.'

'*You* could go,' Madeleine said.

'I could, but I won't. By far the best thing is to ignore Sophia. Penelope knows quite well that if she really wants to leave Ripon she can always come back here.'

Nevertheless, though her fears about the baby were somewhat allayed in the face of Léon's common sense, Madeleine continued to worry about Penelope. When Irvine called at Mount Royd – it was his day for working Helsdon, though he allowed himself to finish early in order to visit his mother and sister and eat a good meal of his mother's cooking – she showed him the letter.

'But it's not myself I'm worried about,' she said. 'It's Penelope. I would like to know if she's all right, and here I am, as helpless as that little baby in its crib! So why couldn't you go, Irvine?'

'Me? Go to Ripon?'

'Why not? You've been talking about going for

175

months, and never done it. Now's the time! You could go on Saturday afternoon when you're off work. I'd be generous with expenses, Irvine. Please!'

We've always helped each other, me and Madeleine, he thought. And he was certainly going to need her help in the near future. Besides, it would get him out of the house, out from under Bessie's feet. She was getting more and more cantankerous.

'Just see that she's all right,' Madeleine persisted. 'And ask her would she like to come back here to work. There'll be enough to do now, with the whole house ours.'

'All right,' he said. 'I'll go on Saturday.'

As he had agreed with Madeleine, Irvine went to Ripon unannounced. He found the house easily enough, went around to the back and beat a sharp tattoo on the kitchen door. Penelope's scream on seeing him standing there was enough to waken the dead. He put a hand across her mouth to stifle it. He had no desire to meet the mistress of the house just yet.

'Whoa!' he said. 'It's only me, not the devil incarnate!'

'Oh Irvine, you startled me!' Penelope cried. 'You're the last person in the world I expected to see! Emerald, look who's here!'

'Well aren't you going to ask me in?' Irvine asked. 'Or am I to stand all afternoon on the doormat?'

'I'm sorry!' Penelope said, smiling. 'Come in, sit down. Emerald, do you suppose we could give Irvine a cup of tea?'

'Of course, silly. Who's to know? Put the kettle on.'

'So you're not really allowed to entertain your brother?' Irvine asked.

'We might be, if we'd asked permission beforehand. Naturally we're not allowed to have male persons in the kitchen,' Emerald said. 'Not unless they're tradesmen with orders.'

'And you don't give them cups of tea?'

'Certainly not!' Emerald said.

Penelope reddened. Only two days ago, when Emerald

176

was out with the children and Mrs Chester engrossed with a visitor, she had given Archie a quick, illicit cup of tea before taking the tray up to the drawing-room.

'Why have you come?' she asked her brother. 'Not that we're not pleased to see you.'

'Madeleine thought it would be a good idea. It seems you sent her a letter. . .'

'I told you it was a stupid thing to do,' Emerald snapped. 'I'd have thought you of all people wouldn't have wanted to frighten her.'

'She wasn't frightened,' Irvine said. 'At least not by the time I got there. She was more concerned that Mrs Chester might be taking things out on Penelope. She wanted me to see if everything was all right.'

'Yes thank you,' Penelope said quietly. 'Please tell Madeleine I didn't want to upset her. I wouldn't for the world. I just thought I ought to warn her.'

'Well I daresay you were right at that. But what about you, love? Is your mistress taking it out on you?'

'She is a bit,' Penelope confessed. 'I can't do anything right, even more than usual. But I don't care.'

'Well Madeleine wanted me to tell you that if you want to leave here, there's a job for you at Mount Royd. You're not to hesitate.'

'Oh I don't want to leave Ripon!' Penelope said quickly. 'Please tell Madeleine I'm quite all right.'

'You could have a worse place,' Emerald said. 'Here's your tea, Irvine.'

He was just taking the first sip when Sophia Chester walked into the kitchen. She stood stock still in front of him, staring. He rose to his feet and faced her, taking in her luxuriant red hair, the whiteness of her skin, and her blue eyes, now sparking anger. She was a looker all right. A bit too plump for her height perhaps, but he liked a woman to be well-covered.

'And what is the meaning of this?' she demanded icily. 'What is a man doing in the kitchen?'

'Please ma'am, he's not a man . . . I mean, he's our brother!' Penelope said nervously.

'A likely tale!' Sophia said.

'He really is our brother, ma'am,' Emerald said smoothly.

When she looked at him more closely, he *was* like Madeleine Bates, Sophia thought; those bold features, that thick, dark hair. All the more reason why she did not wish to have him in her house. The sisters were different. She had them under her thumb.

'I do not remember a request that you might have your brother visit you,' she said.

'He happened to be in the neighbourhood, so he dropped in,' Emerald explained. Penelope could say nothing. Her tongue stuck to the roof of her mouth in fear.

'So! You live in Leeds, but you just happened to be in Ripon?' Sophia said. 'How very strange!'

'That was what I told my sisters,' Irvine lied. 'As a matter of fact, ma'am, I came specially. I had this funny feeling that everything might not be right. Do you understand?' He looked her straight in the face. His words were polite enough but his tone was only a shade away from insolence.

'No I do not understand,' Sophia said. 'And now that you have seen your sisters and ascertained that they are alive and well, and not chained up, I think it is time you left.'

'I was just going,' he said nonchalantly, 'when I've finished my tea. I'm pleased to see everything's all right. I think a lot of my sisters, Mrs Chester, all three of them. But we're like that as a family. Anyone who's up against one of us finds he – or she – is up against the lot!'

The smallest narrowing of Sophia's eyes told him that she recognized a threat when she heard one. Good!

He turned to Emerald and Penelope.

'I'll be off then, girls! Keep in touch! I'll see you again before too long. I daresay I shall come to see you more often in future!'

He walked jauntily out of the house and away down the drive. He'd put the fear of the Lord into that little madam, he reckoned.

In the centre of the town he thought, shall I spend a bit of time and cash here, or go back and do it in Leeds? He had quite a bit left from the money Madeleine had given him to cover his fares. She'd expect him to treat himself – a bit of a reward for a job well done.

In the end, since there was a train due, he decided to go back to Leeds. A bit more lively. In Leeds he bought a *Leeds Mercury* and took it with him into the pub, where he ordered a pint of beer and a beef sandwich. He studied the newspaper carefully. He was looking at the advertisements of businesses for sale. He checked his money again. He could treat himself to a whisky – or two.

It was late when he arrived home. He was a bit unsteady – but no one could say he was drunk; not actually drunk!

'You're drunk!' Bessie said. 'Where have you been?'

'You know where I've been,' he said with dignity. 'I've been to Ripon to see my little sisters. An errand of mercy!'

'You didn't get that skinful in Ripon,' Bessie said sharply. 'You smell like you've drunk the Horse and Groom dry. As for mercy, I wouldn't mind a bit of that – in the shape of the money you've just spent on drink. Don't you know, you stupid fool, that if we don't pay the rent soon we'll have the bailiffs in? Though what they'll find worth taking in this hell-hole beats me!'

'Oh Bessie, don't go on!' he pleaded. He was beginning to get a headache. 'Now look at this – just look at this!' He pushed the newspaper into her hand.

'What do I want to look at this for? I've no interest in reading newspapers.'

'This bit at the bottom,' he said. 'Here!' He read aloud, pronouncing his words carefully.

' "A general store to be disposed of in Helsdon. Low rent. Good opening for an ambitious young man with limited capital." '

'Low rent? Limited capital?' Bessie cried. 'What would we use for money? Have you got some, because I haven't. Not two ha'pennies to rub together!'

'Ways and means,' Irvine said solemnly. 'Ways and means!'

TEN

Henry Garston sat behind his desk, his face suffused with anger. He held a letter in each hand and his eyes darted from one to the other, and back again. He could hardly believe what he was reading. And yet, he thought, it fits. It fits in with the rest of the pattern.

The letters were almost identical. 'We venture to ask when your commercial traveller might be calling. We have seen nothing of him in the last month.' 'Kindly inform us when may we expect to see your representative? He has not favoured us with a visit recently.'

Irvine Bates, of course! Well, he'd half expected it. After the last warning he'd given him the man had pulled up his socks for a couple of weeks and since then his orders had gone steadily downhill again. But what I can't forgive, Henry thought, is that he just hasn't called on the customers. It made his blood boil. And how many others did this involve besides those whose irate letters he held in his hands?

Well he'd remedy the situation all right! Bates would have to go, the sooner the better. He raised a hand and rang the bell which brought a clerk running.

'Is Bates in yet?'

'No sir, not yet.'

That was another thing; he was always late.

'Well when he does, tell him. . .' He stopped in midsentence. 'No, don't bother. I'm going out. I'll see him later.'

Oh, he'd definitely sack him, there was no doubt of that. But he'd planned to go Helsdon way today, and that being the case, he'd call in on the Bonneaus. He'd like to tell Madeleine his intentions regarding her brother before

Bates went to her with his own cock-and-bull story. On his present form, that version would be a good stretch away from the truth. It was ridiculous, of course, that he should wish to put himself right with Madeleine before her brother put his two pennyworth in, but there it was. Whoever told her she'd be upset, but at least if he did it she'd know he'd been fair. As for the letters, he'd make personal calls on the writers this very afternoon. They were valuable customers and he certainly didn't want to lose them.

Two hours later Rose Hardy showed him into the drawing-room at Mount Royd, where Madeleine sat with the baby on her lap and Léon hovered protectively close.

'Would you like some tea, Henry?' Madeleine asked.

'Not for me, thank you.'

'Then a glass of sherry wine?' Léon offered.

'That's more like it,' Henry approved. 'It would do you good, too, Madeleine.'

He watched Rose Hardy's retreating figure.

'I've not seen her before,' he said. 'She's a pretty piece!'

'According to my mother that's all she is!' Madeleine's smile took the sting out of her words.

Henry dismissed Rose Hardy from his mind.

'Well Madeleine, I must say you're looking fit enough. Motherhood suits you.' There was a peach bloom to her skin, a melting softness in her dark eyes. She looked like a Madonna in an Italian painting and he envied Léon Bonneau with all his heart.

'Oh I'm very well indeed,' Madeleine agreed. 'Please come closer, Henry, and take a real look at my beautiful Claire!'

Into Henry's mind as he looked at the child rushed the thought of the baby he had lost, and his wife at the same time. But he couldn't dwell on it. He pulled himself together.

'Well, she's a right bonny one!' he pronounced.

He felt in his pocket and brought out a gold sovereign, then, opening the baby's hand he placed the coin in it. At once, the child's fingers curled tightly around the coin.

'See that?' he said laughing. 'She's never going to want! She'll not go short! See how she looks after the money!'

'It's good to see you,' Madeleine said. 'Were you visiting Helsdon, then?'

'I was,' Henry said. 'And though it's a pleasure to see all three of you, in fact I came for something a mite more serious.'

'Nothing wrong, I hope?' Léon said quickly. 'Nothing to do with the business?'

'No, not your business,' Henry said. 'And nothing that can't and won't be put right in mine. No, what I came about was Madeleine's brother.'

'Irvine?' Madeleine was startled. 'What's wrong with Irvine?'

'Only what he's brought on himself. The plain fact is, I can't keep him on!'

'Can't keep him on? You mean you're going to sack him?'

'I'm afraid so, Madeleine. I wanted you to know first, him being your brother, and you having got him the job, so to speak.'

'But why, Henry? Whatever has he done?'

Henry shook his head.

'It's largely a matter of what he hasn't done. He's been unsatisfactory almost from the beginning – and let me say, I did give him fair warning. He can't deny that!'

'But what *is* it he hasn't done?' Madeleine persisted.

'For a start, even allowing for his inexperience, he hasn't taken nearly enough orders. Also, I've very good reason to believe he hasn't been putting in the time. He's been starting late, finishing early, skiving off when it suited him. And now I find that though he's put down in his book that he's made visits, *and* claimed expenses, he's not been near.'

Madeleine listened with a sinking heart.

'Is this true, Henry?'

'Take a look at these two letters. They speak for themselves.'

Madeleine read the first letter, handed it to Léon, and perused the second one.

'And these two firms are on Irvine's round?'

'They are!' Henry said grimly.

'But this is awful!'

'I think so,' Henry agreed. 'And I'm feared there might be more letters to come. Oh, I daresay I'll be able to repair the damage. These are good customers who've dealt with me a long time. But what would you do if one of your workers carried on like this?'

'I'd dismiss him at once,' Léon said sharply. 'I wouldn't keep him a day longer!'

He wasn't the least bit surprised at the turn of events. His previous conversation with Henry had forewarned him, but he'd kept that from Madeleine, not wanting to worry her.

'Oh Léon!' Madeleine sounded near to tears.

'I'm sorry, love, but so would you,' Léon said. 'You know you would. It's the fact that he's your brother. . .'

'Which is why I gave him every chance, and why I came myself to tell you,' Henry said.

'Which was very courteous of you,' Léon said. 'We appreciate that, don't we, Madeleine?'

'Yes. Yes, I suppose so,' Madeleine said reluctantly. 'No, that's wrong! Of course we do, Henry – and I'm more than sorry it's turned out like this. I feel partly responsible!'

'Nothing of the kind,' Henry said. 'How were you to know? The truth is, your brother's competent enough, but he's not suited to the job.'

It was a half-truth. The whole truth was that Bates was a lazy good-for-nothing, not fit to tie his sister's shoelaces. But he wasn't going to distress her further by saying so.

There was a silence, and then Madeleine said:

'Would you do me one more favour, Henry?'

'Madeleine, you can't. . .' Léon began.

'Will you allow Irvine to resign instead of sacking him, Henry? It would make a big difference when he comes to look for another job.'

And where he'll get another job, heaven alone knows, Madeleine thought. Oh how stupid he'd been! How utterly stupid!

'Well,' Henry said slowly. 'I suppose I could – but I want him out from under my feet quickly, before he does any more harm. But if it'll please you, I'll give him the chance to resign, then when he's done it I'll give him a week's wages to leave at once!'

'He'd be damned lucky at that,' Léon said.

'Yes it *is* good of you, Henry,' Madeleine said softly. She reached out and touched his hand.

'Aye, well! There it is. I'd best be going!'

'No don't go just yet,' Madeleine said. 'There's something I've been wanting to talk to you about.'

Henry's face dropped.

'Now don't tell me, now that you're a mother, you're going to give up your designing? That would be a big mistake. In fact, we can't do without you!'

'No, no! I've no intention of giving it up,' Madeleine assured him. 'Quite the opposite. I want to do something extra.'

'Madeleine, now is not the time!' Léon interrupted. 'It's not a sensible idea, and in any case it's too soon after the baby's birth!'

He knew what she had in mind. It was this silly idea of doing some fashion designing. He didn't approve of it and she knew he didn't. 'I'm not thinking of starting today, or even this week,' Madeleine said. 'Though I'm perfectly fit to do so.'

'Well come on! What is it you're fit to do but won't start this week?' Henry asked. 'Out with it!'

'I want to do some fashion designing for you,' Madeleine said. 'In particular, I want to design some of the garments for which my cloth will be used. I'd like to know that the cloth was being used to the very best advantage – and who knows better than I do what it's suitable for? You would have to approve the designs, of course.'

'Thank you,' Henry said dryly. 'Thank you very much. And do you reckon, then, that Garston's present designs aren't good enough for your cloth?' All the same, Joe Sims had said as much to him after a visit to Lester's. Joe was one of his best travellers. He took a lot of notice of what Joe said.

'Now I didn't say that, Henry! For a start, I don't know all your designs.' There was no way she would ever tell him of the criticisms which had been voiced by Irvine. 'But I'm interested in fashion. It's always changing and I see the trends. Can I ask if your designers are all men?'

'That's right.'

'Then I might bring a new point of view,' Madeleine said. 'And what I'm proposing could work both ways. There'd be times when I could design the cloth to fit in with a new fashion.'

'Well it's an interesting thought,' Henry conceded. 'I won't dismiss it out of hand. But what makes you think you could do it?'

'That is exactly what I have asked her,' Léon interposed.

'I just reckon I could,' Madeleine said. 'I have this feeling. I wouldn't only be drawing pretty pictures, you know. I'd make sure I could explain how the fashion worked, why it worked – and so on.'

'Well,' Henry said. 'I'll think about it. In the meantime you could let me have a few ideas – whenever you're ready. No hurry.'

'You shall have them quite soon,' Madeleine said. 'I already have lots of sketches.'

'Right you are. And now I must be going. I'm really sorry about your brother, Madeleine.'

'Thank you,' she said. 'It's a blow, but please don't think I'm blaming you.'

When Léon returned from seeing Henry on his way, his face was like thunder.

'Madeleine, how dare you put your nonsensical proposals about fashions to Henry? You know perfectly well we didn't agree on the subject between the two of us!'

Madeleine stared at him in astonishment. It was seldom he spoke to her so harshly.

'Nonsensical? Léon, how can you say they're nonsensical? I know you and I don't agree on this subject but I didn't think you felt so strongly. I bow to you in most things, my love, but about this I think you're being a bit perverse, and I don't understand why.'

'You do too much!' he snapped. 'Why can't you take things easy, like other women in your position?'

'Because I'm not made that way. You've always known that. I haven't suddenly changed.'

'I don't forbid you to do this, Madeleine,' Léon said. 'But if you continue with it you know it will be very much against my wishes. Doesn't that mean anything to you?'

'Of course it does! I'm very sorry. But I don't think you're being reasonable. All you can say is that I'd be doing too much. But would you say that if I spent my time socializing, going to tea-parties, indulged in trivialities? Is that what you *really* want me to do?'

'You know it isn't.'

'Then will you do something for me, Léon? Will you look at some of my drawings, let me explain them to you?'

He sighed.

'Very well. But not at the moment.'

'No,' Madeleine agreed. 'It would be better some other time. Then may we talk about Irvine? What can I do to help him?'

'Madeleine, you have no further responsibilities towards Irvine,' Léon said forcefully. 'You have done everything you could for him. You got him a good job, and look what he did with it. No, you owe him nothing!'

'I shall always be in Irvine's debt,' Madeleine said quietly. 'If it hadn't been for Irvine, you and I wouldn't be sitting here now. Apart from that, he's my brother.'

Léon sighed.

'Well I don't have the slightest doubt he'll be here pretty quick to tell you the tale. Unfortunately I shall be in Roubaix.' He was due to set off for Marie's wedding the next day. 'You must deal with him as you think fit. But please, my dear Madeleine, don't make any rash decisions.'

'I won't,' she promised. 'I'm sure there's nothing that can't wait until you get back.' He would be gone no more than three days.

'I wish you were coming with me,' Léon said.

'Oh, so do I! I do hope Marie will like her wedding present. You must take the greatest care of it.' They had chosen a pair of handsome Wedgwood vases.

'I promise I will,' Léon said. 'And you must promise to take the greatest possible care of yourself and our daughter. You are infinitely more precious than fine china!'

'But nowhere near as breakable,' Madeleine said, laughing.

Now that she was up and about again, free from the restraining influence of the monthly nurse, she felt imbued with new strength, both mental and physical – as if there was nothing she couldn't do, no task she couldn't undertake. Energy surged in her, so that she found it almost impossible to remain idle. Léon observed this new-found energy with distrust. It was too soon.

'All the same, you must rest,' he ordered. 'I shall tell your mother to make sure that you do.'

'Well if Ma doesn't succeed it won't be for want of trying,' Madeleine said. 'She's always on at me!'

But only at the times when she fed Claire was she content to rest, to let everything glide by in the pleasure of nursing her baby. As the baby suckled, Madeleine felt something of her own strength and vigour flowing into the small person she held in her arms. Oh, it was wonderful having this baby. Already she knew she wanted another child, and without waiting too long.

'Perhaps we shall have another baby by this time next year?' she said to Léon. 'It's a perfect time, with all the summer in which to grow strong.'

Léon was suddenly immersed in a painting which hung on the wall over the sideboard.

'Did you hear me?' Madeleine asked.

'What? Oh yes, yes I did. I think it will be too soon.' He would have to tell her what Doctor Hughes had said – but not yet, not today. It would wait until he returned from France.

'Well we'll see, won't we?' Madeleine said happily. Already they were lovers again, and it was better than it had ever been, as if the birth of the baby had deepened and sharpened every feeling. How could she not become pregnant, she asked herself?

'I want to enjoy you and Claire,' Léon said quietly. 'We seem complete in ourselves, the three of us. I wouldn't mind if it was always so.' He didn't believe what he was saying, but somehow he had to learn to believe it. And to convince Madeleine.

The next morning Madeleine saw Léon off.

'Give my love to your family,' she said.

'I will,' Léon promised. 'And I will complete the arrangements for *Maman* and Marie to visit us in July.'

The plan was that her mother-in-law, with Marie accompanying her for the journey, would visit for two or three weeks, during which time Claire would be baptized. Marie would return to her husband in Paris soon after the baptism and Léon would take his mother back when he had to go to France on business.

'Tell them both how much I look forward to it,' she said. 'As for you, my darling – keep safe, and come back to me soon.'

When she had waved Léon out of sight she fed Claire, then handed her over to Flora Bryant. In a way, she would have preferred to look after Claire by herself, but if she was to work at her designs, which she wanted to do, then Flora must take over for much of the time. That was the reason Madeleine had agreed to having a nursemaid in the house. The only thing she adamantly refused to do was to wean the child early. No one was going to deprive her daughter of what was best for her.

'The little love!' Flora cried. 'I do declare she's smiling at me!'

'Well I believe you,' Madeleine said. 'Even though everyone says it's simply wind!'

In the middle of the afternoon Irvine arrived at Mount Royd. He sought out his mother in her parlour and sank exhausted into the nearest chair.

'Why, whatever's the matter with you, love?' Mrs Bates cried. 'You look done in!'

'I am, Ma. I've walked all the way from Leeds.'

'Walked from Leeds? Whatever for?'

'I didn't have the train fare, that's why. Give us a cup of tea, Ma, and a bite to eat. I'm worn out and starving! Oh, I've done route marches twice and three times the distance, but nothing seemed as long as this!'

But why was he here at all in the middle of the day? Mrs Bates asked herself uneasily. And what was so urgent that he had to walk from Leeds? She had a nasty feeling in the pit of her stomach about it.

'Is there something wrong?' she asked. 'Is there something wrong with Tommy or Bessie?'

'Not with them, only with me. I've got the sack, Ma!'

She stared at him, open-mouthed.

'Got the sack? You can't have! It was a good job! You were doing well!'

'I can and I have. Anyway, it wasn't all that good a job; not what I wanted at all. And actually I didn't get the sack. I resigned. I told Mr Henry Garston what he could do with his job!'

'You did *what*? Oh Irvine, I don't believe it! How could you?'

'Well I did. Come on, Ma! Don't nag. I've had all the nagging I can take from Bessie.'

'Well for once I'm on her side,' Mrs Bates snapped.

'Ma! I'm tired out! I've walked all the way from Leeds!'

'And I don't understand that, either. Surely you had some wages to come? Surely you had enough to pay your fare from Leeds?'

'I would have had,' Irvine said. 'He paid me a week's wages – if you can call that miserable pittance a wage – but with my usual luck, when I got home the bailiffs were in. It was either pay them off or lose the furniture!'

'The bailiffs! Oh Irvine, how could you let it come to that? The bailiffs!' Never, even when times were at their worst, had she had the disgrace of the bailiffs coming.

'I was unlucky, wasn't I? If you want to make a living out of Henry Garston you have to sell and sell and sell. You have to flog your guts out. I did flog myself, Ma, but I didn't get the orders. That's the long and short of it. Now is there a cup of tea?'

She rang for Rose to make a pot of tea.

'Strong,' she requested. 'And butter a teacake or two, and bring some cheese.'

'Now!' she said when Rose had left the room, 'tell me what you're going to do. I've got a bit of money put by, but it's not much.' She'd always been able to save most of the small wage Léon paid her. She had a roof over her head and food in her stomach, and apart from a few clothes now and then she didn't seem to need much more.

'I don't want to take your money, Ma,' Irvine said. But he would have to borrow a bit to tide him over. 'Though I'll pay you back, of course. No doubt about that!'

'So what are you going to do?' Mrs Bates pressed him. 'Where will you find another job? Oh Irvine, you'll be the death of me!' But he was her life as well, her only son. There was nothing she wouldn't do for him.

'I'm not going to,' Irvine said. 'At least, not what *you*

mean. I'm sick of working for other people, being ordered about, do this, do that, go there, come here! First the army and then Garston's. I've had enough.'

'If you don't work, you can't eat,' Mrs Bates said tartly. 'Not to mention you've got a wife and child to think of.'

'I never said I wasn't going to work, Ma. No, what I want to do now is work for myself.'

He took the cutting from the *Leeds Mercury* and put it on the table in front of his mother.

'Read that! That's what I want to do!'

She read it, then lifted her head and looked at him straight.

'Have you gone daft? This needs capital. Where are you going to find it?'

'A hundred pounds would do it, Ma!'

'A hundred pounds! You might as well say a million! If I scraped together everything I had in the world it wouldn't amount to more than fifteen pounds!'

'I know,' Irvine said. 'But I wasn't thinking of you. I thought Madeleine might help.'

'We're beholden enough to Madeleine as it is,' Mrs Bates said shortly.

'Well she's one of the lucky ones in life,' Irvine said. 'I'm not. Though if I had my own business everything would be different. I'm certain of it. Anyway, I'm sure Madeleine could lend me the money. Is she in?'

'Yes.'

There was some truth in what he said. Irvine had never had Madeleine's luck. If a small voice inside Mrs Bates said that Irvine had never worked half as hard as Madeleine had, she stifled it.

Rose came in with a laden tray.

'Then I'll have a cup of tea before I go and see her,' he said. 'And a teacake! You still make the best teacakes in Helsdon, Ma!'

'Don't soft soap me, Irvine,' Mrs Bates said. 'I'm not in the mood.'

'And don't try to pull the wool over my eyes, Irvine,'

Madeleine said fifteen minutes later, as he started to tell his tale. 'Henry Garston was here yesterday. I know all the details, thank you!'

For a fleeting moment Irvine looked shocked. It had never occurred to him that Madeleine would have heard anything. It was not a good beginning.

'And I suppose you choose to believe him before your own brother?' he said bitterly.

'As a matter of fact, yes. I believe every word he said. I also read two letters he'd received from valued customers. I daresay he showed them to you!'

'I can explain that. . .'

'Don't bother! In my view Henry Garston was very restrained in saying as little as he did. Most men would have sent you packing long before.'

'He didn't send me packing. I've told you, I resigned!' Irvine said.

'I know that, too. I asked him to allow you to resign so you'd find it less difficult to get another job. So where are you going to start looking?'

Irvine took out the cutting and put it in front of her.

'Here,' he said. 'This is what I want to do, Madeleine. I'm sure this is what I'm cut out for, working for myself! As I have said before, I'm not made for taking orders from every Tom, Dick and Harry. Oh, I wish I could make you understand, Madeleine!'

Madeleine read the advertisement, then looked at her brother thoughtfully. She understood. But he was not to know that she was remembering the time – it seemed so long ago now, though in reality it was only eight years – when she'd decided that she could no longer go on being a servant, not if her life depended on it. She'd been in Paris, with Sophia Parkinson and Sophia's father, when it all came to a head. She'd gone to Mr Parkinson and told him. He hadn't liked it, but he'd been understanding. If he hadn't been, if he'd not agreed to her request to let her learn weaving in his mill, where would she have been now?

It wasn't quite the same as with Irvine, of course. She'd still remained at other people's beck and call in the weaving; she'd had to work as hard as ever. Would her brother do that? But at least she'd been given her chance.

'So how much would it cost to take on this shop?' she asked.

'I reckon a hundred pounds would do it. I'd have to pay a bit of the rent in advance, and the stock at valuation I suppose. But if you lent me the money I'm sure I could pay you back out of the first year's profits – and with interest too!'

He was full of enthusiasm. With every word he uttered the prospect seemed brighter and brighter. Why hadn't he done this when he'd first left the army?

'What about the goodwill?'

'That I don't know until I see it. Perhaps, if it's a bit run down, there isn't much goodwill left. I'd have to build it up.'

'And how do you know you could run a shop?' she asked. 'You've no experience.'

'I have this feeling I could!'

They were the exact words she had used to Henry Garston yesterday. Once again, she knew well enough what Irvine meant.

'And I expect there're rooms over where we could live. Bessie could help me in the shop. We wouldn't be too far from Ma – she'd like that. Oh Madeleine,' Irvine implored. 'If only you could see your way, it would change my life!'

What more could he say? He'd never felt so nervous. In the silence which followed he twisted his hands together until the knuckles showed white. He felt the perspiration breaking out on his face.

'All right,' Madeleine said at last.

He let out a long sigh.

'You mean you'll let me have the money? Oh Madeleine, I can't thank you enough! And I'll not let you down, you can depend on that.'

'I can't let you have it, not just like that,' Madeleine said. 'What I mean is, I'll consult Léon.'

'Oh!' He hadn't thought of that. 'Then when will he be back? You can see it's urgent, Madeleine.'

'In two days' time,' she said. 'I'll ask him then.'

On his way back to his mother, Irvine put his head around the kitchen door. As he'd hoped, Rose Hardy was there.

'Hello, beautiful!' he said.

'Don't be cheeky!' she replied. 'My name's Rose, and don't you forget it!'

'As if I could!'

He stepped into the kitchen and began to sing; he had a pleasant, tuneful, tenor voice:

> ' "Oh, my love is like a red, red rose
> That's newly sprung in June. . ." '

He moved nearer, put his arm around her slender waist.

'Mr Bates! Stop it, do! What if your Ma was to come in – which she might do any minute?'

He was a right card, this one. All the same, you couldn't help liking him. And it was a pleasant change to have a nice-looking young man's arm around her waist. She gave him a half-hearted shove. He took not the slightest bit of notice. Continuing to sing, he led her in a slow dance around the kitchen. He had reached the last verse when they heard his mother's steps in the passage.

'Let me go!' Rose whispered. She jerked away from him and was sitting at the table, her head bent as she industriously polished a teaspoon, as Mrs Bates walked into the kitchen.

Irvine went on singing:

> ' "And fare thee well, my only love,
> And fare thee well awhile
> And I will come again, my love,
> Though it were ten thousand mile." '

Rose raised her head fractionally and met his look. Then she lowered her eyelids and he knew she had got the message. Oh well, it might be a bit of fun, once he was back in Helsdon. Brighten things up a bit. Not that he'd have a lot of time once he was in business for himself!

'You sound as if you'd lost a ha'penny and found a shilling!' Mrs Bates said. 'A bit different from half an hour ago.'

'The world's a different place from half an hour ago!' Irvine said.

So Madeleine has said 'Yes', Mrs Bates thought.

He means me, Rose thought, stifling a giggle.

'And now, much as it pains me, I have to leave you lovely ladies,' Irvine said. 'Leeds awaits me! Ma, a word with you before I go!'

He followed her into her own room.

'It worked!' he said. 'Our Madeleine turned up trumps! She's going to lend me the money. At least she is if Léon agrees,' he amended.

'Then you're a very lucky young man,' Mrs Bates said. 'See to it you don't let her down.'

'Oh I won't! I really won't!' Irvine promised.

She went to her purse, took out a coin and handed it to him.

'Here you are, here's your fare back to Leeds. No need to wear out more shoe leather.'

Two days later, late at night, Léon returned from France. The ground floor of the house was in darkness, everyone gone to bed, which was as he expected. But from the drive he had seen the square of light which was the window of their bedroom and he knew that Madeleine had stayed awake for him. He took the stairs two at a time. When he went in she was sitting up in bed, her dark hair loose around her shoulders, her arms outstretched to welcome him. Then he was in her arms and she was unfastening the buttons of his jacket.

'Oh Léon!' she said. 'I thought you were never coming!'

'There was a thick mist in the channel. Don't ask me why, since it's June. I missed the train I should have caught.'

'Well you're here now, my love. Are you hungry?'

'Only for you!'

'Well then, here I am! Oh Léon, only a few days away and it seemed like half a life time. Did everything go well? What was the wedding like?'

'It was good,' he said. 'Everything went well. Marie was a beautiful bride. I think she will be happy with Jules.'

'And how was your mother? And Hortense? Hortense was there of course?'

'Naturally,' Léon said. 'They have known each other since my sister was born.'

When he had met with Hortense in Roubaix he'd been surprised by how little real feeling he had for her, though she was as beautiful as ever. It was as if Paris had never happened. He knew now that he would never tell Madeleine that Hortense had been in Paris. She would be quite needlessly upset.

'Well dearest, I'm glad you enjoyed it,' Madeleine said. 'And sorry I couldn't be with you.'

'And what happened here, if anything?'

'Irvine came.'

'I knew he would. What had he to say?'

She recounted her conversation with Irvine. 'I'd like to help him,' she added.

'You do realize we might never see the money again.'

'I do,' she said. 'Even though at present he means to pay us back. But perhaps this is something he *would* make a go of. And Léon, you and I are so very happy, we have so much. It's for that reason that I'd like to help Irvine. A sort of thanks offering to life!'

'Very well, my love, we will,' Léon agreed. 'You are a very generous creature.'

At the beginning of July Irvine moved into the premises

in Helsdon. The shop was roomy, but dark, with an even darker store-room behind; but the position was good, on a corner where four streets crossed and, moreover, where workers coming to and from a couple of large mills would have to pass. He had been right in thinking that there was little goodwill left.

'It belonged to an old man who'd been ill for a long time before he died,' he told Madeleine. 'He'd let things go. So I've next to nothing to pay for goodwill. His daughter, who inherited the business, wants nothing to do with it. She was only too glad to let it go. But there's not much stock. I shall have to build that up before I can hope to get the customers.'

'And will the hundred pounds cover that?' Madeleine asked.

'Yes. Yes I reckon so. You don't know how grateful I am, Madeleine.'

'Yes I do,' she said. 'You keep on telling me. And I don't want you to think about paying the money back for at least the first two years. We'll talk about it then. So how does Bessie like it?'

'She's pleased,' Irvine said. 'The upstairs rooms are lighter than the shop. They need a lot of cleaning, but she'll soon see to that. And Ma's as pleased as punch she's got Tommy a bit nearer.'

In fact, Bessie was not pleased. Oh, it was better than the hovel in Leeds, no doubt about that. And they wouldn't have to worry about the bailiffs – the rent had been paid for six months ahead. Also, she'd do her bit and serve in the shop when necessary. But she'd never settle down in Helsdon, nor anywhere else in the West Riding. What she wanted was to be back in Brighton. That was the place.

Ten days after Irvine's move, a letter came from France for Léon. At the breakfast table Madeleine watched a frown spread over his face as he read it.

'What is it?' she asked. 'What's wrong?'

Without thinking, he passed the letter to her, but she waved it away.

'It's in French,' she said. 'Please translate. I'm still slow.'

'It's from *Maman*. Marie cannot accompany her to Helsdon. It seems she cannot tear herself away from her new husband! My mother suggests that Hortense should come with her. Hortense has been to London, but never to the north of England. She would like to see it and, *Maman* says, renew her acquaintance with you – and of course, see the baby!'

'Oh!'

'I'm sorry, my love,' Léon apologized. 'It's not what you wanted, nor I for that matter. But no doubt it will be all right.'

'Of course!' Madeleine said. 'Please tell your mother that both she and Hortense will be welcome.'

ELEVEN

'I wouldn't have believed,' Mrs Bates said to Madeleine, 'that two people visiting could cause such a to-do!'

'I know, Ma, and I'm sorry,' Madeleine said. 'But I do so want everything to be just right.'

'Oh, no need to be sorry, love!' Mrs Bates assured her. 'And no need to worry, either.'

'Why am I so nervous?' Madeleine asked. 'No one could say that Hortense wasn't friendly. So is Madame Bonneau, though perhaps a bit more reserved.'

'You're nervous because she's your mother-in-law, because she's never been here before and you want to make a good impression. Well, you will, love!'

'I hope so,' Madeleine said dubiously.

When, at breakfast next day, she revealed her anxiety to Léon, he laughed at her, but in a kindly way.

'You silly goose! Everything's going to be all right. I know how much *Maman*'s looking forward to seeing you – and Claire, of course.'

'It's such a long time since I saw your mother,' Madeleine said.

'You got on well enough with her then. You will again,' Léon assured her. 'As for me, I'm looking forward to showing her Mount Royd.'

'I remember the flurry here when you were due to visit for the first time,' Madeleine said. 'Sophia was all for poor Mrs Thomas serving nothing but French menus!'

'Instead of which I learned to like roast beef and Yorkshire pudding,' Léon laughed. 'Well, *Maman* and Hortense will do the same!'

'I do really rather wish Marie was coming instead of Hortense,' Madeleine said. 'I liked Marie so much.'

'I wish that too,' Léon admitted. 'But there's nothing we can do about it. Hortense won't be here for more than a few days.'

He was every bit as disappointed as Madeleine that Hortense was coming. It was not that he any longer felt particularly guilty about Paris – it was over and done with, it meant nothing. But if Madeleine found out she would be deeply hurt, and that was the last thing in the world he wanted. Hortense, he reckoned, would say nothing – though if she was so inclined she could convey a whole world in a look or a gesture. Oh damn Hortense, he thought irritably! He finished what was left of his breakfast and jumped to his feet, then moved around the table to give Madeleine his customary embrace before leaving for the mill.

When he'd left, Madeleine went in search of her mother, and found her in the kitchen.

At the kitchen table sat Jane, the new maid Léon had insisted they must have in addition to Rose Hardy. There was the whole house to keep in order now, including the nursery.

Jane was polishing silver. Every piece the house contained was there, sitting on old copies of the *Yorkshire Post*, the *Bradford Observer* and the *Leeds Mercury*, which had been spread to protect the scrubbed table top.

'Do you want a hand with anything, Ma?' Madeleine asked. 'Where's Rose?'

'She's doing the bedrooms.'

'Then shall I help you here?'

'No, love,' Mrs Bates said. 'But it would be a good idea if you'd go round and check the bedrooms when Rose has finished. Make sure everything's in order. She's a bit slapdash, Rose is.'

Madeleine thought later, in spite of her mother's misgivings, Rose had done well. All the rooms were in order, the furniture polished so that you could see yourself in it. And at least there was plenty of room for visitors now.

In the newly-furnished guest bedrooms she admired

the bed linen and curtains, approved the prettily-patterned ewers and basins and matching chamber pots which she had been to Bradford to choose only last week. Yes, it all looked very nice. She hoped her guests would think so. Of course everything would look even better when she had added flowers from the garden, but that she would leave until just before they arrived tomorrow evening.

When Léon came home at the end of the afternoon she said: 'I'm sorry I was so doubtful about everything this morning. I'm sure it's going to be all right.'

He stopped her words with a kiss.

'Of course it is, *chérie*! And now that you have learnt so much more French, and Marie has been teaching *Maman* English, everything will be easier still. You'll see!'

Madeleine had adhered firmly, sometimes gritting her teeth to go through with it, to the promise she had made to herself after that visit to Roubaix, that every single day she would learn a few words of French. Now she and Léon could sometimes actually hold a conversation in French, though she was still not good at reading or writing it.

'You've been a very patient teacher,' she said.

'And you've tried hard as a pupil,' he told her. 'Now, where is my beautiful daughter? I want to see her.'

'Asleep, in the nursery. You can take a peep, but please don't waken her.'

They went together into the nursery and, arm-in-arm, gazed at the sleeping child.

'She grows more beautiful every day,' Léon whispered.

'And she's so good,' Madeleine said. 'She hasn't been a bit of trouble all day.'

'In any case she shouldn't be to you,' Léon said as they tiptoed out of the nursery. 'That's why you have Flora.'

'I know,' Madeleine agreed. 'Though if I hear Claire cry I just can't stop myself going to her. But today she hasn't cried. So in spite of the fact that I've been busier than usual in the house, I've managed to do two quite good drawings for Henry Garston. At least I think they're good. Would you like to see them?'

'Later,' Léon said. He still had little time for this venture of Madeleine's. It was of no use to forbid her but he wouldn't encourage her. He hoped it would come to nothing in the end, but experience told him that nothing Madeleine set out to do ever came to nothing.

'So when is your Irvine moving into his new shop?' Rose asked Mrs Bates. 'Tomorrow, isn't it?' She knew perfectly well when it was; she just liked to bring Irvine into the conversation.

'Tomorrow it is,' Mrs Bates confirmed. 'So let's hope and pray for fine weather!'

They would be bringing their few goods and chattels from Leeds on an open cart. It was all they could afford, and she knew that because she'd lent them the money for it. Given more like, she thought, but Irvine vowed he would pay back every penny, including what she'd let him have to help tide them over the last week or two.

Now she had very little left in her purse in the dresser drawer, and what she had was to be spent on a christening present for Claire. Fair's fair, she thought. She'd done plenty for Irvine's family; now it was her granddaughter's turn. Besides, she didn't want to be shown up by the poorness of her baptismal gift against that of the child's French grandmother. She had seen a silver spoon – real silver it was – in the window of a jeweller's shop in Helsdon, and that she meant to have. Moreover, she would have it engraved with the baby's initials. With what she had in her purse and what was due to her from Léon any time now, she'd just about manage it.

'I could wish it wasn't tomorrow,' she said to Rose. 'I'd have liked to have given a helping hand, but with the visitors arriving it'll be all hands aloft here.'

She was no less nervous than Madeleine about the arrival of the two women from France, but for a different reason. She was landed with the cooking.

Cooking was the only chore she did nowadays, except for overseeing the domestic staff. She was, after all, still officially the housekeeper, and paid as such. She valued her independence, but in every way Madeleine and Léon had seen to it that she was part of the family.

'You needn't be afraid,' Madeleine had said when her mother had voiced her apprehension. 'You're as good a cook as anyone I've come across. I'm sure whatever you serve will be more than acceptable. And I'll help you whenever you wish. But if you really and truly don't want to do it, well then, I'll hire a cook for the duration of the visit. I sometimes think we should have a cook anyway, not because she'd be better than you, but now that we have the whole house and more people in it, I don't want you to have too much to do.'

'That I don't have,' Mrs Bates said. 'And I'm pleased to do the cooking as long as it's good enough. I'm not mad keen on a strange woman cooking in my kitchen.'

'We'll get Mrs Partridge to come in more,' Madeleine said. 'I don't want you spending hours in the kitchen.'

'Would you like me to give your Irvine a hand getting straight in the new place tomorrow, Mrs Bates?' Rose now offered. 'I'd be pleased to do so.'

'I'm sure you would,' Mrs Bates said. 'But you'll have plenty to do here.'

'I can't think what,' Rose said. 'Everything in the house has been cleaned within an inch of its life. I defy anyone to find so much as a speck of dust.'

'Every day brings its own work,' Mrs Bates said. 'Not to mention a fresh coating of dust!'

'Please yourself,' Rose said. 'I just thought with you and me and Jane and Mrs Partridge – not to mention Flora, and the mistress – we'd be falling over each other.'

'Don't worry. I'll see you're well occupied,' Mrs Bates promised.

I'll bet you will, Rose thought. But don't you worry either. It'll not be long before Irvine sets foot here again.

It wasn't. Halfway through the next afternoon the door

opened and in walked Irvine, holding Tommy by the hand. Mrs Bates held out her arms and Tommy came to her.

'This is a surprise! I didn't expect to see you today,' she said to her son. 'I thought you'd be too busy.'

'We are,' Irvine said. 'We've just arrived with the stuff from Leeds. I wondered if you'd look after Tommy while we get straight?'

'Well you've chosen a bad day,' Mrs Bates said. 'I'm up to the eyes in cooking. But of course I will. Sit him at the table, then.'

'You don't need to tell me you're cooking,' Irvine said. 'It smells like heaven in here! Makes me realize how hungry I am!'

'I never knew you when you weren't!' Mrs Bates said indulgently. 'Here, sit you down with Tommy and I'll serve you a bit of something. Will a plate of ham and eggs suit you?'

'Down to the ground,' Irvine said, seating himself.

When his mother had gone to the larder to fetch the ham, Irvine spoke to Rose.

'And how are you, beautiful?'

'Well enough,' she said. 'I offered to come and give you a hand today but your Ma said I was needed here.'

'That was very civil of you, Rose of Tralee! Perhaps you can persuade Ma to send you to buy something from the shop? We'll be open for business from tomorrow. Always glad to see a customer – especially a pretty one!'

He turned away from her, concentrating on Tommy as his mother came back into the room.

'I'll fry a bit extra and you can take it home for Bessie,' Mrs Bates said. 'She can have it cold with a bit of bread.'

'That reminds me,' Irvine said. 'Have you got a spare loaf – and a bit of butter? And a pot of your jam wouldn't come amiss.'

Irvine had been left an hour or more when Madeleine came into the kitchen to check, not for the first time that day, that everything was going ahead as planned. She was

205

still there when Léon, arriving unexpectedly early from the mill, came to search for her.

'I didn't expect you so soon,' Madeleine said.

'I left a little early. I thought it would be as well to have something to eat before I went to Leeds – just in case the train is delayed and we're all late for dinner.'

'Indeed I hope that won't be the case,' Madeleine said. 'Ma is doing something quite special.'

'Don't worry,' Mrs Bates said. 'It's a casserole. It won't spoil.'

'Good!' Léon said. 'Then if someone has time to make me a simple meal I can eat in the next hour or so?'

'I'd be pleased to,' Rose said swiftly, before Mrs Bates could answer.

There was nothing she wouldn't do for the master. She'd give Irvine Bates the go-by for this one any day of the week. What woman wouldn't? He was so handsome, so well-dressed, so polite, so . . . so *French*! And so passionate, she wouldn't wonder. You could see it in his eyes, in his glance. The mistress was the luckiest woman on earth – and to think she'd been no more than a servant! So swiftly did Rose plunge into dreams of what life might bring that she almost failed to hear Léon's request.

'An omelette would do very well,' he was saying. 'Can you cook an omelette, Rose?'

'Oh yes, sir!' she replied. 'I'll do it right away.'

'Thank you. I'll have it in my study.' He caught sight of Tommy, standing in front of a stool which served as a table, shaping a piece of pastry which his grandmother had given him.

'Hello, young man! I hadn't seen you!' He smiled at the child, ruffled his hair and chucked him under the chin. Tommy responded with a wide grin and offered Léon a piece of grey pastry.

'Give it to Grandma to cook,' Léon said. 'Then I'll eat it for my supper.'

He was an engaging little chap. How lucky Irvine Bates

was to have such a son; to have any son, Léon thought bleakly.

Madeleine, watching her husband with Tommy, saw the longing in his look. When Léon rose to leave the kitchen she went with him, slipping her arm through his as they went upstairs to their own rooms.

'Oh Léon, don't you agree we should have another child? And I'm sure next time it will be a son!'

'It's too soon,' Léon said. He sounded sharper than he meant to. She *must* be told – but once again it was not the time, not with his mother and Hortense arriving within a very few hours.

'Please excuse me,' he said. 'I have some work I must do before I go to Leeds.'

He walked away from her abruptly and went to his study, leaving her staring after him. After a moment she went to the nursery to see Claire. Why hadn't Léon done so, she wondered? It was usually the first thing he did when he returned home at the end of the day.

When the sun, streaming through the window, caused Madame Bonneau to open her eyes, she thought at first that she must be dreaming. This was not the room she had awakened to almost every day since she was a bride of eighteen. This was not the bed to which her husband had brought her all those years ago; in which she had conceived and borne her children, and in which she had lain alone and lonely for the last fifteen years, still occupying only one side, still stretching out a hand to the husband who wasn't there.

She let her gaze wander around the room, remembering now every detail of how she came to be here. That terrible crossing of *La Manche* on the night boat! Then the long train journey to Yorkshire. She had been pleased to have Hortense with her to while away the journey, and even more pleased to see Léon waiting on the platform when they arrived in Leeds.

But this room, she thought, was quite pleasant, and the

207

bed comfortable. The soft feather pillow was *not* to her liking. She was used to a hard sausage of a pillow – so much better for one. Perhaps if she asked her *belle-fille* – no, my daughter-in-law, she reminded herself; I am in England now – she would provide something firmer?

There was a knock at the door.

'*Entrez!*'

It was Madeleine.

'*Bonjour, Belle-mère!*' Madeleine said. 'I hope you have slept well?'

'Very well, thank you. You are up early.'

'I waken early to feed the baby,' Madeleine explained. 'I thought you might also be awake, being in a strange place, and I wondered if you would like some coffee.'

'That is very kind,' Madame Bonneau said. 'I *would* like it.'

She spoke carefully, determined to use the English she had been learning in the last year.

'Then Rose shall bring you some,' Madeleine said. 'Perhaps you would like a breakfast tray in your room?'

'*Merci.* I would prefer to take my breakfast with the rest of you.'

'And Mademoiselle Murer?' Madeleine enquired. 'I'm afraid I forgot to ask her last night. Would she like some coffee, do you think?'

'*Certainement!* I am sure of it.'

'You must let me know if there's anything you want, at any time,' Madeleine said.

'I will,' Madame Bonneau promised. But in fact she would not mention the pillow just yet. She had no wish to complain. Perhaps she might even get used to it, though she doubted that.

When Rose brought the coffee Madame Bonneau was already up, though not dressed, wearing her *peignoir*. She was sitting in the armchair, looking out of the window at the surprisingly pretty view. Rose placed the tray on the low table beside her. Well, she thought, she doesn't look all that French first thing in the morning! She looks exactly like any other elderly lady – except her night-cap's a bit more fancy. But she'd been a good-looker in her time, you could tell that even now, and you could see where the master got his looks from.

When Rose had gone Madame Bonneau poured a cup of coffee. It was better than she'd expected. Léon must have taught them how to make it. Everyone knew that the English made coffee far too weak – which was perhaps the reason why they drank so much tea?

She had had her fears about the food, also, but last night's meal had been a pleasant surprise. Country cooking, of course, but well done. She herself preferred country cooking. She had been brought up to it.

'Last night's meal was delicious!' Madeleine said to her mother.

'I thought it went down well,' Mrs Bates said modestly. 'I think if I stick to my English cooking – steak-and-kidney pie, roast beef, Yorkshire pudding, apple pie, hot-pot – it'll be best.'

'Of course it will,' Madeleine agreed. 'Mind you, I doubt we'll ever get either of the ladies to eat bacon and eggs for breakfast. I remember when Léon first came to England he used to shudder at the sight of it!'

'And now he eats it every day,' Mrs Bates said. 'Speaking of which, I'd best set Mrs Partridge on doing the breakfast. There's some fresh bread just out of the oven.'

'I can smell it – and I'll have a slice,' Madeleine said. 'I'm always hungry!'

'It's feeding the baby,' Mrs Bates said, cutting a thick crust from the crisp new loaf, spreading it thickly with butter. 'Here you are then.'

Both Madame Bonneau and Hortense appeared for breakfast on the dot, Hortense looking elegantly attract-ive in a pale cream gown with a deep border of Greek key pattern, in rich brown, around the hem and on the sleeves. To Madeleine's eyes, it had the stamp of France all over it. Not that it was ornate – it was entirely suitable for breakfast in the home – but there was something in the cut... She tried to analyse it. It was a quality she would like to get into her fashion drawings.

'And what would you ladies like to do today?' Léon asked. 'I shall be free later this afternoon, but for this morning I must go to the mill. Of course if you would like to take a look at the mill you would be very welcome.'

'I think I shall remain close to your very nice home this morning, Léon. I am tired after my journey, and your garden looks inviting,' Madame Bonneau said. 'Also, the day is quite warm,' she added in a surprised voice.

'And you, Hortense? What would you like to do?' Léon asked.

'I too will remain here,' Hortense said. 'I have never been able to understand what goes on in a factory!' She turned to Madeleine. 'Have you?'

'Oh yes! I understand most of it. Some of it I can actually do!'

'Really? How clever of you!'

Sitting in the garden, the three women discussed the baptism which was to take place in two days' time. Madame Bonneau had brought down the gown in which her two youngest children, Léon and Marie, and all her grandchildren had been baptized. Now she displayed it for Madeleine's approval and admiration.

'Oh, Claire will look beautiful in this!' Madeleine cried. 'Look at the fineness of the lace – like cobwebs! And this dear little cap to match! It's all quite perfect. Thank you so much, *Belle-mère*, for lending it to me. I shall take the greatest possible care of it.'

'I shall carry it back to France with me when I return,' Madame Bonneau said. 'But I promise to lend it to you for each of your children as they are baptized. Now tell me more about this lady whom I have not met, who is to be one of Claire's godparents.'

'Her name is Mrs Barnet. I have known her a long time and she is a dear friend. I was married from her house. She is also a Catholic. Unfortunately none of my own family are of the Catholic faith, so they cannot be godparents. Mrs Barnet works for Léon.'

'Works for Léon?' Madame Bonneau said. 'In what capacity?'

'She is a weaver. His best and most highly-skilled weaver.'

'A weaver?'

'How very unusual,' Hortense said. 'I mean that she should be your daughter's godparent. Had I but known...'

'I can think of no one I would prefer to Mrs Barnet,' Madeleine interrupted. 'No one!'

'And who else shall we be privileged to meet on this occasion?' Hortense enquired.

'At the church, only my mother and Mrs Barnet in addition to ourselves, but afterwards a few friends will take a glass of sherry wine with us. Our lawyer, and his wife. My brother can't come because he has just opened a business and he's very occupied. Then there will be Mr Henry Garston, a manufacturer from Leeds, who is a good friend of ours.'

'How interesting!' Hortense said with polite insincerity. 'I shall look forward to it.'

The day of the baptism was clear and bright.

'Let's hope it's an omen for the rest of Claire's life, the little darling!' Mrs Bates said to Madame Bonneau. They were arranging their wide skirts in the carriage which was to take them to the church.

'But it is the meaning of her name!' Madame Bonneau exclaimed. 'It means "clear" and "unclouded".'

'Well I never!' Mrs Bates said. 'That's something I didn't know! I don't suppose "Martha" means anything special. I'm very complimented that she has my name as her second one, but I'm equally glad she won't be known by it. I never liked it.'

Nor did my name give me a clear and unclouded life, Madame Bonneau thought. She had had as much shadow as most. But one came out of the shadow – and today was

211

one of the sunny times, even though she was so far from home. There was the baptism to look forward to, and then they would be back in her son's home.

This has been truly wonderful, Madeleine thought a little later. The baptismal service was over and Father O'Malley was pronouncing the blessing, but she would never forget it: the oil of the catechumen, a reminder of the faith her child was to be taught from the cradle; the giving of her name – she had cried a little at the coldness of the water; the anointing with chrism – the oil for strength, perfumed for the sweetness of Christ's life in the world: and then the lighted candle for the light of Christ.

Madeleine had not been so moved since the day she and Léon had married in this church. She caught her husband's eye, wondering if he was remembering that. From the smile he gave her she felt sure he was.

Back at Mount Royd, carrying the baby in her arms, she crossed the room to where the two grandmothers stood together.

'Wasn't it wonderful?' she said. 'Isn't it a pity that Claire won't remember it? *Belle-mère*, would you like to hold Claire for a minute? Henry Garston has arrived and I must speak to him.'

She went to where Henry, for the moment, stood on his own. Thank Heaven Irvine wasn't able to come, she thought. It would have been awful to have had them both together in her drawing-room. 'Henry, I must ask you, did you like my drawings?' she said.

'Indeed I did. I want to talk to you about them, but I daresay this isn't the time.'

'I suppose not,' Madeleine agreed. 'But I'd like it to be soon. And now I'd like you to come and be introduced to my mother-in-law.'

'Hold on a minute!' Henry said. 'Who is the beautiful lady standing next to Ormeroyd? I can guess she's every inch a Frenchwoman by her style, but she's surely not Léon's sister?'

212

'No. Marie is newly-married and couldn't be persuaded to leave her husband. That is Mademoiselle Murer, a family friend of the Bonneaus.'

'Then you can introduce me to her at once!' Henry said. 'She looks far too charming to be wasted on old Ormeroyd!'

Madeleine took him across to Hortense.

'May I present Mr Henry Garston, an old friend. Miss Hortense Murer, from Roubaix.'

Hortense offered Henry her hand and, totally unexpectedly, even to himself, he raised it to his lips.

'I would have thought from Paris, Mademoiselle!' he said. 'Not Roubaix!'

'How kind!' Hortense said. He was not at all what she had expected. 'A manufacturer from Leeds'. It had sounded so dull! He was perhaps a little too stout, but he was handsome enough, fashionably dressed, and he had a twinkle in his eye. Was he rich, she wondered?

Madeleine left them together and went to join Léon. He was standing by the table on which were displayed the baptismal gifts.

'Henry seems quite taken by Hortense,' she said.

'He would be,' Léon said. 'Henry is always taken by a pretty face.'

She glanced at the display on the table.

'How generous people have been. Your mother with the silver rattle which belonged to you. That will be very precious. And the monogrammed silver spoon from my mother.' Only Madeleine could guess what sacrifices that had meant to her mother. The same might be said for the ivory-backed prayer book which was Mrs Barnet's gift.

'The bone teething ring is from Emerald and Penelope jointly,' Madeleine said. 'It's entirely typical of Sophia Chester that she wouldn't give either of them a few hours off to be here!'

And then there was the doll, a present from Hortense. Fifteen inches high and superbly dressed, down to the

213

jewels around its neck and in its hair, it outshone everything else on the table.

'The French make the finest dolls in the world,' Léon said. 'And this one is quite splendid! Do you realize that its dress is a copy of a crinoline worn by the Empress Eugénie herself?'

'So Hortense told me. And it comes with a complete wardrobe of clothes for every occasion, all almost equally fine. But of course it is no good to Claire?'

'What do you mean, my dear? It's quite exquisite.'

'Of course it is, and it's a most generous gift. But it will be years before she's old enough to play with it. Still, it's beautiful. Anyway I must relieve your mother of Claire,' Madeleine said. 'Any minute now she'll cry to be fed. I expect people will leave fairly soon, so will you please make my farewells for me, if necessary.'

It took longer to feed and change the baby than she had expected. In the first place she had to take off the exquisite christening gown before anything dire happened to it; and when it came to feeding, after the first few hungry gulps Claire was in a mood to look around, to take her time. Following the baptism Madeleine had allowed Flora to take the two hours off which were her due, so that she could visit her mother in Helsdon. Perhaps I should have asked her to stay, she thought. At least she could have put clean clothes on the baby, remained with her until she fell asleep.

As it was, by the time Madeleine returned to the drawing-room it seemed as though all her guests had left. Only Léon was visible.

'*Maman* has gone to the kitchen with your mother,' he said. 'I suspect she is teaching her how to make *coq-au-vin*, since she firmly believes it is my favourite dish and that I cannot live without it!'

'Anyway, I'm pleased that your mother and mine appear to get on so well,' Madeleine said. 'But where is Hortense? Don't tell me that she's in the kitchen!'

214

'No. She is showing Henry Garston around the garden – or he is showing her. Whichever way, they seemed not to need me!'

'Henry is still here?'

'And seems unlikely to depart. I think you will be obliged to ask him to stay to dinner, my love.'

Henry, when he finally appeared, was duly invited and accepted with alacrity.

'I get tired of eating on my own,' he confessed.

'I expect you do,' Madeleine said. 'But you know you are always welcome here. I wish you would come more often.'

She felt suddenly sorry for him. She hadn't given enough thought to his loneliness because he seemed always so self-sufficient, so much in control. But he seems quite smitten by Hortense, she thought. Well there was no future in that. Hortense was leaving in the morning.

After dinner they moved back into the drawing-room. Léon served himself and Henry with cognac, and his mother with a peppermint liqueur which he had laid in especially for her, and which Mrs Bates also decided to try.

'It is very good for the digestion,' Madame Bonneau informed her.

The six of them sat in a semi-circle, overlooking the garden. The shadows had lengthened, but it was not yet dark. Flower scents, more powerful now at dusk than in the heat of the day, drifted in through the open windows.

'There's nothing to beat an English garden at dusk,' Henry said. 'That wonderful smell!'

'It *is* lovely,' Hortense acknowledged. 'But French gardens can also be very beautiful.'

'Well I'm sure you'd benefit from seeing a bit more of this one,' Henry said. 'Not to mention a lot more places in this part of the world. A pity you have to go back to France tomorrow!' She was a knock-out, this one, and he was only just getting to know her, damn it!

Hortense looked at him wide-eyed.

215

'Well. . .' she said hesitantly. 'It's not that I actually *have* to return. I am after all a free woman. . .'

'Then why . . . ?'

'I was invited only for two or three days,' Hortense said demurely. 'A guest does not outstay her welcome!'

Madeleine glanced at Léon and he gave an almost imperceptible nod of his head.

'You are most welcome to stay as long as you wish, Hortense,' she said.

'Oh, but that is very kind of you!' Hortense cried. 'If you're really sure. . .'

'Quite sure.'

'Then I should like to stay a little longer.'

'If it is agreeable to Léon and Madeleine,' Madame Bonneau said, 'it would make sense if you were to stay until I returned, so that we could travel back together.'

For a brief moment, Madeleine felt a pang of disappointment. She was not sure how she felt about Hortense. But it was good to see Henry looking so happy. Also, the arrangement meant that Léon wouldn't need to go to France again quite so soon. The two women would travel back without him.

'Of course it's agreeable,' she said. 'Let's consider it settled!'

'So! We must think up a few things to amuse you ladies,' Henry Garston said happily. 'Oh, you'll find there's plenty to see and plenty to do around here. Concerts, the theatre, the countryside to explore. I'd be pleased to escort you. It's a long time since I allowed myself much leisure so I think I'm due it! Yes, I can promise you a good time!' His words were for all, but his eyes were on Hortense.

It was late when he left, and quite dark. He had driven himself over from Leeds and now, when the horses were harnessed, he set off to drive himself back.

'I must say,' Madeleine said to Léon when they were getting ready for bed, 'Henry was in good form! I haven't seen him look so happy for a long time.'

216

TWELVE

Henry Garston wasted no time. Two days later a letter arrived announcing his intention of driving over to Mount Royd early the following day and taking everyone for an outing to the dales. 'Since the weather seems set fair, we will take a picnic,' he wrote.

'Which means that *we* must prepare the picnic!' Madeleine said to her mother. 'Knowing Henry, he won't have given a thought to that!'

'No matter,' Mrs Bates said. 'Me and Mrs Partridge will do it. Five of you. You'll have to take your carriage as well as his.'

'I can't go because of Claire,' Madeleine pointed out. 'She has to be fed. And I doubt that Léon will take a day away from the mill. So it will just be Madame Bonneau, Hortense, Henry and you.'

'I hadn't thought of going,' Mrs Bates said. 'I've never been much of a one for picnics.'

'But you might enjoy it, Ma!'

'Well as a matter of fact, if I've got the time to spare, I'd quite like to go and give Irvine a hand.'

'Poor Irvine!' Madeleine said. 'And poor Bessie. We're really neglecting them. Well you do what you think is best, Ma.'

'It's a shame *you* can't go on the picnic,' Mrs Bates said.

Actually, Madeleine thought, she would be pleased to have the time on her own. Since the moment of their arrival she seemed to have spent all her waking hours with her mother-in-law and Hortense. She didn't mind, but there were so many other things she wanted to do. For more than a week she hadn't even entered her workroom, or spent a minute on her textile designs, let alone on the fashion drawings she was so eager to develop. And though Hortense had been kind enough to bring her several fashion magazines from France, she'd given them no more than a cursory glance.

'I shan't be fast for something to do!' she said to her mother.

'I think perhaps I shall go with them,' Léon said when she showed him Henry's letter that evening.

'I thought you were very busy in the mill.'

'So I am,' he admitted. 'But I owe something to *Maman*. Rob Wainwright will manage without me for a day.'

In the event, the party went to Ilkley, stabling the horses at an inn and carrying the picnic basket and the rugs up the steep path which climbed, immediately behind the town, to the top of the moor. When the rug had been spread, Madame Bonneau sank thankfully down.

'I had not thought to climb so,' she said when she had her breath back. 'But all is *magnifique*! And how do you call the flowers which cover the ground everywhere?'

'Heather,' Léon told her. '*Bruyère*. It is always like this in August.'

They found a spot where huge rocks cast welcome shade, and set out the picnic. Between them, in no time at all, they ate the ample contents of the picnic basket and drank both bottles of lemonade.

'I feel better for that!' Henry said, patting his stomach. 'I suggest we take a bit of exercise now, walk it off. There's a splendid view if we climb a little higher.'

'No! Please, not for me!' Madame Bonneau begged. 'I cannot do it. I will wait here.'

'Then I shall happily stay with you,' Léon said. 'I can't leave you alone.'

'I shall be perfectly all right,' Madame Bonneau insisted.

She was by no means sure that Hortense should go off

218

on her own with this man who looked at her as if he could eat her. On the other hand, Hortense wasn't a child. She was well able to look after herself.

'I insist on staying,' Léon said.

It was exactly what Henry had hoped for. He held out his hand and pulled Hortense to her feet before anything more could be said.

'We'll not be long,' he promised. 'We'll not go far.'

And I, alone with my son, will be able to speak in my own tongue, Madame Bonneau thought. What a relief that would be. Before the others had moved a yard, she began to chatter to Léon in French.

'Are you happy here, in Yorkshire, *Maman?*' he asked her presently.

'Oh yes. It is better than I thought. It is quite beautiful.' In fact it was more beautiful than Roubaix, but of course she wouldn't admit it, even to Léon. And it was not home. What was it the so popular English song said, which now everyone sang all over the world? 'Home, Sweet Home. There's no place like home!' It was very true.

'I am glad to see you settled,' she confessed. 'Though naturally I would prefer you had settled in France.'

'I know. But my life is here now, *Maman,*' Léon said gently.

'And I know that.'

It was no use to argue. It was all too late anyway. Your children did what they wanted to do; and if they didn't, and were not happy, they blamed you.

'I can see that you are happy here. And Madeleine is a good wife and a dear girl.'

They went on to talk about the family back in Roubaix, and about Marie in Paris.

'I did so want her to come with me,' Madame Bonneau said. 'But wild horses won't drag her away from Jules, and he couldn't leave his work.'

'Well, another time,' Léon said.

'Hortense seems taken with your Mr Garston,' Madame Bonneau remarked presently.

'I would put it the other way round,' Léon said. 'I haven't seen Henry like this before. He has been very subdued since his wife died. I hope Hortense won't lead him a dance and then drop him.'

'It might be worse for him if she did not drop him,' Madame Bonneau said dryly. 'But no! That was unkind of me. And it's time Hortense settled down. She gads about too much. Now can you see them anywhere? My eyes are not good enough.'

'Yes, they are almost at the top.' He could see Hortense hanging on to Henry's arm, and then the next moment they were over the crest of the hill and out of sight.

The day continued warm and sunny. When Henry and Hortense returned, looking pleased with themselves, Madame Bonneau wakened from a short snooze.

'Why don't we pick up the carriage and drive along to Bolton Abbey?' Henry suggested. 'It will be cooler by the river.'

It was early evening before the picnic party arrived back at Mount Royd. Henry immediately accepted Madeleine's invitation to stay to dinner.

'I don't know when I've enjoyed myself as much as I have today!' he said as they sat at the table. 'I hope the same can be said for everybody?'

The question was directed at Hortense, and it was she who answered it.

'It was quite wonderful!'

'A pity you couldn't come, Madeleine,' Henry added.

'Yes indeed. But I was well occupied,' she said amiably.

She had done some work, and after that she had allowed herself to start on Mr Dickens's latest book, which was enthralling.

'So where shall we go tomorrow?' Henry asked. 'What would everyone like to do?'

The outing to Ilkley was the start of a round of pleasure trips, each one organized by Henry. Nothing was too much trouble, too far or too expensive. They visited the theatre in Leeds, attended a concert in Bradford, went to Harrogate, an outing which Mrs Bates joined and was delighted by. They made a second trip to Ilkley, and on one day took the train to Skipton, from where they hired a carriage to take them into Wharfedale. And every day the sun shone, the heather bloomed, the rivers sparkled.

Madeleine could seldom make one of the party, though she went to the theatre and was desperate, when the performance was over, to get back to feed Claire. Nor could Léon go every time, though Helsdon Feast week, when all the mills in Helsdon were closed down, gave him some opportunities.

'Even so,' he said to Madeleine, 'I don't like leaving you behind. But we cannot let Hortense go unchaperoned, and it is easier for my mother on the occasions when I'm there. She and I can go at a slower pace.'

'Don't worry, I understand,' Madeleine said.

In fact, though she wouldn't say so to anyone, she was a little depressed. Her period had come and gone; she was not pregnant and she'd been so sure she would be. Was she to have that long, long wait which she had endured before Claire was conceived? Looking back, she was reminded of her visit to Akersfield Fair and Romany Rose. It was nonsense of course, but at the time she had been comforted.

'Why don't we all go to the fair?' she suggested to Léon.

'The fair?' He sounded astonished.

'Yes. Why not? I'm sure everyone would enjoy it. I could go too, since it's near at hand. And think how Henry would enjoy taking Hortense on the roundabouts!'

'Very well, if you really want to,' Léon said, amused.

While Henry Garston and the visitors were dashing around the countryside, Irvine was busy settling into the shop. Starting on the day after they'd moved in, Bessie had swept and scrubbed and cleaned from top to bottom, every floor, every wall, every shelf.

'I've never seen anything as filthy in all my born days!' she said. 'And let me tell you, we've got mice! I've seen their traces. We've got to get rid of 'em quick, or they'll eat the stock. Anyway, I don't fancy mice running around where I live. I can't abide the horrible things!'

'I'll set some traps,' Irvine said. 'We'll soon get rid of them.'

Though trade wasn't as brisk as he'd expected, he was optimistic. He was as pleased as Punch at the thought of being his own boss, not being at anyone's beck and call nor having anyone nag at him. Except Bessie, of course – but half the time he didn't listen to her. And she'd made a good job of putting things to rights; he had to admit that.

'So how much have you taken today?' Bessie asked. They had closed the shop at nine o'clock and now Irvine was cashing up.

'Not a lot,' he admitted. 'Ten shillings and three-pence.'

'We'll not get rich on that,' Bessie said. 'Not when we've paid the rent and the wholesalers' bills – not to mention keeping ourselves alive.'

And paying back the loan to Madeleine, and to his mother, Irvine thought, though he knew neither of them would press him.

'I daresay it's a slack time of year,' he said.

Bessie clicked her tongue impatiently.

'Don't be daft! There's no slack time of year for food. People eat every day – if they're lucky!'

'And don't forget those book debts,' Irvine said. 'There's quite a few folk owe money to the shop. I suppose some of them might pay up.'

'Pigs might fly!' Bessie said. 'I reckon they wiped those debts off their minds the minute the old man died. Anyway, I'm going to bed. I'm dead tired.'

She was always tired these days. She couldn't remember when she'd last felt well, really well. Not since they'd left Brighton. If I could get back to Brighton, she thought, if I could just get back for a week or two. And she would, somehow she would, she and Tommy. She was determined on it.

And now there'd be Irvine coming up to bed, pestering her for what was due to him, demanding his rights. Well he'd not get anything! She'd lost interest in all that, and in any case she didn't want another kid. Oh, she loved Tommy all right; he was the brightest star in her dark sky; but she couldn't do with another.

She undressed quickly, not bothering to wash – it was too much trouble – then got into bed and lay straight out on the very edge, eyes closed, snoring gently, pretending to be asleep. When Irvine came into the room and began to curse at the sight of her feigning sleep, she lay rigid.

'Damn and bugger!' he swore.

He kicked hard at the foot of the bed, kicked the chamber pot, then took off his boots and hurled them to the other side of the room. Had she really been asleep there was no way he wouldn't have wakened her, but now she kept her eyes tightly shut and continued to snore. He banged into bed, pulled the blanket from her to his own side of the bed, so that she was immediately cold. They'd played this scene many times. Sometimes he'd shake her until she *had* to waken, and then he'd do what he wanted with her, but tonight she sensed he was going to leave her alone. It was worth being cold.

After that she fell asleep quickly. Not so Irvine. He lay awake for a long time, angry and frustrated, his optimistic mood of an hour ago vanished.

'Would you believe, we've run out of candles?' Mrs Bates said to Rose Hardy next day. 'I can't understand it. I'd have sworn there was another bundle in that low cupboard!'

There was, Rose thought, until I moved them.

'Well there's none there now,' Mrs Bates affirmed. 'I've searched thoroughly. And we can't manage without candles.'

'I'll nip down to your Irvine's and get some,' Rose offered. 'It won't take me a minute. I daresay he'll be glad of the custom.'

'I daresay he will,' Mrs Bates agreed. 'But it's very inconvenient, running out of things like this. Now don't take long, Rose. Fifteen minutes there, fifteen back, say five minutes being served, unless you have to wait. You should be back in three-quarters of an hour at the most.'

'Yes, Mrs Bates,' Rose said. If anyone thought she was going to watch the clock once she was let out, they had another thought coming!

'Hello, Rose of Sharon!' Irvine said. 'This is a pleasant surprise! It's the best thing that's happened to me all day!'

'Things not going too well, then?' Rose asked. There wasn't a sign of another customer.

'Oh not bad! Not bad at all. But we don't get many pretty young ladies in! So what can I do for you? Well, we both know what I could do for you, but now's not the time nor place, eh?'

'Cheeky!' Rose said.

'Go on! You know you'd enjoy it!'

Yes, she knew she would, but she wouldn't let on. It was a long time since she'd been in a man's arms. Too long. Sometimes she could hardly sleep for wanting it – and she'd taken a shine to Irvine from the first minute. If only he hadn't been married she'd have had him long before now.

'I've come for some candles,' she said. 'We've mysteriously run out.'

'Right,' he said. 'I'm your man!'

Everything he said had a double meaning, Rose thought. But he was a bit of fun.

'While there's no one in the shop, come upstairs and see where we live,' he invited. 'Oh it's all right! Bessie's in – and Tommy! You'll be quite safe!'

She followed him through the small stockroom to the

narrow stairs which led to their living quarters. Bessie
was standing at the table, ironing. Rose was shocked by
her appearance. She was white-faced and looked deathly
tired.

'Are you all right, Bessie?' she asked.

'I suppose so,' Bessie answered. 'Do you want a cup of
tea?'

Rose shook her head.

'I'd best not stay. Your mother-in-law's timing me
with a stop watch!'

'That's the shop bell!' Irvine said suddenly. 'Bessie,
will you go down and answer it, love? I want to write a
note for Rose to take to Ma.'

Bessie put the iron on the range and went downstairs.

'Here, Tommy,' Irvine said. 'Go down after your Mam
and tell her I said you can have a sweetie out of the jar.
Any jar you like!'

Tommy was hardly out of the room before Irvine
had Rose in his arms, pressed hard against him, his
hands everywhere on her body; fondling the softness
of her breasts, squeezing the roundness of her
buttocks.

'Irvine Bates!' she began.

His lips, crushing hers, stopped her words. She tilted
back her head, pressed her body closer against him, gave
up all pretence of protest.

'Oh Irvine! Oh Irvine!'

Dimly, they heard the shop bell again as the customer
left, and then Bessie's tread on the stairs. Rose pushed
Irvine away from her and when Bessie came in she was at
the far side of the room from him.

'Fourpence three-farthings,' Bessie said. 'Not worth
trailing downstairs for!'

'Oh, I don't know, love,' Irvine said smoothly, looking
at Rose. 'Every little helps. Perhaps she'll come back for
more!'

'I'll have to go,' Rose said.

She was halfway back to Mount Royd when she

remembered she was supposed to take a note to Mrs Bates. Or was she?

'I suggested the fair to Henry,' Léon said. 'He was all in favour.'

'He'd be in favour of going to the moon if Hortense was in the party,' Madeleine said.

She had observed the ripening affair between Henry and Hortense with a certain amount of disquiet. They seemed ill-matched and she didn't want Henry to get hurt. She hadn't always thought of Henry as being vulnerable. He'd seemed strong, immovable.

'I think I will not go to the fair,' Madame Bonneau said to Madeleine. 'I will stay behind and join your mother in her little *salon*.'

'So it will be the four of us,' Léon said.

'I'm lucky to have this room to myself,' Mrs Bates said when the two women were together. 'Your son has been very kind to me.'

'He was always the most considerate of my children,' Madame Bonneau acknowledged. 'And I have to say that I believe your daughter has made him happy, though I admit I was against it in the first place. . .'

'Oh, so was I!' Mrs Bates said quickly.

She had come to like and respect Madame Bonneau, but there was no way she was going to let her think that Léon had condescended in marrying Madeleine. Her daughter was the equal of anyone.

At the fair the four of them, between them, tried just about everything. Henry excelled at the weight-lifting; Léon sent the coconuts flying – and gave away his winnings to the children in the crowd. Henry and Hortense decided to go together on the roundabout and then the swing-boats, but Madeleine would have none of it; it made her squeamish even to watch.

'You go, Léon,' she said. 'I'll wait here for you.'

If Léon went on the swing-boats, would she have the nerve to pay a visit to Romany Rose, whom she had already ascertained was here again this year? But it seemed there was no chance of putting it to the test.

'I wouldn't dream of leaving you on your own,' Léon said. 'You're far too attractive! You and I will stroll around and meet up with the others in twenty minutes' time.'

When Henry and Hortense returned from their rides, Hortense looked pale, and clung heavily to Henry.

'Oh!' she cried 'The swing-boat was terrible. You were wise not to try it, Madeleine. If Henry had not been there to support me I don't know what I would have done!'

'But I *was* there,' Henry said happily.

And thoroughly enjoyed it by the look of you, Léon thought.

'There's just one thing more I would like to do,' Hortense said. 'I know it's very foolish of me, and you'll laugh at me, but I would like to visit the fortune-teller. I have never visited a fortune-teller in my life and it would be such fun. Surely there must be one here?'

'Not twenty yards away,' Madeleine said. 'Romany Rose.'

'But how wonderful! And have you ever visited her yourself?'

'No,' Madeleine lied.

'I should hope not!' Léon said. 'Stuff and nonsense!'

'Who can say?' Hortense challenged him. 'In any case, it would be fun. Don't you think so, Henry?'

'If that's what you want to do, then you shall do it,' Henry said. 'Why not?'

Romany Rose and her daughter watched Hortense approaching, noted her wealthy-looking escort, and the proprietary way he took her arm; noted also that she wore neither a wedding nor an engagement ring.

'This one's dead easy!' Romany Rose muttered.

She also recognized and remembered Madeleine. That one had a face and presence you wouldn't forget in a hurry. The same was true of the man she was with; handsome enough to be a prince! But no way would she ever let on that she remembered, though she had seen the recognition in *her* eyes too.

'Well here you are, my dear,' Henry said. 'I shall wait on this very spot. Here, let me give you a coin, for luck!'

'Oh I couldn't!' Hortense protested. 'It must be my own coin!'

Which is a pity, Romany Rose thought, for the way he was looking at her, as if he could eat her up, he'd probably have slipped her a half-sovereign.

There was no doubt that Romany Rose gave Hortense value for money, piled high and running over. It was plain to be seen when she emerged from the tent to rejoin the others. Her face was no longer pale; her cheeks were flushed with pleasure, her eyes shining.

'Well then,' Henry said, 'what did she tell you that makes you look so pleased?'

Romany Rose, who had hurried out after Hortense, called out to Henry.

'She's a lucky lady, sir! Come and let me tell you *your* luck!'

He laughed, and turned away, but not before he had tossed a half-sovereign in the gypsy's direction. She caught it deftly. She'd been waiting for it.

'Come on then,' Henry encouraged Hortense as they walked away. 'What did she say?'

'Oh I couldn't possibly tell you!' She was all embarrassment. 'You of all people.'

If it's what I think it is, Henry vowed to himself, I'll get it out of her before the evening's over!

Yet again he was to eat dinner with the Bonneaus. Hortense was changed, and downstairs again, before anyone else appeared – anyone except Henry, that was. He was already waiting for her.

'Why don't we take a turn in the garden?' he said. 'It's a lovely evening.'

They walked around, admiring the borders, and then sat, close together, on a seat just out of sight of the house.

'Now come on, my dear, tell me what the gypsy said?' Henry persisted.

'Oh I couldn't, Henry! Please don't ask me!'

'Then let me guess!'

'If you must.'

He put a finger under her chin and turned her head so that she was obliged to look at him. 'She told you you had met a man who had taken a real shine to you. . .'

'She didn't put it quite like that,' Hortense murmured. In Romany Rose's words it had sounded much more romantic.

'She told you that he wanted to marry you. And that if you were wise, if you took her advice, you'd accept him, because then you'd both live happily ever after.'

'How did you know?' Hortense asked softly.

'Because I'm that man. If she said all that, it was the truth. So what *did* she tell you?'

'Exactly what you have said.'

'And will you take her advice, Hortense? Will you marry him?'

'I think I must, Henry, don't you?'

He jumped to his feet – though she had half expected him to fall to his knees.

'Well Hortense,' he cried. 'You've made me a very happy man! And I'll make you a happy woman. I'll be good to you, I promise!'

When he kissed her she was surprised at his clumsy passion, and not sure she was ready for it.

'We must break the news,' Henry said when he finally let her go. 'I can't wait to tell them!'

As they went back into the house, Madeleine was descending the stairs. As Henry watched her, the whirlwind of the last three weeks was suddenly wiped out, and for a moment he was filled with doubt. What had he done?

You were the one I wanted, he thought. But am I to spend my life, go to the grave, wanting a woman I can't have? Am I to pass by every other woman because I can't have you? Then with an effort of will he pushed the doubts away from him. Everything would be all right. Hortense was a prize any man would be fortunate to win.

While Henry's eyes were fixed on Madeleine, Léon was looking at Hortense. He saw the look of triumph on her face. She caught his look, and half-closed her eyes and turned away, unable to bear his scrutiny. Don't dare condemn me, she wanted to cry out. I chose you long ago, but you didn't choose me.

Later, after they had drunk toasts, offered and accepted congratulations, spent the evening in a convivial manner, Hortense lay awake in bed and realized that at no time had Henry said he loved her. And, come to think of it, nor had she used those words to him. But they would do very well, she was sure of it. It was time she settled down. At twenty-nine, she wasn't getting any younger. Feeling slightly chilly, though it was August, she drew the bedclothes up around her neck, and went on staring into the darkness.

Henry was at Mount Royd in good time next morning, but not so soon that he had not been to the best jeweller in Leeds and bought an engagement ring which, in the privacy of the conservatory, he now placed on the third finger of Hortense's left hand.

'Oh Henry, it's beautiful!' Hortense exclaimed. 'How did you know that diamonds and rubies were my favourite stones?'

'I didn't. But I reckoned you couldn't fail to like this. It was the best in the shop,' Henry said proudly. 'You shall always have the best of everything, my dear. You're not marrying a poor man! And now tell me how quickly I can add a plain gold band to it?'

'You're very impatient!' Hortense teased.

'Of course I am! Anyway, the sooner we get married and settled down, the sooner I can get back to work and earn a bit of brass to buy a few more trinkets!' he said, laughing. 'So what's to stop us getting married quickly?

You're due to return to France by the end of this week. I'd like all the details settled before you go.'

'Oh Henry! So soon?'

'Why not? What's to prevent us?' he demanded.

'Nothing I suppose. Nothing at all!'

She had wakened in the night, wondered if she was doing the right thing – and decided she was. So what was the point in delaying?

They fixed a date in mid-September. They would be married, without fuss, in the Register Office in Bradford.

'But surely you wish to be married in Roubaix?' Madame Bonneau said when they told her their plans.

'Not really,' Hortense said. 'As you know, I have no family now. We can't be married in church, so it will be much better here. I've already spoken to Léon and Madeleine and they've agreed to let me be married from Mount Royd. I shall take you back to Roubaix, gather a few things together, and return quite soon.'

'But your trousseau?' Madame Bonneau protested. 'You won't have time to prepare a trousseau!'

'She'll not need to do that,' Henry interrupted. 'We can buy her trousseau after we're married. Hortense need bring nothing to her marriage except herself.'

He took his fiancée's hand in his, stroked her fingers, his eyes glinting with pride at the sight of the huge engagement ring.

'Henry is so kind,' Hortense said.

She hoped to persuade him – indeed she thought she would have little difficulty in doing so – that they should spend their honeymoon in London and Paris. She could buy a far better trousseau in those places, and in Henry's generous company, than she could ever put together in Roubaix.

Madame Bonneau sighed.

'Well, I suppose you are free to please yourself! But it is not what your mother would have wanted.'

Oh yes it is, Hortense thought. My mother would have

been delighted to see me marry a rich man, no matter if he was a Hottentot!

In the three days which remained before Hortense must return to France with Madame Bonneau, Henry took her to see his house in Leeds.

'It's a nice house,' he said with pride. 'Plenty of room – plenty of room for children. You would like children, wouldn't you?' Rarely for him, he sounded nervous.

'Of course, Henry dear!' Hortense murmured.

'Once we're installed you can have every room done up just as you want it. Your choice entirely!'

'You spoil me,' Hortense said happily.

'I mean to,' he said. 'I'm going to enjoy spoiling you.'

All the arrangements went without a hitch. They were married on a golden day in September, Henry looking uncommonly handsome in his morning dress and tall silk hat, Hortense almost breathtaking in the wedding dress which was the one garment she had insisted on bringing from France. Madeleine noted every detail: the overskirt of gold *moiré* silk, revealing the frilled under-skirt of pale cream; the close-fitting bodice intricately ruched between bands of narrow lace; the neck modestly high. It could only have originated in France, she thought, as could the bonnet, fashionably spoon-shaped and perched well forward on Hortense's abundant hair, trimmed and tied with gold-coloured beads, silk ribbon and flowers.

'It will certainly be the finest gown Bradford Register Office has ever seen,' she said enviously. 'And you look lovely in it, Hortense! Even the Prince of Wales's new bride couldn't outshine you!'

Until now, Hortense thought, the Danish Princess Alexandra and I have shared the same problem, not enough money to spend on dress. Well, from now on it will be different for both of us!

'You don't think it is too elaborate?' she asked.

'Not for your wedding.'

232

Since Hortense knew no one in the West Riding and Henry seemed not to have many friends, it was only a small reception which Léon and Madeleine gave at Mount Royd. Within a couple of hours the newly-weds were on the London train. After three days in London they would move on to Paris for at least a week.

'Please take note of all the fashions,' Madeleine begged as they were leaving. 'Bring me back lots of details!'

She wished that Léon would take her with him on one of his trips to France, so that she could see things for herself. She had a little niggling worry that Hortense might now be the one to design the garments for Henry. No one could deny she was fashionable – and she was a Frenchwoman. On the other hand, Madeleine consoled herself, the bright star of the Paris fashion world was a certain Mr Charles Frederick Worth – and Mr Worth was an Englishman born and bred!

Hortense was agreeably surprised and pleased at the consummation of her marriage to Henry. She had expected, been resigned to, a certain clumsiness, a lack of sensitivity. He prided himself on being a blunt Yorkshireman and she had thought his lovemaking might follow suit. It was not so. He was ardent, skilful, and considerate. Afterwards, she went to sleep highly satisfied, and with the last, lovely thought in her mind that in the morning they were to go shopping for whatever delights London had to offer.

Since the departure of her visitors, though she had enjoyed getting to know her mother-in-law better, Madeleine had felt a new freedom. It seemed as if all the summer had been taken up with other people's affairs. Now their lives were their own again, and it was with this feeling of liberation that she made love with Léon on the night of the wedding.

'I'm sure now it won't be long before we have a child,' she said to Léon. 'I know they say a woman can't conceive when she's breastfeeding, but that can't be true because I know so many families where it's happened. Wouldn't it be strange if both Hortense and I conceived at the same time?'

Léon had been on the point of falling asleep. Now he was wide awake again. She had to be told. It couldn't be put off any longer. He sat up in bed, put a light to the candle.

'Léon, why have you lit the candle?' Madeleine asked. 'Is something wrong? Do you feel ill?'

'I have to talk to you,' he said.

'What about? Why do you look so grave? You *are* ill! Or there's something wrong at the mill? Please, Léon, you must tell me!'

'I am trying to tell you – and it is none of those things. Please listen to me, Madeleine.'

'Very well. I'm listening.'

'You must be very brave. . .'

'Why? Oh, Léon, why?'

'What I have to tell you is not easy for me, and will be difficult for you to bear. I have to tell you that you will not conceive from tonight's lovemaking. Or from any occasion, now or in the future.'

'What do you mean?' She stared at him in astonishment.

'What I have just said, my darling. That we shall not have another child. For you it is impossible.'

She didn't believe him. How could it be true? She had already had a child. She was not barren. But searching his face she saw the truth.

'How do you know this?' she said quietly.

'Dr Hughes told me soon after Claire was born. Perhaps I should have told you sooner. I didn't know what to do for the best. But tonight I knew I couldn't let you go on hoping.'

There was nothing to be said; no reply. It was the end of her hopes. She recognized now, in a way she had never known before, the strength of her desire for more

234

children. She felt herself suddenly bereft of those sons and daughters she might have had. She wanted to weep for them, but no tears came. She turned away from Léon and buried her face in the pillow. He took hold of her and turned her gently towards him.

'Don't turn away from me, Madeleine! It's my sorrow as well as yours. Do you think I didn't want a son to bear my name? Do you think it doesn't hurt me?'

'And do you think that doesn't make me feel even worse?' she asked passionately. 'Do you think I don't care that I'm a bitter disappointment to you?'

'But you're not,' he protested. 'You could never be a disappointment to me, never in a thousand years. I didn't marry you so that we could have children; I married you because I loved you – and still do, and always will. And we have Claire. Don't let's forget that we have Claire. For Claire's sake, you must be brave. We must both thank God that we have one child to love.'

'Even though we don't have a son?'

'Even though we don't have a son,' he repeated.

She was silent for a long time, staring at the ceiling, at the shadows thrown by the light from the candle. At last she said:

'You are right, Léon. We have Claire. Please let's not ever mention this conversation again. It is better to forget it.'

'You are wrong,' Léon said. 'It is better to talk about it whenever we need to.'

'From this moment we will live our lives as if Claire was the sum total of all the children we ever wanted,' Madeleine said. 'I shall try never to think otherwise.'

'Give yourself time to heal, my darling.' Léon begged. 'Yes, you must come to terms with it; we both must. But give yourself time.'

'All the time in the world won't give me another child. Therefore I shall cease to think about it. I shall never think about it again.'

*

In the September weekend which saw the beginnings of Henry and Hortense's marriage and the shattering of Madeleine's hopes of a son, Penelope and Archie lay on the ground in a field by the river. The corn was high and golden, waiting to be cut. Its height blotted out the world, hid everything but the blue dome of the sky. In a few days from now, when they had harvested, there would be nothing except harsh, dry stubble, and after that the weather would turn cold and the frost would come. But for now, for a little while longer, it was summer.

Her eyes closed, feeling the warmth of the sun on her face, Penelope was hardly conscious of what Archie was doing; but then when he touched her breast she became acutely aware. It was a sensation she had never known, never dreamt existed. She wanted it to go on for ever, never to stop. While he caressed her breasts she thought of little else – she didn't think at all, she was all feeling.

What he did next seemed to follow naturally; there was no question of right or wrong, it was what had to be, what she wanted, what he wanted. There was no one else in the world. She cried out with the sharp pain of his penetration and then gave herself up to the exquisite waves of pleasure which swept her from head to foot, until it was all over and they were lying quietly again, still hidden by the corn.

'Oh Penny, I do love you so,' Archie said.

'And I love you!'

'We'd best be going,' he said.

236

THIRTEEN

It was well into October before Henry and Hortense returned from their honeymoon in Paris. In Helsdon the days were shortening. It was not fully light now as the millgirls set off for work; also some mornings there was a distinct nip in the air which made them draw their black shawls closer around their heads and shoulders. Evenings saw them scurrying home to sit close by the fire.

'I don't know how Henry manages to stay away from business so long,' Léon said to Madeleine. He passed her the letter he'd been reading. 'Shall we accept their invitation for Sunday?'

'But of course!' Madeleine said. 'I'm quite curious.'

They drove over in time for the midday meal. The signs of autumn were all around them, the trees changed from their summer green to shades of red and yellow and gold; the bracken brown, and drying at the edges. There was no longer a purple haze over the distant moor, which meant that the heather had died back. All it needed now was an early November gale – than which nothing was more certain – to strip the trees bare: and for winter; that longest and dampest of seasons here in the Pennines, to start its assault, freezing the fingers and toes, invading the lungs. Madeleine hated the winter. All that made it bearable was Christmas.

'Here we are, then!' Léon said. He turned through the iron gates to the circular drive which wound to the front door of Henry Garston's substantial house. Henry, hearing the sound of the carriage on the gravel, came to the door himself to greet them.

'Well this is a pleasure! Isn't this a pleasure?' he said to Hortense as she joined him.

'We began to think you two were never coming home,' Léon told them.

'Who wants to return from a honeymoon, eh?' Henry said, smiling at his wife. 'But come in out of the cold, the two of you. Melton will see to the horses.'

They followed him into the spacious hall. Hortense turned to Madeleine, took her by the arm.

'Come up to my room. You'll want to leave your cloak, and tidy up, and I've got so much to show you, you'll never believe!'

I wouldn't have, Madeleine thought a few minutes later, if it hadn't been here in front of my eyes! She had never seen so many clothes in one woman's possession, and all of them, she guessed, newly purchased. Two huge wardrobes were crammed across their width with gowns, skirts, blouses, jackets, capes. In the shelves above, hats, shrouded in tissue paper, filled every inch of space, and in the cupboards, which Hortense triumphantly threw open for inspection, were more shoes and boots than Madeleine had possessed in her life. She stood open-mouthed at the profligacy of it all.

'I'm afraid I'm *rather* extravagant!' Hortense apologized. 'But dear Henry encourages me.'

'May I take a closer look? At your gowns, especially.'

'Please do.'

Curiously, though the clothes were without exception expensively beautiful, Madeleine felt no envy. She liked to be well dressed, but she wouldn't have known what to do with so many garments. When would Hortense wear them all?

What made her wish to look more closely, to handle the cloth, note the cut, check the details, was professional curiosity. And that, as she examined the garments, was quickly followed by an appreciation of something well done. The details – the buttons, the lace (every inch of it handmade), the linings – were perfection, the work of skilled craftswomen. And some of the materials were new to her.

'What's this cloth?' she asked. 'I haven't come across it before.'

She held the dress against her cheek, soft and sensuous, then crushed it in her hand. When she released it, it fell and flowed into its original folds as if it had a life of its own.

'I don't know,' Hortense confessed. 'It's new.'

'I've not seen anything like it before,' Madeleine said. She examined it closely. 'It seems to me that it has a fine wool warp and a silk weft?'

Hortense shrugged.

'I have no idea of these things. I just know I like it.'

Madeleine returned the dress to the wardrobe. 'I'd like to show it to Léon,' she said.

'I expected you to bring Claire today,' Hortense remarked. 'Since you are nursing her. Why haven't you done so?'

'I had to wean her,' Madeleine said shortly.

'Had to?'

'My milk dried up. But she's taken quite well to the bottle.'

Her milk had begun to dry on the morning after Léon had told her there would be no more children. Within a week her breasts, which had been so bountiful, were as dry as an abandoned river bed. Not a drop of milk remained. All that week, holding her baby close, the thought uppermost in her mind had been that she would never feed a child again. But she had kept her thoughts to herself, said nothing to anyone, nor would she.

'So do you think the crinoline is going out?' she asked Hortense, steering the conversation along more acceptable lines.

Hortense raised her eyebrows, shook her head.

'Who can say? You know we've had that rumour for years, but it seems women won't give up the crinoline easily. They say Mr Worth has done his utmost to persuade the Empress Eugénie to abandon it. If she were to do so, then the whole of France would follow.'

'But she won't?'

239

'It seems not,' Hortense said. 'Though the crinoline *has* changed. In Paris most of the fullness is now drawn to the back of the skirt. The front is almost flat.'

'I've thought for some time that that would happen,' Madeleine said.

Hortense looked at her curiously.

'You have? But why?'

'I just had a feeling for which way fashion would go. Women get bored with the same style, and this one has been in far too long. Not a single one of the sketches I've brought for Henry features the crinoline as we know it in England.'

'How very clever of you,' Hortense said. And how could anyone living in Helsdon know about fashion, she wondered? 'But before we join the gentlemen I absolutely *must* show you Henry's wedding present to me – or one of them. Every day he seemed to buy me a new one!'

What she showed Madeleine was a silver-backed hairbrush, with two hand mirrors and combs, scent bottles, small boxes, all to match.

'It's exquisite!' Madeleine said.

'We bought it in London. Henry says there's no better place than London for silver.'

They went downstairs.

'Isn't it time we ate, my love?' Henry said. 'I'm starving!'

After the meal the men smoked a cigar and took a glass of port while Hortense persuaded Madeleine to walk in the garden. A month ago, Madeleine thought, it had probably looked quite beautiful: now, with the exception of a few dark evergreens, everything was in a melancholy state of fading and dying.

'I don't think much of this,' Hortense said suddenly. 'Also, I'm chilly. Shall we go in?'

Madeleine was glad to be back in the comfortable drawing-room, with its fire piled high and glowing with best Yorkshire coal.

'Henry, I've brought you lots of sketches,' she said. 'May I show them to you?'

When he agreed, she spread them out on the small tables, on the furniture, some on the floor. Henry picked up a few and examined them closely.

'Very interesting!'

'I'm convinced that Bonneau's materials, made up in these styles, would sell well,' Madeleine said eagerly.

'Well I don't know about the fashions,' Henry said. 'I leave that to you ladies. I need to know whether my seamstresses could make them at not too great an expense. Are the designs practical from that point of view?'

'I think you'll find they are,' Madeleine said. 'I've taken all that into account. Of course some are more elaborate than others, and for those a woman would expect to pay more. Sometimes it's no more than the trimming which makes the difference, though there's a lot of variety here, plenty for the customer to choose from. And everything is new!'

'I can see you've been hard at it while we've been gallivanting in Paris!' Henry acknowledged.

That was certainly true. The moment Madeleine realized that Claire must be weaned, she told Léon that she wanted to do her work in the mill again.

'I'll occupy the same room, until you can find me something bigger – which I really shall need if I'm to branch out into fashion designing as well.'

'But there's nothing you can do in the mill that you can't do here at home,' Léon protested.

'You're wrong,' she said. 'I need the atmosphere of the mill, and the contacts. I need to be able to go into the weaving, or the spinning; or sometimes to talk to the dyers. I'm cut off from all that at home.'

He wanted to argue with her, but one look at her face, at the fire in her dark eyes, told him it was no good. She had the most loving of natures, but for all that there was a core of steel in her, and recently he had felt it strengthen. He knew the reason why. She was throwing herself into her work, filling every hour, so that she wouldn't have time to dwell on her deep disappointment. He would have been happier to see her give way to her feelings.

But looking at her now, in the Garstons' drawing-room, she seemed utterly composed, totally in control, as if everything in her life was exactly as it should be.

'Hortense has shown me all her beautiful clothes from Paris,' she was saying to Henry. 'They're quite an inspiration, I must say.'

She was a little worried that Hortense, if life in Leeds became boring, might wish to take over the fashion designing – and that Henry might allow her to do so. She badly needed reassurance on that.

'I just hope Hortense won't do me out of a job,' she said lightly.

'Me, do that? Me do your fashion drawings?' Hortense sounded astonished. 'Never in this world!'

She had not the slightest intention of working for her living. She could think of far better ways of rewarding Henry for his kindness to her.

'But what will you do with yourself all day?' Madeleine asked.

'Oh, I shall find plenty to occupy myself,' Hortense assured her. 'There are good shops in Leeds, and you know how much I like shopping. And I daresay I shall get to know people, make calls.' Leeds society, she thought, though not Parisian, would be at least as exciting as Roubaix's. 'And my dear Henry has promised to take me to London from time to time. Oh yes, I shall do very well!'

Why am I the opposite of all this, Madeleine wondered? But if she lived that kind of life, then Léon would come home to a wife bored and frustrated.

'Madeleine, we forgot to bring the dress down!' Hortense said. 'The one you wanted to show to Léon. I'll fetch it.'

When Hortense returned with the dress Madeleine said: 'Will you take a look at the material, Léon? Don't you think it's a silk weft and a wool warp?'

Léon examined it closely.

242

'Yes,' he said. 'You're right. I haven't seen this done before. And I daresay if it can be done this way, it can be done the other way on; a silk warp and a wool weft. Silk, for all its fine appearance, is very strong, though wool is perhaps more flexible, and warmer.'

'Silk is also extremely fashionable in France,' Hortense said. 'That again is due to the Empress. She's doing her best to encourage the Lyons silk trade.'

'But the Lyons silk is heavy,' Léon said. 'Especially if the dress is very full. Woven like this, it would be lighter. And it doesn't need to be spun, of course. The silkworm does that for us. It needs only twisting and winding.'

'When you go to France, Léon, will you see if you can find out about it?' Madeleine asked.

'Certainly I will – and it will help if Hortense will tell me where she bought this particular dress.'

'You should get Léon to take you when he goes to France,' Hortense said to Madeleine. 'You would enjoy it, I'm sure. And now that you're not tied down to Claire you would be free to go.'

Madeleine smiled, but said nothing. The same thought was in her own mind, but now was not the time to discuss it.

It was late afternoon when they left Leeds, and dusk when they reached Helsdon. In the stretches of country between the two towns, where the canal and the river ran like two parallel snakes, the fields which bordered the roads were bare where corn had been harvested, the stubble brown.

'There's a smell of woodsmoke in the air,' Madeleine said. 'It's one of the things I *do* like about autumn!'

The days, through the autumn and into the winter, went by more quickly than Madeleine had dared hope, perhaps because she seldom stopped working. In the mornings she was at the mill before daylight and in the evenings it was dark before she was back home. After supper, more often than not, she would sit with her sketch book and

243

work at her fashion designs. Of these she destroyed more than she kept, impatiently tearing out the page, crumpling it into a ball and throwing it in the fire. When, once, she missed the fireplace, Léon picked up the crumpled sheet and opened it out.

'Why have you thrown this away?' he asked. 'It looks perfectly good to me – rather attractive, in fact.'

He had by this time ceased to show his opposition to her work. It was a battle he couldn't win. Also he recognized it as a solace to her, as his was to him. They both worked far harder than they need.

They were busier than ever in the mill. Things had changed since the time when Léon had taken over, on borrowed money, with every day a struggle to keep things going. Now, his greatly increased number of workers were all on full-time and he had become known as one of the best employers in Helsdon. Yet only the other side of the Pennines the Lancashire cotton mills were in deep trouble; most of them not working more than three days a week because the war in America meant the raw cotton wasn't coming over.

'I've discarded the drawing because I can't get the style right,' Madeleine answered. 'In fact, it lacks style. It's ordinary, too like a hundred other dresses. That's not what I want.'

'What do you want, then?'

'I want my designs to be different, to have their own stamp. I want the woman who buys one to recognize that it's by me: to like it, and therefore to look for another. And then I intend to help her to find one.'

'How?'

'I'm going to tell Henry that I want the dresses from my designs to carry my name. I want a label, stitched into the seam, to say ''Bonneau''. What do you think?'

'What I immediately think is that Henry won't agree to it,' Léon said firmly.

'I shall persuade him to do so.'

'But your dress designs have been on the market a bare

244

two months,' Léon protested. 'Hardly time to know whether they'll be successful or not. And women are much more used to having gowns made for them.'

'That's changing,' Madeleine said. 'And will change more than ever when they have good garments available. And if it's *my* name that's in the gowns, Henry has nothing to lose.'

She spoke with quiet confidence, hardly looking up from the new sketch she had started on. She never ceased to surprise him.

'Claire was crawling when I came home at dinnertime,' Madeleine said. Her voice softened when she spoke of her daughter.

The only break she made from her rigorous timekeeping was that when the dinner-time hooter sounded, and all work stopped, she would hurry up the hill to Mount Royd. She would go straight to the nursery and spend a half-hour playing with Claire, at the same time eating whatever her mother thrust into her hand.

'I wonder you don't get indigestion!' Mrs Bates grumbled.

When the hooter sounded to recall the workers she left Claire in Flora Bryant's care again, and ran back to the mill. She never failed to feel refreshed from the short spell with her daughter, though once at work again she effortlessly put the child out of her mind until it was time to go home.

'She crawled halfway across the room,' Madeleine continued. 'Really, at not yet eight months I think that's quite forward, don't you?'

'I'm sure it must be,' Léon agreed. 'My only experience of children is those of my brothers. I'm certain Claire is well in advance of any of them at the same age!'

'There speaks a proud father!' Madeleine said, smiling. How cruel, therefore, that he was not to father a whole brood of children. But at once she put the thought from her.

'I shall tackle Henry Garston when he comes to the

245

mill tomorrow,' she said. 'About my name on a label, I mean.'

'I wish you luck,' Léon said.

'Is that really necessary, lass?' Henry said next day, when the three of them met.

'To me it is,' Madeleine said. 'And I don't see what harm it can do. You know the dresses will be well up to standard. I wouldn't want my name on them if they weren't.'

'I suppose not,' Henry allowed. 'But it's a bit unusual.'

'And what's wrong with being unusual?'

'Oh, go on then!' he said. 'But nothing conspicuous. Just a small label with the name. I think "Bonneau" will be quite enough. No need for "House of Bonneau"!'

'Thank you, Henry! You're a love! I shall get them embroidered at once and send you the first batch.'

She went back to discussing the garments Henry had brought to show them, dresses made from cloth woven in Bonneau's to Madeleine's fabric designs and made up to her latest fashion drawings.

She examined the garments carefully.

'They've been very well done,' she said approvingly. 'Were there any difficulties?'

'Not that I know of,' Henry said.

'Well obviously you have a very talented cutter, as well as good seamstresses.'

'They wouldn't be working for me if they weren't,' Henry said firmly. 'I don't employ incompetent people.'

Madeleine picked up a dress and draped it over the back of a chair.

'I think I'd like to see this one in our new striped design,' she said thoughtfully. 'The basic cut could be the same, but it would look quite different in an arrangement of stripes, which I would work out. Especially if it was worn with the striped stockings, which Hortense says are the thing in Paris.' She turned to Léon. 'Wouldn't it be fun if we could show the garments on real live people – I mean show them to the buyers from the stores?'

'I doubt you'll persuade Henry into that,' Léon said, with a smile.

'Leeds isn't Paris,' Henry said. 'I keep telling Hortense that. Let's not try to run before we can walk!'

'Why not?' Madeleine said. 'If Claire decides to run before she's walking – which on present form she may well do – I shall certainly let her!'

'Come on!' Henry said. 'You've got your name on the label. Let that be enough for one day! How's that brother of yours faring?'

'All right,' Madeleine said. 'Nothing spectacular.'

Spectacular was something Irvine Bates never would be, Henry thought – unless it was spectacularly idle. It beat him how a brother and sister could be so different.

It was true that as far as trade in the shop went, Irvine wasn't doing too well. But he refused to let it worry him. Drawing a pint of porter, Irvine took a deep and satisfying draught, then placed the tankard on the shelf under the counter as a customer came into the shop. He was not quite quick enough.

'Sampling the wares, Mr Bates?' the woman said.

'That's right, Mrs Blakeley!' he said. 'I wouldn't want to sell my customers anything which wasn't up to standard. But I can confidently say that this porter is first class!'

'Then perhaps you'd like to taste a spoonful of treacle,' Mrs Blakeley said, 'since that's what I've come for.'

'I did that too!' Irvine said. 'I spread some on a bit of bread only this morning! You won't find better treacle than mine, neither.' Silly old cow, he thought.

'Then fill that,' Mrs Blakeley said, pushing a jar, tied around with a string handle, across the counter.

He hung the jar in place and turned on the barrel tap. The dark brown, sticky substance oozed into the jar.

'Mind you fill it,' the woman said.

She was just leaving when Bessie came down the stairs, holding Tommy, muffled up to the eyeballs, by the hand.

'I'm off then!' she said. 'Any message for your Ma?'

'Well you could tell her I fancy a bit of her baking,' Irvine said. 'Especially if she's made a parkin. There's nothing to touch a bit of Yorkshire parkin!'

'So you keep saying,' Bessie said.

'Don't hurry back, love,' Irvine said. 'Enjoy yourself!'

She didn't bother to reply. It wasn't to enjoy herself that she spent every Thursday afternoon with her mother-in-law, though admittedly she liked Mrs Bates better than she had done at first. She went there to get out of the chill of the rooms over the shop and to make a change from staring at the same four, peeling walls. It was always warm at Mount Royd, and certainly there was no place where Tommy was more welcome. She chose to visit on a Thursday, partly because it was baking day, partly because it was Rose Hardy's afternoon off. She didn't particularly like Rose Hardy.

When Bessie walked into the kitchen at Mount Royd, Rose was just leaving.

'Where's she off to then?' Bessie asked her mother-in-law as Rose scurried away.

'She's going to Bradford,' Mrs Bates said. 'She has family there. Mind you, she doesn't know she's born, having three hours off every week. Madeleine's very generous with her servants.'

Mrs Bates would have been surprised if she could have seen the route Rose took to Bradford. She walked briskly into Helsdon, but passed the railway station without so much as a sideways glance. Ten minutes later the bell on the spring behind the door clanged as she entered Irvine's shop. At the moment when Bessie finally succumbed to the heat of the fire and took off her shawl, Rose, in the bedroom over the shop, was taking off considerably more. Her skirt, bodice, petticoats, stays; in fact, the lot.

Irvine gave a long, low whistle at the sight of her nakedness.

'You beauty! You little beauty!'

'Are you sure you've locked the shop door?' she asked prosaically.

'Of course I am, silly!'

'What if any customers come?'

'You ask that every time. They'll rattle the door, then they'll go away again. And if they want something urgent, they'll come back. Never mind them – I certainly want something urgent, and you know what!'

She lay on the bed and held out her arms to him, smiling a wide, welcoming smile. It was one of the things he liked about Rose; she took pleasure in the act and didn't mind showing it.

'You can have whatever you want,' she said. 'Within reason!'

'Don't talk to me about reason!' Irvine said. 'You're enough to drive a man mad!'

He went on to the bed and she pulled him down on top of her, holding him close, winding her legs around him, digging her nails into his back until she nearly drove him crazy. Within seconds she was frenzied, and so was he, both of them like two people who, after being starved of food, see a rich meal spread before them, ready for the taking. They took and ate to the full.

Afterwards she dressed quickly.

'I'm supposed to be in Bradford,' Rose said. 'There'll be no time to go there now. You were a greedy boy today, weren't you?'

'Hungry,' he corrected. 'I'm on a starvation diet most of the time.'

'What about me, then?'

'I should hope you are,' Irvine said quickly. 'If I hear of you nibbling anywhere else, you'll be in trouble!'

He went downstairs first, unlocked the shop door and peered out into the street, making sure the coast was clear.

'Ta-ta then!' he said. 'See you next Thursday!'

'One of these days. . .' she began.

But she wasn't really worried. She was always careful not to leave Mount Royd until Bessie actually showed up. And Bessie will stay until the minute I get back, she thought. No doubt of that. It was all as regular as clockwork.

Disappointingly, Mrs Bates was in the kitchen when Rose walked in.

'You look flushed!' she observed.

'I got warm, walking up the hill,' Rose said.

'Bradford seems to agree with you,' Mrs Bates remarked. She wondered what Rose had been up to there. She looked for all the world like a cat which had been at the cream.

'I'll be off then,' Bessie said. 'Thanks for everything.' She picked up the basket which she had brought empty, and was now full.

'See you next week,' Mrs Bates said. 'Give Grandma a kiss then, Tommy!'

It wanted ten days to Christmas when Penelope arrived at Mount Royd. When she walked into Mrs Bates's parlour, Madeleine was there, but not her mother. Madeleine stared in disbelief at her sister. It was not only that she was there, for which there seemed no reason, it was the way she looked. Her eyes were red-rimmed and frightened in a chalk-white face; her hair hung down in untidy streaks from beneath her bonnet. She looked near to collapse.

At once, Madeleine held her arms wide and Penelope ran into them. The sisters held each other close. Penelope was now sobbing. For a moment Madeleine held her without speaking, then she said: 'Why, Penelope love, whatever is it? Now come and sit down and let me take off your cloak and bonnet, and you can tell me what it's all about. Why are you here?'

'I've left!' Penelope said in a whisper. 'I couldn't stand it another minute, Madeleine. I honestly couldn't. Please don't be angry!'

'Of course you couldn't,' Madeleine said. 'And no one's going to be angry. I just want you to tell me what it's all about. And I'm on your side, remember. Nobody knows better than I what Sophia Chester can be like! I'm sure you had good reason to leave.'

Penelope started to cry again, noisy sobs tearing.

'Oh Madeleine, you won't be on my side when you hear what it is! And I didn't decide to leave. I was sacked!'

'Sacked? But that's preposterous! What could *you* have done to be sacked?'

'Oh Madeleine, I don't know how to tell you!' Penelope said.

'Come on, love,' Madeleine urged. 'Nothing can be that bad!'

'But it is! The truth is . . . I'm going to have a baby! That's why she sacked me. I'm going to have a baby!'

Madeleine stared. She couldn't be hearing right. Not Penelope, not her little sister!

The horror of that other December day, which until this moment had receded until it was like something which had happened in another life, swept over her like a cold dark wave. Her flesh crawled, feeling again the horror of George Carter's hands on her body. And then, when it was over, the terrible shame; the dirtiness and filth of her. She would kill whoever had done this to her sister!

'I'll kill him!' she cried. 'I'll kill him! Oh, my dear little Penelope! But don't fret – he'll not go free!'

At the sound of Madeleine's voice Penelope immediately stopped crying. She looked with horror at her sister. She'd got it all wrong.

'No Madeleine! No! You mustn't say that! I love Archie! I love him more than anyone in the world. You can hate me, but you mustn't hate Archie.'

Hearing her sister's words Madeleine, with an effort, quelled the rage which had risen with such terrible and sudden force in her.

'Archie? I don't understand. Who is Archie?'

251

'I've known him for months now. We love each other.'

'And Archie is the father of your child? Is that what you're telling me, Penelope?'

'Yes. Oh, we only did it once. You must believe me. We didn't mean to . . . we didn't think. We were going to save up and get married.'

But would they have done it again, Penelope wondered, given the chance? They had longed for each other – but the cornfield was harvested, the rain came, then the cold. There'd been nowhere they could be together again like that. She liked to think they would have waited until they were married but she couldn't be sure. It would have been so long.

'Oh Penelope!' Madeleine said. 'My dear little Penelope! What have you got yourself into?'

Penelope looked frightened again.

'How am I going to tell Ma?' she asked. 'I can't tell her!'

'If you don't, time will,' Madeleine said. 'How did you tell Mrs Chester?'

'I didn't tell her. She guessed. I was sick in the mornings and she heard me.'

'Does Emerald know?'

'She does now,' Penelope said. 'She's terribly ashamed of me! She says I've let down Mrs Chester.'

'Damn Mrs Chester!' Madeleine cried. 'If she'd been looking after you properly this wouldn't have happened! You were in her care, she was responsible for you. One thing's certain, *she* won't get away with it. I've a good mind to go and tell her what I think of her!'

'Oh please, Madeleine! I couldn't face it! She was so angry. She said the most terrible things! And then she told me to pack my box and get out.'

'Does she owe you wages?' Madeleine asked.

'Yes, four months. But I couldn't go back for them.'

'I could,' Madeleine said. 'The money's yours by rights and you'll need it for the baby. Does Archie know about this?'

'I told him about the baby last week,' Penelope said. 'He doesn't know I was turned out, or that I'm here. I just came. But he is going to marry me, Madeleine. He promised.'

Madeleine put a finger under her sister's chin, tilted her face and looked into her eyes.

'And is that what you want? Is that what you truly want, love?'

'Oh it is, Madeleine! It really is. More than anything in the world!'

'You don't want it just for the sake of the baby? Because you needn't, you know. I'll look after you.'

'I love Archie,' Penelope said steadily. 'I'd want to marry him whatever else.'

'Then I shall go to see him also,' Madeleine said.

'You won't be angry with him, Madeleine? It was my fault as much as his. I didn't try to stop him.'

Madeleine shook her head. She felt perplexed. She couldn't and wouldn't judge her sister. In any case it was too late.

Mrs Bates came into the room carrying a tea tray. At the sight of Penelope she almost dropped it.

'Penelope! What in the world . . . !'

'Oh Ma, please don't be angry! Promise you won't be angry!'

'Why should I be angry? What are you talking about? Why are you here?'

'Let me tell Ma,' Madeleine said. 'Ma, you'd best sit down.'

She told it calmly and factually, aware as she did so of the mounting pain and horror in her mother's eyes.

'Try not to take on, Ma,' Madeleine said when she'd finished. 'What's done is done!'

'How can I not take on?' Mrs Bates cried. 'Oh Penelope, you of all people!'

Of all her children, Penelope had seemed the purest, the most innocent and unworldly. She hadn't yet come round to thinking of her as much more than a little girl.

'I know, Ma!' Madeleine said. 'I know!'

'Oh Ma, I'm sorry!' Penelope whispered. 'I wouldn't have hurt you for the world! But you won't disown me, will you?' she pleaded. 'You won't turn me away?'

There was a tense pause. Madeleine watched her mother and Penelope looking at each other. Then Mrs Bates moved to her youngest daughter and took her in her arms.

'Of course I'll not turn you away, love! I'm your mother. I'd never do that.'

But her father would have, Mrs Bates thought: as he did Irvine, as he would have Madeleine had she not been too strong for him. Without a qualm, Joseph Bates would have thrown out his youngest, his most vulnerable child; and he would have done it in the name of religion. Well, he was beyond the power to hurt any of them now.

Penelope, held in her mother's arms, was weeping again – but now they were tears tinged with relief.

'Oh Ma, thank you! I'm ever so sorry and I will try to be good.'

'Of course you will! Now dry your eyes, love. I'll pour us some tea and we must think about what we'll do.'

'Archie wants to marry me,' Penelope said. 'If we can find just one room to live. . . We'll have to live in Ripon because he'll need his job. He doesn't earn much but I'm sure we'll manage.'

'We'll sort out all that,' Madeleine said. 'I'll go and see him. And while I'm in the neighbourhood I'll call on Sophia Chester!'

'Whatever for?' Mrs Bates said. 'She only did what any employer would have done.'

'She owes Penelope four months' wages,' Madeleine said. 'I intend to get them.'

'But what if she takes it out on Emerald?' Penelope said anxiously. 'What if she gives Emerald the sack?'

'She'll not do that,' Madeleine said. 'That I'm certain of! Sophia Chester knows which side her bread is buttered. She knows she'll never find another willing slave like Emerald.'

'I still think. . .' Mrs Bates began.

'Don't try to stop me going, Ma,' Madeleine interrupted.

Léon, when told later of Madeleine's proposed visit, was of the same opinion as his mother-in-law.

'I quite see why you should go and see the young man responsible,' he said. 'And if you wish I will go with you.'

'I don't mind going on my own,' Madeleine said. 'She's my sister. You've done so much for my family already.'

'Then make whatever arrangements seem best,' he said. 'But must you go to see Sophia? The money doesn't matter. I will make it up. You'll only upset yourself further.'

'I must!' Madeleine said. 'Why should you pay for what Sophia Chester owes?'

Bradshaw's butcher's shop was close to the market-place. Peering in at the small window, through the joints of meat hanging from the rafters, Madeleine could see a young man who, from Penelope's description, was most likely Archie. The older man beside him was presumably Mr Bradshaw. She went in, thankful that the place was empty of customers, for she had no clear idea how to set about this business. There was no point in getting Archie into further trouble, yet she had to talk to him.

'Good-morning!' she said pleasantly.

'Good-morning, ma'am,' the older man said. 'What can I do for you?' A new customer, he thought.

'As a matter of fact I didn't want to buy anything, not at the moment. I wondered – that is, do you think I might have a word with Archie? I was just visiting the town and. . .' she faltered.

Mr Bradshaw looked at her keenly.

'Would you be Penelope Bates's sister?'

'Yes. Madeleine Bonneau.'

'I thought so. You favour each other. Well you'd best come through to the back. Archie, lock the shop door for five minutes.'

Madeleine followed the butcher through to a back

room, and when he had locked the door, Archie joined them. So far he had not spoken.

'Do you know Penelope then?' Madeleine asked Mr Bradshaw.

'Oh aye! And I know why you've come, though I only learnt it last night and I told Archie he had to get over to Helsdon the minute he'd finished his rounds today. Me and my wife are both very sorry. We think a lot of Penelope. I was tempted to take the boot to my nephew!'

'Archie is your nephew?'

'Did Penelope not tell you?'

'No. So what's to be done?' Madeleine asked.

'Ask him!' Mr Bradshaw said, pointing at Archie.

'I want to marry Penelope,' Archie said. 'I do truly love her, and I'll look after her.' He was an earnest-looking young man with a gentle voice, and he was clearly very worried. Madeleine couldn't help but like him. But what babes in the wood her sister and this young lad were!

'And what will you live on, keep a wife on?' she queried. 'You understand I have to ask?'

He blushed to the roots of his fair hair.

'I don't earn much,' he said. 'I'm still learning the trade, Mrs Bonneau.'

'But he'll get a rise when he's married, and when he's learnt his trade he'll get another rise,' Mr Bradshaw put in. 'They'll not have it easy, the pair of 'em, but they'll manage. I'll see to that.'

'It strikes me you're a lucky young man to have an uncle like Mr Bradshaw,' Madeleine said to Archie.

'I know,' he said. 'I appreciate it. But my biggest luck is getting Penny. So I'd like me and Penny to get married as soon as maybe.'

'The circumstances being what they are, I think you'd better,' Madeleine said dryly. 'Also it might be best if it took place in Helsdon.'

The three of them discussed plans, briefly, until Mr Bradshaw said: 'I mun get back into the shop, and Archie here has his second round to do, if you'll excuse us.'

'And I still have another call to make,' Madeleine said. 'Thank you for speaking so warmly of Penelope. I feel much happier now.'

'Oh we'll look after her, never fret!' Mr Bradshaw assured Madeleine. 'The wife will be only too pleased to do what she can. We've no bairns of our own, you see.'

'I'll write to you tomorrow, when I've spoken to my husband and Penelope,' Madeleine said to Archie. 'Also I was to tell you that Penelope sends her love.' She smiled at him for the first time.

When Madeleine rang the Chesters' bell the door was opened by Emerald, whose face fell at the sight of her older sister.

'Hello Emerald,' Madeleine said. 'I came to see Mrs Chester.'

'I'm not sure. . .'

'Don't tell me she's not at home. In fact, if that's really the case I'll wait here until she is!'

'Oh Madeleine, I do hope you haven't come to make trouble,' Emerald protested. 'Mrs Chester was very upset by Penelope. And I was terribly ashamed, I can tell you.'

I expect you were, Madeleine thought. It was predictable that shame, rather than compassion, would have been Emerald's reaction.

'I'm not here to make trouble,' she said. 'I'm here on legitimate business. Penelope is owed four months' wages and I've come to collect.'

She followed close behind as Emerald went to announce her, and as her sister crept out of the drawing-room, Madeleine went in.

Sophia Chester jumped to her feet.

'What in the world . . . ? How dare you walk into my house like this? Who let you in? Please leave immediately!'

'I don't wish to stay,' Madeleine said. 'The minute I have Penelope's wages in my hand I'll be pleased to leave. Four months' wages, that's four pounds exactly.'

'How dare you!' Sophia spluttered. 'Your sister's behaviour warrants no consideration at all. She's nothing more than a common little hussy! How do you think I could possibly keep her in my house a minute longer than I did, with three innocent children at risk of being contaminated?'

'Be careful what you say, Mrs Chester,' Madeleine said quietly. 'There's such a thing as slander.'

'It would be no slander, would it?' Sophia countered. 'You're not denying that your sister is pregnant by the butcher's boy. Lying in some field, I expect, like the peasant she is! But then what can you expect, seeing who she's associated with all her life?'

She hated Madeleine Bates – she refused to call her Bonneau. She hated her guts. *She is a low-born little upstart who has taken what is rightfully mine*, she thought. *Léon Bonneau should have been mine! Mount Royd should belong to me and my children! And now it's all hers, every stick and stone!*

'Your sister Penelope is fast and loose, she's no better than a whore . . . !'

It was too much! Madeleine leapt across the space which separated them and fetched Sophia a stinging slap across the face.

'How dare you, Sophia Chester! How dare you!'

Tears of pain filled Sophia's eyes as she lifted her hand to her face: but the pain only enraged her further.

'And she gets it from you!' she cried. 'Don't forget that I saw the way you went after Léon Bonneau. I was there. Well, I daresay he regrets it, now that it's too late and he's saddled with you and your awful family.'

She went on and on, each thing she dredged up more bitter than the last. *But she degrades only herself*, Madeleine thought.

'If you've quite finished,' Madeleine broke in, 'I will take Penelope's wages, and leave.'

'I'm not paying any wages,' Sophia said. 'Not a penny piece!'

'Then I'm not leaving,' Madeleine said.

She sat down firmly on a chair and calmly started to remove her gloves, and then her bonnet. Sophia gave a cry of impotent rage and ran out of the room.

'Blast you!' she cried as she slammed the door.

A minute later she returned – and threw four sovereigns on the floor at Madeleine's feet.

'Take the money and get out!' she yelled. 'Don't ever set foot here again.'

'I won't!' Madeleine promised, re-tying her bonnet strings, pulling on her gloves.

I suppose I should feel sorry for her, she thought, walking back to the railway station. I have everything that poor woman wants! But she didn't feel sorry at all, only sorry that she had been so undignified as to hit her.

FOURTEEN

'The first three months of this year have flown by,' Madeleine said to Léon. 'Usually, the winter drags on and on, I suppose because I hate it. But we seem to have been so busy.'

Battling against the blustery wind, they had walked home together from the mill, just catching the daylight, for now the days were lengthening. Supper over, they sat in the drawing-room with the fire piled high and the heavy velvet curtains drawn against the wild March evening. Every so often the wind whistled down the wide chimney and blew the flames awry.

'I think we're likely to remain busy,' Léon said. '1863 was a good year for us, but 1864 will be better, you'll see!'

He was speaking of the life of Bonneau's mill, Madeleine thought: of trade and industry, of orders taken, profits made.

'Yes,' she agreed. 'It was a good year for the mill. But for us it was ups and downs, wasn't it? You bought Mount Royd, and I love the feeling that we own it, but then. . .'

'But then, best of all,' Léon interrupted, 'is that we have Claire. What else can compare to that, my dear? Our daughter has made the greatest difference to our lives.'

'Of course, Léon!'

But the other great difference in our lives, Madeleine thought, though never to be discussed, is that now we know that Claire is the first and last, the one and only. They might not speak of it, but it was there.

Léon leaned over and took his wife's hand, kissed the tips of her fingers.

'We must count our blessings, *chérie*.'

'Oh I do!' Madeleine assured him. 'Believe me, I do!'

Léon took the firetongs, and picking up a live coal which had fallen to the hearth, replaced it on the pyramid in the grate.

'Did I tell you that Ma had had a letter from Penelope?' Madeleine asked. 'It seems that Mrs Bradshaw is teaching her to cook the hams and the legs of pork they sell by the slice in the shop; not to mention making the brawn, which I happen to know Penelope would never touch. She hates the stuff!'

'Nevertheless, she'll do it well,' Léon said. 'She's a conscientious little soul, your sister. Archie Freeman is a lucky young man.'

Penelope and Archie had married in the second week in January, at which time Mr Bradshaw and his wife had decided to leave the rooms over the butcher's establishment and move into a cottage.

'So you and Archie can live over the shop,' Mrs Bradshaw said. 'As we've done all our married lives, and been happy here.'

'I just hope Penelope isn't working too hard,' Madeleine continued. 'I'd really have liked her to stay here until she'd had the baby. So would Ma.'

'That would have been quite unfair both to Archie and Penelope,' Léon said. 'Would we have wanted to live apart when we were first married? You are too protective of Penelope, my love. You must allow her to stand on her own feet.'

'I know,' Madeleine admitted. 'But I'm glad she's agreed to come back to Mount Royd in June, to have the baby. It will be much better here.'

'So long as it's Penelope's own wish,' Léon insisted.

'When I'm in France,' Madeleine said, 'I mean to look out for something very special for her baby. Perhaps even an entire layette. Hortense tells me they have the most beautiful baby clothes there.'

Léon frowned. Madeleine was a little too interested in this child her sister was expecting, as if she were trying to

261

share it. That would solve nothing for Madeleine and would be unfair to Penelope. It was a situation upon which he intended to keep a close watch.

'Did your French lesson go well today?' he asked.

Each week since Christmas Madeleine had taken lessons from a man who had once taught French at Bradford Grammar School. She could get by reasonably in conversation, but now she wanted to be able to read and write in French. For one thing, with the orders from France came a fair amount of correspondence. The fact that only Léon could translate it made her feel less than efficient.

'Also, I'd like to be able to read the books you read,' she'd said to him. 'You still read far more in French than in English. And another thing is, how nice it would be if I could write to *Belle-mère* in French!'

But also she wanted command of her husband's language because one day, though this was not the time to say so, and in any case it would have to wait until Claire was a little older, she desperately wished to travel with Léon on his buying trips to the continent. She was determined, however ludicrous it seemed, that one day she would break into the French market with her fashion designs. It was this, most of all, which drove her to struggle every Wednesday morning under the patient tutelage of Mr Fairbrother.

'It went quite well,' she said. 'Though I must say, French is a difficult language!'

'So is English,' Léon countered. 'As for the language of the West Riding – I sometimes think I shall never master that!'

'It will be wonderful *at last* to be in Paris in the spring,' Madeleine said. 'So often it's been promised, and every time something has happened to prevent it.'

Léon had visited France in the New Year, refusing to take Madeleine because the weather was bitter. He had consulted with his brothers about the possibility of manufacturing the silk-and-wool cloth Madeleine had admired in Hortense's gown. Marcel and Pierre had

262

known nothing of the process themselves, but a mill had been located, not far from Lyons, which wove such material. He had been received at the mill, though the owners had been reticent about the process.

'It's not yet clear,' he'd told Madeleine on his return, 'whether we would need to import new machinery from France – in which case it might not be worthwhile – or whether we would be able to make adjustments to our own machines, both for twisting and weaving.'

'John Hartley is very gifted with the looms,' Madeleine said. 'He might be able to do it.' John Hartley was the weaving overlooker.

'And then there's the dyeing. Different fibres take the dyes differently,' Léon pointed out. 'Also, the weavers would most likely have to learn new techniques.'

'Oh, I don't think you need worry about that!' Madeleine said. 'Once a weaver, always a weaver! They'd soon learn!' On that she could speak from experience.

'Titus Salt is the one for producing beautiful cloth from mixed fibres, though whether he'd advise us I'm not sure,' Léon said doubtfully. West Riding manufacturers were no readier than the French to share their expertise.

'Well I'm sure we'll find a way,' Madeleine said. 'And I feel in my bones that we're going to need softer materials when the crinoline goes out of fashion.'

At nine-thirty they were, as usual, interrupted by Rose Hardy who brought Madeleine her nightly cup of chocolate. When she had gone, Léon poured himself a measure of brandy.

'Rose looks very chirpy these days,' Madeleine said.

'She's an attractive woman,' Léon answered. 'It's sad she was widowed so young.'

Mrs Bates had the same thought as Madeleine.

'Rose seems to have taken out a new lease of life,' she remarked the next afternoon to Bessie. 'And I must say, she's very attentive to her family. Goes to visit them every single week!'

I wish I could visit my family, Bessie thought. Though her parents had both died, she had two sisters living in Brighton, and she longed to set eyes on them. But one day, and it wouldn't be too long now, she *would* see them. Not only had she worked out a plan, she had begun to put it into action and she was determined it would succeed.

'You look a bit peaky,' Mrs Bates said.

'I'm all right. A bit tired.'

It was an understatement. She was desperately tired. Today she had felt so weak that she had hardly known how to drag herself, not to mention Tommy, pulling at her hand, up the hill to Mount Royd.

'You mustn't come when you feel it's too much for you,' Mrs Bates said kindly. 'Though you're always welcome.'

'Oh I wouldn't stay away unless I had to,' Bessie said. 'And Tommy would be very disappointed not to see his grandma. He likes coming here.'

'And we like having him,' Mrs Bates said. 'Not just me, but Madeleine and Léon. I've seen Léon quite disappointed when you've left before he's got home from the mill.'

'He's always been very good to Tommy,' Bessie acknowledged. 'That's a lovely coat he gave him. It's kept him warm right through the winter.'

Nothing kept her warm. But it would be different in Brighton. She would be warm again there. Even when the wind blew, even when it was so strong that it whipped the sea into great, foam-topped waves, even when it was from the south-west and had nothing of the biting chill of the wind in Helsdon, which blew from the north and felt like it was straight from Iceland.

'Now, Tommy love, what would you like to do?' Mrs Bates asked. 'I've saved you a bit of bread dough. You could make a nice little loaf and take it home for your daddy's supper. Or you could put currants in and make a teacake. Your daddy likes those.'

264

Tommy would miss his grandma when they went to Brighton, Bessie thought. No doubt at all about that. But he'd have his two aunties and three cousins, so he'd soon settle down. She gave no thought as to whether he would miss his father. Irvine didn't come into her scheme of things at all. Anyway, she doubted he thought a lot about Tommy. He didn't talk to him much and practically never played with him like you'd expect a father to. To her mind, he hadn't earned the right to keep Tommy.

As for herself and Irvine, well she considered their marriage was as good as over. He practically never wanted her in bed now, never so much as touched her – not that she cared, it was quite a relief. She reckoned he must be getting his two pennyworth somewhere else. When he went down to the alehouse after the shop closed he must also be visiting some woman. She knew Irvine: he'd not go without.

'And how is Our Irvine?' Mrs Bates enquired. 'I haven't seen him for a while. I expect he's busy in the shop.'

'Not as busy as we'd like,' Bessie said. 'Trade doesn't seem to pick up much.'

'Well perhaps it will in the summer,' Mrs Bates said.

It can do what it likes in the summer, Bessie thought. In the summer me and Tommy will be sitting on the beach in Brighton.

'Do you serve much in the shop, then?' Mrs Bates asked.

'Oh, I do my share. We more or less take it in turn.'

In fact she did more than her share, and from choice. And she mustn't grumble about the door opening as long as it brought a paying customer and she was there behind the counter; for every customer, unknowingly, made a contribution to her flight to Brighton. A copper or two each time, only a small proportion of the sale, found its way into the strong calico pocket fastened around her waist and hidden under her skirt, instead of into the till drawer.

She saw nothing wrong in what she did. She worked as

hard as Irvine, and if he could take his ale money from the drawer, she was entitled to her Brighton money; only he could do it openly and she must do it in secret. She wrapped the coins in a bit of muslin before putting them in the pocket, so they wouldn't jangle when she moved. Even when she went to bed she kept the pocket securely tied to her person. It was getting pleasantly heavy. One day very soon she would go down to Helsdon station and enquire the cost of tickets to Brighton.

'Well pull up to the table,' Mrs Bates said. 'I've made some potato scones.'

'Want to see Claire!' Tommy said when he had eaten his fill of the hot, buttery scones.

'Bless you, so you shall!' his grandmother said.

He followed her out of the room. Bessie immediately helped herself to two more scones and was just swallowing the last morsel when her mother-in-law returned.

'He'll be all right for a bit,' Mrs Bates said. 'He and Claire seem to get on very well – and Flora's always pleased to see him in the nursery.'

'Is Claire walking yet?' Bessie asked.

'Not quite. But I reckon she'll be off before her first birthday. It only wants six weeks. How time does fly!'

An hour later Bessie echoed Mrs Bates's words.

'How time does fly! We must be off!'

'Very well, love. It'd be best to get home afore dark,' Mrs Bates said. 'Will you fetch Tommy from the nursery? I'll be warming his coat.'

She took his coat, held it to the heat of the fire, so that when she put it on him a moment later the lining was warm against his back and arms.

'There!' she said. 'Now that'll keep you cosy. And think on you come and see Grandma next Thursday!'

When Irvine Bates wakened on the following Thursday he was surprised to find Bessie still in the bed beside him. Usually she was up first, had already lit the fire and put the kettle on to boil by the time he surfaced. When they were first married she used to make the tea and bring him a cup, but it was a long time since she'd done that.

'Wake up, Bessie,' he said.

'I am awake.'

She had been awake for hours, in fact she had hardly slept, but Irvine wouldn't know that. As usual, he'd lain like a log from the minute his head touched the pillow, oblivious to her cough, her fierce, burning heat, and then the sweating and the shivering. Her night-dress was soaked with sweat.

'Time for you to get up,' he mumbled. 'I'll just have another ten minutes!'

'I'm not getting up,' Bessie said.

'What? What did you say?'

'I'm not getting up.'

'It's not like you to have a lie-in. We've got to open up the shop, you know.'

'I'm not having a lie-in,' Bessie said. 'I can't get up today. I'm poorly. You'll have to see to things.'

She didn't care whether he saw to things or not. It didn't matter what he did or didn't do – except that she'd like a drink of water.

There was something in her voice, a flatness, a deadness, which cut into Irvine's half-sleep. He raised himself on one elbow and stared down at her. The flush on her cheeks, the brightness of her eyes, he took for health. She looked a damned sight fitter than he felt right now. She was just being more awkward than usual.

'What about Tommy?' he complained. 'He'll be awake any minute. I can't manage Tommy *and* the shop if you're going to lie here in bed.'

'You'll have to,' Bessie said flatly. 'Otherwise you'll have to lock up the shop while you take him to your Ma. That would be best. Tell her I'll not be able to come today. She won't mind looking after Tommy.'

But if Bessie didn't go to Mount Royd, Rose couldn't come here, Irvine thought. Damn it all!

'Happen you'll feel better by dinner-time?' he suggested

hopefully. 'You know how you like going to Mount Royd on a Thursday.'

'Not this Thursday,' Bessie said. 'I shan't be going this Thursday.' Oh, if only he'd get out of the bed and leave her alone, just fetch her a drink of water and then let her be. Grunting and sighing, he heaved himself out of bed, pulled on his trousers and a shirt. He'd have to go to Mount Royd. He'd have to warn Rose. They had an arrangement that she wouldn't leave there until Bessie arrived, but she could be a bit careless, he couldn't trust her not to jump the gun. Oh, damn it to hell!

'I'll take Tommy to Ma, then,' he said reluctantly. 'Are you sure you can't look after the shop while I'm gone?'

'Quite sure. You'll have to lock up.'

'Very well then. I'll go as soon as he wakens. Is there anything you want?'

He asked the question grudgingly. A day in bed was what *he'd* like, but fat chance he'd got!

'Only a cup of water,' Bessie said. 'But see Tommy gets his breakfast.'

When he brought the water she drank it greedily, then lay back on the pillow. She felt so weak, and so very, very tired. If only she could sleep and sleep and sleep! As it was, she lay on her back and thought what it would be like in Brighton.

She was lightheaded, which somehow made her thoughts more vivid, almost as if she was there and it was happening. With her eyes closed against the drabness of the room, she saw the sun sparkling on the water, smelt the salt sea air, felt the short, springy turf under her feet as she walked along the cliff top towards Rottingdean; and then came the change to the hard, round pebbles when she climbed down the chalky path to the beach. There, in a leisurely manner, she dabbled in the rock pools, watching the creatures who lived in them: crabs, sea anemones, other things of which she didn't know the names. Well, it wouldn't be long now. She placed her hand on her money pocket and was comforted by the feel of it.

After that, she *had* slept. She'd heard nothing of Tommy getting up, or of the two of them leaving, though she was sure by the stillness that there was no one else in the building. But she'd wakened with her body on fire and a raging thirst in her throat. She would have to have a drink of water and there was none left in the cup. She called out but there was no answer.

When she got out of bed to fetch a drink, the room spun round, and she clutched at the bedpost to steady herself. She was uncommonly weak. Gradually she made her way to the scullery, drank deep, refilled the cup and started back for the bedroom. She was halfway there when she heard the knocking at the shop door, the impatient rattling of the latch. Should she go down, though she really didn't feel strong enough? She stood at the top of the stairs, wondering.

It was then that the second bout of dizziness came, much worse than the first. She tried to clutch at the banister, and missed it. She felt the first, quick sensation of flying through the air, and then nothing more until – and she didn't know how long after it was – she opened her eyes and found herself lying at the bottom of the stairs. In those few seconds she wasn't aware of any pain. There was more knocking at the shop door, and she knew she ought to answer it, but when she tried to call out, no sound came. Very soon after, either the knocking ceased, or Bessie ceased to hear it.

Mrs Bates was in the kitchen when Irvine arrived with Tommy.

'Of course I'll be glad to have him,' she said. 'In fact it might be best if he stayed the night, then Bessie can have a good rest. She hasn't been looking too well lately.'

She turned to Tommy.

'You can sleep in Grandma's bed tonight! You'll like that, won't you?'

'Want to see Claire,' Tommy said.

'What, already? Well come along then. We'll go and see what Flora says to that.'

'It's all washed up for today, Rose of Tralee,' Irvine said when his mother had left the kitchen. 'Here, give me a kiss to keep me going! Quick, before she gets back!' He grabbed Rose and kissed her hungrily.

'Eh, stop it!' she cried. 'What if your Ma walks in on us?'

He let her go.

'So when am I going to see you?' he demanded. 'I can't wait until next Thursday.'

'Looks like you'll have to,' Rose said. 'Unless. . .'

'What?'

'I'll tell your Ma I'll not take time off today. I'll very nobly stay and help her with Tommy. That'll leave me a couple of hours in hand for another day.'

'Clever girl! And the minute Bessie's on her feet again, I'll see she comes up here.'

'Well, he's set up for the moment,' Mrs Bates said, coming back into the kitchen.

'I've just been saying to your Irvine, I'll not take my time off this afternoon,' Rose said. 'I'll stay and help you with Tommy.'

Mrs Bates looked at Rose in astonishment. Everyone knew that Rose didn't actually like children. On the occasions when Tommy was there she ignored him, unless he put a foot wrong, and then she was sharp with him.

'Well I never!' she said.

'I could take him for a walk, if it's fine later on,' Rose offered. It would be slightly less boring than working in the kitchen on baking day; greasing tins, washing messy dishes.

Wonders never cease, Mrs Bates thought.

'Right, well I'll be off,' Irvine said. 'I'll let you know how Bessie gets on.'

'You do that,' his mother said. 'And if you think she ought to have the doctor, well then, call him.'

'Oh I don't think there'll be any need for that, Ma,' Irvine replied.

He unlocked the shop door and let himself in. Because he'd not stopped to raise the blind before he left for Mount Royd, it was dark. This he now did, before walking through to the back of the shop, but there was never much light at the bottom of the stairs and he almost fell over Bessie's body.

Though her face was hidden, he knew at once that she was dead; it was something in the way she was lying, the angles of her limbs. Holding his breath, he bent down and touched her with one finger, turning her head to look at her face. It was curiously peaceful, all fatigue vanished.

He had seen death in the Crimea; death from wounds, death from fever, death from the cruel frosts. There, he had seen it so often that he had ceased to be afraid of it – but now he was terrified. He sprang to his feet and rushed out of the shop, shouting.

The day of the funeral was everything Bessie would have disliked most. Snow showers fell from a leaden sky and were blown into flurries by a cruel wind which seemed to come from every direction at once, and to find every inch of unprotected flesh, chilling the spaces between collar and hat, between glove and wrist, stinging the faces of the mourners.

Not that there were many mourners. It was too far for Bessie's sisters to journey from Brighton. The weather was considered too inclement for Penelope and there was no question of Emerald attending her sister-in-law's funeral. She hardly knew her and, besides, Mrs Chester was far too busy to let her go.

It was a cheap funeral, too – though in the end, even then, Madeleine had to pay the bills, since Irvine confessed that he had failed to keep up the burial club payments. Full of sympathy though she was in every other particular, Mrs Bates found that difficult to forgive. You paid your burial club no matter what else went short, otherwise it was that last and worst disgrace of all, a pauper's funeral.

It was a relief to all when the clergyman hurried through the final prayer and they were free to leave the graveyard.

'You'll come back with us, Irvine?' Madeleine asked. 'Have something to eat?'

'Very well,' Irvine said. 'But I'll not stop long. I ought to open up the shop again.'

'Nay, you'll not be expected to open on the day of your wife's funeral!' Mrs Bates remonstrated. 'In fact it hardly looks respectful.'

'I mean no disrespect,' Irvine said.

Poor lad, he looks distraught, his mother thought, tucking her arm through his as they walked along. It had been a terrible shock to all of them – and him finding her like that, and rushing out into the street and running all the way back to Mount Royd.

'Of course, love! Of course,' she said. 'And you'll find you'll feel better, more able to face things, once the burial's over.'

He didn't know that he would ever face it. Why had Bessie done this? Why had she left him to fend for himself? How was he going to look after Tommy?

'Now don't forget,' Madeleine said when they were back at the house, and he'd been given a warming drink of brandy by Léon, 'Tommy can stay with us for a while, until you get settled.'

'He is no trouble,' Léon said. 'Indeed, he is company for Claire. He can share her room. So take him back only when you are ready, and not before.'

'He'll be better here for a bit,' Irvine admitted. 'I'm not good company for a little 'un at the moment.'

When Irvine was ready to leave, Mrs Bates went into the kitchen with him and handed him a basket.

'A few bits to help out,' she said. 'There's potted beef I made yesterday, and a custard tart and so on. You've got to keep up your strength.'

272

'That's right,' Rose agreed.

Irvine seemed to have gone off her since his wife's death. She couldn't think why. It had all been very unfortunate, quite shocking in fact, but none of it was her fault, was it? Or even his.

Back home, Irvine drew up the blinds and opened up the shop. There were no customers, so in the end he locked the door again, poured himself a pint of porter, and when he'd drunk it, poured another. He was steeling himself to do the job he dreaded most, to sort out Bessie's few possessions. He poured a third pint and took it upstairs with him.

She hadn't had a lot. There was a brooch he'd given her when they were courting, and a string of beads she'd won at a fair in Brighton. What puzzled him most – he found it on a chair where the undertaker's lady had presumably put it – was a calico pocket with money in it.

He tipped the contents out on to the table, unwrapped the coins and counted them. Nineteen shillings and sevenpence. Where had she got it? What was she saving it for? He couldn't imagine, and he'd never know now. He scooped the coins up and put them in his trouser pockets. Poor Bessie!

On Thursday afternoon, a week to the day since Bessie had fallen down the stairs, the shop bell rang, the door opened and Rose Hardy walked in.

'I've come to cheer you up!' she said.

He stared at her.

'Don't look so surprised,' Rose said. 'You didn't think I'd desert you, did you?'

'But Rosie. . .'

It was so soon after Bessie's death, only a week. It didn't seem . . . well . . . quite right. But he was pleased to see her. It had been a lonely week; he hadn't had the heart even to go and see his mother and Tommy.

'Well,' Rose said. 'What about locking the door and inviting me upstairs for a bit. I don't want to stand in the shop and you don't seem to be swarming with customers.'

273

Without waiting for Irvine's reply, she shot the bolt across the shop door, then walked past him through the shop and up the stairs. Irvine followed.

'What you need,' Rose said, making straight for the bedroom, 'is what I can give you! Right here and now!'

She pushed him down on the bed, took off his jacket, undid his waistcoat buttons, slipped his braces off his shoulders, started on his collar.

'I'm not sure. . .' Irvine began. It was his only resistance.

'I am,' Rose said. 'It's just what you need – and I most certainly do!'

In the event, she was right. When it was over he felt tons better, more of a man again. She was a wonder, Rosie was. They dressed, and went through into the living-room.

'All the same, Rose of Sharon,' he said, 'I don't see how we can go on like this, me locking the shop every Thursday afternoon.'

And life wasn't just Thursday afternoons, was it? There were all the other times. He'd never have thought he'd have missed Bessie so much. Only a week without her and the whole place was looking dirty and dingy, a real mess. Also, he'd hardly eaten a thing.

'Why can't you?' Rose demanded. 'I haven't heard anyone rattling the shop door in the last hour – though I admit I've had my mind on other things!'

'I don't suppose there *was* anyone,' Irvine admitted gloomily. 'Thursday is the worst day of the week. The day before pay day; nobody has enough left for a penny candle!'

'I'll tell you what,' Rose said, looking around, 'it's a right old mess in here! I doubt you've washed a pot in the last week.'

'It needs a woman's touch,' Irvine said. There was a pleading note in his voice.

'It needs a wife's touch,' she said.

'It's not a man's job,' Irvine complained. 'In fact, I don't think running a shop is a man's job, not a job for a *young*

274

man. I have to say, I don't think I'm much good at it – and that's because I'm not interested, Rose.'

'And what do you reckon you are good at?' Rose asked. 'Well, we both know one thing you're good at, *and* interested in,' she added with a wink. 'But that won't put bread in your mouth, more's the pity.'

'I've been thinking a lot this last week,' Irvine confessed. 'Do you know what I've been thinking I'd like to do?'

'No.'

'Well go on, have a guess!'

'I don't like guessing games,' Rose said. 'You tell me.'

'I've been thinking I'd like to emigrate. . .'

'*Emigrate*?'

'To Canada!'

'I don't believe it!'

'And why not? There'd be more for me there than in this country. I could live a man's life there. There's farming – I could have my own land in no time. And there's gold. If you go west, there's gold!'

'Well you do come up with some surprises, Irvine Bates! But perhaps you're right,' Rose added thoughtfully. 'We might do very well in Canada.'

'*We*?'

'Now you weren't thinking of leaving me behind, were you?'

'Well, I . . . I don't know what to say! Except that I'm not the only one to come up with surprises.'

'If I were your wife,' Rose said, 'I'd be able to look after you in every way. In *every* way!'

'It might be a hard life – just at first, anyway,' Irvine said. 'Almost certainly it would be.'

'I know. I daresay I could stand that, with the right person. At least we could expect it to get better.'

Anything, she thought, was better than being a skivvy for the rest of her life. Irvine Bates wasn't a bad sort. Nobody could say he wasn't good-looking, and he could be quite exciting in some ways. It just needed the right woman to bring him out. And if he was the means of getting her to Canada – which she'd heard was a land full of opportunities and with an abundance of men and a shortage of women – well, that was a start, wasn't it?

'You mean you wouldn't mind roughing it?' Irvine said.

'Course I wouldn't. Not to begin with, anyway.'

'And you'd be a mother to Tommy,' he mused. 'Tommy's going to need a mother.'

Rose frowned. She'd completely forgotten Tommy.

'I hadn't thought. . .' she began. 'I reckon I'm not really cut out to be a mother, not unless it was to my own kids, in the fullness of time of course.' If ever, she thought.

'But I couldn't leave Tommy,' Irvine protested.

'Well, that's a pity,' Rose said. 'We'd have travelled faster and got further, just the two of us – and it's probably no life for a little lad of four. Still, it was a nice idea – while it lasted.'

'Wait a minute,' Irvine cried. 'Don't be so hasty. If I decided to leave Tommy – not that I could permanently, but just till I got settled – where would I leave him?'

'That's a silly question,' Rose said. 'Why, with your Ma of course.'

Irvine sighed.

'It would kill Ma, me emigrating.'

'People don't die that easy, love. True, your Ma thinks a lot of you, but she's tough. And if you were to leave Tommy it would make up for a lot. You know how fond they are of each other.'

'That's true.'

'Still, I'll say no more for now. And I'll be off.' She fastened her cloak, tied her bonnet strings. 'You think about it, love. Only don't think about it too long. Who knows, somebody else might come along and pick your Rose!' They might at that, she thought, though she'd seen no one on the horizon.

She gave him a long and loving kiss, and departed.

It won't be easy to leave her, Irvine thought.

276

FIFTEEN

Irvine twisted a piece of paper into a 'poke' and tipped in the two ounces of tea from the scales. His customers were mostly poor and tea was expensive. Every brewing would have to be left in the teapot and used again and again until there was no strength left in it.

'There you are, Mrs Holmes! Will there be anything else?'

The woman looked with longing around the well-filled shelves, for Irvine, since taking over the business, had made it his first priority to build up the stock.

'No lad, that's it!' she said reluctantly. She'd have liked to have filled her basket.

'Very well.'

He pushed the tea across the counter. He felt sorry for Mrs Holmes, and all the others like her – but how could he ever make a living selling two ounces of tea, a pint of vinegar, a pound of treacle? He couldn't, and that was the long and short of it.

In the last few days, since Rose had paid her visit, he'd thought more and more about emigrating. What had he to lose? Yet the answer was plain. If he didn't lose Tommy, then he might have to lose Rose. He'd known by the tone of her voice that Rose was serious about not wanting Tommy, and he was well aware that the two of them didn't get on. Rose was not a maternal woman.

He, who usually fell asleep quickly and slept all night, was now regularly awake in the small hours, weighing and sifting, tossing and turning. But when he'd wakened this morning, he'd been immediately filled with determination; quite sure of himself. Canada was it. Who he took with him – Tommy or Rose – he'd decide pretty soon: but go to Canada he would.

It was also high time that he went to see his mother. If he didn't go soon, she'd surely be down here, and though he'd have liked her help in cleaning up the house, which got worse every day, he was inexplicably ashamed at the thought of her seeing it.

He'd not mention Canada to his mother yet. Time enough when everything was cut and dried. He'd see Tommy, he might manage a word with Rose. So he'd not wait any longer, he'd go today. He'd close the shop about six, be there in time to see Tommy before he went to bed.

'I'm glad you've come, love,' Mrs Bates said when he walked in. 'In fact if you hadn't turned up today, I was coming down. How are you?'

'All right, Ma. A bit in the dumps, as you might expect. How's Tommy?'

'Tommy seems fine. I don't think he realizes what's happened – which is just as well, the poor lamb!'

'Where is he, then?'

'In the nursery with Claire,' Mrs Bates said. 'He spends a lot of time there. They've really taken to each other, those two, in spite of the difference in their ages.'

'Can I go and see him?' Irvine asked.

'What a question, lad! Of course you can!'

Irvine, following his mother out of the kitchen, sidled past Rose, stroking his fingers across her shoulders as he went. She gave a small, answering wriggle of pleasure.

In the nursery Tommy and Claire were sitting on the floor, Tommy building wooden bricks into a pile which Claire, with shouts of glee, immediately knocked down again. Flora Bryant sat at the table, mending. Neither child looked up as Mrs Bates and Irvine came in.

'Here's your daddy come to see you!' Mrs Bates said brightly.

'Hello Tommy!' Irvine said.

Tommy, his tongue sticking out between his teeth in concentration, began building up the bricks again.

'Say ''hello'' to your daddy,' Flora urged.

Tommy looked up at Irvine.

'Where's Mammy?' he demanded.

'Like I told you,' Mrs Bates said hastily, 'Mammy's gone away for a bit.'

'I thought you might like to come home with me, Tommy,' Irvine suggested. 'Would you like that? I'd play with you. Or you could help in the shop; you could weigh things.'

'No,' Tommy said firmly. 'Want Mammy to come here. She's gone to Brighton. Mammy said she'd take Tommy to Brighton. On a puffer.'

'He keeps saying that,' Mrs Bates said. 'I don't know what he means.'

'Some tale Bessie used to tell him, I expect,' Irvine said.

'Then you'll not come home with me, Tommy?' Irvine asked.

'No. Mammy come here.' Tommy didn't look up; he was busy with the bricks.

Irvine shrugged his shoulders. He was upset by Tommy's attitude, though he wouldn't show it.

'I'm ever so sorry, Mr Bates,' Flora said. 'He gets caught up in his games with Claire. He's so good with her, looks after her lovely.'

'I can see he's happy enough,' Irvine acknowledged.

He turned to his mother.

'Is Madeleine in?'

'Yes. Léon isn't back yet, but I'm sure Madeleine won't want to miss you.'

'I'll be with you later then, Ma,' Irvine said.

'There's something I want to talk to you about, Maddy,' Irvine said the minute the preliminaries were over between them. 'But I'd rather you didn't tell Ma, not just yet.'

It was immediately clear to Madeleine that her brother wasn't his usual, jaunty self, but it was early days yet. Bessie's death had left them all feeling stunned. She herself had worried that she hadn't ever done much for her sister-in-law, had been so busy that she'd hardly taken any notice of her, though common sense told her that her attitude couldn't have made any difference to Bessie's end. But Irvine clearly had something more on his mind.

'What is it?' she asked.

'I want to emigrate, Maddy. What's more, I mean to do so!'

'*Emigrate*?'

'To Canada.'

'Irvine, you can't mean it! You're not serious!' Madeleine cried. 'I know you must feel terrible, I understand that, we all do. . .'

'I'm serious all right,' Irvine interrupted.

Madeleine fell silent, looked at her brother closely. His mouth was tight, his eyes hard, in dark-ringed sockets. He looked older than his twenty-six years. Filled with a rush of pity for him, she leaned forward, touched him gently.

'I do believe you are, love. But I'm equally sure you're being too hasty. Things won't always seem so bad. You'll feel better as time goes on.'

'I daresay. But I'll not change my mind. I've given it a lot of thought. I've thought about it for hours and days. Maddy, I know it's what I want to do.'

Yes, it would be, Madeleine thought sadly. The decision was typical of Irvine; it followed the usual pattern of his life. At sixteen he'd left home because he couldn't face inhabiting the same house as his father; after that he'd left the army as soon as he could get release; then when the job with Henry Garston didn't work out he'd quitted that. Now he was about to do the same thing again. Irvine would always run away.

'If it's what you want to do,' she admitted reluctantly, 'I suppose you'll do it. But I can't say I agree with you, and I'm not surprised you don't want to tell Ma, though you can't get out of it in the end.'

'I thought it would be best not to tell her until everything was decided.'

'But Irvine, what will you *do* in Canada?' Madeleine asked. 'How will you live?'

'I'll be all right,' Irvine said. 'It's a big country, Canada. There'll be plenty of ways of earning a living. I'm young enough, and strong.'

He was jaunty again, he sounded so sure. But that was typical, too, Madeleine thought. He was always brimful of confidence at the start of something new.

'But what about Tommy?' she asked. 'How will you manage with Tommy? In fact, have you thought at all whether it will be good for Tommy?'

'Of course I have!' Irvine snapped. 'I've thought about it a lot, and the truth is, I don't know. That's one of the things I want to talk to you about.'

In the nursery, sensing Tommy's lack of feeling for him, he'd made up his mind in an instant. If he *had* to choose between Rose and Tommy, though he still hoped it might not come to that, then he'd choose Rose. But he could only do that with Madeleine's help, and it was too soon to tell her about Rose.

'I want to ask you a big favour, Maddy,' he said. 'If it seems to me that it might be best not to take Tommy to begin with, then would it be possible to leave him with you, just till I get settled? Say for a year?'

Madeleine stared at him in disbelief. How could he bear to be parted from his son, and so soon after losing his wife? She could never consent to be parted from Claire. Never! And if she had a son...

'To tell you the truth,' Irvine went on, 'I think he'd miss Ma, and you, more than he'd ever miss me. He's always been a mother's boy, really. He'll not miss me like he would Bessie, and you'd be the most comfort to him there.'

'You may be right. I'm not sure,' Madeleine said thoughtfully. 'I think we could look after him, but naturally I'll have to ask Léon. I don't suppose there'll be any difficulty there. Léon is very fond of Tommy. But I must ask him.'

'I understand.'

'Oh Irvine, don't you reckon you should think it over a bit longer, about going at all?' Madeleine pleaded. 'Give yourself more time.'

Irvine shook his head.

'I've thought about it all I need. I've made up my mind. What I want to do now is get on with it.'

'Very well,' Madeleine said. 'I'll speak to Léon this evening and I'll call in at the shop before I go to the mill. That way Ma won't know before she has to.'

'I'm grateful,' Irvine said. 'And there is one other thing. I don't quite know how to say it. . .'

'You're not usually stuck for words,' Madeleine said. 'So what is it?'

'I'm well aware that I still owe you money,' Irvine began, 'but my only way of raising the passage money and a little bit to keep me going – though heaven knows there'll not be much left over for that – is to realize on the shop. The stock's good, and I can get a bit back on the rent if I do it quickly, since it's paid in advance – but by rights that money's yours.'

'That's the least of my worries,' Madeleine said. 'It needn't worry you.'

'I *will* pay it back in the end,' Irvine assured her. 'Once I've got settled, started earning, I'll be able to send something to you. And for Tommy's keep also.'

He'd had it in mind to ask her for a further loan, to help set him up when he got to Canada, but perhaps he'd best wait a bit.

'I'll be off then,' he said. 'I'll just see Ma before I go. Thanks again, Maddy. You're a real sport!'

'Well there's just one condition on my side!' Madeleine said. 'I reckon the minute it's settled – about Tommy I mean – you must tell Ma. We can't all conspire to keep her in the dark. It wouldn't be fair and she'd never forgive us. It's going to be a bitter blow for Ma.'

'But less so if Tommy stays,' Irvine pointed out. But what he wouldn't tell his Ma or anyone else about, except the lady herself, was Rose. That he'd keep to the last. There'd be an almighty fuss, and the less time for it the better.

Returning to the kitchen he was pleased to find Rose on her own.

'Everything's going to be all right,' he said. 'You, me and Canada, I mean. But I've got to see you, we've got to make plans. Will you come on Thursday?'

Rose treated him to a provocative smile.

'I might!' she said.

'You'd better,' he warned. 'This is no time to play games!'

'Ooh! Aren't you masterful! All right then, I will!'

'And in the meantime, not a word!'

'I'm not daft!' Rose said.

He went in search of his mother, found her in her own room.

'I'm just off, Ma!'

'You'll surely have a bite to eat before you go,' Mrs Bates offered. 'There's a nice bit of cold beef and some pickles.'

'No thanks, Ma. I'd best be off.' He knew he couldn't bear to sit at the table, knowing what he knew, while his mother remained in blissful ignorance.

Madeleine could hardly wait to break the news to Léon, but wait she did, until they were sitting in the drawing-room, after supper. Léon was reading and Madeleine ostensibly working at her French.

'Irvine was here today,' she said.

'How was he?'

'Not quite himself. He came partly to see Tommy, to suggest taking him home again, and it seems Tommy didn't want to go. He didn't want to leave Claire, so I hear.'

'Well, much as we enjoy having him, we mustn't try to keep Tommy here once his father wants him back,' Léon said. 'It wouldn't be right.'

'Of course not. And that's what I have to tell you, Léon. You see – and I'm not sure you're going to believe this – Irvine wants to emigrate. He wants to go to Canada, and what's more, he's determined to do so. But more than that, he wants to leave Tommy with us. Oh Léon, do say he can! I mean leave Tommy.'

Léon held up a hand to stop the torrent of words.

'Wait a minute! Wait! You mean your brother is seriously thinking of emigrating? And he'll give up his son to do so?'

'Oh no!' Madeleine said. 'He would leave Tommy with us just for a while, until he'd got things sorted out in Canada. Perhaps a year – I don't know.'

'And how would he get Tommy to Canada at the end of that time?'

'I hadn't thought,' Madeleine confessed. 'We didn't go into that. I have the feeling that Irvine isn't sure himself what he'd do.'

'It seems to me that Irvine is more than ready to abandon Tommy, whereas the child should be his first and greatest concern.' Léon's voice was passionate with disapproval.

'I think perhaps you're judging him harshly,' Madeleine said.

But is he, she wondered? She hadn't been at all satisfied with her brother's too casual arrangements about Tommy.

'I'm not sure that he quite knows what he *is* doing,' she said. 'It's no time at all since Bessie died. I told him he shouldn't be making such decisions just yet, but there's no changing his mind. I'm sure he'll go, and if we don't say we'll look after Tommy, then he'll take him with him. I don't think that would be a good idea, do you? So please say he can stay with us, Léon!'

'Of course he can, you silly goose! There's no question of that. In fact the best thing for Tommy would be for him to stay with us permanently!'

The words rushed out of him without the slightest premeditation. He broke off suddenly, stunned by his own thoughts. He and Madeleine stared at one another.

'You mean . . . ?'

'I think what I mean,' Léon said slowly, 'is that perhaps we should offer to adopt Tommy. If I'm right, and Irvine doesn't want to be bothered with his little son, then it would be better all round if we gave him a real home with us.'

'Oh Léon! Léon, do you really think . . . ?'

'You like the child, don't you?' he demanded. 'You're quite sure about that?'

'Oh Léon, of course I do! Like him? Why, I love Tommy! I really and truly love him!'

'And so do I,' Léon said soberly.

How many times had he looked at Tommy and wished that by some miracle he could have such a son? And now perhaps that miracle could happen.

'And I'm sure he loves us,' Madeleine said eagerly. 'He's much warmer towards you than he ever was towards Irvine, though I know that's a sad thing to say. And there's no doubt he adores Claire.' She paused. 'Léon. . .'

'Yes?'

'I know we don't ever mention it now – but perhaps Tommy could be the son we thought we could never have.'

'We will speak with Irvine,' Léon said gruffly.

In his state of emotion his accent became so much more French. Whenever he was deeply moved he felt the English language almost deserting him. Madeleine recognized such a moment now.

'The sooner the better,' she said. 'Shall I get him to come here tomorrow evening?'

Léon nodded.

'I promised to go down to the shop before I went to the mill in the morning,' she went on. 'He was anxious to know whether we'd look after Tommy.'

'*Très bien*! But tell him that in any case, if he eventually wants Tommy in Canada, we will care for him until then. We cannot take a man's son away from him if he does not want it, so don't build up your hopes,

Madeleine. And do not take a quick answer of any kind in the morning. Ask Irvine to come here in the evening.'

'Oh Léon!' Madeleine said. 'I'm already praying for what I want him to say! I know I shouldn't, but I am!'

'Come here, my love!'

She went across to him and he put his arms around her.

'No, you shouldn't,' he agreed. 'Nor should I. We can hope – but we must be prepared to be disappointed. A man's tie with his son is very close.'

Irvine walked home with a lighter step. The worst, for him, was over – the task of telling Madeleine and getting her to agree that he could borrow what proceeds there were from the shop. The question of further money he'd need to consider. Perhaps Rose has a bit tucked away, he thought? Who knows?

As for Tommy, well that seemed to be working out. He was sure Léon would let him stay at Mount Royd for a year, and after that he'd see how the land lay. It would certainly be better all round for the lad to stay with his aunt and uncle, and grandma, until things were more settled.

So, after he'd seen Rosie on Thursday, made sure that she was coming with him, he'd set about selling the shop and booking passages. The sooner it all happened, the better.

With his spirits raised, he felt more able to tackle the mess in the upstairs rooms. It took him until midnight, but when he crawled into bed he fell asleep at once and slept until morning.

He was in the shop when Madeleine arrived.

'Will you come upstairs?' he asked her. 'I can lock the shop door.'

'No thanks,' Madeleine said. 'I'm in a hurry, a busy day ahead.' Now that she was here, she felt horribly nervous, didn't know how to begin.

'Did you speak to Léon?' Irvine asked.

'Yes.'

'What did he say?'

Why was she looking so worried? Was it possible that Léon had refused? If he had, if he'd got to take Tommy with him, it was ten to one Rose wouldn't go. In the seconds before Madeleine replied, Irvine saw his plans crashing to the ground.

'He said. . . Oh Irvine, I don't know how to say it! It seemed so easy last night, and now it isn't at all!'

'Oh come on, Maddy!' Irvine said harshly. 'Spit it out!'

'Very well,' Madeleine said. 'What I have to tell you is that Léon and I would like to adopt Tommy. It isn't. . .'

'Adopt him? You mean for good and all?'

'Yes. Bring him up as ours. Oh Irvine, we love him already as if he were ours, we'd care for him, we'd give him a good life!'

'Adopt him?' Irvine was bemused. Such a possibility had never entered his head. 'What can I say? I don't know what to say. It's a bombshell, Maddy!'

'I know,' Madeleine said quietly. 'I'm sorry. I couldn't think of any less sudden way of putting it. But Léon said I was particularly to tell you two things.'

'And what are they?'

'That whatever you decide about *that*, we'll still keep Tommy for a year, or however long you want – and that he'd rather you didn't make any decision here and now. Will you think it over, Léon says, and come to see us both this evening?'

'You mean you expect me to decide by tonight?'

'Not necessarily,' Madeleine said. 'But we can talk about it then, can't we?'

It seemed an age before Irvine answered.

'All right,' he said at last. 'But only to talk about it, mind.' Thoughts were whirling around in his head. He'd never felt quite like this before.

He had to see Rose. Somehow he had to see her today.

In the end she saved him the bother of deciding how, by walking into the shop as bold as brass.

'What are you doing here?' he demanded. 'It's not Thursday.'

'I'm a real customer,' Rose said. 'Your Ma needs some nutmegs. She can't make a rice pudding without a sprinkling of nutmeg, and hers have unaccountably disappeared. I wonder where they could have got to?' She looked at Irvine wide-eyed, then winked.

He shook his head.

'You are a wicked woman, Rose Without a Thorn,' he said.

'I wanted to know what was happening. You were a fair long time with your sister last night and you didn't say much about it.'

'I told you it was going to be all right. I couldn't say more, not with Ma coming back into the kitchen.'

'So?'

Before he could answer, a customer came into the shop. She took a very long time to buy half a pound of currants and a piece of cheese. Irvine could see Rose growing impatient.

'I'll lock the door, pin a note on it,' he said when the customer, at long last, departed.

He took a piece of wrapping paper and began to write a message. 'Back . . . in. . .'

He looked up. 'Back in half an hour?'

'Certainly not,' Rose said. 'We've no time for that sort of thing today. Your Ma'll skin me alive if I'm not back soon!'

'All right,' Irvine said. 'I'll put "back in ten minutes".'

They went upstairs. He took her in his arms and they kissed long and passionately, then she pushed him away.

'That's quite enough of that! Now tell me what's happening.'

'I've told you,' Irvine said. 'We're going to Canada.'

'You mean *you're* going. Speak for yourself!'

'I mean you are if you want to. Madeleine has agreed to let me have what I get from the shop. It'll pay the passages and maybe a bit left over. It's very generous of her.'

Rose sniffed.

'She's got plenty more where that comes from!'

'Even so, she didn't have to do it. I reckon it's pretty decent.'

'And what about young Tommy? Where does he fit in?' Her voice was flat, her face wary.

'That's what we have to decide,' Irvine said. 'First choice, we could take him. . .'

Rose shook her head.

'Not possible! Not fair either to us or to him.' She knew who'd be lumbered with looking after Tommy, and it wouldn't be Irvine Bates.

'Second choice, I could leave him here for a year or so, till we got settled. Then I'd have to find some way of getting him out to Canada, or come back for him.'

'And the third choice?' She could tell there was more to come.

'Third choice has only just been made to me. Madeleine and Léon want to adopt him.'

'That's the one!' Rose said quickly. 'Absolutely the best, all the way round! Best for Tommy, best for you and me. Come to think of it, best for your poor old Ma, too!'

'Well I'm sure I don't know,' Irvine said hesitantly. 'I have to go and see them about it tonight. I'm not sure what I'll do.'

'I told you,' Rose said. 'Take the offer. Much the best thing for Tommy. Good home, good education, no roughing it like he might have to do in Canada. And there's another thing. . .'

'What?'

'Have you not thought that if you're letting them have your lad, they'll want to compensate you? They'll want to see you get a fair deal. It needn't be only the money from the shop. I daresay you'll get quite a fair whack, if you play your cards right.'

'I hadn't thought of that,' Irvine admitted.

'Then it's as well you have me to think for you,' Rose told him. 'Anyway, I have to be off. I'll see you tomorrow, being Thursday, and think on you to do the right thing! The right thing by all of us.'

He thought about it all day. It came between him and his customers, so that he kept giving them the wrong goods or the wrong change.

'Poor lad!' one woman said to another. 'He's fretting for his wife!'

Rose was right, he reckoned. To let Tommy be adopted was the sensible thing to do, though she didn't take account of his feelings as a father. Somehow they were stronger now than they'd ever been in Tommy's four years. But also he had the notion that Rose might not be so keen to go to Canada, might even refuse outright, if he didn't take the chance of leaving Tommy behind.

When he thought of the money which Rose seemed so certain Léon would offer him, he felt guilty, almost as though he'd be selling Tommy: yet he needed the money, he needed it badly.

But in the end, when evening came and he set off for Mount Royd, he'd made up his mind. He'd put things plainly.

'So have you thought about it?' Léon said.

'All day long,' Irvine admitted. 'It's a big step, to let your only son go.'

'Of course,' Léon acknowledged. 'I do realize that.'

'We'd take great care of him,' Madeleine said quickly. She was standing beside Léon, clasping his hand. 'He'd be loved and looked after as our very own. And he'd want for nothing.'

'I know,' Irvine said. 'But there's more to it than that, isn't there?'

'What do you mean?' Madeleine asked.

'Well first off, there's a father's feelings. And then. . .'

'What then?' Madeleine persisted.

'Well then, there's the practical point of view. He won't always be a little 'un, will he? Before we know where we are, Tommy'll be grown. Likely he'll be a big strong lad, ready to be a help to his father. In places like Canada, children are an insurance against the future!'

Léon felt the anger surge in him. This man was putting a price on his son's head! What sort of a man would do that? From this moment, Léon thought, I stop being sorry for him. I now think of us and I think of Tommy; especially of Tommy.

'I presume we are talking now of money?' he said. His voice was like steel.

Madeleine recognized his seething anger, and put a restraining hand on his arm.

'What sum do you have in mind?' Léon continued. His voice was as chilly as a winter wind.

Irvine's look was direct.

'Five hundred pounds.'

He heard Madeleine's gasp and wondered if he had pitched it too high. Well, he could always come down if he had to.

'You shall have it,' Léon said. 'I think you are aware it is a lot of money; on the other hand if I had a son I would not let him go for five million pounds.'

The contempt in his voice stung Irvine like a whiplash. If it wasn't for the thought of Rose, he'd fling back the offer in the Frenchman's face.

'No,' he said. 'I don't suppose you would. I don't suppose you'd ever need to. Some of us are born rich and some of us are born poor, and I reckon neither lot knows how the other feels!'

'The adoption must be entirely legal,' Léon said. 'I will see Mr Ormeroyd tomorrow and start the process. When the final papers are signed, I will hand over five hundred pounds.'

'I'll need something before then,' Irvine said boldly. 'I've got to book passages, get a few things together.'

'Passages?' Madeleine queried. 'More than one?'

'Two,' Irvine said. 'You may as well know now as later, I'm taking Rose Hardy with me. And I'd rather you didn't give Ma that bit of news just yet. I'll tell her myself in a day or two.' He'd given it away, damn it, but perhaps no harm done.

He wanted no slip-ups now. He still had to get the final say from Rose, but with five hundred pounds to come, he thought there'd be no difficulty about that.

'Rose Hardy! I really can't believe it,' Madeleine cried. 'With poor Bessie. . .'

'Lay off me!' Irvine shouted. 'I'll marry who I like and when I like! I can't exactly do a year's mourning, leave Rose behind, if I'm going off to Canada. And that I shall be doing the minute I lay hands on what's due to me.'

'You can be quite sure I shall have the papers ready for signing as quickly as ever I can,' Léon said. He was trying to be civil for Madeleine's sake, but he wished Irvine would go. He had never liked him, but now his dislike was intensified.

'Then I'll be off,' Irvine said.

'I do think perhaps you were a little hard on him, dearest,' Madeleine said when Irvine had left.

'I don't think so, Madeleine. I would have offered him the money even if he had never mentioned it. I had it in mind to do so all along. But a man who will sell his son. . .'

'Soon to be our son,' Madeleine said gently. 'It might be better to remind ourselves of that!'

Léon looked at her.

'Yes, you are right,' he conceded. 'I will try to do that. But I hope not to see too much of your brother between now and the day he sails.'

The next day, being a Thursday, Rose was at the shop by half-past two in the afternoon. With no more than a word of greeting, Irvine locked the shop door before they hurried upstairs. But when he took her in his arms, attempted to kiss her, she pushed him away.

'Not yet! I want to know what happened. What did you say? What did *they* say?' Her voice was sharp with eagerness, excitement. He was overwhelmingly glad that he didn't have to report failure.

292

'Everything's going to be all right, Rose of my heart! It's all going to happen!'

'What about Tommy? What did you decide about him?' The news had better be good. *She* had decided that there was no way she was going to be encumbered by someone else's kid, no way at all.

'I agreed. . .' Irvine faltered for the first and last time: then he pulled himself together and spoke firmly. 'I agreed that they should adopt him.'

'And the arrangements? What arrangements did you make?'

'You mean the money?'

'Of course I mean the money! What else? Don't tell me you did nothing!'

'I won't then. I asked for five hundred pounds, and that's what Léon will pay me when the papers are signed.'

Rose looked thoughtful.

'I daresay you could have got more.' Then her face brightened. 'But never mind, love. There'll be other opportunities. Letters and money can cross the ocean quite successfully.'

'I hadn't thought in terms of asking for more,' Irvine protested. 'Five hundred pounds is a lot of money.'

'Well we'll see. We're going to need a lot of money.'

'Does that mean you're definitely coming with me?' Irvine asked. 'Please say you are, Rose. I've done most of this for your sake.'

Left to himself, he thought, if he hadn't been so keen on Rose, he'd just have upped sticks and gone, left Tommy with Madeleine and Léon and never mind the brass.

'Of course I'm coming with you,' she assured him. 'Just one condition, that's all.'

'And what's that?'

'That you marry me before we set sail. In fact, I'll not sail if you don't!'

'Oh Rose!' he cried. 'You know I'll marry you. I've

already told Madeleine, and the minute I've told Ma, we'll be wed. After that you can come and live here, over the shop, until it's time to go – which I hope won't be long.'

'Right then!' A smile of satisfaction lit up Rose's pretty face. 'So why don't we have a bit of practice for married life – that is if you can keep the shop closed for a bit longer?'

'Bugger the shop!' Irvine said.

She was already halfway to the bedroom, taking off her clothes as she went. He followed her, doing likewise.

Much later, they dressed again.

'I could do with a cup of tea,' Rose said. 'Funny how it always makes me thirsty.'

'You shall have one,' Irvine said.

They drank the tea, and when Rose was putting on her bonnet Irvine said, 'I'm coming up to tell Ma tonight. There's no point in keeping it back, now that we've made up our minds.'

'She'll not like it,' Rose said.

'I know. But at least she'll have a few weeks to get used to it before I go.'

'I'll be out,' Rose decided. 'I'll go to Bradford, see my Ma. I'll not come back till the last train.'

Should I tell her all at once, Irvine thought, walking up to Mount Royd to face his mother? Or should I just tell her about me and Tommy and leave Rose until later? Right to the moment of walking into her parlour he hadn't made up his mind, but when he started to speak, everything came out.

Mrs Bates sank heavily into the nearest chair, her face the colour of parchment, her hand clutching her chest.

'I don't believe it!' she whispered. 'I don't believe it! You can't do this to me, Irvine. You walked out once before and nearly killed me. Have you ever asked yourself what I went through when you joined the army, got sent to the Crimea?'

'It'll be nothing like that, Ma!' Irvine said. 'I'm not going to fight in any battles, I'm not going to get wounded or killed.'

'You're going away,' Mrs Bates insisted. 'You'll be thousands of miles away. I'll never see you again!'

'Of course you will, Ma. There's ships go both ways across the Atlantic ocean. Why, when we get settled you might even come to visit me!'

'Don't fob me off!' Mrs Bates cried. 'You know I'll do no such thing! You know very well I'll never get to Canada. No, son, it's goodbye!'

'Then I'll come back to see you,' Irvine promised. 'When I've made my pile, which I mean to do, see if I don't come back on a visit!'

She shook her head in denial. She would accept none of it.

'Please try to understand, Ma,' Irvine pleaded. 'I've got to make my way in the world. I can't do it in Helsdon. And you'll have Tommy. He'll be happy to stay with his grandma.'

'Bless his little heart!' Mrs Bates said. 'And him losing his Dad!'

'He'll have Léon Bonneau for a father,' Irvine said. 'He can give him more than I ever could.' He was filled with a deep jealousy at the thought.

'You could give him a father's love,' Mrs Bates said. But perhaps that wasn't true? Perhaps Léon would give him more love than Irvine had ever done. She was well aware that her son hadn't been the best of fathers.

'And Madeleine loves Tommy,' Irvine said. 'I wouldn't leave him, else.'

'Well there's one thing certain,' Mrs Bates said fiercely, 'Madeleine will be a better mother to the lad than Rose Hardy could ever be! What's come over you to think of marrying Rose Hardy I shall never understand! She's a. . .'

She's a trollop, she wanted to say, but thought better of it.

'Rose will make me a very good wife,' Irvine insisted.

'And so soon after poor Bessie!' Mrs Bates said. 'I'm shocked to the core.'

'Happen if I hadn't been going to Canada we'd have waited a bit,' Irvine said. 'As it is, you can see we can't.'

On and on it went, Mrs Bates veering from anger to sorrow, from shouting to bitter weeping. When Madeleine came into the room her mother's hands were covering her face while tears trickled down between her fingers. Madeleine put her arms around her and held her close.

'Oh Ma, I am sorry! But you'll see Tommy grow up, and you'll mean a lot to him. And rejoice a little bit for Léon and me because we'll have a son at last.'

'I do rejoice for you, love,' Mrs Bates said, drying her eyes again. 'I only hope he doesn't grow up to desert you!'

'Irvine isn't deserting *you*, not *you*, not *me*. And we'll see him again. I'm sure we will!' She wasn't at all sure, it simply seemed a lie in a good cause.

'And what I'll say to that . . . that *hussy* when she gets back – how I'll bide in the same house with her, I don't know!' Mrs Bates said.

'Poor Ma!' Madeleine sympathized.

Poor Rose, Irvine thought.

In spite of all Léon could do to hurry the proceedings, it was mid-June before the adoption papers were ready for signing. In the waiting period Rose married Irvine and went to live over the shop, thankful to be out of Mrs Bates's way. The two women had not spoken to each other since Irvine had broken the news to his mother.

Penelope's baby was due at the end of June and Madeleine went in the carriage to fetch her sister from Ripon to wait for the birth at Mount Royd. On the day on which Irvine and Rose sailed from Liverpool, having earnestly requested that no one should go there to see them off, Penelope went into labour with her first son.

It was not quite certain, even to herself, whether the

tears which raced down Mrs Bates's face were of sorrow for the loss of her only son, or for joy at the sight and feel of her new grandchild in her arms.

That same night Léon and Madeleine stood arm in arm in the nursery, looking down at their sleeping children: their daughter and their son.

SIXTEEN

Madeleine slipped into her *peignoir*, crossed the bedroom to the window, drew back the heavy brocade curtains and looked out.

The lawns, benefitting from what had so far been a wet April, formed a brilliant green backcloth to the yellow daffodils and white narcissi which crowded the borders and beds. Every year nature increased their numbers, and each September Madeleine planted more. They were almost her favourite flower, partly because their appearance meant that winter was over, partly because they had been in bloom in the garden, though in less profusion, when Claire had been born seven years ago. Seven years to this very day, in fact.

'I do believe it's going to be a fine day,' she said. 'There isn't a cloud in the sky, and as far as I can tell. . .'

Her words faded because she remembered she was talking to thin air. Léon was away, somewhere in the Midlands, but he had promised to be back in good time for this afternoon's birthday party, and he would never break a promise made to Claire or Tommy.

She gazed out of the window a minute or two longer, admiring the large chestnut tree in the middle of the lawn. At the moment it was clothed in fragile leaves of the palest, silver-tinged green, but by summer the leaves would have grown and darkened to cast a patch of dense shade, sometimes welcome even in Helsdon. And then, in the autumn, there would be the conkers for the children. She just loved that tree.

There was a knock at the door and Jenny came in with Madeleine's morning tea. Jenny had joined Jane in the kitchen to replace Rose Hardy. Flora Bryant was still the devoted slave of Claire and Tommy.

'Good-morning ma'am!' Jenny said. 'It looks like being a nice day.'

'Thank heaven for that!' Madeleine replied. 'Those hordes of children can let off steam in the garden after tea.'

In fact, she thought, sipping her tea, nibbling at a Marie biscuit, there wouldn't be hordes: Penelope's three, Mr Ormeroyd's two grandchildren, the children of two or three families they had got to know in Helsdon over the last few years; no more than fifteen in all, including their own two. There would be almost as many adults present as children.

She was finishing her tea when Claire burst into the room. Claire never entered a room quietly, she always made her presence felt at once. Now she stood there in her frilly white night-dress, her dark hair cascading down her back, her brown eyes shining with excitement.

'Many happy returns, my darling!' Madeleine said.

'Seven years old!' Claire exclaimed. 'Do you think I look any older, Mama? Do you think I look taller?' She stood on tiptoe, trying in vain to see herself in the large mirror over the mantelpiece.

'I think perhaps you do,' Madeleine said gravely.

'Where's Papa?' Claire demanded. 'Why isn't he here?'

'You know perfectly well that he had to be away, but he'll be home well before your party. He wouldn't miss that for the world!'

'Will he bring me a present? Will everyone who comes to the party bring me a present?' Claire asked eagerly.

'Wait and see,' Madeleine reprimanded her daughter.

'It's awful waiting,' Claire grumbled. 'I'm going to waken Tommy. And then *Grandmère*.'

Madeleine looked doubtful.

'Tommy, certainly. But you must creep into *Grandmère*'s room, and if she's asleep you must not disturb her.'

Claire had already dashed away.

Madame Bonneau was here specifically for Claire's birthday. She has aged since she was here two years ago, Madeleine thought. She seems frail. The journey from Roubaix was a trying one, and although Léon had fetched his mother three days ago, she still looked tired.

Madeleine washed in the new bathroom Léon had had put in last year – such an improvement from the ewer and basin in the bedroom – then dressed quickly and went downstairs to see her mother. Mrs Bates would be up and about. She was still the earliest riser in the household.

'Where's Claire?' Mrs Bates enquired.

'Gone to *Grandmère*. I warned her not to wake her, but will she take the slightest bit of notice?'

'More'n likely not,' Mrs Bates said. 'She's a young monkey, that one!'

'Now tell the truth and shame the devil, Ma! You think the sun shines on her!' Madeleine said, laughing.

'Oh I admit it!' Mrs Bates said cheerfully.

But what she would not admit, and never show, was that her favourite grandchild was Tommy. She knew she shouldn't favour one above another, but there it was. Irvine had been her favourite child and Tommy had inherited his mantle. And the fact that she had not seen her son in six years, and knew full well, no matter what promises he made in his letters, she might never see him again in this life, made Tommy doubly precious.

'Jenny had best take Madame Bonneau's tray up, then,' she said.

She could never refer to Madeleine's mother-in-law as other than Madame Bonneau, though they were on the friendliest terms and admired and respected each other.

'Yes. If she wasn't awake, she will be now.'

Madame Bonneau had been awake for some time. She slept less well now than she used to. It was always a relief when morning came. She had been reading her missal when Claire ran in. She put it down on the bedside table and held out her hand.

'*Bonjour, ma petite!*'

'*Bonjour, Grandmère!*' Claire dropped the little curtsey which she knew this grandmother expected.

'Your French accent is getting better,' Madame Bonneau said. 'But it is not perfect, there is something of Yorkshire in it. So we will continue to practise a little every day while I am here. Does your Papa not speak to you in French?'

'Sometimes. But mostly we all speak in English,' Claire admitted. 'It's a lot easier.'

'It is nothing of the kind!' Madame Bonneau contradicted. 'It is a terrible language to learn, as I well know.'

'Tommy thinks French is difficult,' Claire said.

'Tommy has no French blood in him,' Madame Bonneau said. 'I daresay he will always speak what French he does learn with an English accent. Just as I,' she added in fairness, 'will always speak your mother's language with a French accent. With you it is different. The blood of France flows in your veins!'

'But when I fell and cut my knee, the blood looked just the same as Tommy's!' Claire persisted. 'It was as red as red, and ran down my leg.'

'Well never mind about that now. I have not yet wished you a happy birthday! Come here and let me give you a birthday kiss!'

'Have you brought me a present?' Claire enquired hopefully.

'*Certainement*! Though you should never ask for a present.'

'Oh *Grandmère*!' Claire cried. 'Is it under your pillow?'

'No. If you can reach to open the second drawer from the top, in the chest, you will find a parcel wrapped in white paper. . .'

Claire was already at the chest. With squeals of excitement she took the parcel from the drawer.

'Bring it here,' Madame Bonneau said. 'I want to see you open it!'

Claire tore off the wrapping paper and threw it to the floor.

'Oh *Grandmère*, it's beautiful! Oh, it's just what I wanted!'

It was a muff, in blue velvet, not only edged with the softest brown fur, but also lined with it, and with a gilt chain to hold it safely around her neck. She put it on at once, thrusting her hands into the warmth of the fur.

'Oh thank you, *Grandmère*! I shall wear it all the time, even when my hands aren't cold! I must show it to Mama!'

'It really is beautiful,' Madeleine agreed when Claire showed her the muff. 'And even though it's April, there'll still be cold days to come.'

'I shall wear it for ever!' Claire said solemnly. 'I'm going to show it to Tommy.'

'I want you both back here in ten minutes!' Madeleine said. 'We must get breakfast over with. There's a lot to do today.'

On Saturdays, now, she didn't go into the mill. The weekends were for her children, though sometimes she fitted in a little of her own work at home. She still had her workroom in the house, and when it came to fashion ideas she could jot them down wherever she happened to be. There were scraps of paper, pencil drawings, scribbles no one but she understood, in every part of the house.

In the mill her own place was no longer the single room she'd had when she'd first started to design cloth. In the last three years, an extension had been built on to the mill, with enough space for her to work not only on her textile designs, which were still important, but on her fashion designs, which were now an increasingly profitable part of Bonneau's trade.

The extension also housed half a dozen workers who made up sample garments to her designs. There was also a showroom where the textiles manufactured in the mill, as well as Madeleine's portfolio of sketches, and several made-up garments, could be seen by visiting wholesalers. She would have preferred more people to come to Bonneau's, rather than Léon going out so assiduously in search of orders.

'We could make it a pleasant thing for buyers to do,' she frequently said to Léon. 'We could have a young woman – or two – who would model the clothes. For buyers who came from a distance, prepared to spend a lot of money, we could offer hospitality in our own home. There's certainly enough room.'

There was no limit to her ambitions. She felt in her depths of creativity which had hardly been tapped. But Léon would not be convinced. He was always telling her she did too much. His love for her was like a citadel around her; sometimes it felt like a fortress. Though her love for him was equally strong, she didn't want to be imprisoned. Sometimes Léon seemed not to comprehend her strength and energy.

'Has Sam set off for Ripon?' she asked her mother.

'An hour ago. It was very thoughtful of you to send the carriage for Penelope, love. She'd willingly have come by train.'

'I know,' Madeleine agreed. 'But it wouldn't be easy with three little ones, and Lucy only two. If it had been Sunday, and the shop closed, Archie could have come with her.'

'You couldn't have a party on a Sunday!' Mrs Bates protested.

At one-thirty precisely Léon arrived. When he walked in at the door Madeleine felt that lurching of her heart which she never failed to experience at the fresh sight of him. At thirty-eight he was more handsome than he had ever been. There was no grey in his dark hair, which he now wore a little longer so that it touched his collar at the back, nor in his neat, imperial beard. All the other men she knew were heavily bearded, usually also with abundant side whiskers, but Léon took his fashion from his Emperor. He could never be mistaken for other than a Frenchman.

As he came into the house he doffed his Homburg hat – which he had bought in Paris, for the fashion had not reached Helsdon, and bowed to her, with the courtly manners which most men reserved for strangers, but which he lavished on his wife.

'Oh Léon, it's so good to see you!' Madeleine cried. 'I didn't expect you so soon!'

'I was up with the lark and caught a very early train,' he said. 'It's good to be back. And I've brought some orders you'll like, but we'll talk of that later. So where is my birthday girl?'

'I'm happy to say that Flora has taken both children out for a walk. Claire is all excitement and she needs to calm down before the guests arrive.'

'Where is *Maman*?' Léon asked.

'In the conservatory. It's quite warm in there, with the sun on the glass. So while you see *Grandmère*, I must get myself ready. Hortense said she and Henry would come early because it's so long since we saw them.'

Hortense was often in London these days, persuading Henry to take her on trips. Leeds society had long ago palled and even the best shops had too little to offer, compared to those in the capital. Shopping, spending Henry's money, remained her favourite pastime. It was a pity she had no children to occupy her, Madeleine thought – though she never heard Hortense bemoan the lack of them. Henry did. In that respect he was a disappointed man, and since Hortense was now rising thirty-seven he was, it seemed, likely to remain so.

By three o'clock Madeleine and the children, Léon and his mother, were assembled in the drawing-room. Claire preened herself in a white dress, trimmed with broderie anglaise, with a wide blue sash around her waist and a matching bow on top of her head.

'Do you think people will notice my slippers?' she asked anxiously. New for the occasion, made of brocade and embroidered with tiny silver beads, they were the current pride of her life.

'If they don't,' Madame Bonneau said, 'I am sure you will find a way to draw attention to them!'

'Perhaps you should wear them on your head?' Léon suggested gravely.

'Oh Papa, you are silly!' Claire giggled.

'Tommy looks very smart,' Mrs Bates said.

'Indeed, I was thinking the same thing,' Léon agreed.

Tommy, in his long narrow trousers, his short blue jacket and his bow tie, flushed with pleasure. Praise from the man he had long ago learned to call Papa was dear to him, not because it was rare, far from it, but because of the deep affection between them. Mama, who once, a long time ago, he had called Aunt Madeleine, was also dear to him – but Papa was special.

He knew that he had once had another father, who was now thousands of miles away, in a place called Winnipeg, in Canada, a distant land which Flora had pointed out to him on the globe; and that this other father was Grandma's son. Sometimes, though not very often, she had a letter from him, and she would read out bits to him.

He could no longer remember what his first father looked like. When Grandma showed him the sepia photograph, which she kept in the drawer so that the light wouldn't fade it, it was like looking at a stranger. In fact he seldom gave him much thought. He was happy here, with his very own family. His one dread was that in two years' time, when he would be thirteen, he might be sent away to school. He tried not to think about it.

'It's so boring, waiting for people to arrive,' Claire complained. 'Why can't me and Tommy play with the toy theatre?'

The toy theatre had been the wonderful surprise present from Mama and Papa. It was exactly what she had longed for, and already Tommy had started to write a play for it. He was good at writing plays.

'Well off you go then,' Madeleine said. 'But the minute I send for you, you must come at once. It would be very bad-mannered not to be here to greet your guests.'

'*And* to see what my presents are!' Claire said.

The Garstons were the first to arrive. Hortense, though

fashionably-dressed as ever, was not looking her usual bandbox self.

'I am frozen stiff and blown to bits!' she complained. 'Henry would insist on having the carriage-hood down, and it is far too early in the year!'

'Nonsense!' Henry said heartily. 'A breath of fresh air never did anyone any harm! It's put colour in your cheeks, my dear!'

'And coarsened my skin, I have no doubt!' Hortense retorted.

'Come up to my room,' Madeleine suggested.

'Indeed I must,' Hortense agreed. 'I must repair the damage before your other guests arrive!'

In Madeleine's bedroom she removed her hat and set to on her hair, surveying herself critically in the mirror.

'I look a wreck!' she complained.

'Nonsense, Hortense. Just a bit untidy, that's all.'

Hortense picked up the silver-backed brush and began to titivate her hair.

'I like your dress,' Madeleine said.

'I bought it in London. So much better than Leeds!'

'Stand up and let me look at you properly,' Madeleine said.

Hortense, her hair finally put to rights, obeyed.

'Look!' she said. 'Only a bit of a curve at the front and all these frills and flounces at the back of the waist.'

'You're wearing a bustle,' Madeleine commented. 'They've not taken on in the West Riding yet, but they will.'

'Give it a hundred years!' Hortense said. 'But this bustle thing's quite good. It's padded, and you tie it with tapes round your waist, then all the frills disguise it.'

'In a year or two we shall all be as flat as pancakes in front and have quite huge bustles behind,' Madeleine predicted. 'Yes, even in Yorkshire, which isn't nearly as backward as you like to pretend!'

'Anything for a change,' Hortense said. 'And in that case we shall certainly need the new corset. Have you seen it? It comes much further down the body and moulds the hips and the stomach.'

'Well, whatever the fashion, women will change their shape to accommodate it,' Madeleine said.

'I see you are wearing the new Louis heels,' Hortense said enviously. 'You didn't get *those* shoes in Helsdon!'

'Léon brought them from France,' Madeleine admitted.

'Oh, how I wish I could go to France whenever I wanted,' Hortense sighed. 'Henry is so pig-headed about going abroad!'

She had crossed the room and was looking out of the window.

'You have more guests arriving!' she said.

'Then I'd better go down. Join us when you're ready, Hortense.'

From then on the guests arrived thick and fast. Claire curtsied prettily and accepted her presents with eager hands and shining eyes. Mrs Barnet brought a doll which she had dressed herself.

'I shall call her Evelina,' Claire said.

The children ate heartily at the lavishly-spread dining-table while their parents nibbled more daintily in the drawing-room.

'The way they're stuffing themselves, these kids will be sick,' Jenny said to Flora Bryant. 'I only hope it's not on the carpet.'

In fact it was one of the Ormeroyd grandchildren who succumbed, and in the discreet manner which he must have inherited from his lawyer grandfather, he waited until the meal was over and they were all cavorting around the garden before throwing up neatly and quietly in a flowerbed.

A sharp April shower drove everyone indoors.

They played endless games – musical chairs, kiss-in-the-ring, Old Roger is Dead – and after that performed their party pieces.

'Surely the hours between three-thirty and six-thirty

must be the longest in the day?' Madeleine said. It was the recognized span for a children's party. 'Thank heaven we have the Magic Lantern!'

She turned to Henry, whose gift it had been.

'It was a stroke of genius on your part,' she said quietly. ' "Famous Foreign Places" and "British Flora and Fauna" will see us through until it's time for everyone to go. . . Oh Henry, I don't mean you!' she added. 'I do hope you and Hortense will stay on a bit.'

Eventually it was all over. Claire was prised away from her presents to bid mannerly farewells and everyone went home, except the Garstons, and Penelope and her children who were to stay the night and return to Ripon next day.

'Your turn next, Tommy,' Madeleine said. 'Shall you want a party?'

'I don't think so,' Tommy said. 'I'll be eleven in August. It's a bit old for a party.'

'Quite right, Tommy!' Léon said. 'We shall think of some other treat. Perhaps we'll go somewhere special.'

'I think you children should go to bed now,' Madeleine said. 'Penelope is already putting the little ones to bed. I know it's a bit early for you, Tommy, so you may read for an hour or so.'

She envied him. At the present moment there were few things she would rather do than go to bed with a book.

While Madeleine went upstairs with the children, and Henry was talking to Madame Bonneau, Hortense cornered Léon.

'Why don't we sit in your beautiful conservatory,' she suggested. 'It is so peaceful there, and so sweet-smelling.'

'Certainly!' Léon said.

They seated themselves in comfortable wicker chairs, facing out over the garden.

'Oh Léon, life is so *boring*!' Hortense exclaimed. 'The same routine day after day, the same boring people. I know you must agree with me that Yorkshire people are very dull!'

'I don't. . .' Léon began.

'You don't know how I envy you, Léon – travelling all over the place, going to France whenever you feel like it!'

Why, oh why, she asked herself, had she not, somehow, managed to marry Léon Bonneau? She could have, she was sure of it. She could have caught him before ever he set eyes on Madeleine. What had she been thinking of to let him go? He was – she faced the fact – the only man she had ever cared about.

Was it too late? Oh, they were both married and there was nothing to be done about that, but marriage wasn't the only thing, especially for a Frenchman. A Frenchman would take a mistress as easily as he would eat his dinner. And where Léon was concerned she would willingly be that mistress!

He found me attractive in Paris, she thought. On that occasion he found me irresistible. So why not again? True, they were not in Paris, but the very fact that they were aliens in this cold, dull place might be fruitful.

'We are two of a kind, Léon,' she said softly. 'Old friends who have known each other all our lives, and now incredibly find ourselves stuck here. How strange that our paths lie so close! Is it meant, do you think?'

'I don't feel "stuck" here,' Léon said, ignoring her question.

'That's because you move around,' she said. 'If I were your wife I'm not sure I'd let you roam. You're far too attractive!'

Did he stray? Surely he must. What Frenchman wouldn't? Well, she must make sure from now on that he strayed in her direction.

She considered Madeleine. One must admit that at thirty-three she was as attractive as ever. Also she was clever and talented. But was a clever wife what Léon wanted? Madeleine never went anywhere with him. She stayed at home, working like a beaver at her designs. No, Hortense thought, I don't really see Madeleine as a stumbling block.

'Here comes Madeleine!' Léon said.

'Why, it's almost dark in here,' Madeleine said. 'Shall we go in?'

Léon rose to his feet and held out a hand to assist Hortense. She gave his hand a small, but distinct, pressure, and let hers linger in his for a brief moment as she stood up.

Henry was on his own at the moment they returned to the drawing-room.

'The two grandmothers have gone together to look at something or other,' he explained.

'I've been envying Léon because he travels around so much,' Hortense said. 'How lucky he is! New places, new faces!'

'In fact,' Léon said, laughing, 'I see the same faces. Faces of businessmen, not nearly as pretty as yours and Madeleine's!'

'But I'm like you, Hortense,' Madeleine confessed. 'I envy him also. I would dearly like to take my own designs around, at least take a share in the selling.'

'We've been through all this before,' Léon said. 'You know it wouldn't do. The fact that you are a woman would tell against you from the start. The buyers I meet wouldn't know how to begin to treat you.'

'But I wouldn't want any special treatment,' Madeleine argued. 'I would just want to be treated as you are.'

'That would be impossible,' Léon said firmly.

Hortense broke in. 'Do you mean that the people you sell to don't know that Bonneau's designs are created by a woman?'

'Of course they don't!' Léon said. 'They wouldn't sell half as well if they did. Women buy dresses, but they like to think they are designed by a man. It's the way of the world!'

'It's a stupid way,' Madeleine said. 'I'd like to help to change it.'

But a woman could not defy her husband. He was the head of the household and in the end his word was law. Nor did it please her to defy Léon. He was kind and generous, he begrudged her nothing – except credit for her own work. In spite of the labels in her garments, she was anonymous.

'Well *I* know the clothes are designed by a woman, and I'm more than happy to have them,' Henry said. 'Especially since I've got them exclusively in the West Riding.'

'As you always will have,' Léon said. 'We don't forget how you helped us when we needed it.'

'But do *your* customers know that "Bonneau" is a woman?' Madeleine asked. 'Do you tell them that?'

'Well, no, I don't,' Henry admitted.

What spirit she had! How beautiful she was, he thought. Why hadn't he tried to take her away from Bonneau before she'd gone and married him? He'd known from the first, from the minute she'd walked into his office, a raw eighteen-year-old, that she was what he wanted. And then because he couldn't have Madeleine, he'd married Hortense on the strength of a three-week infatuation, and look where it had got him! As far as she was concerned, he was simply a source of spending money! Not that he couldn't afford her, but he didn't get value for money.

So not everything is sweetness and light between Léon and Madeleine, Hortense thought. There were chinks in the armour. Good!

'So what about the French market?' Henry asked Léon. 'How is that going?'

'With our materials, very well,' Léon said. 'We have a good trade. With the fashion designs, not yet – though I live in hopes. The problem is that there are so many good French designers.'

'But don't forget that the first and foremost designer in Paris is English,' Madeleine said. 'No one comes within a mile of Charles Worth.'

'And when do you return to France, Madame?' Hortense asked.

'On Wednesday, I think,' Madame Bonneau said. 'It

depends whether it is convenient for Léon to take me then.'

'Quite convenient, *Maman*,' Léon said. 'I have to go to France in any case.'

'I wonder. . .' Hortense began. 'Oh, Madame Bonneau!' she said in a rush. 'I do so long to see my native country. Would it be an imposition if I were to come with you, to stay with you for a little while? I get so homesick!'

What a golden opportunity, she thought. Fate is being kind to me. She turned to Henry.

'You wouldn't mind, would you, my dear?'

Henry shrugged.

'If that's what you want!'

SEVENTEEN

Madame Bonneau checked once more the contents of the hand grip, which she would carry with her on her way back to France. Her most precious possessions were in this bag – her string of small but good pearls; her jet brooch; her prayer book, worn with a lifetime's use; the new photographs of Claire and Tommy which Madeleine had given her. The silver bracelet which had been her husband's last gift was, as always, safely on her wrist. When she had ascertained that everything was in place, she closed the bag again, and locked it.

As far as the journey was concerned, she had no other responsibilities. Léon would see to everything – her trunk, the tickets, the food basket which Mrs Bates had prepared for the journey: it was all taken care of. All that was left to her was to fill in the short time until the carriage would be ready to take them to Leeds, to catch the London train.

She seated herself on the chair by the window, and looked out. Mount Royd was a pleasant house and even Helsdon wasn't as bad as she'd expected it to be before she'd paid her first visit, almost seven years ago. She was sorry to be leaving, but it was always good to be back in one's own home. Crossing on the night boat, she would be in Roubaix by this time tomorrow.

Madeleine came into the room. She was already dressed in her outdoor jacket, with her bonnet, because fashion said hair must now be piled high on the top of the head, tipped precariously to the front.

'Is there anything I can do for you, *Belle-mère*?' she asked.

'Thank you, Madeleine. I am quite ready, except for putting on my cloak.'

I shall be sorry to see *Belle-mère* go, Madeleine thought. She had enjoyed this last visit more than any other, had felt more at ease.

She helped her mother-in-law with her cloak. Madame Bonneau took a last, long look at the garden and then at the room, and together they went downstairs. Tommy and Claire, already dressed for the small private school they attended, were waiting in the hall to make their farewells. Claire flung herself into Madame Bonneau's arms, the tears starting in her eyes.

'Oh *Grandmère*, I don't want you to go!' she cried.

'I know!' Madame Bonneau agreed. 'And I don't want to leave you. But *Maman* has promised she will bring you to see me in France next year, so that is something we can all look forward to. And in the meantime you can practise your writing by sending me letters.'

Tommy, looking serious, offered his hand.

'*Au revoir*, Madame Bonneau!'

'Oh, but you must never call me *that*!' Madame Bonneau cried. 'You must always call me *Grandmère*! I am sure I have said that before.'

But perhaps she had not, and when she came to think of it, Tommy had not really called her anything during the whole of her visit. It was remiss of her. He was a nice boy, and her son was so fond of him. Her repentance showed in the warmth of the hug she now gave him.

Tommy flushed with pleasure.

'I hope you have a safe and pleasant journey, *Grandmère*,' he said. 'May I also write to you?'

'Indeed, I shall expect it!' Madame Bonneau said.

She turned to Madeleine.

'There is no need for you to accompany Léon and myself to Leeds, my dear! I know how busy you are.'

'I wouldn't dream of doing otherwise,' Madeleine assured her.

'And now we really must go,' Léon advised.

'First you must allow me a minute to make my fare-wells to Mrs Bates,' his mother said.

They were to meet Hortense and Henry at the station in Leeds. When they arrived there was no sign of them, though it wanted only ten minutes to departure time.

'Perhaps Hortense has changed her mind,' Léon said.

'I think that highly unlikely,' Madame Bonneau said dryly.

She did not approve of Hortense going to France in this fashion, leaving her husband behind, especially as no time limit had been set on the length of her visit. But there had been many things about Hortense of which she had not approved on this visit. If she could have refused her hospitality in Roubaix, she might well have done so – but of course that was not possible.

I wish Hortense *would* change her mind, Madeleine thought. In her heart she had always suspected that Hortense was too fond of Léon; and on the day of Claire's party she had become sure of it. There had been various signs – the way she had held on to his hand in the con-servatory, the expression in her eyes when she looked at him, the too-lingering farewell when the Garstons had left. Small signs, but they added up to the fact that Hortense hankered after Léon.

If Léon was aware of it, he showed nothing. And Madeleine would not insult him by mentioning it. She trusted him. It would be wrong to do otherwise. But Hortense is a very attractive woman, she thought, and she is used to getting what she wants. Look how she wound Henry around her little finger!

The sight of Hortense, now walking along the platform towards them, looking exceedingly smart and hand-some, did nothing to console Madeleine.

'I'm sorry if we've kept you waiting,' Henry apol-ogized. 'My wife had difficulty in deciding which gloves to wear with which bonnet!'

'Henry can never take dress seriously,' Hortense said

315

lightly. 'But no matter, I'm here now. And I knew Léon wouldn't let the train go without me!'

'We must board at once,' Léon said, 'or it will go without any of us.'

He turned to embrace Madeleine, and was surprised by the way she clung to him. In the end he had gently to disengage her.

'Come back soon!' she whispered.

'I will, *chérie*!'

Meanwhile Hortense and Henry bid each other a cool farewell.

'I shall keep an eye on your wife, Monsieur Garston!' Madame Bonneau said lightly.

Henry smiled.

'I wish you luck, Madame! And I hope you have a pleasant journey, not too boring.'

'Oh it won't be,' Madame Bonneau assured him. 'Léon sits there with Black's guide open on his lap and informs us of every single thing we pass, even the length of every tunnel! He did it all the way from Dover and I'm sure he'll do it all the way back!'

Henry stood with Madeleine on the platform, both of them watching until the train was out of sight, the last wisp of smoke evaporated; then he turned to her.

'And who will keep an eye on us?' he joked.

'We don't need it,' Madeleine said shortly.

And that was unfortunately true, Henry thought, at least for Madeleine. She was as true as steel to Léon. For his part, chance would be a fine thing. If he thought he could tempt her to be otherwise, he might, he just might, try it.

'Well at least come and have a cup of chocolate with me,' he invited.

'I'm sorry, I can't,' Madeleine said. 'Sam is waiting with the carriage.'

'Then I'll tell him you'll be another hour,' Henry said. 'It's a fine day, he'll not mind waiting. He can pick you up at the Queen's Hotel in an hour's time.'

'Well I'm not. . .'

'Now surely you can spare me one hour?' Henry urged.

Madeleine hesitated, then suddenly said, 'Of course I can! And I would love a cup of chocolate. We breakfasted so early.'

She linked her arm through his as they left the station to walk the short distance to the Queen's Hotel. As they were shown to a table Madeleine recalled the last time the two of them had done this; when Léon had been in France and Henry had taken her to Bradford. Oh, but Léon had been so cross!

'So tell me how things are with you?' Henry said when he had given his order.

'Quite good.'

'No complaints?'

'Only the usual one, that Léon won't let me travel around, won't let me try to sell my own designs. That's quite frustrating. But you've heard it all before, so I won't bore you with it. It's a hardy perennial.'

'I know. But Léon's quite right, of course. It wouldn't be suitable. If you were my wife I'd never let you out of my sight!'

'But you've just let Hortense out of your sight,' Madeleine reminded him.

He shrugged.

'Try stopping her!'

'How long will she be away?' Madeleine asked.

'Your guess is as good as mine. What's more, I frankly don't care!'

'Henry, I don't think you should talk like that,' Madeleine said.

'I daresay not. You wouldn't, would you? But I'm sure you know, love, that our marriage isn't working. The trouble is, I rushed into it. She swept me off my feet.'

'I'm sorry. I really am sorry,' Madeleine said gently.

'Aye well, there it is!'

'I must say. . .' Madeleine began. She had been about to confess her own worries about Hortense, in relation to

Léon, but she mustn't do that. It would be disloyal to Léon; it would sound as though she didn't trust him.

'What must you say?'

'Nothing, really.'

Henry looked at her keenly. He had seen the way she had clung to Léon at the station, and the sidelong glance she had given Hortense which she thought no one had noticed. He also recalled Madame Bonneau's remark about keeping an eye on his wife. The old lady wasn't blind!

'Perhaps I can guess,' he said.

'Please don't, Henry!'

'Very well. But you've no cause to worry, lass. No man who had you for a wife would be tempted to stray.'

'Really, I don't know what you're talking about, Henry dear!'

'Then just remember this, love – even though you don't know what I'm talking about. Any time you need me, any time at all, I'm there!'

'Thank you, Henry.'

But with his words, the hope that what she had been thinking about Hortense might all be in her own imagination, flew out of the window.

'Then we'll change the subject,' Henry said.

Usually, there was no difficulty in making conversation with Henry. They had the easy familiarity of two people who have known and respected each other for a long time. It was different today. They discussed the weather, work, railways – all the time skirting around what was uppermost in their minds. Madeleine was relieved when the page came to tell her that the carriage was waiting.

'Thank you, Henry,' she said.

He accompanied her to her carriage.

'Think on what I told you,' he said as he handed her in.

Madeleine had promised to take the children to Ripon on Saturday.

'You'll have to be up bright and early,' she said to them on Friday evening. 'We can only spend the day there. Aunt Penelope doesn't have room for us to sleep. I'm beginning to wonder if it would have been better to have had Sam take us and bring us back?'

'Oh no, Mama!' Tommy protested. 'It's much more exciting by train! And you promised.'

'I did – so I'll stick to it.'

They left the house in good time and were at the station well before the train arrived. They were lucky enough to get an empty compartment.

'Bags me sit by the window, facing the way we're going,' Tommy said.

From the moment the train drew out of the station he pressed his nose against the window, looking out, and every so often writing down a word or two in a small notebook.

'We shall see three rivers today,' he announced. 'The Wharfe, the Nidd and the Ure.'

'I think you've been reading Papa's railway guide,' Madeleine teased.

'He lends it to me any time I want it,' Tommy said. 'Did you know that they had the plague in Ripon?'

Claire let out a scream, and clutched at her mother.

'I don't want to go! I don't want to go! We'll get the plague and I'll be covered in horrible spots!'

'Not *now*, silly!' Tommy said. 'I mean hundreds of years ago! Oh Claire you are stupid!'

'I am not stupid!' Claire retorted. 'You're stupid not to say in the first place it was hundreds of years ago.'

'I know a lot of other things about Ripon but now I'm not going to tell you any of them,' Tommy said.

'I don't want to know!' Claire said loftily.

'If you two don't stop bickering we shall take the next train back,' Madeleine threatened.

Since their mother's threats were seldom idle ones, both children were immediately subdued.

It was while they were walking from the railway

station to Penelope's home that Madeleine saw Sophia Chester coming towards them. How plump she had grown; she was all curves: but she was still undeniably pretty, Madeleine thought, her hair still the vibrant auburn it had always been.

Sophia hadn't seen Madeleine and her children. Truth to tell, she was short-sighted and getting more so, though she pretended not to be because there was no way she would *ever* wear spectacles. By the time she did see them, it was too late to cross to the other side of the street. She did the only thing possible to her. At the very moment Madeleine bade her a cool, but civil 'good-morning' Sophia drew her skirts aside in an exaggerated manner and turned away. How dare that upstart servant girl speak to her!

Madeleine now rushed ahead, her face burning with anger.

'Do you know that lady, Mama?' Claire asked.

'I used to,' Madeleine said shortly.

'Who does she think she is?' she demanded of Penelope a little later. She was still angry, more with herself for speaking than with Sophia for not doing so.

'The Queen of Ripon!' Penelope said.

'How can Emerald continue to work for her? How does she stand her?'

'I don't know,' Penelope said. 'We hardly ever see Emerald, though we live so close. Archie hasn't delivered the meat since his uncle promoted him soon after we were married. There's been a succession of boys delivering the orders since then.'

'Doesn't Emerald come to see you when she has a half-day off?' Madeleine asked.

'Hardly ever. I expect she doesn't get much time off. And when she does, Mrs Chester more than likely persuades her to take the children with her. She wouldn't bring them here because Mrs Chester wouldn't approve – and I can't go there because she's forbidden me the house.'

'Well she'll not forbid me,' Madeleine said. 'I stopped being frightened of Sophia Chester a long time ago. I've a good mind to go and see Emerald. I'd like to make sure she's all right.'

'Oh Madeleine, must you?' Penelope sounded alarmed. 'Supposing you make it worse for Emerald?'

'I promise I won't,' Madeleine said. 'In fact if I go now, as likely as not Mrs Chester will be out. She looked as if she was on her way to somewhere.'

'Then hurry,' Penelope urged. 'And leave Tommy and Claire here with me.'

'No!' Madeleine said. 'I shall take them with me. They've got a perfect right to see their aunt. I shall take them with me. Come along, children.'

In less than twenty minutes they were knocking on the Chesters' kitchen door. Emerald, opening it, gave a short scream at the sight of them.

'Oh! Oh it's you!'

'How are you?' Madeleine said. 'I've brought your nephew and niece to visit you.'

They were still standing on the doorstep, Emerald holding the door half closed.

'Well aren't you going to ask us in?'

'I'm not sure. . .'

'Mrs Chester is out. We saw her in the town less than an hour ago. Anyway, surely you can have your own family call?'

'I suppose you'd better come in,' Emerald said.

Grudgingly, Emerald opened the door and they trooped in.

'How's Ma?' Emerald asked.

To Madeleine's ears her sister sounded a bundle of nerves. Her voice was thin and jerky; she'd lost weight too, all her chubbiness gone. Fine lines – worry lines, Madeleine decided – showed on her face. At twenty-nine she looked nearer forty.

'Ma's all right,' she answered. 'She'd be all the better for seeing you. Nobody can make up for Irvine's going,

321

but you could help, love. You were the one she always saw to most when we were little, because you were the delicate one. Many's the night she sat up with you.'

'I know!' Emerald retorted. 'Have you come here just to upbraid me – because if so you needn't have bothered!'

'I'm sorry, love! Of course I haven't. I came because I wanted to see you. I wanted to make sure you were all right.'

'Of course I am! Why shouldn't I be? If you came to criticize Mrs Chester, don't bother to do that, either. I get along quite well with Mrs Chester – partly I suppose because I know my place – which I daresay you never did.'

'Never for want of being reminded!' Madeleine said.

'Well just because you're rich, and I'm a servant, don't think you can tell me what to do,' Emerald said.

Tears sprang to Madeleine's eyes; tears of anger as well as of hurt.

'That's quite unfair, Emerald! I might be rich, or on the way to it, but I'm not ashamed of it, or guilty. We've been lucky, but we've also worked very hard, and taken risks. And I'm the same person inside as I was when I hadn't two ha' pennies to rub together, when we all lived in Priestley Street. I came to see you because you're my sister, and I love you – not so I could boss you about, tell you what to do!'

'I'm sorry,' Emerald said.

'Please could I have a drink of milk?' Tommy requested loudly.

He'd thought it would be pleasant, visiting his aunt – but there she was, looking sulky, not a bit pleased to see them, and his mother almost crying.

'Can I have a drink of milk, too?' Claire asked.

Emerald, glad of something to do, took two cups from the dresser and filled them from the large milk jug on the table.

'There you are,' she said. 'I daresay you'd both like a biscuit?'

Emerald was taking the biscuits from the barrel when she – and the others – heard the sound of the front door opening, and then closing with a bang. She turned pale, and dropped a biscuit on the floor.

'It's the mistress!' she gasped. 'You'd better go. No use asking for trouble.'

'But I've only just started my milk,' Tommy protested.

'And you promised us biscuits,' Claire reminded her aunt.

'So you did, Emerald,' Madeleine said gently. 'And really, I don't think we should rush away. We're doing nothing wrong – nor are you.'

The words were not quite out of her mouth when Sophia Chester stormed into the kitchen, not having bothered to take off her jacket or her bonnet. Whatever her reason had been for coming into the kitchen in such a temper, it was forgotten at the sight of Madeleine.

'What is the meaning of this?' she cried. 'What in the world is happening?'

She addressed the words to Emerald, but it was Madeleine who answered. Her voice was deliberately calm.

'Nothing very extraordinary, Mrs Chester. I merely brought my children to see their aunt. They don't often see her.'

'I'm sure I didn't mean. . .' Emerald began.

Mrs Chester had no time to listen to Emerald.

'And a meal at my expense!'

'A drink of milk for the children,' Madeleine said. 'Children get thirsty, as I'm sure you know.'

'Then kindly see that your visitors drink up as quickly as possible and leave my house!' Mrs Chester spoke to Emerald, not looking at Madeleine.

'They were promised a biscuit,' Madeleine said smoothly. 'I see they are Shrewsbury biscuits and my son is particularly fond of those.'

She had said the wrong thing. She knew it as soon as she saw Sophia's change of expression, the way she now looked directly at her. She had given her the weapon, sharp as steel, with which to wound not only herself but, far worse, Tommy.

'Your son?' Sophia Chester drawled. 'Your son?' She gave Tommy a slow, lingering look from top to toe. Madeleine watched him flush, and then go white. 'He's not your son! Why, the whole county knows that you're not capable of having a son! Didn't some woman put a curse on you, say you'd never have a son? Well it worked, didn't it?'

Madeleine moved to Tommy and put her arm lightly around his shoulder. She could feel him trembling.

'Tommy is my son,' she said steadily. 'He is legally my son. He knows I didn't bear him, but he also knows that he's every bit as dear to me as if I had. Perhaps even more precious since I chose him. So you see, the curse didn't work! I have a son in a million!'

'He's your brother's brat!' Sophia Chester spat out the words. 'And we all know what a ne'er-do-well your brother was!'

'Once again, you're misinformed,' Madeleine countered. For the sake of the children she kept her voice level. 'My brother is doing exceptionally well. He is just about to buy his own farm, in Winnipeg. And now, children, I think we should leave. Say "goodbye" to Aunt Emerald. Tommy, don't you want your biscuit?'

He shook his head, then rushed out and was sick in the garden.

'I'll have it,' Claire said brightly. 'I'll take it with me.'

Mrs Chester turned to Emerald.

'See that those two mugs are extra specially washed. We don't want any nasty infections, do we?'

'I'm sorry I was sick,' Tommy said as they walked back into Ripon.

'Don't apologize,' Madeleine said. 'Mrs Chester makes me feel sick too. In fact, if it hadn't been for your Aunt Emerald, I'd have been happy for you to throw up on the kitchen rug!'

'But is it true what she said?' he asked anxiously.

'Tommy love, you know what's true and what isn't,' Madeleine said. 'Most of all you know that what I said is true. You are my son and Papa's son, and you're a son in a million!'

'Does Papa think so?' It mattered so much what Papa thought.

'Papa thinks you're a son in *ten* million!' Madeleine assured him. 'Every day we thank God for both our children.'

Then she stopped right where they were, in the middle of the market square in Ripon, and took him in her arms and hugged him.

'Now what were all those things you wouldn't tell Claire about Ripon?' she demanded. 'Because I should like to hear them.'

The journey from Yorkshire had been more tiring than Madame Bonneau had expected. But thankfully, before they'd left Mount Royd, Léon had insisted on an overnight stay in London and had booked rooms for the three of them in an hotel in Bloomsbury. Now, after dinner, though she was almost too fatigued to put one foot before the other, they were strolling in the evening sunlight around the square in front of the hotel, she on her son's left arm, Hortense clinging to his right.

'We might just manage to get in at the theatre,' Hortense had said over dinner. 'Or failing that, the second house at the Music Hall.'

'I am far too tired to go to the theatre,' Madame Bonneau said. 'As for the Music Hall, even if I were fresh as a daisy, I have never been to such an entertainment in my life. Nor do I think you should go!'

Hortense pulled a face.

'I thought it might amuse you. But if you don't want to go. . .'

'I don't!' Madame Bonneau said.

Oh dear, Hortense thought, it's going to be rather dull

325

in Roubaix! But it couldn't be as dull as Leeds, could it? In any case, she had no intention of staying there long. She would go on to Paris as quickly as possible; hopefully as soon as Léon went there. He wouldn't have time to stay in Roubaix long.

'So perhaps a gentle stroll,' Léon had suggested. 'You do look rather tired, *Maman*, but some fresh air would help you to sleep.'

And perhaps she will go to bed early, Hortense thought hopefully, and I shall have some time with Léon. For this reason she fell in graciously with the idea of walking in the square.

'It was thoughtless of me to suggest the theatre,' she said as they ambled. 'An early night will do you the world of good, Madame.'

Madame Bonneau looked at Hortense keenly. She had known her since she was a little girl and she could read her like a book.

'An early night would do us all good,' she said. 'We have a prompt start in the morning. It's a long way to Dover.'

When they came in from their stroll she was too tired to fight against Léon's suggestion that she should retire at once, and powerless to prevent Hortense doing exactly as she pleased.

'I will accompany you to your room, Madame,' Hortense said graciously. 'See you have everything you need.'

She turned to Léon.

'In fact I am not in the least tired. When I have settled your mother I shall come downstairs again for a little while, and join you. That is, if you don't mind.'

'Not at all,' Léon said politely.

Hortense insisted on seeing Madame Bonneau into bed before she finally bade her good-night.

'*Dormez bien*,' she said.

'You too sleep well. And do not stay up too late,' Madame Bonneau said firmly. 'And see that Léon doesn't stay up late, either!' she added.

326

'Why, Madame Bonneau, Léon won't take the slightest notice of me!' Hortense said sweetly. 'He won't do what *I* want!'

I hope he won't, Madame Bonneau thought. But she was far from sure. All her sons were hot-blooded Frenchmen, like their father before them. Hortense was an attractive woman and she had always had an eye on Léon. Once I thought it might be a good thing for them to marry, she reminded herself: now she was glad they had not. Léon was better off with his Madeleine.

'Your mother seems very tired,' Hortense said as she rejoined Léon. 'I think she will fall asleep as soon as her head touches the pillow. As for me, I am wide awake. It is much too soon to go to bed!'

'What would you like to do?' Léon asked.

'Perhaps another walk in the square?' Hortense suggested. 'Or even further afield. I know it's dark now, but the gas lamps are so pretty.'

She took his arm as they left the hotel. It was almost dark, and with the lamps illuminating the trees, the square had a totally different feeling from an hour ago.

'The older people and the children have gone home,' Hortense observed. 'There are only young couples here now. Don't they look romantic? Do you suppose they look at us and think the same, Léon?'

'I doubt it!' Léon said prosaically. 'Of you, perhaps,' he added politely. 'But in two years' time I shall be forty – hardly a romantic figure!'

'Oh Léon, how can you say that?' Hortense cried. 'You are quite, quite wrong!' She tucked her arm further into his, leaned more closely against him. 'You were always a romantic figure in my eyes, Léon, and now you are more attractive than ever! You don't mind me saying so? We are old friends, *n'est-ce pas?*'

'We have certainly known each other a long time,' Léon allowed.

'If only I had not. . .' She broke off. 'Oh, why was I so foolish as to let you go!'

'It is a long time ago,' Léon said. 'We are still good friends, we always will be, but we are both happily married now.'

She sighed deeply.

'*You* are happily married – though perhaps your marriage is – will you be cross with me if I dare to say it? – a little dull at times! But I am not so fortunate. Oh Léon, you must know I am *not* happy with Henry!' She took out her handkerchief and dabbed at her eyes.

He couldn't bear it if she was going to cry! He had no defence at all against a weeping woman – added to which, Hortense was the only woman he knew who looked even prettier when she cried.

'Please, may we sit down for a minute, until I compose myself?' Hortense begged. 'I am so sorry!'

They sat on a secluded seat, overhung by trees, through which the light from the nearest gas lamp hardly penetrated.

'I am very unhappy, Léon!' she said. 'You can't imagine how unhappy I am! And I know I shouldn't burden you with my troubles except that you are the most sympathetic person in the world!'

She leaned her head against his shoulder and he put an arm around her, then she raised her head and he looked into her beautiful eyes, shining with tears. Her perfume teased his nostrils, her body pressed close against him and he felt the softness of her breasts. Dear God, how could he stand it?

He was not the slightest bit deceived. He knew exactly what she was doing, as he had on the day of Claire's party. He knew what she was after, and though it went against his will, he couldn't prevent his body responding to hers. He longed to give in to her. And who would know, what harm could there be?

'I think you are overwrought, my dear. Also it is chilly and I wouldn't want you to catch cold. We must go back to the hotel.'

He was about to rise to his feet when she leaned further

against him, clasped her hands around his neck, and fastened her lips on his. Her lips were cool, and trembled a little. Her body was close and pliant against his; he felt its warmth through her thin dress. He kissed her long and passionately, then, with an effort which was almost too much for him, he gently removed her arms from around his neck and pulled her to her feet.

'We must go!' he said.

She was more than willing. She saw only one end to this, the end she longed for.

In the hotel he said: 'I think you should go straight to your room and I will get the waiter to bring you a nightcap. After that you must go to sleep quickly.'

'I will go to my room, dearest Léon, but only on condition that you yourself bring me a nightcap.'

'No, Hortense! That is not a good idea.'

'Then I shall stay downstairs,' she said. 'Surely you wouldn't want me to do that? Oh Léon, please! I shan't eat you! I only want you to bring me the nightcap and then I promise I'll go to sleep. Is it so much to ask?'

'Very well,' he said hesitantly.

When he went into her room with a glass of cognac she was already in bed. He placed the drink on the bedside table.

'Sit on the bed while I drink it,' she said.

She stretched out an arm and pulled him towards her, and he sat on the bed.

'Oh Léon, make love to me!' she pleaded. 'Léon, let it be like it was in Paris!'

He was desperately tempted. Who would know? Who could it harm? Then on the point of taking her into his arms he pushed her away and jumped to his feet.

'No, Hortense!' he said. 'No!'

She sat up in bed and watched him rush out of the room. Round one to Léon. But no matter. Even though her body was crying out for him, she could wait. There was time. They would be together in his mother's house in Roubaix and then, better still, perhaps in Paris. She was well aware how much he'd wanted her, how difficult it had been for him to resist. Well, he would want her again, and next time he wouldn't resist. She would see to that. Perhaps life wasn't going to be so dull after all.

It was the afternoon of the next day when they reached Roubaix. Pierre and Charlotte were there to greet them.

'You look worn out, *Belle-mère*,' Charlotte said. 'The minute we are in the house, Brigitte shall make you a *tisane*. You will feel better when you have drunk it.'

'Thank you,' Madame Bonneau said. 'I am rather tired but it is good to be home.'

'I'm sure it is,' Charlotte agreed. She did not approve of her mother-in-law gadding off to Yorkshire. Who could know what influences she came under from her English daughter-in-law, of whom she seemed far too fond?

'We have arranged for Hortense to sleep at our house,' Charlotte went on. 'We thought it might be easier for you, and we haven't seen Hortense for such a long time.'

'What a good idea!' Madame Bonneau said. 'Don't you think that's a good idea, Hortense?'

'Certainly. If it's not too much trouble to you, Charlotte!' She could have screamed.

'None whatsoever,' Charlotte said. 'Perhaps we should go soon, leave *Maman* to rest. We shall come to see you in the morning, *Maman*.'

When they came in the morning it was too late.

It was Brigitte, taking coffee and a croissant to her mistress, who found Madame Bonneau dead. At first, since the bedcovers were half-hiding her face, she thought she was asleep: but when she touched her on the shoulder there was a rigidity, a coldness about the old lady which set Brigitte screaming and brought Léon running.

'She died in her sleep, I would say several hours ago,' the doctor said when they brought him. 'You can see from her features that it was a peaceful death. And to me it was not a surprise.'

'What do you mean?' Léon demanded. 'My mother was never ill!'

'Her heart had not been good for some time. She knew and I knew, but she forbade me to tell anyone else. She didn't want to be fussed over.'

But if I had known, I would have spared her the long journey to Helsdon, Léon thought. I would have taken better care of her. Why didn't she tell me?

'I daresay I can guess what you're thinking,' the doctor said. 'That there are things you would have spared her. But you would have been wrong, Léon. She wanted so much to go to your home in England.'

'She told me she enjoyed this last visit more than any other,' Léon admitted.

There was a great deal to do.

He telegraphed Madeleine, though advising her not to make the long journey for the funeral. He sent for Marie, who came at once from Paris. Everyone was suddenly in the house – Marcel, Pierre, their wives, Hortense.

'Jules will be here for the funeral,' Marie said.

'And afterwards, if I may, I will go to Paris with you,' Hortense said.

'Of course!' Marie said. 'And what will you do, Léon?'

'I shall go home,' he said. 'To Helsdon. I shan't have time, now, to go to Paris.'

Ah well, Hortense thought. He would not be good company, not at all. She must find her own amusements in Paris. And when she returned to Yorkshire, Léon would still be there.

'I shall come to Paris in September,' Léon told his sister. 'I have business commitments in France then, and I shall certainly make time to come to see you.'

EIGHTEEN

'You know I would have come to the funeral if you had wished me to,' Madeleine said.

'Of course! But it was better not,' Léon said. 'In any case, you would hardly have been there in time. Everything happened so quickly.'

He had been back in Helsdon three days now, after spending the better part of a week in Roubaix. Even after the funeral there had been so many matters to attend to: lawyers, the will, possessions: everything to be divided equally between himself, his brothers and his sister. There was also the position of Brigitte to consider. She had been with his mother a long time.

'In the end Simone decided that she would take Brigitte,' Léon said, 'though they don't actually like each other. But I think that she might eventually end up with Marie, in Paris.'

'Brigitte would be happier with Marie,' Madeleine said.

'As a matter of fact,' Léon said, 'I think *Maman* grew to love you more than any of her daughters-in-law.'

'I think in the end she even forgave me for having taken her son away to a foreign country!' Madeleine said. 'And she did enjoy her last few weeks with us, so I'm pleased about that.'

She was deeply pleased to have Léon back. Never before had she felt so anxious about his absence. Her anxiety had had nothing to do with his mother's death; it had been at its height before she had known of that, in fact from the moment when she had seen him off in Leeds.

Hortense was the reason, of course – though she

chided herself for the thoughts which had raced through her head. They were an insult to Léon, yet to apologize for them was the last thing she could do. He would be hurt even to know she had entertained them.

'Was Hortense very shocked by your mother's death?' Madeleine enquired.

'Yes. Afterwards, she didn't want to stay in Roubaix a moment longer than she had to. She never got on well with Charlotte or Simone.'

'So when do you think she might return home?'

Léon shrugged.

'I have no idea!' He went back to reading his *Yorkshire Post*.

'Léon!' Madeleine said suddenly. 'Léon, please tell me you love me!'

He looked up in surprise, then put down his newspaper and held out his arms.

'Come here!'

She came to him and he pulled her on to his lap.

'How many times have I told you in the last few days?' he said. 'I love you. You are the sun and the moon and the stars to me.'

'I needed to know,' Madeleine said. 'You can go back to your newspaper now!'

He knew the root of her anxiety. He'd sensed it when he was leaving for France. And how close he had come to proving her right! What a fool I am, he thought! What a lucky fool. With a wife like Madeleine, how could he even think of Hortense?

'I've been thinking about Tommy's birthday treat,' he said. 'I'd been considering taking him to Roubaix, but now isn't the time.'

'He was very upset about *Grandmère*'s death,' Madeleine said.

'So I thought instead I might take him to London when I go to the Wool Sales in July. It's just before his birthday. I need spend no more than half a day at the sales, and he can attend them with me. Since one day he will be buying wool, he might find it interesting.'

'He would like to go to London,' Madeleine said. 'Most especially, he would like to go just with you. He adores you, Léon. You know that, don't you?'

'I do. And I love him. I never think of him as other than my son.'

Tommy, when given the news, went crimson with pleasure.

'London? Do you really mean it, Papa?'

'Of course I do,' Léon said. 'It'll be just you and me. Claire and Mama can come with us on another occasion, but not this trip.'

'Oh Papa, it will be the best birthday present in the world!'

A whole week in London with Papa! Tommy almost burst with joy at the thought of it.

'What will we do, Papa?' he asked.

'Lots of things,' Léon promised. 'The Zoological Gardens, the museums. Or we can take a boat on the river. And then there's Madame Tussaud's Waxworks. . .'

'Can I have a sheet of drawing paper from your workroom, Mama?' Tommy asked.

'I think so. Why do you want it?'

'I'm going to make a calendar. I'm going to fasten it to the wall and mark off every day until we go! When do you think we might go, Papa?'

'Do you want to know exactly?'

'If I could.'

'Very well. Let me see now. . . We'll go on Monday, 11 July, and return a week later.'

While Tommy eagerly marked off the days on his calendar, the weeks meanwhile passing through pleasant northern weather, with warmth in the Helsdon valley and a fresh breeze on the top of the moor, France moved languidly through the hottest summer in all but the longest of memories.

In the countryside farmers counted the days since they

334

had last had the rain for which they now prayed constantly. And when the ground was baked as hard as a rock, when the crops failed and the horses were likely to die from lack of fodder, their owners reluctantly led them to market and sold them off as horsemeat for the people in the towns. It was a matter of fine judgement as to precisely when this moment had arrived.

It was hot in Paris, of course, but nothing seemed to stop the comings and goings, the parading in the latest fashions up and down the boulevards, the river trips on the *bateaux-mouches*, each of which held a hundred and fifty passengers all intent on pleasure, and, if possible, on cooling off by the water. The exhibitions, the theatres, the balls, continued unabated.

Hortense was having the time of her life.

Naturally it was not possible for Marie and Jules to visit the theatre, or any other entertainments, since they were in mourning. But to Hortense it seemed reasonable, when friends offered to escort her where propriety banned Marie and Jules, graciously to accept such offers.

'You see very little of Hortense, my dear,' Jules said to his wife. 'Don't you mind?'

'Not really,' Marie confessed. 'I like Hortense – she's fun – but we never did have many tastes in common. Now that my interests are in my home and my son and daughter, and Hortense's definitely are *not*, we have less than ever to talk about.'

'How long will she stay?' Jules asked.

'I don't know. I don't feel it's a question I can ask outright. And whenever I skirt around the subject she quickly changes it. She's enjoying herself too much. She's made too many friends to want to leave.'

'Especially the Colonel!' Jules remarked.

'Especially the Colonel.'

Colonel Maurice de Beauvoir was stationed, at least for the time being and hopefully for the rest of the summer, in Paris. Hortense had met him in an art gallery. She had felt faint, and had therefore been obliged to sit down for a moment on a seat already partly occupied by this hand-some man in his officer's uniform.

She had, to be plain, picked him up – but since he clearly had money which he wasn't averse to spending, came of an impeccable family, had beautiful manners and no wife in sight, then that was all right.

What would I have done in Paris without him, she asked herself? Marie and Jules were so circumscribed by their mourning. Really, in relieving them of respon-sibility, she had done her hosts a good turn.

As a consequence of going to bed at all hours, she rose late in the mornings. Today it was almost noon when she appeared, still in her *peignoir*, her hair tousled, her hand to her mouth, covering a yawn.

'Oh, but I am so tired, Marie!' she cried. 'And I daresay you have been up hours!'

'You look tired,' Marie said unkindly. 'And yes, I have been up since six. If you want the best value, you have to be out doing your marketing early.'

'How wonderful you are!' Hortense said.

'No,' Marie said. 'Just an ordinary French housewife.'

Hortense repressed a shudder. The only thing worse was to be an ordinary English housewife in a place like Leeds!

'No, you really are wonderful!' she insisted. 'It would all be quite beyond me!'

'Sometimes I think it will get beyond me,' Marie said. 'Everything costs so much, and prices are rising up all the time.'

'But you're not poor, *chérie*! Jules has a good job.'

'We are not poor, thank the good Lord – nor are we rich. To be poor in Paris now is not good. In spite of all Emperor Louis Napoleon has done – and one has to admit, he has really tried to help in many ways – the working man must still spend a third of his wages on rent, and a great deal of the rest on food. There is very little left after that.'

'Oh dear, you are getting so serious, Marie!' Hortense

lamented. 'You used never to be. I must say, I blame Jules!'

'Jules is a good man!' Marie said hotly. 'He thinks of others besides himself!'

'But he doesn't like the Emperor?'

'Neither of us has much time for the Emperor, and even less for his extravagant, vain-glorious wife. She should go back to Spain where she belongs!'

'I think I shall have a cup of chocolate,' Hortense said in a bored voice. 'And perhaps a croissant – though I mustn't eat too much. The Colonel is to take me out to lunch. And tomorrow I *must* be up early. The Colonel and some of his officers are to go hunting in the Forest of Fontainebleau. Of course I can't hunt because I don't have the proper clothes, and between you and me I'm frightened to death – but a few ladies are to go along in the carriages and join the men in a picnic. It will be such fun!'

'Well I suppose the Colonel and his officers might as well take their fun while they can,' Marie said. 'There won't be much fun for them when the war comes!'

'War? Don't be silly, Marie! There's not going to be a war!'

'Don't you read the papers, Hortense?'

'Indeed I do! Why only last week the British Foreign Secretary said there wasn't a cloud in the sky! Those were his words: "Not a cloud in the sky!"'

'Last week's newspaper is old news,' Marie said. 'Events move on; change.'

'Well you can't expect me to keep up with the newspapers,' Hortense complained. 'I'm much too busy. And now I really must go and dress. Maurice hates to be kept waiting!'

In Helsdon, Tommy crossed off the last date on his calendar before he was to set off for London. His valise was packed. His new suit of clothes waited to be put on first thing in the morning. His boots had been polished until he could see his face in them. He had had a bath, washed his hair, eaten his supper, the last only because Grandma Bates had stood over him and made him do so. He wasn't the least bit hungry.

'Now you must go to sleep quickly and get a good night's sleep,' his mother said. 'You have a long journey ahead of you tomorrow.'

'I'll try to, Mama,' he promised. He knew he would never sleep.

But when Madeleine looked in on him on her way to bed, he was fast asleep. He looked so young, much younger than his years. There were times, and this was one of them, when he reminded her of Irvine at the same age. But apart from his looks, which were also her looks, he had nothing of his real father in him. In temperament he was uncannily like Léon: strong, yet gentle; tenacious, passionate, caring.

It was all rush and bustle next morning, with Grandma Bates giving him terrible warnings about putting his head out of the train window, Mama fussing about whether she had packed everything, and Claire fretting and fuming because she wasn't going. Tommy was glad when Sam brought the carriage to the door and they set off for Leeds.

From the very first moment when the train drew up in the high, smoky station, London was a joy, a delight, a city of magic. They went everywhere together: Hampton Court, the Tower of London, Kensington Museum; to the Zoological Gardens in Regent's Park where for a shilling they spent almost a whole day. And in the evenings – it was almost the high spot of the day – Tommy sat at a table in the dining-room with his father, man-to-man, choosing whatever he wanted from the menu: no restrictions, no discussions about what was or wasn't good for a growing boy to eat.

On the Friday evening just as they were starting dinner they heard the newspaper boy shouting in the street. Léon immediately summoned the waiter.

'Get me a newspaper!'

When the waiter returned he snatched the newspaper from him and began to read, after which it seemed as though he had suddenly lost his appetite. He sat at the table, white-faced and serious, eating nothing.

'What's the matter, Papa?' Tommy asked. 'What does it say in the newspaper?'

'It says that France has declared war on Prussia,' Léon said quietly.

'Is that bad? Whose fault is it?'

'I'm afraid most people will say it's the fault of France,' Léon said. 'The English like the Germans better than the French. As for whether it's bad – all war is bad. We have to hope and pray that it won't last long.'

'Does it mean . . . shall we have to go home?' Tommy asked fearfully. He couldn't bear the thought. There was a whole, glorious weekend before them. And tomorrow they were to go to Madame Tussaud's. How could he bear to give it up?

'We ought. . .' Léon began, then saw his son's anxious face.

'But I don't think we will, old man! I think we can stay until Monday without changing the course of history!'

Madeleine would hear the news, of course. She would be one of the few people in Helsdon who would be worried by it. Helsdon was a long way from France: its inhabitants went about their business with little thought for foreign parts.

'I'll write a few lines to Mama at once,' Léon said. 'She'll receive it before she sees us.'

On the following morning, passing by Charing Cross station, they saw a long column of German soldiers going for the train which would start them on their journey to the war. People in the Strand stood and cheered as they marched past.

'You were right, Papa!' Tommy said. 'The people are cheering the Germans. But *I* shall be on the side of the French!'

For the rest of the weekend Tommy, his whole being

concentrated on the delights of London, gave no thought to the war. Léon thought about it most of the time, but said nothing. He was not sorry when it was time to board the train for home.

'It's been the best week of my whole life!' Tommy said when they were on the train. 'Nothing will ever be as good as this.'

'Lots of things will be,' Léon assured him. 'But I shall be happy if you remember it with pleasure.'

At Mount Royd Madeleine met them with an anxious face, but said nothing of what troubled her until Tommy had gone off with Claire and she was alone with Léon.

'What will happen?' she asked him anxiously.

'Who knows? I only know what I read in the newspapers – and how much of that is rumour, anyway?'

'Will it affect our trade with France? I mean Bonneau's trade.'

'It depends how long it lasts.'

'Well thank heaven you didn't take Tommy to Roubaix,' Madeleine said.

'Oh I think we would have been all right,' Léon said. 'I doubt that there's fighting anywhere near Roubaix.'

'All the same, I'm glad you didn't go. And of course you won't be able to go to Paris in September.'

She was watching him as she spoke. There was a look on his face which alarmed her.

'You won't, will you, Léon?' she pressed him.

'I can't promise, my dear. September is two months away. And we must do everything we can to keep up our business contacts. Once lost, it might be difficult to get them back. That's important. Also, I did promise Marie I would go.'

'In any case,' he went on, 'the war might be over by then. And even if it isn't, it probably won't affect Paris. No enemy would be so barbarous as to march on Paris. Even the Prussians acknowledge the importance of Paris to the civilized world.'

'And who will win this war?' Madeleine asked.

Léon looked at her in astonishment.

'Why France of course! The Prussians are all talk. They'll be no good when it comes to a fight.'

'I still wish you would promise me not to go there,' Madeleine persisted.

'You are worrying unnecessarily,' Léon said. 'Put it out of your mind. Now let me tell you what a wonderful time Tommy and I had in London.'

The next day Henry Garston came over from Leeds.

'I'm worried about that wife of mine,' he said. 'I telegraphed her to come home at once, but I've had no reply. Now I've written to her. Goodness knows if she'll take the slightest notice. I daresay she's having too good a time, but how do I know if she's safe?'

'Léon thinks Paris will be quite safe,' Madeleine said.

'Well, perhaps he's right,' Henry said grudgingly. 'But I can't risk it. She's got to come home, even if I have to go and fetch her.'

He wasn't even sure that he wanted her home – the silly bitch – but he felt responsible for her.

As a matter of fact Hortense, in Paris, was no longer having such a good time. Colonel de Beauvoir and his regiment had been packed off to the war front at less than a day's notice. There had scarcely been a moment for him to take her shopping for a farewell gift. Luckily, she had known exactly what she wanted – a pair of diamond earrings – and where to find them – otherwise it would have been hopeless.

The next morning she stood in the street and watched them as they rode out of Paris. Oh, but they looked so splendid in their colourful uniforms, and every officer with a neat imperial beard. And Maurice looked especially fine! She was truly moved. The tears hovering in her eyes, though she must not give way and let them fall, were almost as bright as the diamonds in her ears. She hoped that Maurice saw her waving as he passed.

'Heaven knows where they were going!' she said later

to Jules and Marie. 'Maurice thought perhaps Metz, which sounds very dreary. *Not* a fashionable place!'

'In any case, he shouldn't have told you,' Jules said disapprovingly.

'He was only guessing,' Hortense said. 'It was probably somewhere quite different. Personally, I don't see why they should have had to leave Paris. Surely we need someone to look after us here?'

'There's no fighting here, Hortense,' Marie pointed out. 'They need the soldiers where the fighting is.'

'Well no one seems to know where that might be,' Hortense said. 'They say the army is turning up in all the wrong places. Isn't it a scream!'

'All the same,' she added, 'it's not very nice at the moment, is it? I mean – all those rough-looking crowds in the street, shouting "*Vive la guerre!*" and the students singing "*La Marseillaise*" in the most threatening manner. I felt quite frightened this afternoon.'

Jules looked at his wife. When their eyes met she gave him an almost imperceptible nod.

'Hortense, I think the time has come for you to return to England,' Jules said firmly.

She was startled by that.

'Oh, but I didn't mean . . . I'm sure I shall get used to it. I'm not *really* frightened, Jules dear. I daresay I was a little tense over Maurice's departure.'

Besides, she would soon make new friends. In no time at all things would be just as they had been.

'I was just having a little grumble,' she said pleasantly. 'You mustn't take the slightest notice of me!'

'But you must take notice of me,' Jules said. 'You really must go home, Hortense. You have had your husband's telegraph and I don't believe you've even replied to it. Think how worried he must be!'

'Oh, I doubt that Henry worries,' Hortense said brightly. 'But I will reply. Of course I will! I'll tell him everything's perfectly all right and I'm staying just a little longer.'

How could she possibly bear to leave Paris, even with a war on, to go back to Leeds?

'No! No, no, no! You will tell him nothing of the kind!' How stern and cold Jules sounded. 'I am formally asking you to leave, Hortense. For our sakes, if not for your own.' But when would she do anything for the sake of anyone else, he asked himself? 'It is my belief that things are going to get really difficult – yes, even here in Paris. Prices will go sky high, we can be sure of that; and then there'll be shortages. If that happens it will take me all my time to provide for my own family. I cannot take on extra responsibility.'

Hortense turned to Marie. She was really quite appalled by Jules's behaviour. And why did his wife stand there and say nothing?

'Can I believe that you, my oldest friend, are *turning me out*?' she demanded.

'If that is how you like to put it,' Marie said. She sounded every bit as determined as her husband.

'I most certainly do!' Hortense said. 'And I can assure you that I shall telegraph Henry first thing in the morning. I can see that I have outstayed my welcome.' She took out her handkerchief and dabbed at her eyes.

'It's not that, Hortense!' Marie protested. 'It's that the circumstances are wrong!'

But in any case she *has* outstayed her welcome, Jules thought. She is a tedious, tiresome, light-minded woman. He wondered what his wife could ever have seen in her.

A week later, Henry Garston came to Helsdon again.

'I've heard from Hortense,' he said. 'Here, read this!'

He handed Madeleine the letter he had received that morning. Madeleine felt her lips twitching as she read it, but from the look of Henry he was clearly not amused. She straightened her face and passed the letter to Léon.

*

'. . . the strain of living in Paris in these difficult times has told on me [Hortense wrote], I am sorely in need of a little diversion and would like you, therefore, to meet me at Dover and arrange for us to have a few days in London before I return to my housewifely duties in Leeds.'

'Shall you do so?' Léon asked, handing back the letter.

'I suppose so,' Henry said. 'But I know very well what the diversion will be. It'll be shopping!'

When Henry left, they saw him to his carriage and watched him being driven away. When they went back into the house Madeleine closed the door, then leaned against it, convulsed with laughter.

'Oh Léon!' she gasped. 'That letter! I don't know how I kept my face straight! ''The strain of living in Paris''! ''My housewifely duties in Leeds''!' She mimicked Hortense's voice, with its delicate French accent, surprisingly well. 'Oh, my goodness! Poor Henry!'

'I should think the strain has fallen entirely on Marie and Jules,' Léon said.

'Oh Léon, to think I was ever jealous of Hortense!' Madeleine cried. 'And I was, you know. I confess I was very worried about her. But really she's just plain silly.'

No, there's more to her than that, Léon thought. And you almost had reason to be jealous, but you never will have again. Of that he was certain. It was over.

Ten days later Henry brought Hortense to Mount Royd. He had, as requested, met her at Dover and they had spent a hectic four days shopping in London.

'You are looking exceptionally smart,' Madeleine said as she took Hortense up to her room. 'You look a true *Parisienne*! And your beautiful earrings! They're new, aren't they? Did Henry buy those in London?'

'No,' Hortense said smoothly. 'I bought them myself, in Paris.'

Their eyes met in the mirror. Hortense saw the amazement in Madeleine's.

'They're fine diamonds. They must have cost you a year's allowance.'

'Oh, they did!' Hortense said.

Where is dear Maurice, she wondered? Where is he on his coal-black horse? She did so hope he was safe and sound.

Hortense's account of her stay in Paris lost nothing in the telling, except, of course, that there were parts of it not touched upon.

'Of course there were things I couldn't do because of your dear mother's death,' she said to Léon. 'But Marie and Jules absolutely insisted that I met people, made friends, did whatever was possible.'

'And I'm sure you did, my dear,' Henry said.

Hortense gave him a sharp look. Was there a teeny hint of sarcasm there?

'And now may I borrow Henry for a few minutes?' Madeleine said. 'There are some designs in my workroom I'd like to discuss. Do you mind, Hortense?'

'Not at all.'

You may have him whenever you like, Hortense thought, as long as I can have Léon in exchange.

An opportunity to see Léon alone was what she'd been waiting for. She had returned to Leeds determined to continue the affair which had been interrupted by his mother's death. It would all need careful arrangements, but she had no doubt at all that she could see to that, or that she could persuade Léon to fall in with them.

'So why don't we take a turn in your beautiful garden?' she asked Léon.

'Very well. And you shall tell me how my little sister is. When is she going to write to me?'

Hortense took his arm as they began to walk across the lawn. At the far corner of the lawn an arch led through to the kitchen garden, which was screened from most of the house.

'Marie will write to you soon,' Hortense said. 'She told me to tell you that. She is always so busy; shopping, cooking, sewing. And she sacrifices herself to those demanding children!'

'Well I look forward to hearing from her,' Léon said. 'Why are we going in the direction of the kitchen garden?'

'Why should I not wish to see your delicious fruit and vegetables?' Hortense said. 'Every Frenchwoman is interested in such things.'

But you are not every Frenchwoman, Léon thought. There is more to it.

The moment they were through the archway Hortense turned towards Léon and took both his hands in hers.

'Oh Léon, you know why we're in this corner of the garden! It's so that we can be quite alone. Now at last you can take me in your arms. Oh my love, it's been so long!'

She closed her eyes and swayed towards him. He was acutely aware of the scent and the feel of her body. Then he took her by the shoulders and held her at arm's length.

'No, Hortense! This is impossible! You know that every bit as well as I do!'

She opened her eyes wide, spoke in hurt, disbelieving tones.

'But surely, Léon . . . you're not pretending you find me unattractive?'

'Of course not.'

'And desirable?'

'I don't deny it.'

'Then what is wrong? You were not like this in Paris. Or in London. I'm not asking you to make love to me here and now – but now that I am back in Yorkshire there will be opportunities, times and places. . . Oh, Léon, we have so much to offer each other!'

'No, Hortense! We have nothing to offer each other, nothing except friendship.'

'I have everything to give you!' Hortense cried passionately. 'I love you, Léon! I've always loved you. Are you throwing that back in my face?'

'I'm not accepting it,' Léon said firmly.

'You will change your mind,' Hortense said. 'I know you will!'

'I shall never change my mind, Hortense. Madeleine is the only woman I love, or ever shall.'

She looked at him long and hard now. Her defeat came as a total surprise to her, but she recognized it when she saw it. He was implacable. She hated him. From this moment she detested him with an ice-cold hatred.

She started to run away from him. He put out a hand to stop her but she was too quick, and ran into the house. When he went in Madeleine and Henry were also there. There was no sign of distress in Hortense's manner and the atmosphere seemed normal.

'Time for us to be off!' Henry said. 'Get your cloak, Hortense!'

All the way home to Leeds Hortense thought of Léon with mounting anger. Henry recognized it and kept quiet. Also, from the side window of Madeleine's workroom he had seen his wife and Léon together in the kitchen garden. He didn't watch them long; his efforts were all on preventing Madeleine looking out of that particular window. But somewhere, there was trouble brewing, which was why he'd made the quick decision to leave.

Bonneau must have turned her down, he thought. That was why she was angry. Well it wasn't the first time for Hortense and he doubted it would be the last. But he wouldn't have overlooked this one, not with Madeleine involved.

'What a boring day!' Hortense said sharply as they were nearing Leeds. 'Madeleine is so provincial, don't you agree?'

'Well since I'm a provincial myself, I wouldn't find much wrong with that!' Henry said.

'And she has made Léon almost as dull as herself. He never used to be like that. No!' she said. 'What they both need is something to waken them up!' And who better to deliver it than she? She didn't know which of them she disliked the more.

Henry was at once alert to the danger signal in her voice.

'Really? And what have you thought of then?'

'I haven't yet. But I will!'

Her tone was controlled, but that was a threat if ever he'd heard one. He knew by now when to ignore his wife and when to take her seriously. This was serious. He must watch and wait, but he doubted he'd have to wait long. She was seething with anger, which would find an outlet.

Less than an hour after they'd reached home Henry went into the morning-room and found Hortense sitting at the desk, pen in hand, a deep frown of concentration on her brow. So intent was she on what she was doing that she didn't hear him enter. It was an unusual sight. Hortense never put pen to paper if she could help it.

'Who are you writing to?' He wasn't sure he needed to ask.

She jumped at the sound of his voice and covered the sheet of paper with her arm.

'Oh! You startled me! I'm just writing a thank-you note to Madeleine.'

That was even more unlike her.

Henry crossed the room in two strides, pushed her aside, picked up the letter and began to read.

'Dear Mrs Bonneau
Ask your husband what he got up to in Paris, not to mention London. Don't believe him if he says nothing. All men are liars.'

It was unsigned. She had not had the time.

As he read, his face went white with anger. When he

reached the end he tore the letter into several pieces, threw them into the empty grate, and set a match to them. He watched the letter burn until there was nothing left of it but a few charred flakes. When it was done he turned to Hortense. She was alarmed at the sight of him. His eyes blazed, his face was a mask of fury.

'You . . . you guttersnipe! You dirty little guttersnipe! And it was to be an anonymous letter, wasn't it? Signed "A wellwisher" I don't doubt.'

'It was . . . a joke! I wouldn't have sent it!'

'Do you seriously expect me to believe that? So what has Madeleine Bonneau ever done to you?'

'She hasn't. . .'

'Don't tell me! I can guess! She married Léon Bonneau, didn't she? And now you want him. And my guess is you can't get him. This is your dirty little revenge.'

'We didn't do anything. . .' she began.

'Do you think I care whether you did or you didn't? But let me tell you this, if you harm a single hair of Madeleine Bonneau's head, either by deed, or word, or innuendo – if you cause her a minute's unhappiness, you're out of this house, lock, stock and barrel! Do you understand?'

Hortense found her voice.

'Oh yes, I understand all right. It's Madeleine Bonneau you care about, and always have done. You'd like her for yourself, wouldn't you?'

The pain in his eyes told her that she'd hit on the truth. What a pity she hadn't known earlier. It might have been useful.

'Well we've both married the wrong people, haven't we?' she said.

'*We* have,' Henry said. 'They haven't. They love each other in a way you and me can never know. If I catch you interfering with that, remember what I said. Out you go, and not a penny piece goes with you!'

Tears of frustration filled her eyes. Why was everything against her – and now even Henry. She couldn't do without Henry. Even in her wildest dreams about Léon she'd always known she couldn't do without Henry.

'I'm sorry, Henry,' she said. 'I'm truly sorry. I don't know what got into me!'

In August a letter arrived from Marie. It was full of the things that Hortense had failed to tell them about France. Léon opened it at the breakfast table and fed the information in snatches to Madeleine.

'She writes about the French victory at Saarbrücken and the capture of the Crown Prince of Prussia. . .'

'But we already know about that,' Madeleine interrupted. 'We've read all about that in the newspaper.'

Each day they avidly scoured the newspapers for every bit of news from the war. They knew that Louis Napoleon, egged on by the Empress, had ridden to war at the head of his troops. They knew that since the victory at Saarbrücken things had not gone at all well for the French.

'Does she say how she is, how Jules and the children are? Are they safe?' Madeleine asked.

'Of course they're safe, Madeleine! She doesn't need to tell us that.'

'She does me! If you're persisting with your idea of going to Paris, it's what I want to know most of all.'

'Well the fact that she doesn't mention it I'm sure means that they are,' Léon said.

I don't want Marie and Jules to be having a hard time, Madeleine thought. Of course I don't. But in a way she was disappointed that there was nothing at all in the letter to deter Léon from visiting Paris.

'I'm somewhat amused,' Léon said, 'that *Le Figaro* has launched a fund to give every French soldier a cigar and a glass of brandy. Since my countrymen don't seem to be able to get either the troops or their ammunition where it's needed, how are they going to organize all those glasses of brandy?'

'Just like a newspaper!' Madeleine said.

Léon rose from the table.

'I've been thinking,' he said. 'I might go to Paris in August, very soon, rather than wait for September.'

Madeleine gave him a long, steady look.

'I can guess why. You do actually think it's going to get worse there!'

'It might,' he admitted.

'Oh Léon, must you go at all? Let the trade go hang! It's nothing compared to your safety. I'd rather lose it all than have you in the slightest danger.'

'I won't be,' Léon said. 'I really must go. And if I go soon, I'm sure there'll be no danger.'

'Well, since you seem determined to go, my love, no matter what I say, the sooner the better! The sooner you go, the sooner you'll be back where you belong!'

Where do I belong, Léon wondered? When my country is at war, where do I belong?

NINETEEN

Losing no time, Léon travelled to France on 13 August, a Saturday.

'I shall be back this time next week,' he said to Madeleine.

'I don't want you to go,' Madeleine said. 'But it seems I can't stop you. So God speed, my darling!'

'If I come back with some good orders we shall both think it worth while,' said Léon. 'And I really do hope to get orders for your fashion designs. I feel in my bones that this time we might break into the Paris market.'

'That would be really wonderful!' Madeleine said. 'But don't you think the people of Paris will have their minds on other things? Won't they be too preoccupied to think of fashion?'

'Paris is never too preoccupied to think of fashion,' Léon assured her.

Travelling by train from Calais to Paris, he saw no signs of a country at war; no troop movements, no sounds of battle. Except that it was dried to a bleached brown from the long summer's drought, the countryside was much as usual. But once in Paris, a city he had known all his adult life, he was aware of the difference.

It was nothing dramatic: no columns of marching soldiers, no fortifications. The streets were crowded, as always, with citizens going about their business; but to Léon, who brought a fresh eye to the scene as he saw it from the *fiacre* on the way to Marie's home in Montparnasse, the signs were there.

Groups of people, not twos or threes but larger groups, stood on street corners not pleasantly chatting, but shouting and waving fists. Or, sometimes, they stood grave and silent while an impassioned speaker harangued them.

Some shops were boarded up, or had closed altogether. Twice he saw families pushing carts piled high with their worldly goods. Of course they could have been moving no further than the next street, but they had about them the look of people starting on a much longer journey.

Once he witnessed a street fight, with a gang of youths attacking three middle-aged men.

'Stop! Stop at once!' he commanded the cab driver. 'We must do something!'

On the contrary, the driver whipped the horse into increased speed.

'It's not wise to stop, *Monsieur*,' he insisted. 'Not an affair to get mixed up in. Anyway, it's not an uncommon sight these days.'

'I was appalled,' Léon said later to Marie and Jules. 'People stood around and watched, didn't lift a finger!'

'Well as your *cocher* said, it's not uncommon,' Jules remarked. 'Every time we get bad news from the war front, the French go out and beat up Germans, poor devils who've lived quietly in Paris half their lives.'

'But why?'

'The excuse is usually that they reckon they're spies.'

'Put it out of your mind for the moment,' Marie begged. 'Come and eat. You must be starving.'

'I am hungry,' Léon admitted. 'And the meal smells delicious.'

'How long will you stay with us, Léon?' Jules asked.

'I expect to be home within the week. I have business calls to make on Monday and Tuesday, after that I can spend a couple of days with you all before I return.'

'You know you are always welcome,' Jules said. 'But in fact I don't advise you to stay long. Paris might soon be a bad place to be.'

'But the war isn't here yet, and perhaps it never will be,' Léon said.

'That's true – though to hear some people talk you'd

think the Prussian army was about to march through the streets! Those are the stupid people who will cause the rest to panic. They're the idiots who beat up innocent Germans.'

'The English aren't too popular in Paris at the moment,' Marie observed. 'As for your Mr Gladstone – he's positively hated!'

'He's not *my* Mr Gladstone,' Léon objected.

'Well you know what I mean, Léon. In any case, do you see Louis Napoleon as your Emperor?'

'Not really,' Léon admitted. 'But I see France as my country. I don't want it overrun by Prussians any more than you do.'

'Oh we shall never let them overrun Paris,' Jules said confidently. 'We shall keep them out, never fear!'

But how, Léon wondered? Everyone knew that the Prussian army was magnificent, and the King of Prussia was a soldier to his fingertips. Besides, hadn't they been preparing for this for years? Every time they built a railway in Germany it had a military as well as a civil purpose behind it. Or so it was said.

'Anyway,' said Marie. 'Let's not talk about the war any more this evening. So tell me, how is Hortense? Was she very cross with us for packing her off home?'

'I think she was,' Léon said. 'She warned me you had changed, and I gather she meant for the worse.'

'Well she hasn't changed, that's for certain!' Marie said. 'She was always selfish – though to be fair, she was always charming.'

The next day Marie said: 'We always walk in the Bois de Boulogne on Sunday afternoon. Would you like to do that, Léon?'

'Of course! What else would one do in Paris on a Sunday afternoon?'

War or no war, Prussians at the gates or not, Léon thought, half the city's population seemed to be strolling in the Bois, in the cool shade of the trees. There were the usual knots of people, meeting and chatting – but nothing

354

untoward. No uncomfortable scenes. The whole atmosphere was brighter, as if everyone had taken a day off from the war. This was more like the Paris he knew.

And then, suddenly, on nothing more than taking a new direction, by turning a corner, everything changed.

Marie and Jules, hand-in-hand with Jean and Etienne, Léon a yard or so behind, dozens of others walking near – all came to a dead stop. They had no choice: their way was blocked by newly-felled trees lying across the path. And a little way off, beyond the felled trees, men were at work with saws and hammers and ropes.

'*Mon Dieu!*' Jules cried. 'Look at that! They're building fortifications!'

'Fortifications! Fortifications!'

The word went from mouth to mouth, like a cold wind blowing through the crowd on the hot afternoon. Voices which a minute before had been raised in laughter were now harsh with fear. The smile on the face of the crowd was wiped off as if by a giant sponge.

'Let's go home!' Marie said, shivering.

They returned home almost in silence. In the evening, though they had foresworn to mention the war over the weekend, once the children were in bed it was all they could talk about.

'I seriously think you should come back to England with me until this is over,' Léon urged. 'We have a large house; there would be room for all of you. And Madeleine would welcome you with open arms.'

Jules shook his head.

'I hate war, and I've no desire to fight, but I can't leave France at a time like this. In particular, I can't desert Paris. I was born here.'

'But what will you do if you stay?' Léon asked.

'I don't know,' Jules confessed. 'I might join the *Gardes Mobiles*, though they already have thousands more volunteers than they know what to do with, most of them untrained. I suppose I shall do whatever seems best to help Paris. But that is no reason at all why Marie and the children should not accept your offer. I would be pleased for them to go.'

'Oh no!' Marie said quickly. 'I will let Jean and Etienne go, but I simply refuse to leave you, Jules!'

She went and stood by his chair, her hand on his shoulder as if any minute Léon might take her away by force. Jules reached up and covered her hand with his.

'Do you think I wouldn't miss you every minute you were gone?' he said tenderly. 'But you know there's a very special reason why you should go. I think we should tell Léon.'

'I am pregnant,' Marie said quietly. 'Only just. The baby won't be born until next spring. Even so, I won't leave Jules. But I would be grateful, Léon, if you'd take the children and look after them for us.'

Could either her husband or her brother, though both of them were so concerned, know what it cost her to agree to part with Jean and Etienne? What she wanted most of all at this time was to gather her family around her. Nevertheless, she would let them go.

'Of course I'll take them,' Léon said. 'But surely Jules is right – surely you also should leave with me?'

'He might be right,' Marie assented. 'However, I'm not leaving.'

'Very well,' Léon said. 'When I write to Madeleine tomorrow I shall tell her to expect the children with me. And if you wish to change your mind, you can.'

The next day, after breakfast, he set off on his business calls. The first was to a wholesaler who had been a firm customer for Bonneau's fabrics for some years. He half-expected, seeing the conditions in Paris, that this time he wouldn't get a good order. When it proved much as usual, he voiced the fears he'd had.

'Oh no!' the wholesaler said. 'I wouldn't think of buying less. People have to be clothed, don't they?'

His reception there gave him encouragement for his next call. It was an important one, on an up-and-coming, though not long-established company, on whom he placed his hopes of selling some of Madeleine's fashion designs. On his last call Monsieur André, the owner, had shown more than a little interest in them. He had ordered nothing on that occasion, but the two of them had discussed prices and profit margins in detail. Monsieur André had also kept the designs, with a promise to give the matter further thought, and had encouraged Léon to call again.

Léon had told Madeleine nothing of this. If he couldn't surprise her with an order, at least he wouldn't disappoint her with dashed hopes.

'Ah, Monsieur Bonneau!' Monsieur André held out his hand. 'I have been looking forward to your visit. What have you to show me this time?'

'I have two new patterns of cloths,' Léon said. 'And some fashion designs which have been created specifically to go with them. I think you will approve.'

Monsieur André looked at everything long and hard. While making his examination he said nothing at all and it was impossible, from his impassive expression, even to guess what he was thinking. In the end, he nodded his head vigorously in approval, and allowed himself to smile.

'Ah yes! Yes, I like them! You are a talented dress designer, Monsieur Bonneau! I think you should live and work in Paris!'

Léon felt himself redden with guilt – and knew that Monsieur André would put his increased colour down to modesty, which made him feel even worse. But he still believed, he was sure, that if he were to present the designs – especially in Paris – as his wife's, they would stand no chance.

'Thank you,' he murmured. 'And the designs which I left with you on my last visit? Did you make any decision about them?'

'I liked those also,' Monsieur André said. 'I have costed everything, down to the last button, and I think we could do reasonably well with them – on two conditions, that is!'

'And those are?'

'That you deliver them soon, and that you give me better terms than you have offered so far.'

'I had thought that my terms were reasonable,' Léon said.

'I shall be giving you a large order,' Monsieur André said. 'A large order deserves the very best terms.'

'Well, we will discuss it,' Léon said. 'As to delivery, we will do our part quickly but something must depend on conditions – in Paris.'

'You mean the war?' Monsieur André waved his hands in a gesture which said he dismissed the war as of no account. 'We must not let the war interfere with business! I am sure there will be no difficulty here. Next to food, fashion is most important to Paris. You will not find us holding up either of those things.'

It might not be you who holds things up, Léon thought. It might be the Prussians. But now was not the time to say so. He would take the order and be thankful, and he would try with all his might and main to fulfil it.

'Then let us get down to business,' Monsieur André said. 'The less delay, the better.'

At the back of his mind lurked the thought that eventually things might get a bit sticky, in which case, the more stock he laid in, the better his position would be. Ladies' clothes might fetch quite a high price later on. Also, he liked what this Frenchman from England had to offer.

Léon left Monsieur André's premises cock-a-hoop. Should he take a *fiacre*, he asked himself? No! The day was fine; moreover he was restless with excitement. He strode ahead, feeling all the while as though he were treading on air. On the corner close to Marie's house he stopped to buy an extravagant bunch of roses for his sister. He wished he was taking them for Madeleine. When he went back to Helsdon he would take her the finest present he could find – a piece of jewellery, scent, silk underwear!

'Why, they're beautiful!' Marie said. 'Are we celebrating something?'

'Do I have to be celebrating to give my only sister a few flowers? But yes, you are right!'

'That's wonderful!' Marie said when he gave her the news.

'You look rather pale,' Léon observed. 'Is it the heat? Or perhaps your condition?'

'Neither,' Marie said. 'I've been rushing around getting everything ready for the children to leave. Washing and ironing clothes; mending. I shall have to buy a few things before they go.'

'There's no need to,' Léon said. 'Anything extra they need, Madeleine can get in Helsdon.'

'We'll see!'

She needed to keep busy. She wanted no time on her hands in which to brood. The thought of sending her children away was killing her. She wasn't sure whether she could go through with it, though she knew she must.

'Why don't you leave everything for now,' Léon suggested. 'I will write my letter to Madeleine and then we'll go out and post it and take the children for a walk in the Luxembourg Gardens. The fresh air will do you good.'

He felt so buoyed up, writing to Madeleine.

'I had to do it at once,' he said to Marie. 'Though possibly she will get the letter only hours before I arrive myself. And now let's go out.'

It was peaceful in the Luxembourg, everything as it should be: old ladies sitting on seats, knitting; mothers with children; nursemaids pushing prams.

'Everything is so normal!' he said.

'Yes, that is what is so strange,' Marie replied. 'One day the air is full of rumours and foreboding, and we are all down in the dumps; the next day everything is all right again. I do really wonder whether I need send the children to England after all?'

'Well then, let's put it that you are sending them for a little holiday with their English cousins,' Léon said. 'If everything continues all right here I will bring them back whenever you ask me to.'

'Do you promise?'

'I promise,' Léon said.

At Mount Royd, the postal service between France and England being extremely efficient, Madeleine received Léon's letter a full forty-eight hours before he was due to appear himself.

'Isn't it wonderful news, Ma?' she cried. 'Isn't it absolutely marvellous?'

'About the orders? Yes it is, and no more than you deserve, love. You've worked hard for your success. About Marie's children coming here, I'm less certain.'

'Oh but surely you don't mind having them?' Madeleine said. 'I don't think they'll be a lot of trouble – and Flora will help.'

'Of course I don't mind having them,' Mrs Bates said. 'I'll be pleased to see them here. No, I wasn't thinking that, I was thinking that things must look bad in Paris for Marie to part with her children.'

'You're right, Ma!' Madeleine said. 'You're absolutely right. I was so taken up with my own good news that I overlooked that. We must make them especially welcome, poor little lambs. We must make them feel at home.'

'Do they speak any English at all?' Mrs Bates asked.

'I doubt it.'

'Well then, I shall have to learn at least a few words of French,' Mrs Bates declared. 'And not before time, neither!'

Two days only, and Léon would be safe home again, Madeleine thought. And after that they would be frantically busy getting the orders out. Oh, but it was all so exciting! She would be counting the hours until he came.

Next morning, Léon, getting ready to leave the apartment, said: 'I don't have so many calls to make today. I shall be back by the middle of the afternoon and then perhaps we might take Jean and Etienne on the *bateaux-mouches*. What do you think?'

'They would love that,' Marie said. 'They like going on the river almost better than anything else. And it will leave me free to get on with some jobs.'

'Oh no!' Léon said. 'You are to come too. I insist on it.'

'You are quite right to do so,' Jules said. 'If I didn't have to go out to work I would go with you.'

He knew that Marie had hardly slept all night. She had tossed and turned beside him in the bed, and when daylight came he had wakened, and found her sobbing.

'I can't let them go! Oh Jules I can't!' she cried.

'But you must,' he said. 'And so must I, my love. It's for their sakes. And they'll be well taken care of with Léon and Madeleine. I promise you that the minute the danger is past, we shall have them home again.'

But she had been inconsolable – and now, at breakfast, her face was still pale, her eyelids red and swollen.

'Very well,' she said. 'We'll be ready when you arrive home.'

She wanted to go, of course she did. Between now and the moment when they would be taken away from her, she wanted to spend every possible minute with the children. While Jules was asleep she had gone into them in the middle of the night, stood watching them by the light of the candle while they slept. So peaceful they'd looked. So peaceful and innocent.

Léon took a few orders that morning, but not many. But since André's order was so big – it would mean the mill working overtime – he wasn't worried about the morning's lack of orders.

Madeleine frequently told him that there was no reason why he should still travel around, seeking orders. They were successful enough now to employ someone else to do the job. That was true, and it would work for the English side of the business, but for France, he maintained, it was different. No one in Helsdon, certainly no one who understood textiles, spoke French as he did, or would understand the French people and their way of working. The truth also was, it was one of the things he enjoyed most. All the same, he thought, walking through the city streets on his way back to Marie's, it would probably be some time before he was back in France again. Everything seemed against it.

His thoughts turned to Helsdon, to Madeleine, the mill, Tommy and Claire. It was because his mind was so far away that he was in the middle of the fight almost before he was aware of it.

He was walking down a hilly, narrow street, from which at intervals alleyways led off to the left. Ahead of him was a long, steep flight of steps which would take him back into the main street. He was no more than vaguely aware of an elderly man walking in front of him, and it was not until a youth sprang out of the shelter of a doorway and attacked the man, felling him to the ground, that Léon came to.

Instinctively, he sprang forward and grabbed the youth, succeeding in dragging him off the old man, who seized his chance and made off at once. The youth was strong. He knocked Léon to the ground, and might well have run away then, had not Léon raised himself sufficiently to grab the younger man around the ankles; and then they were both on the ground.

Léon was on top now, pinning his adversary down, but at that moment two more men ran from the alleyway and joined in the fight against him.

He was no match for the three of them, but anger – blinding rage – made him try. He lashed out, landing blows where he could. It would have been better had he not done so. They might have run away and left him. As it was, for every blow he attempted, three rained on him: on his head, his jaw, to his stomach.

When finally he lay there, limp and beaten, no strength left in him, they picked him up by his arms and legs and shifted him to the top of the steps. Then the three of them gave him the kicks which sent him rolling down.

The steps were so steep, so narrow, that he didn't come to a stop before he reached the bottom. In a way, it was as

362

well he did reach the bottom, because here was the main street where, though he was now unconscious and knew nothing of it, he was quickly found, and an ambulance called.

When next he opened his eyes he was in a hospital bed, one of forty or so in a large, shabby-looking ward. And with consciousness came excruciating pain; pain in every part of his body. His head throbbed with it; his face was stiff with it; every muscle, from top to toe, ached. What was it all about; how did he come to be here?

He turned his head, wincing at the agony it caused him, and saw a white-robed nun standing by the side of the bed.

'Don't try to move, Monsieur Bonneau,' she said gently.

'How do you know my name, Sister?' His voice was a croak. It was difficult to form the words.

'We found papers in your pocket. It seems that you live in England, but there was no note of where you are staying in Paris.'

'You didn't inform anyone in England?' Léon asked anxiously.

'There hasn't been time yet, *Monsieur*!'

'So how long have I been here?'

'Not more than a few hours,' the nun said. 'But I'm sure there must be someone we should inform, even if it's only your hotel.'

Léon thought hard before replying.

'I'm staying with my sister.'

'Then if you are able to give me her address I will send for her. She must be anxious.'

It was an effort to remember where Marie lived, even more of an effort to get the words out. It was difficult to think of anything except the pain. But in the end he managed it.

'We'll send a messenger at once,' the nun promised. 'In the meantime, the doctor will want to see you again.'

She left him, and returned minutes later with the doctor,

an elderly man who asked questions in a quiet voice.

'Do you remember what happened, *Monsieur*?'

'There was a fight,' Léon said. It was all so difficult to recall. He wanted to go to sleep again now, to escape from the pain. The wider awake he became, the more his body hurt him.

'Obviously! But where? With whom?'

'I think there were three men,' Léon said. 'We were at the top of a flight of steps.'

The doctor nodded.

'I thought so. You have so many bruises and injuries, it seemed certain you had been thrown quite a distance. Whether we shall ever catch the ruffians who did this to you is another matter! Paris is full of such happenings at the moment. I have informed the police. Perhaps by the time they want to question you, you will remember more.'

I don't want to remember, Léon thought. I just want to go back to sleep.

'Many of your injuries are minor ones,' the doctor continued, 'though nonetheless painful for that. But your right leg is broken rather badly, in two places. I shall have to set it quite soon, and it will not be easy for you.'

It was not easy. The nun he had already met – her name was Sister Felicity – and a colleague stood on either side of him, held him firmly and spoke soothingly, while the doctor manipulated his leg. Even so, there was a point at which he couldn't keep back a cry of agony.

'That is the worst moment,' the doctor consoled him. 'Once the plaster is on the pain will be less – at least in your leg. The rest of your body will mend as fast as nature allows. The muscles in your right shoulder are bruised and torn, so that you will find it difficult to use your arm. There isn't much I can do about that, but you are young and healthy, so you should heal quickly. If the pain becomes too much, you must tell Sister Felicity and she will give you something to ease it a little.'

When the doctor had left, Sister Felicity gave him a draught.

'This will help,' she said. 'You should sleep now.'

In spite of the pain he fell asleep. When he wakened it was to see Marie and Jules sitting by his bed, his sister with tears in her eyes.

'Oh Léon! Oh Léon, thank God we've found you! Oh, your poor face!'

He raised his left arm and touched his face. He had realized, from the stiffness, and the difficulty he had in speaking, that his lips were badly swollen, and now he felt the puffiness all around his right eye, traced the cut on his chin, sticky with congealed blood.

'I don't think I look very pretty,' he said.

He tried to smile, but it was too painful. But, thankfully, his head, though still aching, was much clearer.

Marie touched his hand.

'Never mind! You are here, and you're safe. Oh Léon, I was nearly out of my mind with worry when you didn't turn up!'

'I'm sorry . . . !' Léon began.

'It's not for you to be sorry,' Jules said gruffly. 'That such a thing should happen to a man going about his own business is a disgrace! What is the world coming to, I ask?'

'Well, as Marie says, I'm safe – if not particularly sound,' Léon said. 'When shall I be able to go home?'

'If by home, you mean back to England,' Marie said, 'I'm afraid not for several weeks. Jules has already asked the doctor. There is no way, with your leg as it is, that you could travel so far.'

'But if by home you mean to us,' Jules said, 'then perhaps in a week or two. It depends on your other injuries, especially on your shoulder: also on the fact that you have been concussed. But please believe that the moment you are fit to leave the hospital, it will be our privilege to look after you until you are well enough to return to England.'

'I must let Madeleine know something,' Léon said unhappily. 'I must warn her that I won't be home just yet. Will you telegraph for me, Jules? A letter won't reach her in time.'

'Of course I will. What do you want me to say?'

What can I say, Léon thought? He had no wish to alarm her, but he must tell her something. When would he feel fit to write a letter?

'Shall I say "Return home delayed. No cause for worry. Writing."?' Jules suggested. 'Would that do? And I would send it in your name. Then if you don't feel like writing in the next day or two, either Marie or I will do so for you.'

'Yes, that will do,' Léon agreed. 'Though perhaps "slightly delayed" would be better. I don't want Madeleine to feel she must come to France.'

'You're right,' Jules said. 'That wouldn't be a good idea at all.'

And he must try to write the letter himself, Léon thought. For Madeleine to receive it from Marie or Jules would be too disquieting.

Sister Felicity came.

'I think you must go now. Monsieur Bonneau should sleep.'

'Oh Jules!' Marie said on the way home. 'I couldn't be more sorry for poor Léon, but I can't help being glad that I don't have to part with my darling children!'

'Why hasn't he said what's keeping him?' Madeleine, telegram in hand, demanded of her mother.

'You don't give long-winded explanations in a telegram,' Mrs Bates said reasonably. 'It's certain to be business. What else could it be?'

'Well I just wish he'd said so. It's not like Léon. He usually sticks closely to his arrangements. Oh Ma, I can't help worrying!'

'Perhaps one of the children's not well,' her mother suggested. 'Children are soon up and down. You know that yourself.'

'That's true,' Madeleine admitted. But she wasn't

comforted. The closeness that was between herself and Léon told her that all was not well. And the newspaper reports from France, which she read avidly, were not reassuring, not least because they were so contradictory. One day they would say that Paris was preparing for the worst, the next day she'd read that the Emperor wanted his son to be in Paris because he considered it safer there. What was she to believe?

Three days later, during which time she'd found it difficult to eat and even more difficult to sleep, she knew as soon as she saw the envelope, even before she opened it, that something was wrong. This was Léon's writing – and yet it was not. She tore open the envelope and took out the single sheet of paper. The writing was shaky; it sprawled unevenly across the page; and the letter itself was far too short. When Léon was away from home he sent her long letters; three or four pages in his neat, flowing script. This barely filled the page. All this she took in before she had read even the first word.

> 'I am perfectly well except that I stupidly slipped and broke my leg, and sustained a few other bruises [he wrote]. I will keep in touch with you and be home as soon as I can, my darling. You are on no account to come to Paris. All my love as always.'

That was all. The last few words and the signature were almost indecipherable, as if he had been unable to continue.

That, had she known it, was the truth. When he'd reached the end of those few sentences he'd been exhausted, and his shoulder was agonizingly painful. Looking at the poorness of his effort he'd wondered which would disturb Madeleine more, to receive this, or to have a letter written by Marie. On balance he thought that his own effort might be slightly more reassuring.

He said nothing of the fact that he was in hospital, hoping she would assume, as indeed she did, that he wrote from Marie's home.

'Oh Ma!' Madeleine cried. 'I knew there was something wrong! I knew it all along! My poor, darling Léon!'

'Well it's a blow, love, I don't deny it. But worse things happen at sea! I'm sure he'll be back the minute he can.' Mrs Bates tried hard to be comforting without sounding complacent; and to hide the fear in her own heart.

'Of course he will, Ma! But how can I *not* worry? He gives me no idea what his other injuries are, but clearly they prevent him writing his usual letter – so what am I to think? I tell you, if it weren't that he specifically orders me not to, I'd be off on the next train to join him!'

'Well I think you must do as he says.'

'I know,' Madeleine agreed.

She mustn't go to Paris leaving the children in the care of her elderly mother. Who really knew what was happening in Paris?

'I must reply at once,' she said. 'He'll be anxious, not only about us, but about the mill. And I need him to say what he wants me to do about the new order. I only have the barest details. Oh Ma, it could be ages before he's fit to travel!'

And never mind the mill, never mind the order, how could she bear to be without him?

In the hospital in Paris, the doctor's verdict was much the same.

'I'm afraid you'll be some weeks before you can travel back to England, *Monsieur*. First of all we must get your shoulder better so that you can use crutches. When that happens you can go to your sister's, but not so soon to England.'

My poor Madeleine! Léon thought. My darling Madeleine! When shall I see her again?

TWENTY

While Léon lay in his hospital bed, fretting and fuming at his immobility, in the city outside action was the order of the day. He could see nothing of it, of course. The hospital windows were high above the street, and for some reason, barred: but news came in. It came early every morning with the woman who arrived to clean the ward; it came with the visitors, and in the newspapers they brought with them. Some of it came from nowhere, spontaneously breeding and growing in the hospital's own gossipy atmosphere. Only the nuns remained aloof from the rumours. They went about their work with quiet, smiling efficiency, acting for all the world as though nothing which took place outside the walls of the hospital was of the smallest account.

Marie and Jules were Léon's chief, and most reliable, source of information. The cleaning lady had a well-developed sense of disaster and gave only the gloomy news. The newspapers were so contradictory that it was difficult to believe anything they said. His sister and brother-in-law, though anxious, were better balanced.

One or the other, or both of them, visited every evening. Léon's whole day, punctuated by painful dressings, bed-makings, meals, doctor's visits, bedpans, was simply a long prelude to the moment when they would walk into the ward, perhaps even bringing a letter from Madeleine.

That evening they came as usual: Marie smiling as they approached him, Jules, as always, more serious. Marie looked unusually pretty. It was too soon for her condition to be apparent, but she was one of those women who are enhanced by pregnancy from the very first minute.

'How are you, Léon?' she enquired. 'No letter today, I'm afraid!'

He wasn't quick enough to hide his disappointment.

'But you did have one yesterday.'

He didn't need reminding. He knew the letter by heart. He had read it a hundred times. Just the sight of Madeleine's writing on the page, the knowledge that she had handled the paper, brought her nearer. Her letters told him of the small happenings in Helsdon – which was what he wanted to know. She wrote that she had purchased the uniform Tommy would need when he started at Bradford Grammar School in September and that he looked very well in it; that Claire had lost another front tooth and had started to lisp. She also asked for further details of the orders he had taken from Monsieur André in Paris, so that she could make a start on them.

'And I've managed to write a note to Madeleine which I'd like you to send,' Léon said. Their exchange of letters was what made the absence between them bearable.

'So what has been happening in the world outside?' he asked Jules.

Jules raised his hands in a gesture of despair.

'Too much – and all too confused! Now that General Trochu's been made Governor of Paris he's issued a lengthy proclamation. He calls for calm – "calm in your streets, calm in your homes, calm in your hearts," he says. A fat chance he has of getting it with everyone running around in circles! Anyway, I've brought the newspaper and you can read it for yourself.'

'What *I* notice most of all,' Marie said, 'is that Paris is filling up. Everyone's coming in from the countryside. Where are they all going to live?'

'And what are they going to live *on*,' Jules said. 'There's this crazy idea that by bringing in all the produce they can, it will help the rest of us. It won't at all, of course. In the end it will just mean more mouths to feed.'

370

'Have I told you that they're moving sheep and oxen by the thousand into the Bois de Boulogne? Presumably to be eaten when the time comes!' Marie shuddered at the thought.

'Can we talk about something else, Jules?' she added. 'All this sort of talk frightens me, and perhaps to no purpose. And I'm sure it's not cheerful for Léon.'

All the same, she had already started hoarding a little food – flour, oatmeal, beans, sugar, dried fruit; anything which would keep. And also some wine. The price of everything was rising faster than ever.

'I would like to give you some money,' Léon said out of the blue. 'I brought quite a lot to France, and I also collected some money due to me.'

It was strange that his attackers hadn't robbed him of so much as a sou.

'I have no need of money in here,' he said. 'And the moment I'm on my crutches and out of this place I shall be on my way back to England.'

Marie looked doubtful.

'It will be a very uncomfortable journey,' Marie said, 'crossing the channel on crutches.'

'It won't be the first time it's been done, nor the last,' Léon said. 'Anyway, I shall do it. Please don't think that I don't appreciate your hospitality, but more than anything in the world I want to get back to Helsdon. It isn't even as if I could do any good here.'

'How long do you think it will be before you're proficient on your crutches?'

'If it weren't for my shoulder, it would be tomorrow!' Léon boasted. 'Or the next day. As it is, the doctor thinks about three weeks. And he won't let me go until I *can* use them.'

Jules remained silent. It was already becoming difficult at many points around Paris to get out or in. Every day new fortifications went up around the perimeter. Even the Seine was being dammed up. The day would come when the inhabitants were securely sealed in their city,

371

or were caught like rats in a trap: whichever way you liked to look at it. He was sure of it, though there was nothing to be gained by saying so. Since Léon could do nothing about it, he might as well remain in ignorance.

In Helsdon, Madeleine threw down the *Manchester Guardian* which her mother had tried to keep from her, pretending she didn't know where it had got to – and burst into tears. She tried hard not to believe what any of the newspapers said, but now the bad tidings came so thick and fast that it was difficult to ignore them.

She picked it up again and re-read the two short sentences which had caused her so much distress.

> 'Paris will be an island very shortly.
> The cannons are all ready.'

There was more, and none of it the least comfort. And in any case, she couldn't see the print for her tears.

'Oh, my poor Léon!' she cried out loud. 'Oh, my darling Léon, what will become of you?'

In his letters he had given her no inkling of such happenings, though he must surely have known? But was it possible, was it just possible, that he would be able to leave in time? *Before* Paris became an island?

Well, though she would not cease for a minute to pray for his safety, she knew from experience that prayers were not always answered. (Father O'Malley said that they were, but that sometimes God said 'No'.) She must at all costs be strong. It was now up to her to do whatever was best for Léon, best for their children, best for Bonneau's. She had had her weeping, and that must be the end of it. It was time to dry her eyes and to carry on as best she could.

For Léon, the important thing was that she should continue to write to him, frequently and cheerfully. It's worse for my darling than it is for me, she told herself. And nothing could be all bad while they continued to have each other's letters.

She re-folded the newspaper and carried it with her into the kitchen.

'Ma,' she said. 'I know you mean it for the best, but I'd rather, in future, you didn't try to keep the news from me.'

Mrs Bates, who liked to bake her own bread, was kneading, pounding the dough as though she would like to thump the whole world. There was nothing like kneading bread to rid yourself of your worst feelings. And observing her daughter's red-rimmed eyes, her worst feelings at the moment were directed to all things German.

'I only wanted to spare you,' she said. 'It'll do you no good to know every detail of what's going on. Any road, it could all be lies!'

'It could be,' Madeleine admitted. 'But you're mistaken in saying it won't do me any good to read it, love. Every word I read about Paris, though it might not comfort me, brings me nearer to Léon. It's the only way I can share what's happening to him.'

'Well if that's how you want it!'

Mrs Bates inverted the mound of dough in the baking bowl, covered it with a clean cloth, and set it in exactly the right spot to rise.

'Have you a minute to spare, Ma?' Madeleine asked. 'I want to talk to you.'

'All the time in the world!' Mrs Bates dusted her floury hands on her pinafore. 'We'll go into my room.'

A minute later they sat opposite each other in Mrs Bates's parlour.

'Now love, what is it?'

'I just need to talk to you,' Madeleine said.

Her daughter looked so strained, so white-faced, Mrs Bates thought.

'I have to face the fact that I might be separated from Léon for some time, perhaps several weeks,' Madeleine began. 'Since he's now confessed that his leg is quite badly broken, he can't possibly be up and doing all that quickly.'

'You never know,' Mrs Bates interrupted. 'They can do lots of things nowadays, especially in Paris!'

'No, Ma! They can't make a broken leg heal any faster,' Madeleine said gently. 'Only nature can do that. I know that Léon will be home as soon as ever he can move safely on his crutches. It's not *that* I'm worried about. What does worry me is what might be happening in Paris while he's still there. And there's no action I can take about that. Oh Ma, if only there was! I'd feel so much better!'

'I know, love. It's hard to have to stand aside.' Hadn't she felt it when Irvine was away at the war?

'The very best I can do for Léon is to see that life goes on here as usual – as normally as it can in his absence. . .' Her voice faltered.

'You're quite right, love,' Mrs Bates said decisively. 'Happen that's what we should all do?'

'It is, isn't it? I must try to be mother and father to the children – though I can never take Léon's place, I must do my best – and I must work for both of us in the business.'

'What do you mean by that?' Mrs Bates asked. 'How can you work harder than you do now?'

'Oh I can,' Madeleine said confidently. 'I can and I must. It's up to me to take on some of Léon's jobs. Of course I can't do them all – Rob Wainwright will have to take on extra, and I know he will – but I can do some.'

'Like what?' Mrs Bates had the feeling that her daughter had it all worked out.

'I've been thinking I shall take on the selling,' Madeleine announced.

'Take on the selling? You mean travel around the country, toting samples, seeking orders? You can't do that, Madeleine love!'

'Yes I can, Ma. At least I can try. And as a matter of fact, there's no one in Bonneau's who could make a better fist of it. That doesn't sound very modest, but it's the truth.'

'I daresay,' Mrs Bates acknowledged. 'But it's not a woman's job.'

'When their menfolk are away, women can do all sorts of jobs they wouldn't usually do,' Madeleine said.

'But whatever would Léon say?' her mother protested. 'He'd not like it, and that's a fact!'

'Oh, if he were here to do it, he'd not let me,' Madeleine admitted. 'And believe me, I'm not doing it as an act of defiance. But it has to be done by someone. We can't afford to lose our contacts or let them be picked up by someone else. We've already had one or two letters from firms wanting Léon to visit them, and several enquiries about orders. Léon isn't here to deal with it, therefore I must!'

Mrs Bates shook her head, clicked her tongue.

'Well I can see the way you're thinking, and I've never known you let go of something you were set on, not from being a little lass. But please love, do promise me you'll try not to work too hard. Mercifully it'll likely not be for long.'

'I'll need all the help you can give me,' Madeleine said. 'The children will need extra love and attention if I'm going to be busy elsewhere, and who better to give it than you. And by the way, I shan't tell Léon what I'm doing. I don't want him to think I'm taking advantage of his absence to disobey him. I'll tell him when I've done it, and made a success of it. Hopefully he'll be back home by then.'

Her words were braver than her thoughts. It was true she'd always wanted to sell, but when it came to the point, would she be any good? Well, it was all to play for!

'I'll start by going over to Leeds,' she said. 'I thought I'd ask Henry's advice. No one knows the trade better, and he's very wise. Also, he might write one or two letters of introduction.'

'I daresay he will,' Mrs Bates said. 'When shall you go?'

'Tomorrow,' Madeleine said. 'The sooner the better!'

The next morning she dressed with great care. Her dress, and the material from which it was made, were of her own design, the waist nipped and close-fitting – how thankful she was that her waist measurement hadn't increased in ten years! – the neck demurely high, and encircled by the coral necklace Léon had once given her. The pink of the coral was repeated in the roses which filled the crown of her tilted little hat, and in the colour which nervous excitement had given to her cheeks. Should she wear a jacket, or should she not? It was a warm day, and she decided not.

She was looking in the mirror, critically adjusting the angle of her hat, when Tommy came into her room, followed by Claire.

'You look lovely, Mama!' Tommy said.

'Why can't we go with you?' Claire demanded.

'Because this is business,' Madeleine said. 'I explained to you last evening that I'm doing this because Papa isn't here. Until he's back with us I shall have to go to lots of other places. So you must both be good so that Papa will be proud of you.'

This was going to be the hardest part of her new task. Also, it would be as well if she never mentioned children to the customers. There'd be a black mark against her for neglecting them!

'I'm off then,' she said to her mother. 'I should be back by the middle of the afternoon.'

'You look delicious!' Henry said when she was shown into his office later that morning. 'To what do I owe this pleasure? I suppose you're shopping in Leeds.'

He had not seen the Bonneaus since that last visit to Helsdon. It had seemed better to keep a distance. Hortense seemed to have simmered down and he had kept a sharp look out for any further hanky-panky and had seen none. Nor had the Bonneaus been mentioned between them.

'No. It's much more than that,' Madeleine said. 'First of all, I must tell you about Léon.'

He was shocked to hear the news.

376

'Why didn't you let me know?' he demanded.

'I should have done so,' Madeleine admitted. 'But it's not all that long since I heard myself. And we've been all hands aloft at the mill. In any case, you couldn't have done anything for him.'

'It's a bad business,' Henry said. 'But breaking his leg could be a blessing in disguise!'

'A blessing? Whatever do you mean?'

'He's a Frenchman, isn't he? I don't know the laws of France, but isn't it possible he could have been conscripted into the French Army?'

'Oh Henry! I didn't think of that! I think of Léon as belonging with me, in Helsdon.'

And if he hadn't been conscripted – the thought came to her suddenly – who was to say he wouldn't have volunteered? He *was* a Frenchman; he *didn't* belong in Helsdon.

'Well the army won't want him now!' Henry said by way of comfort. 'So give me your sister-in-law's address and I'll write to him. But I've a feeling there's something else you've come about, otherwise you'd have sent a letter. So tell me what brings you to Leeds?'

Madeleine drew a deep breath, gripped the arms of her chair and prepared for battle.

'Before we go any further,' she said quickly, 'don't you tell me not to do it, because I shan't take any notice. I've made up my mind and I'll not change it!'

Henry leaned back in his chair and roared with laughter.

'Oh Madeleine! You really take the cake! Here you are telling me not to stop you, and I haven't the faintest notion what terrible thing it is you're going to do!'

'Oh! Didn't I say?'

'You did not!'

She explained what she had in mind.

'I've come to you for your advice about how to do it, Henry,' she finished. 'You know so much about trade. And really, it's no laughing matter.'

'I'm not laughing at the idea – and you don't want to know whether I approve or not – so I'll tell you what I think about how.'

'Please do!'

'Be yourself,' Henry advised. 'That's the most important thing. Explain about Léon first of all, and by the time you've done that, you'll already have everyone's sympathy. But don't be abrasive or pushing just because you're a woman doing a man's job. It won't go down well. You'll do far better by being feminine.'

'Of course I won't be pushing,' Madeleine said. 'But the last thing I want is to be given business just because I'm a woman. I want no favours!'

'Yes you do!' Henry contradicted. 'You want the favour of orders. And you can't hide the fact that you're a woman, so you must allow people to treat you as one.'

She's the most feminine creature I know, Henry thought. Even though she's clever and efficient, and she can run rings round many a man I'm acquainted with, and she doesn't think all the time about fripperies, she's still totally feminine, and totally bewitching.

'I'll try,' she promised.

'Do you remember the first order I gave you?' Henry asked. 'Do you remember that? You came to see me then because Léon was ill.'

'I shall never forget it,' Madeleine said. 'I was eighteen – and scared stiff.'

'You were shabbily dressed and you tried to hide your hands. I gave you the order because I liked what you showed me, but I admit that I was swayed because you were a lovely young woman. It might not be fair, but it's the way of the world!'

'Where do you think I should go first?' Madeleine asked. 'I've looked at Léon's office diary and I see he has a date with Hardman's in Harrogate next week. Then there's been a letter from Sutton and Sons in York, asking him to call when he's that way. I'd as soon not go too far and have to stay overnight on my first trip, because of the children – though later I'll have to go to London and other places down south. We have several customers there.'

'But you'd like to practise on your own people first?'

'That's about it,' Madeleine confessed. 'So should I write for an appointment, or should I just turn up?'

'That's a tricky one,' Henry said. 'If you write first it gives them the chance to say they'll wait until Léon is back. . .' And goodness knows when that might be, he thought. 'If you turn up on the off-chance, you might have a wasted journey.'

'I think I'll risk the wasted journey,' Madeleine said.

'I daresay you're right. And remember, Madeleine, wherever you go looking for business, always look prosperous. Success attracts success! Travel first class. Take cabs. Anyway, you can afford to. It's what Léon would want you to do and apart from anything else, it'll save your strength and energy, which you're certainly going to need.'

'I'll take your advice about that, also,' Madeleine promised.

'Well enough of this serious talk for now,' Henry said, jumping up from his chair. 'I'm going to take you out for a bite of dinner before you get your train back to Helsdon.'

Should she accept? She remembered how annoyed Léon had been when she'd gone out to dinner with Henry in Bradford. But it would be rude and ungracious to refuse. Besides, she wanted to accept; apart from anything else she was now surprisingly hungry.

'Thank you,' she said. 'That would be lovely. I wonder if. . .' She hesitated.

'Yes?'

'Henry, when I came to see you that first time I had my dinner in a café not far from the station. I had the most delicious meat-and-potato pie! I'd like to go there again for old time's sake – if it's still there?'

'I expect you mean Dawson's. It's still there.'

'I could have taken you somewhere much better than

379

this,' Henry said as they threaded their way through the crowded restaurant.

'I know,' Madeleine said. 'But I wanted to come here.'

'Well, has it changed?' Henry asked her a little later.

'Only that there are separate tables instead of everyone at a few long ones. But the pie is as good as ever. And I shall have jam roly-poly to follow, like I did the first time.

'But I've changed,' she continued. 'I'm thirty-three, not eighteen. Fifteen years ago I was almost too scared to come in here.'

A few days later, getting ready to go to Hardman's in Harrogate, she realized she was almost as nervous at the prospect as if she were still eighteen.

She dressed with even more care, wearing a different dress from the one she had worn to Leeds – and again of her own design – but the same hat. When she was almost ready, on impulse she ran down into the garden and cut a rose of the same shade as those on her hat. Back in the bedroom she pinned it carefully just below the coral necklace, then looked in the mirror. Perhaps it was too much? Perhaps it wasn't very businesslike?

She took it out again, and laid it down – then picked it up and re-pinned it. She *would* wear it. Whether it was businesslike or not, it made her feel good. She checked the contents of her satchel, the patterns of cloth and the designs – how terrible if she were to forget something! Then she eased on her new kid gloves and went downstairs.

'I have to change at Leeds for Harrogate on the way there,' she informed her mother. 'But from Harrogate I can get a train straight to York.'

'So you've told me, love!' A dozen times, Mrs Bates could have added.

On the train Madeleine reminded herself of what she knew about Hardman's. They were a wholesale firm, not large, but supplying fashionable and exclusive garments to the expensive shops in and around Harrogate. Mr Hardman – and it was he she would ask to see – always bought the best, Léon had once told her, but he wanted value for money and wasn't at all easy to please. Oh dear, she thought, perhaps I should have started on someone not quite so difficult!

Hardman's wasn't far from the station, nevertheless she took a cab. She wished to arrive cool and composed, not hot and flustered. In giving her business card to the clerk at the reception desk she cheated a little. It was Léon's card. She had debated whether she should write her own name on it, but had decided to make life easier, just this once, by sailing under Léon's colours. The clerk looked at it, and looked at her, but said nothing. She held her breath while he took it into Mr Hardman, and let it out with a sigh of relief when he reappeared almost immediately and said: 'Mr Hardman can give you a few minutes right away, madam!'

Clearly, the clerk hadn't informed his employer that the visitor wasn't Monsieur Bonneau. When Madeleine walked into the room, though he had his hand outstretched, Hardman looked decidedly startled. Madeleine took the hand which the man now seemed uncertain whether or not to offer. He was a tall, cadaverous-looking man, sallow-skinned and serious.

'I thought . . . I expected. . .' Hardman began.

'You expected my husband,' Madeleine said. 'I know. And he will be devastated that he couldn't make this call himself.'

'He's not ill, I hope?'

'Not ill,' Madeleine said. 'But I'm afraid he's detained in Paris with a badly broken leg. Of course I am in communication with him, but it's not quite certain when he'll be able to return. Therefore he was most insistent that, since you are one of our most valued customers, I should visit you in his place.'

She was appalled at the fluency with which she lied. Dear Léon, please forgive me, she said to herself.

'I'm very sorry to hear this, madame,' Mr Hardman replied. 'It was good of you to do us the courtesy of calling. Please give your husband my very best wishes for his recovery, and assure him that when he returns I shall be pleased to do business with him again.'

'Thank you,' Madeleine said. 'I will convey your good wishes when I write this evening. But in the meantime, Mr Hardman, it is my resolve to carry on my husband's business in his absence. I have brought with me all the things my husband would have carried and I'd be greatly obliged if you'd take a look.'

'But I . . . but you're. . .'

You're a woman, Madeleine guessed he was trying to say, but she took no notice. While he was floundering for excuses she was bringing out the samples from her satchel, spreading them on the desk, right under his nose, and keeping up a flow of talk as she did so.

'My husband has often told me how interested you always are in new designs,' she said. 'And how knowledgeable you are about what will be popular. I've taken the liberty of bringing you half a dozen of my new designs for next spring and summer, as well as some new fabrics I think you might like.'

Without being downright rude, he could hardly fail to look at them; and as he did so Madeleine saw the gleam of interest in his eyes.

'Now that one,' she said, 'the one you're looking at now – is one of my favourites. And here's the design of how we propose to make it up. You see how all the fullness is at the back again. It's the new bustle.'

'But will it last?' Mr Hardman asked gloomily. 'You ladies are always changing your styles.'

'Oh I think it will, Mr Hardman. It's going to be an important feature of gowns for some time to come.'

'It looks highly inconvenient for the wearer! But I expect you'll all put up with that if you think it's smart!'

'Oh you're so right, sir!' Madeleine agreed. 'Look how

many years we endured the crinoline – a most inconvenient garment in any circumstance.'

She had lost all her fear. She was talking with confidence and enthusiasm about matters she understood.

'But to give a proper balance to the bustle, the bodice will now be slightly shorter-waisted, and coming to a point in the front. And I do believe that wide sleeves are going to be fashionable again in the seventies,' she said. 'And in this evening dress design here, you'll see there's a square *décolletage* instead of the usual round one, and the underskirt forms a short train at the back. Don't you think it's pretty?'

Mr Hardman grunted, but as far as Madeleine could tell, it was an approving grunt.

'Take a look at this one,' she went on, 'and consider it in this material here. Of course it wouldn't be cheap, but then my husband has always told me that yours wasn't a cheap trade. . .'

'It certainly isn't,' he agreed. 'I sell to the nobility and the gentry, of which Harrogate isn't short.' And to those with plenty of brass, he thought, even if they've made it in manufacturing.

'All the same,' he said, 'I'd want a fair price!'

'Of course you would!' Madeleine agreed. 'And you shall have one.'

'And a quick delivery and the latest style,' he added. 'My customers can afford to be choosy. So can you assure me that these "Bonneau" designs are quite new? Your husband hasn't sold them to anyone else?'

'Oh Mr Hardman, you are the very first person to see them!' Madeleine assured him. 'In fact, some of them I finished only two days ago! And whatever you decide to take, I shan't show to anyone else in this area.' She expected he knew that Garston's had the first choice in the Leeds area. In any case, these weren't Henry's type of merchandise.

'Of course if there's anything you'd like me to alter . . . though I have been quite careful with the details. . .'

She broke off, aware that Mr Hardman was staring at her.

'You say you finished some of these two days ago, and you say you've paid attention to the details. Are you trying to tell me...'

'Oh! That I'm the designer of "Bonneau" garments?' Madeleine said. 'Well yes, I am.' She hadn't meant to say so. It had slipped out. 'But my husband and I work so closely in everything that he must have forgotten to mention it!'

'Well I'll be damned! Oh, beg pardon!' Hardman said.

'I'm so glad you like the designs,' Madeleine said. 'Do you want to talk about prices and delivery?'

He'd admired them, he'd found no fault, surely he *must* give her an order.

'Well, if you're sure. I mean . . . your husband. . .'

'My husband trusts me to do that in his absence,' Madeleine said. 'Though of course I shall inform him at once. No, Mr Hardman, I can give you prices and dates here and now, and whatever I quote, you can be sure Bonneau's will stick to!'

By the time Madeleine was ready to leave, with a substantial order tucked away in her satchel, Mr Hardman, though still looking dazed, had managed a smile or two. It changed his whole face, she thought.

'Well, thank you very much, Mr Hardman,' she said.

'It's been a pleasure, Mrs Bonneau,' he assured her.

She walked back into the town as if there were wings on her heels! It was difficult not to break into a run for the joy that was in her. And now for a quick bite to eat, she thought, and then the train for York.

Except that Mr Percy Sutton, of Sutton and Sons, York, was physically the very opposite of Mr Hardman, being round, fat, and rosy-faced, the interview with him was much the same. She came away with a similar-sized order, though of different designs.

When she had completed everything she said: 'I wonder if I could call upon your clerk to get me a cab to take me to the station?'

'Why, Mrs Bonneau!' Percy Sutton said. 'There's no need for that! I have my own driver here. He will take you to the station at once!'

He saw her into the cab and watched her as she was driven away. Now why hadn't he taken her himself? He wished her husband no harm, but he wouldn't mind if he was laid up long enough for his wife to make the next call also!

By the time Madeleine reached Mount Royd she was exhausted, though still exhilarated.

'I'm afraid I rashly promised to take the children for a walk when I came home, and so I will,' she said to her mother.

The house seems so empty without Léon, she thought later, when she went upstairs to bed. And how empty her life would be without him! Darling Léon, what are you doing at this minute, she wondered? Are you thinking of me? But at least he was with Marie and she would look after him well.

She took out her writing-paper, her pen and ink and began to write her nightly letter. Should she tell him what had happened today? She decided she would, but she would play it light, so as not to worry him unduly.

TWENTY-ONE

On a day in mid-September Léon demonstrated to the doctor that he could, at last, walk the length of the hospital ward on his crutches.

The doctor would never know, it was important that he shouldn't, what this triumph had cost him. The pain of it made him sick to the stomach. Halfway down the ward there had been one terrible moment when he'd almost lost his balance, felt one crutch beginning to slide away under him. It was a miracle that he hadn't fallen to the floor. And if he had fallen, he knew his plea to be allowed to leave the hospital would have been rejected out of hand.

In fact, the doctor had noted it all. He had heard the sharp intake of breath when the pain struck, seen the beads of sweat on his patient's pallid face when the effort became almost too much. He had been ready to put out a steadying hand when Léon had almost overbalanced.

He shook his head. This man should not be allowed to leave the hospital. He wasn't fit. In normal circumstances he would certainly not be allowed to go, but circumstances were far from normal. It was wartime, and who knew how soon every hospital bed in Paris might be needed.

'Bravo!' he called out as Léon reached the end of the ward and thankfully lowered himself on to the nearest bed. 'You did well, *Monsieur!*'

Léon gathered enough strength to speak.

'So I may go home, Doctor?'

The doctor hesitated. It went against the grain to say what he must say.

'If by ''home'' you mean England, then it is too soon;

but to go to your sister would be a step forward, would it not?'

'It would indeed!'

'Then you may tell your sister that she can fetch you tomorrow!'

Léon had waited and longed for this decision. Though everyone was kind, and the nuns, with their soft voices and gentle hands, were angels of mercy, it was the thought of leaving this place which had spurred him on in his fight with the heavy wooden crutches. They seemed to have a life of their own, a malevolent determination to go in any direction except the one he wanted. And, in spite of all the nursing sisters could do to pad them, they caused painful weals in his armpits and aching muscles in his arms. But now all the effort seemed suddenly worth while.

'I shall need to see you again, of course,' the doctor said. 'And eventually there will be the plaster to remove.'

'Certainly!' Léon agreed.

There was no need to say that once out of here, he wouldn't return. In no time at all, whatever the difficulties, plaster or no plaster, he would be on the cross-channel boat. If the crossing was rough – and there could be gales in September – he might even have to be tied down for his own good. But it didn't matter. The only thing that mattered was to get to England.

For a moment he forgot where he was, no longer saw the hospital ward. He was swamped by the thought of that drab, dirty little Yorkshire town, ringed by wild hills, which had become his home, which now held everything that was dearest to him.

When Marie and Jules came that evening he demonstrated his new-found independence by propelling himself halfway down the ward to meet them.

'Oh please, do go back to bed, Léon!' Marie implored. 'You look so tired!'

'On the contrary, I am much better. The doctor has

said you may bring my clothes tomorrow, and take me home!'

'Why, that's wonderful!' Marie cried. 'I must admit, I hadn't expected it so soon.'

'I will take an hour or two off work to fetch you,' Jules said.

'But when you are home with us you must take plenty of rest,' Marie said. 'I'm sure the doctor will insist on it. And so shall I.'

He didn't look well. Pain showed in his eyes, and the cuts and bruises, though they were healing, marred his handsome face.

'For a little while,' Léon agreed. 'But not for too long. Every day I shall become more mobile, and I'm quite determined to get back to England as quickly as I can. You've both been so good to me, and I appreciate it, but I can't tell you how much I long to see Madeleine and my children again.'

Marie and Jules looked at each other.

'Léon, I don't think. . .'

Marie was silenced by a look from her husband.

'I can imagine how you feel,' Jules said. 'But you must give yourself a little more time.'

There was no point, at this moment when his brother-in-law was so full of optimism, in telling him that time was not on his side; that he had as much hope, in his present state, of taking the ferry as he had of sprouting wings and flying across the channel. And there was still less point in telling him that by the time he *was* physically fit there were other reasons why it would almost certainly be too late. Those who didn't close their eyes to reality knew that the days in which anyone might enter or leave Paris were numbered.

Surely Léon must know this? The hospital was full of gossip; he saw the newspapers. Was it his eagerness to be off which made him turn a blind eye? But once outside the hospital he would see the truth of it soon enough.

'Come for me as early as it's convenient tomorrow,'

388

Léon said. 'I'm impatient to leave!'

They came at ten o'clock the following morning, Marie carrying Léon's clothes in a large bag.

'My dear little wife has insisted on bringing your trousers,' Jules said. 'I've told her there is no way you can get them on. But don't worry, Léon, I have brought my *robe*.'

'But Léon is so much taller than you,' Marie protested. 'It will only reach halfway down his legs!'

'I'm not worried,' Léon said. 'Nothing in the world worries me this morning, not even if I must go naked through the streets of Paris!'

'In any case we have ordered a *fiacre*,' Jules pointed out. 'It will be at the entrance in a few minutes.'

Getting him into the cab was a difficult manoeuvre. By the time the *cocher* drove away Léon was pale with exhaustion from the effort. It was several minutes before he could look up, look out at the streets he had so longed to see.

It was the same scene he had left almost a month ago; and yet it was different, as if he was watching a new play with a new cast of actors. Almost every face wore a look of strain; eyes were wary, mouths were tight lines.

The strangeness of the men's clothing struck him most. Apart from the few, fashionably-dressed dandies, who now looked incongruous, most of the men were wearing whatever was the nearest they could get to military dress, though few were completely uniformed. One man might sport a military cap and belt, another a pair of uniform trousers, or perhaps a soldier's jacket.

'How odd they look,' Léon remarked. 'Neither soldiers nor civilians!'

'They are the Paris National Guard,' Jules told him. 'I myself have joined, in my spare time, along with about three hundred thousand others, and almost all of us are untrained. General Trochu hit the nail on the head when he said we have many men but few soldiers. Goodness knows what the authorities will find for us to do. And as you can see, there aren't nearly enough uniforms to go round. I have been issued with a belt and a cap.'

'I don't see why you had to join at all,' Marie said shortly. 'You're a man of peace, not of war. It isn't even as if you were needed!'

'I might be. Who knows? In any case, Paris is my city and I must be ready to defend her.'

'What *will* you all do?' Léon asked.

'Well for one thing I suppose we shall be needed to relieve the regular soldiers and the *Garde Mobile* on the fortifications around Paris. The fortifications have to be seen to be believed. In fact, if you can bear the thought of being hauled into a cab again, we must take you. To drive around the fortifications is quite the thing to do now on a Sunday afternoon, rather than to go to the Bois de Boulogne, which is no more than a sea of livestock!'

'I refuse to go!' Marie protested. 'I don't want to look at fortifications. It's frightening enough even to think of them.'

'You need not accompany us, *chérie*,' Jules said.

'It seems to me also that a great many men are carrying weapons,' Léon observed.

'True,' Jules agreed. 'They've been issued with whatever was available – and they seem to feel an obligation to carry them everywhere. The trouble is that most of them don't know one end of a gun from the other, but there's a rebellious faction in the city which wouldn't hesitate to use them.'

'It's all quite stupid and quite terrifying!' Marie complained. 'The only good thing *I* can find to say about all these ridiculous regulations is that the *cocottes* have been driven off the streets. They've had to go into munitions! Isn't that a lark?'

'Here we are, home at last!' Jules said. 'Now to get you out of the cab!'

An hour or two later, Léon having rested, Marie placed the huge soup tureen and the loaf of new bread on the table and summoned them all to the midday meal. The soup was tasty enough, Léon thought. Better than hospital fare, but thinner than Marie usually made it.

'Eat plenty of bread,' Marie advised everyone. 'We are not short of bread, thank goodness!'

When she turned to Léon, who of necessity was sitting apart from the table, she had a worried face.

'There is very little meat,' she apologized. 'And I'm sure you will excuse me if I give more to Jules and the children. Jules has to go out to work, and Jean and Etienne are growing so fast that I worry about them not having the proper nourishment.'

'But of course!' Léon said. He felt immediately guilty that he was eating their food. 'In any case I am not very hungry,' he lied.

'It is you who should be eating extra, Marie,' Jules said. 'Don't forget that you are carrying a child. I don't need good food as much as you do.'

'Well let's not make a fuss,' Marie said lightly. 'We're not starving, not by a long way!'

She sounded brighter than she felt. Every day it became more difficult to find food. And who knew how much worse it would get? That was the great worry, and no one knew the answer.

'I didn't realize food was difficult,' Léon said. 'I thought that what I'd been offered over the last few weeks was sparse simply because it was hospital food. But I still have some money, Marie, and when I've taken out what I need to get back to England, the rest is yours.'

'Bless you!' Marie said. 'A little more money will help because what food there is, gets more and more expensive. But the scarcity is the main thing. I worry that one day even money won't buy food. As it is, we have a little meat no more than twice a week, and fish almost never. All the same, Léon, you must never think that we're not pleased to share whatever we have with you. And I have been lining my storecupboard for weeks now, so I'm sure we shall manage somehow.'

Jules scraped his plate clean and pushed it away.

'I must get back to work. I only took the morning off.'

'It was good of you,' Léon acknowledged. 'And I'm afraid I need to ask you another favour. Will you, as soon as possible, get me to the British Embassy? Though I'm not British, I mean to ask for whatever help they can give me to get back to England.'

'I doubt you'll get much help from that quarter,' Jules said. 'They say the place is in disarray. The rumour is that the Ambassador will pull out any day now.'

'The British Ambassador flee Paris!' Léon cried. 'Really, I can't believe that!'

Jules shrugged.

'That's the rumour!'

Marie glanced at the clock.

'The shops will be open again now. I must go out and see what's to be had. I find the best way is to do my marketing as often as possible. You never know when goods come in – but the minute they do, they sell like wildfire. It will help, Léon, if you'll give an eye to the children, so that I needn't take them with me. They'll be very little trouble to you.'

'Of course I will,' Léon said. 'I shall read them some stories.'

How pleasant it was, Marie thought as she left the house, not to have a child on either hand, much though she loved them. And it was a beautiful day yet again. The summer seemed to go on and on, as if in defiance of all the horrible things that were happening in France. The only problem with the warm weather was that the streets had begun to smell, and the air was dusty. The street cleaners and·the water carts seemed to have vanished from the face of the earth. As for the sewage disposal men, well it appeared that most of them were German, so they'd fled, or been driven out.

She was lucky at the shops. She bought coffee, flour, sugar, salt: all things which would keep – and, unfortunately, all things which made her basket heavy. She decided she would sit in the Luxembourg gardens for a little while; watch the world go by and rest in the sunshine before carrying the shopping home. At a street stall near to the entrance gates she bought five apples which would do for dessert this evening – and guiltily treated herself to a pear, which she would eat in the gardens.

What she longed for was peaches; round, ripe, glowing peaches, but the season was over. Why was it that when you were pregnant you always longed for something out of season? The pear was sweet and juicy and she enjoyed every bite. Refreshed, she wiped her hands and mouth on a handkerchief, sat just a few minutes longer, then picked up her shopping and made for home.

Next morning Léon received a letter from Madeleine. He tore it open eagerly and began to read.

'Oh, but this is such good news!' he exclaimed. 'She tells me that the order for Monsieur André is almost ready. What do you think of that? They must have worked exceedingly hard to accomplish it.'

The moment he'd been fit to do so, Léon had written to Monsieur André from hospital, explaining that he was detained in Paris, but that he had sent details of the order to his wife, who could be relied upon to deal with it promptly.

'That's splendid!' Marie said.

'I knew Madeleine wouldn't let me down,' Léon said. 'Would you believe, she tells me it will be ready for dispatch in a week or so. Oh, how I wish . . . !' He broke off.

Marie stood beside him, put her arm around his shoulders.

'I know. You wish she would accompany it!'

'Yes,' Léon said quietly. 'That's what I wish. But perhaps it won't be too long now before I see her again. Every day brings it nearer.'

Marie moved away and began to busy herself with the children.

'I must write to Monsieur André at once,' Léon said. 'He will be pleased to hear the news.'

At midday Jules came home for his dinner. He had a wary expression on his face.

'Did you hear the explosion?'

'I heard nothing,' Léon said. 'What explosion?'

'We have blown up the last of the bridges over the Seine. Now all we can do is to sit tight and wait for the Prussians to pound themselves to death against the fortifications.'

'I don't understand it,' Marie protested. 'They said that all the Prussians wanted was the Emperor Louis Napoleon. Well they've got him, so why don't they just stop the war?'

'What if they never attack?' Léon said quietly. 'What then?'

Jules gave his brother-in-law a sharp look. So was he beginning to see things as they actually were?

'Oh they'll attack!' he replied. 'And we'll beat them!'

He spoke with a confidence he didn't feel, but he had seen his wife's face suddenly turn ashen pale. He hoped that at any rate *she* hadn't thought of the alternative to attack; that instead the Prussians would choose to starve them out. A long, slow death.

When Jules had returned to work, Léon took out Madeleine's letter and re-read it. Then he folded it and put it away with all the others she had sent him. In spite of the conversation over the dinner table, it did not occur to him that this might be the last letter he would receive from Madeleine; that his small bundle of letters would be read and re-read until they began to fall to pieces in his hands.

Madeleine sighed, a deep sigh of relief and fatigue. Putting down her pen, she leaned back as far as the upright office chair would allow it. She pushed back the strands of hair which had fallen over her face, then moved her hands to massage the tense muscles at the back of her neck. It had been a long day.

She allowed herself thirty seconds more to do absolutely

nothing, then began to tidy her desk. She liked everything cleared at the end of each day, everything place
in its exact position ready to start work afresh next
day.

She had been at the mill since seven o'clock this morning, and now it was after eight in the evening. All her days
now started early and finished late. It was the only way she
could get through. She had never quite realized until
recently, how much paperwork there was in a business
which was really concerned with producing goods. Letters
to write, orders to check, her itinerary of calls and visits to
arrange – let alone carrying out the latter.

In Léon's continuing absence – they had now been
parted for five long weeks and four long days – she had
taken on almost all his calls, devoting two, sometimes
three, days of the week to that important business. She
was not able to make the calls as frequently as Léon might
have done, or as she herself preferred, but she saw to it
that no customer, however distant from Helsdon, went
completely without a visit. And if her visit had to be
delayed she kept in touch by letter, written in her own
hand, as often as not late at night. No one must be
neglected, no customer lost.

She gave a last look around the office then picked up a
file of papers she would attend to when she got home.
When she had locked the office door behind her, she went
into the Counting House.

She was not surprised to find Arthur Parker still at work,
his long nose almost touching the ledger he was busy on.
His eyesight was getting worse, though he would never
admit it.

'It's time you went home, Arthur!' Madeleine said.

'Aye, I could say the same to you, Mrs Bonneau,' he
replied. 'Any road, I'll finish Simpson's entry then I'll
pack up. That's all this month's accounts ready to go out.'

He had nothing urgent to go home to. Since his mother
died he had lived alone. He would make his supper, wash
up, read a chapter, go to bed.

'You're a marvel,' Madeleine said. 'What would we do without you?'

He was worth his weight in gold to Bonneau's, and he wasn't the only one. How does it happen that we have the best, the most loyal workpeople in Helsdon, she asked herself? In the whole of Yorkshire, never mind Helsdon. All right, so she herself worked long and hard, but most evenings when she was still at it there'd be others in the mill, working overtime to finish an order, to get it out on time. And it wasn't only the money; there was more to it than that.

'I'm so lucky,' she said to Arthur Parker. 'No one in Bonneau's ever lets me down!'

'Why should they?' he demanded. 'And I don't know that luck's owt to do wi' it. You and the master are good employers. The best. Ask anyone in Helsdon and they'll tell you that.'

'Everyone's been extra good to me while Léon's been in France,' Madeleine said.

'Aye well,' he said. 'We can still show those Frenchies a thing or two. The master excepted, of course!'

You could say most things to Mrs Bonneau, but how could you tell her that there wasn't a man in the mill who wouldn't go into battle for her, if need be? Himself, he'd go to the ends of the earth. And the women liked her, especially the weavers. She spoke their language, understood what they were doing, appreciated the difficulties. They could talk to her, but at the same time, they looked up to her.

He laid down his pen and closed the ledger.

'That's it then! Wouldst like me to walk up to the house with thee?'

'Oh no, it's not necessary. It's not quite dark, and in any case that doesn't bother me. But thank you all the same, Arthur.'

It was good to be out in the open air. Climbing the hill to Mount Royd, she breathed deeply, filling her lungs. Though she had glimpsed it only from her office window, which in any case overlooked the mill yard, it had been another perfect day, the best that September could offer.

She saw that the bracken was already turning colour, and a few of the trees just beginning to do so. Up on the moor the heather would still be in bloom. She longed to see it. She must, somehow she must, make time to climb up to the moor before the weather changed. Perhaps she would manage it on Sunday, take the children with her. She fell to thinking about the scores of times she had walked the moors with Léon. When he returned, as soon as he was fit to walk, they would do it again. She was sure of that.

'Nay, Our Madeleine,' her mother said when she went in. 'What are you doing, working till this time?'

'There were things I had to finish, Ma. Any letters for me?'

'Not today.'

She had hoped there would be. 'Have the children been all right?'

'Right as rain. I'm more worried about you than the children.'

'Well please don't be. Actually, I've been thinking I'd take them up on the moor on Sunday. It would do us all good. In the meantime I'll go up and see them now.'

She went first into Claire's room. Her daughter was fast asleep, her limbs spread-eagled across the bed and the bedclothes thrown off. Madeleine gently drew the covers up around the child's shoulders and planted a kiss on her cheek. She's fast asleep now, she thought. She was also asleep when I left the house this morning, and it'll be the same tomorrow. What sort of a mother am I? But there was no help for it with things as they were.

In the next room, Tommy was still awake, fighting sleep so that he could see his mother. She gave him a hug, then sat on the bed and took his hand in hers.

'Have you had a good day, love?'

'Yes thank you, Mother. I got top marks for my history homework.'

397

'Why that's wonderful!' Madeleine cried. 'Well done!'

'But I didn't do well in arithmetic,' he confessed.

'Ah well,' Madeleine consoled him. 'No one can be good at everything. I was never much use at arithmetic myself.'

So used was she to thinking of Tommy as her own son, bone of her bone, flesh of her flesh, that she found herself again and again tracing his talents and shortcomings back to herself and Léon.

'I thought we might go up on the moor on Sunday,' she said. 'Would you like that?'

'You mean instead of going to church?' Tommy asked hopefully.

'No, I do not! I mean in the afternoon.'

'I'd like it anyway. There wasn't a letter from Papa today,' Tommy said.

'I know. But we can't expect one every day. I'm sure he writes as often as he can.'

Downstairs Mrs Bates brought Madeleine a supper tray.

'Thank you, Ma. This looks good! Where are the newspapers?' She'd left home that morning before they'd arrived.

Mrs Bates frowned. Sometimes she thought she'd like to have stopped all newspapers coming into the house. There was never any good in them, nothing but trouble. On the other hand, you had to know. She herself perused them for news from France as eagerly as did her daughter – which was why she knew that Madeleine would be shocked by today's news.

'I'll get them for you, love. But promise you'll eat your supper first.'

She'd said quite the wrong thing. She knew it the minute the words were out of her mouth.

'Why?' Madeleine asked quickly. 'Why shouldn't I read the newspaper first?'

The minute Mrs Bates returned, Madeleine snatched the papers from her, quickly turning to the news from

France. There was no need to search for the words. They sprang out at her from the page.

> 'All postal communications with Paris from the exterior will cease from Friday.'

No! It wasn't true! It couldn't be true! She had misread it, she must have! She read it again and it was true.

Trembling from head to foot, sick inside, she read further.

> 'The German armies are drawing in upon Paris as Paris resolutely prepares for a siege.'

'Léon! Oh Léon!' she cried out aloud, then threw the paper to the floor and sank into the chair, burying her head in the cushion, sobbing as though her heart would break. It was more than she could bear.

'Nay love!' Mrs Bates said. She felt helpless.

'Why didn't you tell me at once, Ma?'

'Because bad news will always keep. And newspapers aren't the gospel. They're not always right, love.'

It was no comfort at all. And Mrs Bates knew it. But what else could she say?

'Friday it says,' Madeleine cried. 'Today *is* Friday. I'm already too late!'

Mrs Bates touched her daughter gently, stroked her hair.

'Come and eat your supper, love. Everything's worse on an empty stomach.'

'Oh Ma, how can you? Léon's trapped in Paris, who knows for how long, or how dangerous it will be? And however long he's there he's not going to hear a word from me – and all you can say is "eat your supper"!'

'I'm sorry, love. I don't rightly know what to say, or

do.' She felt utterly useless, as though she had let down her daughter when she needed her most.

'He might never come back!' Madeleine was frenzied. 'Don't you see, he might never get out of Paris alive!'

'Now you mustn't say such things,' Mrs Bates said sharply. 'You mustn't allow yourself even to think them. That much I do know. Of course he'll come back! Why, you don't even know that he *is* trapped in Paris. It only says the post is stopped. Léon might still be able to get out.'

'It also says the German armies are getting near and that Paris is preparing for a siege. In that case no one will get either in or out. That's what a siege means, Ma! And even if there was the slightest chance in the next day or two, how could he take it? You know he's only just got on to his crutches.'

'Well we must hope for the best,' Mrs Bates said stubbornly. 'You can't help Léon by such thinking. And there's the children to consider. You've got to keep up for the sake of the bairns, love!'

'I can't!' Madeleine protested. 'I can't think about anyone but Léon!'

'Not just now you can't. But you will, love. I know you. I know your strength, and I know you'll do what's right.'

And to have to think about the children, and about the mill, would be her daughter's salvation. I might be an ignorant old woman, Mrs Bates thought, but I've sense enough to know that.

'And you'd best start off by eating a bit of supper,' she added. 'Just a bit, love.'

Madeleine lifted her head. Mrs Bates caught her breath at the sight of her daughter's ravaged face. All the fatigue, the strain, the worry, the responsibility of the last few weeks. All the longing – and now this final blow, were there to be seen in her. Mrs Bates's heart ached. If only you could bear your children's griefs for them! What mother wouldn't, if she could?

400

'Try to think what Léon would want you to do, lass,' she said gently. 'That way you'll get it right. I know you will.'

There was silence between them for a moment, then it was broken by Madeleine.

'Yes. You're right, Ma! And not for the first time. You always tell me you don't know what to say, but you manage to find the right thing. You're a wise lady.'

'I'm older,' Mrs Bates said. 'Unless you're daft you can't help picking up a bit of something as you go along. Now just eat a little bit of chicken and I'll go and put a hot-water-bottle in your bed and you'd best get an early night.'

I shan't sleep, Madeleine thought. She hadn't touched the papers she'd brought home to work on. Some of them were urgent, but they'd have to wait until tomorrow. What she wanted to do most of all was to write to Léon. She wanted to tell him, perhaps for the last time, what was in her heart. If the papers were to be believed, and she thought on balance that they were, then he'd never get the letter, but all the same, she would write it and send it.

And would she hear from him again? The report said nothing about letters out of Paris. She had little hope that she would.

She slept hardly at all that night. More than at any time during his absence she missed the comfort of Léon's body beside her in the bed. She flung herself across the space where he would have lain and cried his name aloud.

'Léon! Oh Léon, what am I to do?'

Next morning she rose early and was in the mill before the hooter went. As soon as work started she sent for Rob Wainwright.

'Did you see yesterday's papers?' she asked.

'No, Mrs Bonneau, I didn't.'

She gave him the news.

'What I'd like,' she said quickly, 'is for you to get everyone together when we break for breakfast. There are one or two things I want to say.'

Rob Wainwright stared at her, marvelling at the cool resolution in her voice.

'I'll do that, Mrs Bonneau,' he promised. 'And . . . I'm really very sorry.'

It was clear, when Madeleine stood in front of the millhands a little later, that the news had got around. There was no need to call for silence. The minute she appeared all chattering ceased. They stood there grim-faced and mute.

'You've heard the news,' she began. 'You know it's possible that it might be some time before my husband is back with us. But he *will* be back, we must all believe that, and in the meantime we have to carry on. I wrote a few days ago and told him that the order was almost completed for André's, in Paris. I told him just how hard you had all worked to make that possible. I'm sure by now he'll have had that letter, and he'll be as proud of you as I am.'

She stopped, swallowed hard. She wasn't sure she could go on. Then Rob Wainwright handed her a glass of water and she sipped it, and recovered.

'We can't now send the order to Paris. We can't risk it getting lost, or being confiscated. And what's worse, the war in France might mean that we shall lose some of our other valued French customers. For that reason we must try harder than ever to do well in the English market. A lot of that will be up to me. Instead of working here with you, a great deal of the time I'll be on the road, selling, getting new orders. But I know that whatever orders I bring back, I can rely on you to carry them out. We shall support each other!'

She paused again, more briefly this time, then said: 'I can't thank you enough for the way you've supported me, and I'm sure you'll go on doing it. On the day my husband returns to Helsdon I want him to come back to a Bonneau's which has not only kept up its business, but which has grown and flourished. Will you do that for him? For Léon Bonneau?'

She sat down, fighting to keep back the tears. There was a moment's silence – and then a burst of applause. She knew in that moment that everything would be all right with Bonneau's mill. And if the applause hadn't told her, the remarks which came to her ears as she walked back through the workpeople to her office convinced her.

'Of course we'll stand by you!'

'Don't you fret, Missus!'

'We'll do our damndest, love!'

She wasn't sure who said what, there were so many of them calling out at once, until she came to Mrs Barnet. That lady, that staunch friend through so many years, opened her arms and Madeleine went into them.

'Don't you fret, lass,' Harriet Barnet said. 'You'll win through. You always have and you always will!'

Back in her office Madeleine thought, what if he never comes back? What if my darling never returns?

She pushed the thought from her and opened the file of papers which she should have attended to last night.

On the following Tuesday the final blow came, though it was not unexpected. She read the announcement in the paper, then, with scarcely a pause, went back to her work. She would never forget the words she had just read.

'. . . It is now impossible to get anything in or out of Paris.'

TWENTY-TWO

In the small bedroom which had been Jean's, until he had ceded it to his uncle from England and moved in to share with Etienne, Léon struggled to dress himself without calling on Marie for help.

It was an uphill task. He could manage the top half of his body, don his shirt, tie his cravat, even shave himself; but it was impossible to wear trousers. He was restricted to wearing his robe all day and every day, and he was sick of the sight of it. It was amazing how helpless, how invalidish, the lack of his trousers made him feel.

Exhausted by his efforts, he lay down on the bed again. He would have stayed there – what else was there to do? – had he not heard his brother-in-law's key in the door. Jules had been on duty with the guard all night.

Léon got to his feet at once, and made his clumsy way into the living-room.

Jules was the bringer of news, sometimes good, sometimes bad, but at least it was from the outside world. He was a man who kept his eyes and ears open and knew what was going on in a city which was growing more and more confusing. Marie went out, shopping twice every day, but the news she brought back was domestic: the rising price of olive oil, the absence of meat. She treated all other aspects of the siege as if they were inconveniences which had nothing to do with her.

If only I could see things for myself, Léon thought fretfully. But he was as clumsy as ever on his crutches, partly because in the small apartment, cluttered with furniture, there was no room to practise. His leg was painful, and not only his leg. Sometimes his whole body hurt. Nevertheless, he would have ignored the pain if he'd been given the chance to get out of the apartment a little more.

He hobbled into the living-room. When he sat down, Marie at once fixed a footstool for him. She was so kind to him; so was Jules. But however kind, they were, in fact, his gaolers, and he was in prison, here in this apartment, two flights of steps up from the street.

Jules hung up his cap and unbuckled his belt. They were still the only items of uniform he had, though recently he'd been issued with a rifle.

'Which I hope you will never, ever use,' Marie had said when he brought it home.

'Did you have a quiet night?' Léon asked now.

'No one troubled us,' Jules replied. 'We could hear gun-fire, but nothing came our way. I spent the night digging trenches. I would rather do that than sit around playing cards.'

'You look very tired, my love,' Marie said. 'And now you have to go to work.'

'I'll be all right when I've had some coffee. Do we have coffee this morning?'

'We do indeed,' Marie assured him. 'It's weaker than you like it because we must make it last, but it's coffee nevertheless.'

He sat at the table and Marie handed him a bowl of coffee, cut him some bread. He drank deeply and ate with appetite.

'You mustn't go out today, Marie!' he said.

Marie paused in the act of fuelling the stove. She did that less often these days because wood was scarce.

'Not go out? Why ever not? I must go out. I have more shopping to do.'

'Not today, you mustn't,' Jules said firmly. 'The streets of Montparnasse are full of deserters from our own army and the people are in an ugly mood. There's likely to be trouble.'

'Deserters?' Léon queried.

'The Zouaves!' Jules's voice was rich with scorn.

'Those so-called crack soldiers in their fancy uniforms, who are meant to show the rest of us how it's done, met up with the Prussians at Meudon. What did they do, those brave popinjays? They turned tail and fled, hared back to Paris, every man Jack of them. Pity it wasn't a day or two later, then there'd have been no getting into Paris – and serve the cowards right!'

'I'm not sure I wouldn't turn tail, faced with a Prussian gun,' Marie said. 'I saw the Zouaves when they marched off. They looked magnificent, yes certainly – but they were so young. Some of them no more than boys fresh from school, I'd say.'

'They are men, and Frenchmen,' Jules contradicted. 'They're a disgrace to their country. But you're a woman, you can't be expected to understand these things.'

'I understand the stupidity of the whole thing!' Marie said hotly. 'Oh yes, I understand that only too clearly!'

'Which is another reason why you shouldn't go out today,' Jules said. 'It seems the rest of the populace doesn't think as you do. They're in a nasty mood and out for the deserters' blood. If you voiced your feelings you'd really be in trouble.'

'I'm quite capable of keeping my mouth shut,' Marie retorted. 'You want to eat, don't you? Well if you want food, I have to go and find it.'

'I wish I could go for you,' Léon said. 'I feel so useless.'

'You're not useless,' Marie said. 'Today you can be useful in looking after the children so that I can shop on my own.'

That's all I'm fit for, Léon thought. Looking after the children.

He had stopped writing to Madeleine. At first, when the posts gave up, he had continued to send letters in the vain hope that somehow they'd get through. In the end he had faced the fact that it was useless. Nothing was moving. Certainly he had not heard from Madeleine.

He had started to keep a journal, mostly to pass the time. Marie had purchased an exercise book for him, but now paper was scarce and expensive, so he must limit the length of his entries, make the book last.

He had very little money left. He had given all except a small amount to Marie, towards food. That gesture had, at least, given him a small measure of independence.

'Don't forget,' Marie said to Jules as he was leaving for work, 'that you promised the children we'd take them to the Jardin des Plantes at the weekend, to see the animals in the zoo!'

'I shan't forget,' Jules said. 'I'm looking forward to it myself.' He had this urgency in him to do so much with the children. There were things he wanted to show them while there was still time.

'Shall you attempt to go with us?' he asked Léon.

'I shall certainly try,' Léon assured him. It would be good just to be in the fresh air again.

When Jules had left for work, Marie put on her jacket and took the shopping-basket down from its hook.

'You shouldn't go,' Léon said. 'You know what Jules said.'

'Yes I know,' she answered. 'And it's not often I defy Jules. But don't worry, Léon. I promise I'll be very careful. I'll keep my mouth shut and attend only to my marketing. Anyway, the streets might have cleared by now.'

In fact, when she went out they had not. Groups of soldiers wandered around seemingly not knowing where to go. They looked haggard, frightened, dirty and unshaven, and for the most part very young. There was no disguising from the public who they were. Their bright red trousers, so dashing when they'd marched off to battle, marked them out.

Wherever there was a group of Zouaves, there was a larger group of hostile Parisians, shouting and taunting. At one point Marie had no choice but to walk through the middle of the ugly crowd if she were to reach the shop which, rumour said, had a new supply of flour. Though she was apprehensive, there was no question of not going on. She needed that flour.

Head down, looking neither to right nor to left, clutching her basket, she plunged into the throng.

'Traitors!' the citizens were shouting. 'Traitors! They should be hanged!'

'It is we who have been betrayed! We were sent into battle without ammunition!'

The soldier who called out was very close to Marie. She turned and looked at him. He was dirty, he looked hungry and haunted. He was very young, perhaps sixteen, she thought.

'You don't know what it's like!' he shouted. 'You sit here in Paris, on your backsides. You don't know a thing!'

His protest fell on deaf ears. The crowd was shouting now with a loud, raucous voice.

'Traitors! Traitors! Cowards! Cowards!'

It was no more than a second or two before the first stones were thrown. Marie tried to push her way ahead, but the menacing crowd was advancing against her. She could make no progress at all. Suddenly, she was caught on the cheek by a flying stone. She put her hand to her face and felt the blood trickling down.

The mob, who outnumbered the Zouaves ten to one, continued to push. It was difficult for Marie to keep her feet. If I lose my footing, she thought, if I fall to the ground, I shall be trampled on. The citizens grappled with the soldiers, who were so outnumbered that their resistance was useless. They were held fast, then carried away shoulder high by their captors. Marie wanted to follow, she wanted to see what happened to the young man who had been by her side when the stone struck, but common sense told her she must not do so.

The blood was still running down her face and she took out her handkerchief to staunch it before continuing on her way. She was trembling now from head to toe, but as much from anger as from fear.

When she arrived back at the apartment, Léon cried out at the sight of her.

'Marie! What in the world happened to you?'

'It's nothing!' she answered. 'I stumbled and fell!'

'My dear little sister, a fall would hardly cut your cheek and leave the rest of you unscathed! So what did happen? You must tell me.'

'A stone hit me,' she confessed. 'But I'm all right. The bleeding's almost stopped. I'll bathe my face.'

'Let me see!' Léon ordered. 'It looks quite nasty. Does it hurt?'

'A little. I'd rather Jules thought I'd fallen,' she said. 'He'll be quite angry with me.'

'Tell Jules whatever you like. Naturally, I shan't contradict you – but you're deceiving yourself if you think he'll swallow that tale!'

By the time Jules came home from work the area of Marie's face around the cut was swollen and angry-looking.

'What in the world . . . ?' Jules began.

'I was hit by a stone,' Marie said. 'It wasn't deliberately thrown at me. I just happened to be in the way. And no, I wasn't provocative. I kept my mouth shut and didn't utter a word. I was just unlucky, that's all!'

'Unlucky!' Jules stormed. 'Unlucky? Not at all. You were lucky that nothing worse happened to you. I told you not to go out! Do you realize that much worse harm might have come to you? Did it not occur to you that someone might have hurt you so badly that you'd lose the baby?'

'No it didn't.' As Marie said the words she remembered the moment when she'd thought she might fall, and be trampled on. 'But nothing terrible did happen,' she added. 'At least not to me, though I wonder what befell those young soldiers.'

'Nothing that you can do anything about,' Jules said firmly.

'Anyway,' Marie said in a dismissive voice, 'I got the flour *and* some salt – which I prophesy will be more precious than gold before we're through!'

On Sunday, with some difficulty, Léon went with the others to the Jardin des Plantes. Descending the stairs from the apartment down to the street was the worst part, but with Jules's patient help and his own grim determination he managed it. Once in the cab, though sometimes it jolted in an unpleasant fashion over the cobbles, it was easier, and when they reached the Botanical Gardens every minute of pain seemed worth while.

For most of the time he was obliged to sit on a bench while the rest of the party explored, periodically returning to him. He didn't mind. The September sun was like a benison on his face, the scents of the garden filled his nostrils.

It was heaven. Or would have been, he thought, if only his dear Madeleine had been there. When all this was over he would bring her here, and they would sit on this very seat, and they'd be happy together.

Presently Jules and Marie and the children returned.

'We're going to see the animals now,' Marie said. 'We thought, if you're rested, you might like to try it.'

'Willingly!' Léon said.

The children were thrilled by the animals, especially by the large ones: the hippopotamus, the camel, and most of all, the elephants.

'The two young elephants are called Castor and Pollux,' Jean said. 'Don't you think they're splendid, Uncle Léon?'

'Absolutely!' Léon agreed.

At the end of that day Léon felt happier than for a long time. His legs ached badly, his whole body was fatigued, but it didn't matter. He had shown what he could do. Every day from now, if only someone would give him a hand down the stairs, he would go out; and with such progress it wouldn't be long before he could go home. Home to Helsdon.

He made no mention of his hopes that night. Everyone was tired, and Jules had to go on guard duty at midnight.

410

But the next evening, when Jules returned from work, Léon was waiting anxiously to speak with him.

'Jules, I did so well yesterday – as you saw – that I think I am almost ready to leave. I'm sure now that I could manage the journey. Oh, not as early as tomorrow, of course, but very soon now. You will help me, won't you?'

Jules looked grim and serious.

'Don't you believe me?' Léon queried. 'I'm quite sure I can do it.'

'I believe you.' He had marvelled at his brother-in-law's courage yesterday, which made it all the more difficult to say what he had to say.

'Then what is it? What's wrong?'

'It's no use, my dear Léon. You are too late. It's all around the city today – you'll see it in the newspapers tomorrow – Versailles has surrendered without a fight. The Prussians have joined hands there and closed the gap. Paris is now completely encircled. There is no way out for you, or for anyone else. We are cut off from the rest of France. Indeed,' he added bleakly, 'we are cut off from the rest of the world.'

When he saw the sudden quenching of the bright hope which had been in Léon's face a moment ago, watched the light die from his eyes, he felt that in bringing him the news he had somehow betrayed him.

'I wish I didn't have to say this, Léon – but you have to know.'

'Yes. I see. Thank you for telling me. What is the date?'

'20 September. Why do you ask?'

'It's a date I shall never forget,' Léon said.

He dragged himself to his feet and went slowly to his room. Was there any point now in trying to get better?

In the night which followed Léon slept little and thought a great deal. There were moments, in the earliest hours of the morning, when his spirits reached the depths. He felt, as Jules had described the situation of Paris, cut off from the world. But his own isolation was more severe because Paris was no longer his place. His world was in Helsdon. Then at last, towards morning, he fell asleep.

He wakened to a different feeling, as if in his sleep a new and miraculous spirit had visited him, whisking away the previous night's depression. He tried, without success, to remember what he might have dreamed which could have caused this new feeling. All he recalled was that just before falling asleep he had longed with a passionate intensity for Madeleine. So intense had the longing been, that he'd cried her name aloud. But as far as he knew, he hadn't dreamed of her.

But she was at the front of his mind, now, as he left sleep behind. Why had he thought only of his own misery in being cut off, when Madeleine was in a position every bit as difficult as his? She would have no news of him. She would carry the burden of the mill, which was not his idea of a woman's work. If he was absent long, she might have to witness the deterioration of the business they had built up so carefully between them; slow at first perhaps, and then rapid. The more he thought of Madeleine, the more ashamed he was of last night's orgy of self-pity.

He made a new resolve. He would do everything in his power to make himself fit, so that when the opportunity came, as eventually it must, for him to leave Paris, he could seize it at once.

From now on he would go out every day. For a start, he would accompany Marie on her shopping trips, even if it meant taking the children. In any case it would only be little Etienne, since Jean had just started school. He would help in the apartment. Even at the cost of buying a little more paper, he would keep up his journal; write it as if each day it was a letter to Madeleine. In short, he would stop feeling sorry for himself and come to life, make the best of things.

Also, he would conquer those damned stairs, even if it meant practising up and down them three times a day. And *that* he would start on the minute breakfast was over.

He put on his robe and went into the living-room.

'Jules has already left,' Marie said. 'He had to take Jean to school on his way.'

'Have you done your marketing?' Léon asked.

'My early marketing, yes. But I must go again this afternoon, see what's come into the shops. Milk was scarce this morning. Would you believe that with all those animals they put to graze in the Bois de Boulogne, they didn't include any milch-cows? Any woman would have told them that cows were an absolute necessity. If the children don't get milk, how will they thrive! Such fools those men are!'

'Do you think I could go out with you when you go shopping this afternoon?' Léon asked.

Marie looked at him in astonishment.

'You would have to help me on with my trousers,' he said.

'Oh, that's no trouble. After all, I'm your sister. But will you be fit?'

'I intend to be,' Léon said firmly. 'If I fall by the wayside you can prop me against a wall and pick me up on your way back. Oh Marie, I just want to get out and about!'

Marie nodded.

'I can understand that! Well, if you're really determined. . .'

'Oh I am!'

'Then how would it be if we went to the Luxembourg Gardens and you sat and waited for me there. I often shop in that vicinity.'

'It would be splendid!' Léon said. 'And that being the case, will you help me dress as soon as I've drunk my coffee? I intend to tackle that staircase.'

'On your own? Oh Léon, you can't!'

'I intend to try. I think I know a way I can do it. I shall need a little help. I mean to do it without my crutches, but you must be there to hand them to me when I reach the bottom.'

'But what will you do?' Marie said.

413

'I shall hold on to the banister rail, and I shall hop down on my good leg!'

'Yes, I suppose that would work,' Marie said thoughtfully. 'It will be difficult, though. And what if you fall?'

'If I fall, I fall. No doubt I'll shout and swear, and if the *concierge* doesn't come running to help me, then you must fetch him. On no account must you try to get me up. But I don't think I shall fall. I'll take it slowly, and be careful.'

'Very well then.' Marie sounded doubtful.

'It will get easier with practice,' Léon assured her. 'When can I try it?'

'A little later, when Etienne has his morning nap.'

While he waited for Marie to be ready he discarded his crutches and hopped around, testing himself, using the chairs and the table to take his weight. It would be more difficult to hop up and down steps, but thankfully they were shallow ones. He was sure it would work.

It did work.

He was exhausted when he reached the ground floor, the sweat pouring down his face. When Marie handed him his crutches he embraced them as old friends, glad to let them take his weight again. But a minute later he said: 'Now I must go back up the steps.'

He managed that also. It wasn't as easy to hop upwards, but it was somehow less frightening than the descent, when he'd seen the flight of stairs going down in front of him.

'Bravo!' Marie said when he'd made the final hop. 'Now you really must rest.'

'I know. And I will,' Léon said. But oh, he felt good! He felt so good!

Later in the day he took himself down the stairs again – it was easier this time, he'd got the knack of it – and went with Marie and Etienne to the Luxembourg Gardens. There he sat and waited while Marie and Etienne shopped.

'Are you very tired?' Marie said when she came back for him. 'Should we get a *fiacre*?'

'No!' Léon said. 'I can manage.'

There was no money to spare for *fiacres*, and they both knew it.

When Jules came home from work it was to a brother-in-law white-faced with exhaustion, but considerably more cheerful.

'I've brought you some very good news!' Jules said. 'Though in fact, you look as though you've had some already.'

'Good news?' Léon said. 'What is it? Tell me quickly!'

'They're going to start a balloon post,' Jules said. 'The Minister of Posts says the first one might well go tomorrow or the day after. It appears we do have balloons in the city, but most of them are in disrepair. Already they're hard at work repairing the first one they hope to use.'

'A balloon post!' Léon cried. 'I shall be able to write to Madeleine!'

'Can anyone use it, or will it be only for official mail?' Marie asked.

'That I can't say. I've told you all I know. Perhaps we shall find out more in tomorrow's newspapers.'

The details, next day, were still sparse. Also the first balloon which had been repaired had burst while being inflated, so it would be a few days longer before the first balloon could take to the air.

'In the manned balloons,' Léon said, reading from the paper, 'we shall be allowed to send small sheets of paper of a certain size and the cost will be twenty centimes. It's hoped that eventually there might be as many as two or three balloons a week leaving Paris. Imagine that!'

'Where would they go from?' Marie asked.

'Probably from the Solférino Tower in Montmartre. Or outside the Gare du Nord.'

Jules, cautious as always, said: 'You realize there's no way of making sure that the letters will get to their destination? The balloons are at the mercy of the wind, and when they come down, the post they contain will be at the mercy of whoever gets to it. If it's the Prussians that will be the end of it.'

'That's true,' Léon agreed. 'But it says here that they rather hope that the prevailing wind might take some of them to Belgium, and that would be all right. At any rate it's worth taking the chance. I shall send my little letters just as often as I'm allowed to do so.'

'And as long as you can afford it,' Marie said. 'Twenty centimes is a lot of money.'

Her mind ran on money far too often these days. It was so difficult to make it spin out. Without meaning to, she calculated what twenty centimes would buy in the way of food.

Though the balloon post was launched only a few days later, it was more than a fortnight before Léon managed to get his letter into the post.

'It's quite ridiculous!' he complained to Marie. 'We're told that each balloon can carry a hundred thousand of these little letters, yet I have to wait two weeks for mine to be accepted. It's my firm belief that people who don't need to are sending them – people who wouldn't have bothered to put pen to paper in normal circumstances. Now they're doing it for the sake of novelty.'

'At twenty centimes a time the Government is making plenty out of it,' Marie remarked. 'I just hope the balloonist is well paid. He's the one who's taking the risk. And have you thought that he stands little chance of getting back to Paris? The balloons go out, but nothing comes in.'

'I know,' Léon agreed. 'So you'd think that Paris would run out of balloonists, wouldn't you? But it seems they are queuing up to be trained.'

The worst part of the whole business was not knowing what happened to the letters. It seemed that one of the *non-monté* – the unmanned – balloons had been shot down by the Prussians just outside the fortifications; that a manned one had been captured not many miles away;

416

that one had got through to Dreux, fifty miles from Paris. Over the next few weeks it was said they'd got through to Belgium, even to Norway. It was all rumours. No one really knew. But whatever the truth, still more balloons were being made at top speed in the factory, and leaving Paris twice a week with their precious cargo.

Marie was not happy about the balloon business. She said nothing to Léon, but alone with Jules she spoke her mind.

'All this money, all this effort, so that people can send a few letters which they don't even know will get there! And look at the gas they use! It's gas which we badly need in the city. One of these days we shall be without lights – but it seems that we're not to mind, as long as the balloons go up! It's all that matters!'

'I think you exaggerate,' Jules said. 'And the balloon post is such a boost to everyone. It shows we're not entirely cut off from the world.'

'For all practical purposes we are. You'd know that if you had to go shopping. And that's another thing – Léon is spending forty centimes a week on the post, yet he has no money to give me towards housekeeping!'

'Marie! That will do!' Jules said sharply. 'I hope you've said nothing of the kind to Léon?'

'I haven't yet. But I well might!'

'You will do no such thing! Have you no imagination? Here you are, in your own home, with your husband and children around you, and you begrudge a man who is cut off from his wife and children trying to contact them? And your own brother at that! Have you thought how you would feel if you were in his shoes?'

'I'm sorry,' Marie said.

'Haven't you noticed how much happier Léon is on the days when he's got a letter in the balloon post? Does that mean nothing to you?'

She sighed.

'You're quite right, of course. I spoke out of turn. But all I seem to be able to think about is how to feed you all!'

417

Jules put his arms around his wife.

'I know, *chérie*! And you do so well. It's hard – but I'm afraid it will get harder, so we mustn't feel sorry for ourselves too soon.'

Jules proved himself no false prophet.

By the middle of October, fresh meat had disappeared from the shops, milk was seldom to be had, cheese was something one reminisced about.

'There was some butter in the shops today,' Marie said one evening in November as they were eating their meagre supper of soup which was little more than vegetable water. 'But it was more than sixty francs a kilo! Before the siege it was eight francs. It's the same with everything! Potatoes fifteen francs a bushel, and not long ago they were two or three francs.'

'We have to be very thankful that you shopped as wisely as you did in the beginning,' Jules said. 'At least you laid in a few stores.'

'Not nearly enough,' Marie told him. 'Before long they'll be finished.'

'I worry most for you, my dear,' Jules said. 'In your condition you should be eating good food, and eating for two.'

'Well there's no chance of that!' Marie said.

She felt so weak and tired these days. The baby was active in her womb now. Every day she felt it kicking. It's stronger than I am, she thought. It took what it needed from her and left her little to exist on. Would she be able to carry it to full term; and when the time came to give birth, would she have enough strength to do so? Sometimes she felt that the baby might actually take her life.

The next day, when Jules had gone to do his guard duty, Léon came into the kitchen to her. A week ago he had been back to the hospital and had his leg plaster removed, and now he could walk without crutches, but with the aid of a stick. He had a letter in his hand.

'I'm going to take this letter to the balloon post,' he said quietly. 'But I want you to know it's the last one I shall send.'

418

'Why is that?' she asked sharply. She had done as Jules said; she had never complained to Léon.

'I've been selfish,' Léon said. 'I've spent money every week on the post which could well have helped to feed you and the children.'

'I do understand,' Marie said.

'Thank you. It's meant a lot to me, being able to write to Madeleine, whether she gets the letters or not – and I try to tell myself that she does. But in this letter I've told her that I shan't be able to write again for a while.'

'What reason have you given?'

'Oh, not the true one! There's no point in telling her that we're so hungry that those who can afford it are happy to eat rat pie! I've been deliberately vague and put it down to the unreliability of the balloons.'

'You needn't post it,' Marie said. 'You can tear that letter up and go on writing to her as usual.'

'No,' Léon said. 'I've made up my mind. I should have done it sooner.'

He took a bag of coins from his pocket and handed it to her.

'This is all I have left, but now it's yours.'

'Oh Léon, are you quite sure?'

'I am.'

'Then thank you. Thank you very much indeed!'

When Léon had left the house to post his letter Marie tipped the coins out on the table and began to count them, but instead of coins in front of her she saw bread, potatoes, oil, perhaps even an egg each.

Léon took his letter to the collecting place and handed it over. When he turned away his eyes were wet with tears. He felt that he had turned his back on all that was dearest to him in life.

It was mid-December when Madeleine received Léon's last letter. It seemed to have gone a roundabout route from Paris to Helsdon. In fact it was not only the last letter she was to receive from him, it was also the first.

Every other letter, so lovingly written, posted with such high hopes, had gone astray. She knew that a balloon post was in operation. Most of the accounts of the siege had reached England by balloon post, but though she rose every morning with the hope in her heart that today she would be lucky, she never had been: until today. Now the longed-for letter told her that there would be no other.

When it arrived she snatched it from the postman's hand and ran out of the room with it.

'She wants to be on her own to read it,' Mrs Bates said to the postman. 'You can understand that!'

'Aye, I can!' the postman said. 'Happen you'll let me know tomorrow if Mr Bonneau's all right. There's a lot of folk in Helsdon will be glad to have me put their minds at rest. He's right well thought of.'

'Of course I'll tell you,' Mrs Bates promised.

Madeleine, in the privacy of her bedroom, read the letter for the fourth time. The writing was small, sometimes almost undecipherable, because he had tried to cram so much into the limited space. He was cheerful. He was in good health, he said, and his leg was getting better every day. He reported on Marie's pregnancy, and on various other domestic details. Though this was her fourth reading, fresh tears raced down her cheeks at his messages of love and concern, first for herself and his family, and after that for his workpeople in Bonneau's mill.

He wrote not a word of the privations in Paris, nothing of whether he was hungry, or afraid. But she knew. Though he gave nothing away, she knew all right. Every day the newspapers had their horror stories of what was happening in Paris: the terrible food shortages, the epidemic of smallpox, the scarcity of fuel. And now even the weather was against them. The long hot summer had given way to freezing cold. Poor Léon, she thought. He had always hated the cold.

But of all this he said nothing. He sounded full of hope.

*

420

'Who knows, my darling, I might well be home with you by Christmas!' he concluded.

She kissed the letter tenderly, then folded it, put it in her pocket, and went back to her mother.

'Léon is well, Ma,' she said. 'He sends you his love.'

'Oh lovey, I'm that pleased! Praise be to God!'

In a gesture unusual for her, Mrs Bates opened her arms and took her daughter into them, holding her close. Madeleine's tears fell anew.

'Praise be!' she echoed. 'Oh Ma, if only I could write back to him!'

She wanted to tell him everything that had happened: how well Tommy was doing at school, how Claire grew prettier by the day. She wanted to tell him that everything in the mill was going well; that she was travelling around and the orders were keeping up, that she had even found new customers.

Most of all, she longed with her whole heart to tell him how much she loved him and longed for him, and looked forward to his homecoming. She wanted him to know that however full her life was, it was only half a life without his presence. But she could say none of these things.

'I must go down to the mill,' she said presently. 'I want to give everyone the news!'

TWENTY-THREE

Christmas came, but with it no news of Léon. It was stupid of me ever to build up my hopes, Madeleine thought. Only two days ago the *Manchester Guardian* had announced that there was no military movement around Paris, and that the Germans no longer had any hope of a quick surrender of the city.

So what is he doing, and how does he fare, this Christmas Eve, Madeleine asked herself? How would he spend the festival? The agony of not knowing ate into her. Did he long for her as she did for him?

'I've no heart for Christmas,' she said to her mother. 'I shall be glad when it's over.'

'I understand that, love,' Mrs Bates replied. 'But we have to keep up for the sake of the childer.'

'I know,' Madeleine said. 'That's the reason I'm trimming this tree.'

'Happen you'll find that doing the usual things will help you most, take your mind off your troubles.'

'Nothing will take my mind off Léon,' Madeleine said.

'I know. I know. And I daresay he'll be thinking of you, picturing you doing just what you're doing now.' Mrs Bates tried to change the subject. 'It's very pretty, this tree! We never had such things when I was a girl – not until Prince Albert married the Queen and brought the idea from Germany. I wonder if they have Christmas trees in France?'

'More to the point,' said Madeleine, 'I wonder if they'll have any Christmas dinner in Paris. What will they eat while we're stuffing ourselves with roast goose and plum pudding?'

But on Christmas Day, though her heart was like a stone in her breast, she threw herself into making the children happy, smiled as if she hadn't a care in the world. Only in church, when they prayed for Léon's safe homecoming, did she allow herself the luxury of tears, and then for no more than a minute, with her head bowed so that no one should see. Leaving the church, she met everyone's concerned enquiries with cheerful answers.

Minutes later the children were sitting on the floor in the drawing-room, surrounded by presents. Madeleine had been unusually lavish with gifts and toys for them this year, trying to make up for the absence of their father. They seemed so carefree as they played, so absorbed, that suddenly she had to get away, she had to be on her own. No one even heard her leave the room.

She was in her bedroom when there was a quiet knock on the door and Tommy entered.

'Are you sad because Papa's not here?' he asked.

'I am a little,' she confessed.

'So am I,' Tommy said. 'I'm trying not to be, but I can't help it! What do you suppose he's doing?'

'I wish I knew! I suppose, like us, he'll have been to church. Perhaps he'll be playing with Jean and Etienne, your cousins, while Aunt Marie makes the dinner.'

'Will Papa remember us?' Tommy asked. He looked at her with troubled eyes.

'Oh my dear Tommy, of *course* he'll remember us! I'm sure he'll be thinking of all of us, most of the time, and especially today. Papa would never forget us, not in a hundred years.'

Madeleine put her arms around her son and held him close.

'I will never ever forget him,' Tommy said. 'Not in a million, billion years!'

'Of course you won't, love. And one day Papa will come home and we'll all be together again. And when we are we'll have a proper Christmas!'

'Even if it's the middle of June?'

'Even if it's the middle of June and boiling hot,' Madeleine promised. Please God they wouldn't have to wait so long! 'And now shall we go downstairs again,' she said, 'and have a game of ludo.'

On Boxing Day they all, including Mrs Bates, went to Ripon to see Penelope. And as the train service wasn't good on that day, Sam Bennett took them in the carriage, all of them wrapped around with rugs against the cold. I wonder if Léon is cold, Madeleine thought?

'Oh, you all look frozen,' Penelope said when she opened the door to them. 'Come right in by the fire. Sam, will you take a hot drink before you drive off to see your brother?' she asked the coachman.

'Best not,' Sam said. 'Best get on.' He turned to Madeleine. 'I'll be back at seven to take you home.'

'Oh, please not so early?' Tommy begged.

'Very well then. Eight o'clock. But not a minute later,' Madeleine agreed.

'Oh goody! We'll be going home in the dark,' Claire said. 'I like going home in the dark!'

'I've asked Emerald to come for tea,' Penelope said. 'Whether she will or not's another question!'

'Nay, surely Our Emerald'll manage an hour or two on Boxing Day!' Mrs Bates protested. 'She's not been near Helsdon over Christmas – not since goodness knows when.'

After an enormous dinner – there was no shortage of food in a butcher's home – Archie built up the fire and they settled down in front of it, the children, except for Lucy, who was too young, playing a game of 'snap'. Lucy climbed on to her mother's knee and settled herself for sleep.

'There's not a lot of room for you here,' Penelope said. She was six months pregnant with her fourth child.

'Come and sit on Grandma's knee!' Mrs Bates invited. 'Grandma's got a nice lap to sit on!'

Within minutes, both Mrs Bates and her youngest granddaughter were asleep, and then Archie. Only

Madeleine and Penelope heard the knock on the door, followed by Emerald's entrance.

'Merry Christmas!' Emerald said. 'I can't stop long!'

'Merry Christmas!' Penelope said. 'That's a right greeting! "I can't stop long!" Well long enough to take your cloak off, I hope.'

'Why can't you stay?' Madeleine asked.

'We're that busy, that's why. And Mrs Chester has people coming in this evening. It was very good of her to let me come down here at all.'

'She's a slave driver, that one,' Penelope said. 'Well will you stay long enough for a cup of tea and a bit of spice cake? The kettle's on.'

'Very well,' Emerald agreed.

At the clinking of teacups, Mrs Bates wakened.

'Why, Our Emerald!' she cried, pleased and surprised.

'She's come to say she can't stop but a minute,' Penelope said. 'Good thing you wakened, Ma, or you might have missed her!'

'Don't be so peevish!' Emerald snapped. 'I told you, I'm lucky I could come at all.'

Once upon a time, Emerald could take a joke as well as the rest of us, Madeleine thought, but her sense of humour seemed to have left her. She took a cup of tea from Penelope and sipped at it, thinking about what she had to do the next day. Nowadays her thoughts were always either on Léon or on work.

'I'm going to York tomorrow, and Harrogate,' she said. 'I wish you two girls could come with me. You could look at the shops while I made my calls.'

'I can't, though I'd love to,' Penelope said. 'It's a busy day tomorrow and I shall be needed here.'

'And I certainly can't!' Emerald said firmly.

Next morning Mrs Bates opened the door and looked out as Madeleine was about to leave.

'It's a cold one!' she said. 'And yon sky's full of snow, if I'm not mistaken.'

'Well I hope you are,' Madeleine answered. 'Harrogate

and York are cold enough without snow. I reckon the wind blows straight from the north pole to Harrogate!'

She travelled to York first, to call on Percy Sutton. He was pleased to see her, eventually gave her a good order, and when he could detain her no longer in his office he took her into York and gave her some dinner.

'I reckon your husband must be right proud of you,' he said as they drank their coffee.

'Thank you!'

Would he be, Madeleine wondered? She'd told him in an early letter that she was visiting a few firms, but he had no idea just how much she was doing. Perhaps she should have told him more. Even if he didn't approve it would have saved him the worry of wondering if the business was going downhill in his absence. And if he could see the order books she reckoned his disapproval would melt. But it was too late to tell him anything now.

'If you'll excuse me, Mr Sutton, I really must be going,' she said. She was warm and comfortable in the eating house, full of good food. She didn't in the least want to go out into the cold.

'Must you?' he asked.

'I'm afraid so. I have a call to make in Harrogate.'

'Oh aye? Then I reckon you're going to see Hardman.'

'That's right.'

'Well you tell him from me that if he doesn't treat you right, I'll have his guts for garters – if you'll pardon the expression!'

In fact, Mr Hardman's treatment was every bit as good as Percy Sutton's. He gave her an equally good order, then insisted on taking her to a tea-shop at the top of Parliament Street. There he kept her talking so long that she was in danger of missing her train.

'Catch the next,' Mr Hardman suggested. 'Why not?'

'Because I'm expected home. And although the snow's held off so far, I'm sure it's coming. I don't really fancy being out in it. I must catch that train!'

426

'Perhaps you're right,' he said regretfully. He'd enjoyed being seen with this lovely-looking woman: and quite apart from her looks she was good to talk to. She had an intelligence which, in his opinion, didn't usually go with beauty.

Madeleine left Mr Hardman and half-ran all the way to the station. As she raced on to the platform the guard raised his whistle to his lips. By the time she scrambled into the compartment, almost falling over two women who were sitting by the window, he was waving his flag and the train had begun to move.

The two women had been chatting when Madeleine burst in on them, though she became aware of this only when their voices tailed off into an unnatural silence. At that point she turned her head to look at them – and found herself face to face with Sophia Chester. For a moment the silence continued, then it was broken by Sophia.

'I think you have made a mistake! This is a first-class compartment!'

Her voice was as cold as the snow which had begun to fall, settling in thick flakes around the edges of the windows.

'Sophia!'

Her companion sounded shocked; then she giggled. Sophia really was too awful! In fact the woman in the corner was very well dressed. She looked as much the lady as anyone.

Madeleine opened her handbag and rooted around in it, giving no sign that she had heard.

'Will you kindly get out at the first stop along the line,' Sophia said, 'and transfer to a second-class compartment. Or should it be a third-class?'

'Ah, here it is!' Madeleine said. 'My ticket!' She scrutinized it as if she was seeing it for the first time. 'No, there is no mistake! First class. It says so quite distinctly. I would have been surprised if it said otherwise since I always travel first class. So much more comfortable, don't you think?'

427

She spoke with great politeness, which was not at all the way she felt. Seeing Sophia Chester, if Sophia had not been so rude, she would certainly have got out of the train at the first stop, and into another compartment. But not now. Now, nothing on earth would move her!

'Comfortable perhaps, but no longer exclusive!' Sophia spoke to her companion, ignoring Madeleine.

'What did you say, Sophia?' her companion asked.

'I said, Gwendoline, that first-class travel is no longer what it was. One thought that it was supposed to be reserved for ladies and gentlemen – but no longer, it seems. Now any riff-raff with the price of a ticket can invade our privacy!'

Sophia, though she did not look in Madeleine's direction, enunciated clearly so that her words would carry above the noise of the train.

I will not let her rile me. I will *not*, Madeleine said to herself. She took out her book and began to read. Then, unable to contain herself, she looked up again.

'You'll excuse me if I don't change compartments? Actually, apart from minor drawbacks which I can ignore, I'm quite settled in!'

'In that case. . .' Sophia began.

'It's no use saying *we'll* change, Sophia dear,' Gwendoline said. 'I've just remembered, this is the express. It doesn't stop between Harrogate and Leeds.'

Sophia glared at her companion, as if the whole thing was Gwendoline's fault.

'So we're stuck!' Gwendoline said. She quite enjoyed seeing Sophia look uncomfortable.

'My dear Gwendoline,' Sophia said, 'I never had the slightest intention of changing. We were here first. If undesirable people choose to invade our compartment, it seems there is little we can do about it, though of course I shall complain to the proper authorities!'

'What a good idea!' Madeleine murmured, not lifting her eyes from her book. 'I daresay I shall do the same.'

Sophia, for the moment, could think of nothing more

to say. She twisted her hands in her lap and glared out of the window. The compartment was filled with an angry silence, which in its way was louder than the sound of the train as it bumped and swayed, going too quickly along the tracks. It was snowing harder than ever now.

In the end, Sophia could bear it no longer. Rage rose in her throat until she thought it would choke her.

'This compartment *smells*!' she cried. 'Don't you get it, Gwendoline? It's really quite disgusting! I shall have to open a window!'

She jumped to her feet, faced the window, and began to tug at it.

'Must you, Sophia dear?' Gwendoline said. 'It's snowing quite hard.'

'At least the snow is *clean*!' Sophia raved.

The window refused to be opened. Over the top of her book Madeleine watched Sophia pulling and tugging.

'Open, you stupid thing!' Sophia shouted. Then, almost beside herself, she banged hard at the unyielding window.

Madeleine saw it all. She watched in horror as it happened before her eyes, with no time at all to do anything.

The window was set in the upper part of the door. At first it didn't move at all, then suddenly, as Sophia at the height of her temper gave the hardest bang of which she was capable, her fury giving her added strength, the door flew open – and Sophia fell out of the train.

Gwendoline jumped to her feet, backed away from the open door, and screamed. And went on screaming.

In the same instant, Madeleine leapt to her feet, located the communication cord, pulled on it hard, and went on pulling. Would it work? One knew about these cords which had been fitted on the trains. When pulled, they sounded a gong in the driver's cabin and he stopped the train. One knew about them, but had they ever been proved to work?

All these thoughts went through her head with the speed of light, and while Gwendoline was still screaming.

429

Then she realized that the train was indeed slowing down; the cord worked. Presently, with a screech of brakes, the train stopped.

The open door was swinging on its hinges, Madeleine jumped down on to the line and began to run back to where Sophia had fallen. Within seconds, the guard caught up with her.

'She fell out of the train! She was trying to open the window and the door swung open,' she shouted.

'How far back?' he asked.

'I don't know.' Madeleine gasped in the cold air. 'I pulled the cord at once, but the train was going quite fast. It might be quite a way back, though.'

They found Sophia lying on her back on the side of the track. She was unconscious. Apart from a slight bruise beginning to form on the side of her face, and a trickle of blood from her mouth, there was no sign of her injuries – until the guard, kneeling beside her, turned her head slightly and revealed the gash at the back of her head, and the beautiful auburn hair, blood-soaked.

All along the length of the train, doors had opened, and now there was a stream of people running towards the place where Sophia lay.

'One of you run forward. There's a group of four cottages about half a mile along, on the right,' the guard ordered. 'Get someone to fetch an ambulance as quickly as possible. You'll have to guide the men back here with the stretcher.'

As far as he could tell, she was too far gone for an ambulance to be any good to her, but it was the only thing he could do in the circumstances.

'I advise the rest of you to get back into the train,' he said. 'You can't do any good here, except that some of you could lend a coat or two to put over the lady.'

She was covered in snow. It was settling on her so that she looked like a snow maiden. The new snow was the same pristine white as her face. Three or four of the men took off their greatcoats and spread them over her.

'I'll stay,' Madeleine said.

'Were you with this lady?' the guard asked.

'I wasn't with her. But I know her. I know where she lives. She had a companion with her on the train.'

'And where is she?'

Gwendoline, in fact, was walking unsteadily towards Madeleine and the guard. When she reached them, she took one look at Sophia – and fainted.

'She's not going to be any good to us,' the guard said brusquely. 'Get her into the nearest compartment.'

'I'll take her,' a man offered.

In the whole of Madeleine's life so far, no period of time was as long as that which passed while they waited for the stretcher party to arrive. And all the time, the snow fell; great, thick, spongy flakes. At last they saw figures in the distance, white figures against a white backcloth, like so many advancing ghosts.

The men, with skilled hands, lifted Sophia gently on to the stretcher. The snow was blood-red where her head had rested.

'I'll go with her in the ambulance,' Madeleine offered.

'That would be a help,' the guard said. 'Seeing as you know her.'

'Someone had better inform her friend. I don't know her – except that her name is Gwendoline. I daresay she'll be suffering from shock.'

'We'll see to that,' the guard promised.

Why am I not suffering from shock, Madeleine asked herself as the ambulance driver whipped the horses along the snow-covered road to Leeds? She felt nothing – except a profound pity for Sophia, lying there frighteningly still under the blankets.

Was she badly injured? Madeleine had seen an ambulance man, when he set eyes on Sophia, shake his head at the guard, neither of them speaking.

If I'd missed the train, she thought, as I almost did – if I'd been a minute later and missed it, none of this would have happened. Or perhaps if I'd kow-towed to her, not answered back and got her in a temper? But even these thoughts did nothing to break the terrible calm which had descended on her. She felt as if she was not herself, but someone else, watching her.

Sophia gave a little moan, almost inaudible. On an impulse, Madeleine took Sophia's hand in her own. It was icy cold. She chafed it gently, then held it between her own two hands. In whatever far-off country Sophia now was, perhaps she would know that someone was with her, was holding on to her?

Madeleine looked down at Sophia's face. Her expression was tranquil, with no sign of pain. How pretty she still was! When her face was in repose, as now, there was no hint of the selfish, bad-tempered character she'd carried around with her all her life.

They must have been not too far from Leeds for they were there quickly. In the hospital they swiftly took Sophia away. When she had gone, a policeman came to talk to Madeleine.

'Now madam, can you tell me what happened?'

She described what had taken place.

'Did you have any feeling that she opened the door – deliberately?'

'Deliberately? Oh no, most certainly not!' Madeleine said. 'She was simply trying to open the window.'

'Open the window? In a snowstorm? Now why would she do that?'

'She . . . she said there was a smell in the compartment. She wanted some fresh air.'

How trivial, how childish it all sounded now. And she had been as childish as Sophia.

They were interrupted by a nurse. She spoke to Madeleine.

'Were you with the lady?'

'No,' Madeleine said. 'But I know her well. How is she?'

'It's bad news, I'm afraid. She died a few minutes ago.'

For a minute no one spoke. Madeleine didn't know what she felt. She was numb. It was as if what was happening had nothing to do with her.

432

'I'll get you a cup of tea,' the nurse said.

While they waited, the policeman said: 'Do you think you could tell me about her? Take your time.'

Madeleine answered all his questions with the same cool calm she had displayed all along. Have I really no feeling, she wondered? Don't I *care*?

'Will you want me to go to Ripon to tell her husband?' she asked.

'No madam. That's not your responsibility. That's a job for us. You've been most co-operative and I'm grateful. So when you've drunk your tea I'm going to arrange for someone to take you home to Helsdon. When you get home, have something to eat, drink a tot of brandy, and get a good night's sleep,' he advised.

'Thank you. I will.'

She's too contained, he thought. She's far too contained. She doesn't realize how shocked she is – but she will tomorrow! She certainly will tomorrow!

By the time Madeleine arrived home, Mrs Bates was in a state.

'Whatever happened?' she cried. 'Oh, I've been that worried!'

Madeleine watched the horror rise in her mother's face as she gave her the news.

'Terrible! Terrible!' Mrs Bates cried. 'That poor man! Those poor little children! Whatever will they do?'

'I must go to see David Chester tomorrow,' Madeleine said. 'There are things he'll want to know, questions to answer.'

'But you can't, love!' her mother protested. 'I'm sure you're not well enough – not after all you've been through. You've had a nasty shock and you won't be over it in the morning.'

'I must go,' Madeleine repeated.

'But what about the weather? The snow's lying a foot deep in parts.'

'If the road is clear enough for the horses, Sam can take me. If not, I'll go by train. The trains will still run, I'm sure.'

'You'll catch your death of cold,' Mrs Bates warned. 'Then where will we all be?'

'Ma, don't use that word about trivial matters like colds!' Madeleine said sharply.

By next morning the temperature had risen a degree or two and by mid-morning the snow on the main roads had turned to a grey slush. Madeleine set off with Sam Bennett in the carriage.

'If the weather gets worse,' she promised her mother, 'we'll stop overnight in Ripon. I can go to Penelope's. But I don't think it will.'

Though, in spite of the brandy her mother had persuaded her to drink, she had slept little all night, she remained unnaturally calm. She dreaded seeing David Chester – and she must also see Mrs Parkinson. Sophia's mother – they knew from Emerald – was staying in Ripon over Christmas and the New Year.

Emerald, eyes red-rimmed and swollen from weeping, in a chalk-white face, showed Madeleine into the drawing-room where Mrs Parkinson and David Chester sat, on either side of the fireplace. There was no sign of the children. In spite of the huge fire in the grate, David Chester looked pinched and cold – and utterly devastated. When Madeleine entered he looked up at her as if he hardly saw her. Mrs Parkinson was the more composed of the two and invited Madeleine to sit down.

'My son-in-law is badly shocked,' she said.

'I quite understand, Mrs Parkinson. I wouldn't have dreamt of calling at a time like this, except that I thought there might be things I could tell you. But if not, I'll leave at once.'

'No, no!' Mrs Parkinson said quickly. 'It is good of you to come. I appreciate it and I'm sure my son-in-law does. I thought you would come. The policeman gave us your name as the lady who had been at the scene of the accident. He said that Sophia fell out of the train. It seems so strange. How did it happen?'

'It was all over in a flash,' Madeleine said. 'I think Mrs

Chester was trying to get a little air. Although it was cold outside, she felt the compartment was stuffy. The door suddenly opened, and she fell.' There was no need, now or ever, to say more.

David Chester buried his head in his hands and groaned. Mrs Parkinson bit her lips, held herself very upright.

'It happened so quickly. I think it will console you when I say I believe she felt nothing – no pain. She died quite peacefully.'

'Thank you,' Mrs Parkinson murmured.

'I was with her in the ambulance,' Madeleine said. 'I thought how beautiful she looked.'

For the first time, David Chester raised his head. All the despair of the world was in his ravaged face.

'She *was* beautiful!' he said vehemently. 'She was the most beautiful creature in the world. And her nature was as beautiful as her face! My little Sophia was a saint! No one knows how fortunate I was that she chose to love me. How shall I live without the light of my life?'

Tears rolled down his face. He jumped to his feet.

'Please excuse me!' he said, and ran out of the room.

Madeleine looked at Mrs Parkinson, trying not to show the thoughts which tumbled around in her head.

Mrs Parkinson met her gaze with a level expression.

'My son-in-law is very shocked, but totally sincere,' she said. 'Sophia was indeed the light of his life! They were happy in their marriage. For David, the sun shone on his wife. Which of us can say more?'

'Not many of us,' Madeleine said gently. 'Perhaps, in a way, the happiness he had with her will help to console him.'

'In the end it will,' Mrs Parkinson said. 'It was what consoled me when my husband died so suddenly.'

'I'll leave you,' Madeleine said. 'I'm sure you'd like to be alone. May I go and have a word with Emerald in the kitchen?'

'Certainly.'

Mrs Parkinson didn't particularly wish to be left alone.

She would have liked to have talked about the old days, the happy days when they lived at Mount Royd. At this moment she felt unspeakably lonely. Her sister – though she had never truly got on well with her daughter-in-law – had taken to her bed with shock.

In the kitchen, Madeleine found Emerald ironing, the tears running down her face and dropping on to the clothes she was pressing.

'Oh Madeleine, it's so awful,' she sobbed. 'You've no idea how much I thought of Mrs Chester. You never understood her, but I shall miss her always.'

'I'm truly sorry, love! Now if you can leave the ironing, I think Mrs Parkinson and Mr Chester would both appreciate a cup of tea,' Madeleine said. 'And I must be getting back before the snow comes again.'

She hardly knew what to say. She felt totally confused. How was it that Sophia Chester, the Sophia she had known, and known intimately, for so many years, could inspire such love and devotion in her husband and in her servant? There was no doubt whatever that the love was genuine, not something born out of the shock of the moment. She couldn't understand it, but she was glad of it.

In the carriage, all her feelings of the last two days, and her feelings and fears for Léon, came crowding together. She began to cry, and cried all the way back to Helsdon, great sobs which tore at her. Sam Bennett got on with his driving and kept quiet. It would ease her. There were times when the mistress was too strong for her own good. It would do her good to cry.

It would be just about the time that Madeleine was returning to Helsdon from her melancholy visit to Ripon, crying her eyes out, that the Prussians began to fire their shells on Mount Avron, a plateau to the east of Paris. For two days they rained their heaviest shells there, until those few Frenchmen (and women and children) who were not killed, fled.

The noise of the shells was clearly audible in the centre

of Paris. Those who had to, went out. Those who needn't, stayed in. While Marie was out of the room, putting the children to bed, Jules spoke to Léon.

'I'm afraid this is a foretaste of what's to come for us. I want you to promise me something, Léon.'

'Anything,' Léon said.

'I want you to promise that while I'm at work, or on guard duty, you'll never let Marie go out alone. You'll go with her.'

'Of course I will,' Léon assured him.

'There's more! Will you also promise that if anything happens to me, you will do all you can to help Marie and the children?'

'You need hardly ask that,' Léon said. 'But also, as we've learnt that the Prussians fire their shells indiscriminately, if I should get in the way of one, when this is over will you go to England to tell Madeleine? And tell her how much I love her.'

'That also goes without saying,' Jules answered. 'And now we must get on with life as well as we can.'

It wasn't easy. The food situation was terrible. Fresh meat had run out more than a month ago.

'The fact that it's rationed is a farce,' Marie complained. 'What's the use of saying we're entitled to fifty grammes a day when there's none to be had?'

Every time she went to look for food she found more shopkeepers who had ceased to trade, put up their shutters. The game wasn't worth the candle.

Milk had run out; there were no fish in the Seine; the gas was finished, and when the short winter days ended, Paris was left in darkness.

One day Jean had returned from school in tears.

'It's awful! It's awful!' he sobbed.

'Whatever is it?' Marie cried.

'Oh *Maman*, it's terrible! Do you know what they've done? They've killed Castor and Pollux and they're selling them for meat!'

Marie took her son in her arms.

437

'Who told you, love?'

'A boy at school. Is it true, *Maman*?'

'I'm afraid so.' She had known for a day or two now, but she had hoped to keep it from her tender-hearted son.

'Then promise me we'll never *ever* eat elephant meat! I couldn't bear it.'

'I give you my solemn promise,' Marie said.

It was easy to do so. Elephant meat, at forty francs the pound, was for the rich. Rat meat too was an expensive delicacy. They said it tasted like rabbit.

As 1870 gave way to 1871, the weather in Paris was bitter. In Helsdon, Léon thought, the moors would be exquisite under a blanket of snow, and the harsh look of the mills and houses in Helsdon would be softened by the snow. Mount Royd itself, with its beautiful proportions, would be a picture.

And inside the house it would be warm. Coal, which lay under the ground across so much of the West Riding, was plentiful. He thought of the wide fireplace in the drawing-room at Mount Royd. The fire would be halfway up the chimney. He shivered at the thought, and turned up his coat collar.

There was no fire in the stove in the Paris apartment. There was no fuel to be had anywhere in the city. Nothing which was combustible was safe: park benches, wooden gates; doors and window frames in empty properties had been pilfered long ago. On Christmas Day, in honour of the festivity, Jules had chopped up an old table and a surplus chair to feed the stove.

'We don't need more than one chair each, after all,' he'd said.

There was just a little of that wood saved, in case anyone should fall ill. When that was used up, Jules planned to take off one of the bedroom doors.

'I'm freezing cold, *Maman*,' Jean said.

'So am I,' Etienne echoed.

'Let's play a game,' Marie suggested. 'I've just thought

438

of one! You have to clap your hands and run round the room while I sing a tune. When I stop, you stand still – and when I start again, so do you!'

She didn't feel like games. She was seven months pregnant now, and bone-tired all the time. And cold, cold, cold. Nevertheless, she sang as loudly as she could and prodded the children into exercise.

'You too, Uncle Léon!' Jean said.

They were hard at it when Jules walked in. At first, because of the noise they were making, they didn't see him. He stood in the doorway, looking at them.

Marie worried him most. They were all of them too thin – the children's legs were like sticks – but the contrast between Marie's hollow cheeks, her barely-covered frame, and her swollen pregnant belly, was stark. How could they all have grown so thin in just a few months, he wondered? It hurt him to see his family so.

'Papa!' Etienne cried.

'I've been watching your game,' he said. 'You did very well. And I've brought home something very special!'

'What is it?' Jean asked.

'It's outside the door – but you're to guess what it is before I bring it in.'

'Eggs!' Etienne said.

'A great big gâteau, with lots of chocolate cream!' Jean guessed.

'Neither of those things,' Jules said.

'Yorkshire pudding with onion gravy!' Léon offered.

'Sorry! Now your guess, Marie!'

She hesitated. It must be something good; he looked so pleased with himself. Could it possibly be . . . ? Well, she was only guessing.

'Firewood,' she ventured.

'Right! Absolutely right!'

He went out, and came in again carrying a thick plank.

'I found it near the fortifications when I came off guard duty. I couldn't believe my eyes!'

'Why, it's wonderful!' Marie cried. 'It will last us three days. Longer if we're careful.'

Jules sawed it up and Léon lit the stove. Marie made a meal of bread, and thin bean soup, with watered-down red wine for the men. They went to bed warm, and not quite so hungry.

Léon lay awake thinking of Madeleine, as he did every night. He had just fallen asleep when Marie came to waken him. It was time to go to the shops. They left the apartment at three-thirty every morning now, so as to be near the front of the long queue, which would already have begun to form. If they were not back before Jules had to go to work, the *concierge* would keep an eye on the children.

'We should take our blankets,' Marie advised when Léon went into the kitchen. 'We can wrap them around us while we wait.'

A woman in the queue said: 'I hear the Government has sent a warning to Tours, by balloon, that we'll run out of food entirely by the end of January.'

'They sent that two weeks ago,' another woman affirmed. 'Nothing's been done. Perhaps it never got there!'

'Mind you, the rich aren't starving!' the first woman said.

A few days later, the bombardment of the city began.

'It might seem a terrible thing to say,' Léon confessed to Jules. 'But in a way, I'm not sorry. It had to come, and better to come while we have a little strength left to face it. And far better than being starved to death.'

'I agree,' Jules said.

Every day now the shells rained on Paris: on the boulevards, on the churches, on the hospitals, on the parks. A little girl was killed in the Luxembourg Gardens at the very spot where Léon had earlier sat while he waited for Marie. Each day fresh tales of the killed and wounded circulated around Paris. Léon wondered how many of them would reach as far as Helsdon. What was Madeleine doing? What was she thinking? He was tormented by his inability to tell her that, in spite of it all, he was alive and well.

Madeleine was reading the newspapers, all she could lay hands on, and not one of them gave her the least crumb of comfort.

'It's terrible, Ma!' she said. 'All the time more bombs, people getting killed and wounded. Ordinary people, sitting at their meals, going about their business: people like Jules and Marie, people like my Léon!'

'I feel for you,' Mrs Bates said. 'What's more, I understand. I remember what I went through when Our Irvine was fighting in the Crimea, reading about the awful happenings there.'

'Of course. I'd forgotten,' Marie said. 'It seems so long ago.'

'But he came back safe and sound, and so will your Léon. You've got to believe that.'

Irvine might be a long way off, his mother thought, and as long as she lived she'd miss him – but at least he was safe.

All through January the bombardment continued. Every day the shells fell, and at night too, so that it was difficult to sleep.

'It's remarkable that the shells can reach so far into the city,' Jules said.

Funerals, often of small children, became a frequent sight – though whether the deaths were from shells or from sickness or starvation was debatable.

The citizens of Paris became almost used to the bombardment. Life went on. There were even adventurous souls who sought the best vantage points from which to watch the shelling, as if it was a firework display. The Prussians began to wonder if Paris would ever give in to the bombardment.

In the end it was not the bombardment which wore the Parisians down; it was starvation, which each day drew a little nearer, stared them in the face. And when the bread ran out, that was it!

In Helsdon, through the second half of January, Madeleine read with mounting optimism of the to-ing and fro-ing, the meetings to bargain for an end to the siege. But it was not until the end of January that she read in the *Manchester Guardian* the news for which she had prayed so long. She ran at once into the kitchen.

'Oh Ma, it's happened! The siege is over! It's all over! Here it is – read it, Ma!'

She thrust the newspaper into Mrs Bates's hands.

'Oh, when will my Léon come home?' Madeleine cried as Mrs Bates read the paper. 'Will it be long, do you think? How can I bear to wait?'

A week later she received a letter, and two days after that she went to Leeds railway station to meet the London train.

As it drew into the station she stood on the platform, trembling from head to foot. The train stopped, down the length of the train the carriage doors opened.

At first she didn't see him, then the steam from the engine cleared, and there he was, walking towards her.

He walked with a stick, and was limping. She caught her breath at the sight of his emaciated frame, his thin, white face. Then she was in his arms, and he was in hers, and there were tears in both their eyes.

'I've come home, my darling!' Léon said. 'I've come home!'

TWENTY-FOUR

Léon, fire tongs in hand, built up the drawing-room fire still further.

'I can't tell you how often I longed to see this fire when I was in Paris,' he said to Madeleine. 'Sometimes I pictured it so vividly in my mind's eye that it was like a mirage.'

'Well it's no mirage now, my love!' Madeleine said. 'Nor am I, nor are you. We're here, and we're together, sitting in front of the fire in our own house. Oh Léon, I've so longed for this!'

They had finished supper more than an hour ago. It was a meal which the children now ate with them. This pleased Tommy and Claire no end, and was deeply satisfying to Léon, who wanted to spend every possible moment with them.

'After all, I am eleven!' Tommy pointed out. 'I shouldn't be going to bed *that* early!'

What a nice lad his son was growing into, Léon thought. As for Claire, she grew prettier – and perhaps a little more spoilt – every day. But he enjoyed spoiling her. He had missed the children so much. It was Madeleine who, in the end, had bundled them off to bed.

'They'll be fit for nothing in the morning,' she said. 'Besides, I want you to myself for a while!'

'You were quite right,' Léon said, now that they were on their own. 'It's wonderful just to be together.' There had been days, in Paris, when he'd wondered if it would ever happen.

'Did you enjoy your supper?' Madeleine asked. 'I thought you ate better than usual.'

'I did,' he agreed. 'The lamb was delicious.'

Three weeks ago, when he'd arrived back in Helsdon, hunger had gnawed like an animal at his stomach, but faced with food he'd found he could take very little. Mrs Bates had cossetted him like a favourite son, making egg-custards, creamy rice-puddings, calves' foot jelly, beef-tea – everything nourishing – and feeding them to him at short intervals.

'Little and often does the trick!' she said.

Thanks largely to his mother-in-law, he thought, the gnawing hunger was gone and his digestion was almost back to normal.

'But I shall never again take food for granted,' he said to Madeleine. 'Nor, I am sure, will Jules or Marie. Thank God, food had started to pour into Paris even before I left. They'll no longer be hungry.'

'We owe them so much,' Madeleine said.

'Yes. The fact that Jules paid for my journey home out of his wages is something I can repay, but nothing will repay them for the months they looked after me.'

'You are looking so much better,' Madeleine said.

He was still thin, though no longer gaunt. The hollows in his cheeks had not yet filled out, but in spite of them, and in spite of the grey hairs at his temples, he was as handsome as ever. He had lost none of his power to make her pulse race faster at the sight of him.

'I can't ever tell you what it means to me to be back,' he said. 'It was while I was in Paris that I realized that France was no longer my home. Helsdon, this small corner of Yorkshire, is my home now. It holds everything that's dearest to me.'

During the last three weeks Henry and Hortense had driven over from Leeds to welcome Léon back. Hortense had been reluctant, but Henry had insisted.

'He's a friend, and he's gone through a bad time. There's no way we'll not go and welcome him back. But think on you behave yourself!'

'You needn't worry,' Hortense said. 'I'm no longer interested!' She had decided the game wasn't worth the candle, at least when played with the Bonneaus.

'It's good to see you,' Henry said. 'You've been very much in our thoughts, lad. And what about the way your Madeleine has kept the flag flying, eh? What do you say to that?'

He was sorry the minute the words were out of his mouth. Who knew whether Léon Bonneau would be pleased at his wife's success?

'I say it's wonderful!' Léon replied. 'But it doesn't surprise me as much as you might think. I've always known how capable Madeleine was.'

'Such a busy bee!' Hortense drawled.

Henry gave her a warning look.

Léon had been down to the mill three or four times. He'd been astonished and gratified at the warmth of his reception there, both from the managers and the millhands. As he walked through the various departments, men and women broke off their work to shake him by the hand. 'I shall be back at work in no time,' he promised them.

'Please promise me you won't do anything too soon,' Madeleine begged. 'Please wait until you are stronger, and the weather a little warmer.'

'I promise,' Léon agreed.

He had been horrified by Madeleine's account of Sophia's death.

'But strangest of all,' Madeleine said, 'was David Chester's reaction. That poor man really saw Sophia as an angelic woman who had done him the world's greatest favour in marrying him.'

'Then he wasn't such a poor man after all,' Léon remarked.

'And he felt it, he genuinely felt it still, after years of marriage,' Madeleine said. 'And look how devoted Emerald was!'

Now, seated beside him on the sofa, her hand in his, Madeleine returned to the subject which had been uppermost in her mind since Léon had begun to make plans for returning to work. While he had been unfit, there'd been no need to discuss it. Now that he was getting stronger by the day, she had to speak.

'Darling,' she said. 'Promise me you won't do any travelling around for a while. I'm afraid it will take too much out of you.'

'I don't think. . .' he began.

'For my sake!' she begged.

'Very well, for your sake, dearest,' he agreed.

But he was longing to renew all his contacts, to get out into the world again. He couldn't sit around doing nothing forever.

'After all,' Madeleine said gently, 'I can take care of that side of things just as long as it's necessary.'

Sitting beside him, she didn't see his forehead crease into a frown.

'Of course you can,' he admitted. 'You've proved that. But now that I'm back, I want to spare you. I saw how very tired you were when you returned from Manchester yesterday. I want you to have time to sit back and relax.'

'But Léon I don't want to!' Madeleine said quickly. 'That's not what I want at all. You know I always wished to help with the selling. Now that I've shown I can do it, please let me share!'

He was silent. She felt the sudden distance between them.

'I wouldn't expect the lion's share,' she ventured. 'But please don't shut me out!'

He rose quickly and crossed to the window, fiddled with the curtains as if they were not quite closed. It was quiet in the room and they could hear the March wind howling outside. Then, after a minute or two, he turned swiftly and came back to her.

'You are quite right, my dear! I was being selfish. You deserve to have your share, and you shall. We'll come to some arrangement.'

Madeleine jumped to her feet and flung her arms around him.

'Oh Léon, that's wonderful! And do you know what I'd like? Shall I tell you?'

'I can see you're going to, whatever I say,' Léon said, smiling.

'I would like at first for you and me to go together, the two of us, to all the places I've been visiting in your stead.'

'I don't see why not,' he agreed. 'Indeed it would be very pleasant. We'll do that first, and afterwards we'll sort things out. I still think I should do the lion's share of travelling. After all, Madame Bonneau, you are our Chief Designer! We can't do without your talent there.'

'Oh I want to design,' Madeleine cried. 'I've no intention of giving that up. However, there is one other thing. . .'

'Yes?'

'I would like to accompany you on one of your trips to France. Only the one, and I don't expect to do any selling in France – that's where you excel. But I'd like to meet our customers just once; especially Monsieur André. I've a feeling he's going to be invaluable to us.'

She had sent off Monsieur André's order the first minute it became possible, and only yesterday the goods had been acknowledged, and with pleasure and many compliments.

'Then I shall try to take you in April,' Léon said. 'I've always promised you Paris in the spring, and this time you shall have it!

'But at the moment,' he continued, 'I don't want to go to Paris, or any other distant place. I want to go to bed with my wife.'

'Oh Léon! So early? Why, it's only nine o'clock!' She was smiling broadly.

He tended to the fire, so as to leave it safe, then arm-in-arm they went upstairs.

A fire in the bedroom grate welcomed them. The bed was turned down.

'No, don't turn up the lamp!' Madeleine said. 'Why don't we make love in the firelight?'

He moved towards her and began to unfasten the tiny buttons from the neck to the waist of her dress. She reached up and unfastened his tie, took off his collar.

'Why not?' he said.

THE END